The Tortoise Shell Game

This work contains concepts from the award-winning, non-fiction work: *A Primal Wisdom, 2d. ed.* pub. 2015, also by V. Frank Asaro, J.D. (finalist, USA Best Book Awards, 2015, categories: non-fction, and philosophy).

The Tortoise Shell Game is a work of fiction and any similarity to fact, person, thing or circumstance is strictly coincidental.

V Frank Asaro

Disclaimer: This story is fiction and any similarity to fact, person, thing or circumstance is coincidental.

Cover Design by: Text, Tatomir Pitariu; background—not including ship and smoke—Ted Packman.
Text Design by Jane Hagaman
Senior Editor: Mark A. Clements

Bettie Youngs Book Publishers

Bettie Youngs Books are distributed worldwide. If you are unable to order this book from your local bookseller, or wholesaler Baker-Taylor, online or from Espresso, you may order directly from the publisher.

BETTIE YOUNGS BOOK PUBLISHERS
www.BettieYoungsBooks.com
info@BettieYoungsBooks.com

ISBN: 978-1-940784-49-6
ePUB: 978-1-940784-50-2

Library of Congress Control Number available upon request
1. V Frank Asaro. 2. Legal Thriller. 3. Co-opetition. 4. Law. 5. Fraud. 6. Barratry. 7. Latin American Affairs. 8. Political Science. 9. Political Polarization. 9. Comparative Economic Systems. 10. Tuna Fishing.

10 9 8 7 6 5 4 3 2

Printed in the United States of America.

Contents

BOOK I

BOOK II

BOOK III

Acknowledgements

We've known throughout time that no one does it all by himself, which is more evidence of the universality of co-opetition. I thank my publisher, Bettie Youngs of *Bettie Youngs Book Publishers*, who inspired bringing this book to print. Thanks to her group: Adrian Pitariu for the text portion of the cover design; senior editor Mark Clements; designer Jane Hagaman who not only designed my previous books, *Universal Co-opetition*, and A Primal Wisdom, but has worked her magic on this book as well.

Thanks to Ted Packman, superlative digital artist, for the background of the cover, excluding the ship and smoke.

A heartfelt thanks, as well, to all those who contributed: the late Scripps oceanographer Rip Sessions; colleague lawyer James A. Mitchell; Chief Deputy DA John Massucco, retired; author David Bowles, Ph.D., for our Starbucks discussions on co-opetition; my college political science professor Dr. Henry L. Janssen, SDSU; my friend and former Ambassador to Argentina Ted Gildred, for inviting me to the Institute of the Americas banquettes and introducing Latin American dignitaries; uncle Vito Sardo, former tuna vessel crewman and electronics rocket engineer; bestselling author Spencer Johnson who urged me to write books on the philosophical aspects of this novel; and to the speed-reading prowess of Barbara Mansfield Asaro, mother of our children: Dean, Stephanie, Valarie, and in memory of our daughter Audrey, to whom I dedicate this book.

I also thank those who read all or parts of the manuscript and gave valuable insight: Former law partner Dick Gant; my former legal secretary Loxie; my former legal secretary, now public defender, sometime court TV counsel, transplanted from Guernsey, England,

Jane Montague Kinsey; retired attorney David Leaverton; sometime adventure traveling buddy, the late Andy Willis; Alberto Hayek, M.D., UCSD; and, Starbucks dialectic psychologist Andrew Paslawski.

BOOK I

1 Rip Tide

"The Verdict is in! Anthony, the court just called; the jury's reached a verdict!"

Laura's words broke across Anthony Darren's desk and crashed through his fugue. He had been staring out his office window at a rather meager view of San Diego Bay five stories below—the waterfront a couple of blocks away. It was nothing like the dizzy perspective he'd had a few months ago from a different office, a much larger, much higher office, in every possible sense. In deep distraction, he didn't really see the tuna boats in the bay dragging white wakes through the etched waters, the aircraft carriers rising like steel islands along the Coronado Island shore. He glanced at his desk calendar: Thursday, February 10, 1980. *So this is the day.*

Finally he turned and smiled at Laura. "How do I look?"

"Great. But here's your jacket." She took it off the hook on the back of the door. "And I'll let Andrea know you're on your way to the courthouse."

"Thank you." He muscled smoothly into the well-tailored coat, but fumbled flipping back the collar. Laura was on it immediately, straightening out the fabric, squinting through her black-framed glasses. He caught her by the shoulders. "Laura, I need you there, too. Just switch on the answering machine and lock up the office."

"Of course." She smiled and then frowned. "Don't say it like you're uncertain." He walked out between the shelves of law books lining each side.

Two blocks away and thirty stories higher, a mob of executives haggled around an enormous conference table in the Southern California Empire Bank Building. The only man not participating sat at the head of the table behind the only gold nameplate in the room. He wore the expression of a spectator about to win big money at a dog fight. He tugged a gray-flecked handkerchief from his pocket and blotted his forehead and drooping nose, then lifted a cup of coffee toward his lips.

A sharp double rap at the door made him halt the movement of the cup. The bickering among the executives instantly halted.

"Yes?" the man with the gold nameplate said.

An efficient-looking woman in her early thirties popped her head through the doorway. "Mr. Hooks, sorry to interrupt, but I just received a message from the Deputy DA. The jury is in."

Hooks looked around at the assembled men, all of them now focused on him. He stood. "Excuse me," he said, "while I go find out if I saved this bank or not." Imperceptible to all but him, his hand trembled as he set down the cup.

In a red tile-roofed house resting high on Point Loma, a hill overlooking the other side of San Diego Bay, a man sat on the couch in his darkened living room. His trim, muscular arms, tanned bronze, lay limp at his sides while he stared up at an imaginary spot on the ceiling.

He heard the kitchen phone ring. Heard his wife answer in a soft voice. "Yes, Joe Cruz is my husband. I'm sorry, he's . . . oh! Oh, it is? Yes, I'll tell him . . . I understand. Right away. We'll be there right away."

Joe continued to stare at the ceiling.

Anthony Darren crossed a busy street and double-stepped toward the courthouse portico. Along the way he passed a newspaper stand prominently displaying the headline JURY STILL OUT IN CONSPIRACY MURDER TRIAL. A few pigeons fluttered out of Anthony's path and settled atop the Doric columns framing the courthouse entrance. *At least* they *give me some respect*, Anthony thought as he stepped into the building.

He strode down the long marble hall along almost empty corridors. The sense of vacancy was, he knew, ephemeral; the courtrooms and juries were still in session as the noon hour approached. That would soon change. The echo of his footsteps to him evoked images of gavels pounding ominously behind each closed door.

When Anthony pulled on the brass handles of the double doors to Courtroom 12, they didn't budge. He knocked. Through the crack between the doors he saw Jennifer Jackson, the judge's clerk, fumbling with the latch.

"Hello, Jenny," he said as she opened the door.

Her smile struck him like a sunbeam through a blizzard. "Hello, Mr. Darren. Sorry, I called you back, but Laura said you'd already left. The judge just decided it's so close to noon he's sending the jury to lunch. They won't be back until about 1:30."

"Oh. I see." Anthony shuddered with the impact of a violent internal clash between disappointment and temporary relief.

"Why don't you get yourself some lunch?" Jenny asked.

"Thanks, but do you mind if I just sit here and wait?"

"No, make yourself at home. I'll be right around the corner. If anyone else comes in, would you let them know about the recess?"

"Sure."

She adjusted the latch so the door could be opened only from the inside, then turned. "Mr. Darren, good luck."

He sat on an upholstered swivel chair at the defendant's table, in the position farthest from the jury box. Silence closed in. Not even the clock mounted above the witness box made a sound. How come he had never noticed that before? He'd appeared in these courtrooms innumerable times over the past ten years. At first he'd found the dark oak paneling dignified, the high ceilings with their carved crown moldings majestic. In those days the room had inspired in him—a young lawyer, rising fast—feelings of reverence. But now he found the space oppressive, threatening, portentous. When the doors rattled, he got up and walked over. Through the crack saw the tall form and hungry face of Deputy District Attorney Egan James. Anthony hesitated, took a deep, steadying breath, and unlocked the door. When it swung open he wasn't surprised to find Herbert Hooks right behind Egan, peering over the younger man's shoulder. Beside Hooks stood a third man, the weasel-eyed witness, with dark hair pulled back into a tiny pigtail.

At the sight of Anthony all three hesitated a bit.

In what might have objectively been called a smile, Anthony said, "Come on in, guys. Sorry to say the judge sent everyone to lunch. They won't be back until one-thirty." He twisted the latch so the door would no longer lock, then turned and headed back to the defense table.

The three men took seats in the gallery to the far right, near the jury box.

Anthony focused his attention on the door nearest the judge's bench. No Christian waiting for lions to appear on the floor of the Coliseum had ever watched a door so avidly. The jury would eventually re-enter the courtroom through this portal.

Usually when a jury came in to read their verdict he had a yellow legal pad in front of him and a pen in his hand so he could give his eyes something to do while his ears received the kiss or the blow. But today no pad lay before him, and he wasn't sure what he should do when the jury returned. Stare at the tabletop? At the wall? Or directly at the foreman?

A few minutes later the main door to the courtroom opened and Laura stepped in, accompanied by a girl of sixteen, petite yet blossoming into an auburn-haired conversation-stopper. As always, Laura had tried, and failed, to make herself look plain in her sensible suit and horn-rimmed glasses.

Egan called across the gallery: "We're on recess until one-thirty."

The women did not respond, and took seats as far from him as possible. Egan watched with the habitual sneer Anthony remembered from long ago.

All at once Anthony wished Laura and Andrea hadn't come after all. They would suffer even more than he while sitting here waiting for the verdict. They would spend the time dwelling on facts only they and he knew; facts the jury had never heard. *So go over and sit with them*, he told himself. *Hug them. Comfort them*. But an invisible public curtain hung in his way. At moments like this he wanted to be alone, like a performer waiting to go on stage. Besides, he didn't want a show in front of Egan.

Once again the door opened, and this time Anthony watched Sylvia Cruz—frail, her eyes tragic—lead Joe in by the arm. The blankness on Joe's face seemed to blend his features—all but the charcoal-black eyes—into the featureless wall behind him. The couple moved toward Laura, who whispered to them, undoubtedly informing them of the delay. They took seats in the row behind Laura and Andrea.

Again Anthony felt the urge to go back there and dispense comfort, but he knew Sylvia would ask him to predict what the verdict would be. He felt the reticence as he waited for the curtain to rise.

As he turned away, his gaze crossed briefly with that of Egan James, a square-jawed and slightly pug-nosed man, his once-athletic body growing thick in an expensive suit. But in that second, Anthony was sure he saw Egan's sneer expand.

I'd like to think he's just overzealous at his job, Anthony thought. I'd like to think that what's happening now, has nothing to do with the past. Nineteen sixty-two was so long ago.

Nineteen sixty-two. The year an American astronaut orbited the earth for the first time. The year the number of American soldiers sent to an obscure Southeast Asian country called Vietnam first exceeded fifteen thousand. The year the United States and the Soviet Union almost swapped nuclear missiles across the Gulf of Mexico between Florida and Cuba.

The year Anthony Darren graduated from college.

Whoever knows, at the moment of occurrence, how one event might lead to another? What the consequences of even the most innocuous decision might be? The most reflexive choice? Even the most noble one?

Who could pinpoint the precise moment that this day in court, this arc stretching between the known past and the unknown future, became . . . inevitable?

I can, Anthony thought. I can pinpoint the moment.

It happened in 1962, yes. On the warm white sands of La Jolla.

That was when and where it began. For him, for Joe Cruz, for Egan James, and by extension, for many others, it began on the last perfect afternoon.

Anthony stretched out on his beach towel and squinted out at the surf line. The breakers seemed unusually big today, even scary, shouldering in against an east wind, a desert wind, a Santa Ana. Three of his friends sprawled about him as if they'd been deposited there by a tidal wave: Joe Cruz, lanky and tan, resembling the great Portuguese-style bullfighter Carlos Arruza; John Parkins, chunky and already getting burnt, wearing the pathetic mustache he'd nursed along for six months; and Nate Adams, pale as the sand. They recharged themselves like solar panels in the rays of the sun.

A hundred yards offshore the green translucent tubes of seawater grew and fell over, smashing themselves into frothing heads that raced and collapsed toward Anthony in overlapping lines. As he shaded his eyes he noticed dark stains on the heel of his hand— blotted ink from the pages of his final exam blue book.

He and his friends had jogged to Black's Beach from the UCSD campus, descending hundreds of steps carved into the sandstone cliffs before plunking themselves down on the sand north of La Jolla. He let his muscles absorb the warmth of the sun-struck Southern California air. The beach was almost deserted today: a weekday before tourist season. Within shouting range he saw only one small boy and his mother. The child played happily in the sand. Anthony had noticed that children instinctively started to draw pictures or build sand castles the moment they were turned loose on the shore. Man, the Great Modifier, always changing his physical surroundings to serve his needs or whims. *Something seems to drive us to compete with nature,* he thought. *Or maybe we think we're enhancing nature, cooperating with it.*

John reached for their sandy Nerf football and bounced it off Nate's head amidst a halo of sprayed grains. "Oooh," he said, "The field goal hits the upright!"

Nate clutched the ball and jumped to his feet. "Run out, run out!"

He and John tore off down the beach, tossing passes back and forth against the wind.

"Not even playing with a real football," Joe Cruz muttered into his beach towel.

Anthony chuckled and eased onto his back. The surf thundered and died, thundered and died, as rhythmic as breathing. *We deserve this day—and the big party Joe's throwing tomorrow night, too.* Yet he couldn't entirely relax. Couldn't quite crowd out a certain uneasiness.

As if reading his mind, Joe said, "So are you going to take the scholarship or not?"

Anthony sighed. "I'd be a fool not to. Law school's not cheap anywhere, but Berkeley? I'd be stupid not to accept."

Joe sat up, his dark eyes pensive. "I thought Dr. Smith had you all lined up to stay here and get your Ph.D. in Poli Sci."

"Yeah. He went out of his way for me. But the law appeals to me, too."

"What about those published papers of yours in the school library? Or the book you were going to write about our trip to Costallegre last year?"

Anthony laughed. "Yeah. My Summer Vacation; or, How to Get Caught in a Failed Military Coup Without Really Trying. I don't know; I might still write about that someday."

"You wouldn't have the time, judging from the young lawyers I've met"

"Hey, I'm not going to be *just* a lawyer any more than you're going to be *just* a . . . what is it you're going to be again?"

"Ha, ha. A tuna fishing mogul, even bigger than my dad." Joe brushed sand off his arms. "Okay, what about the other little problem with going away?"

"I knew you were going to get to that." Anthony sat up. "I know Berkeley's a long distance from here. I know it means Cheryl and I will have to split up for a while." He pried a chalky clam shell up with his toes, grabbed it and spun it toward the water. "And she's talking about marriage."

Joe's head turned. "Already? She doesn't want to finish college first?"

"I guess not. She's intelligent, but it looks like we have different goals right now. Not like you and Sylvia."

"Well, I got lucky."

"Lucky, hell. You knew what you wanted and went after it every step of the way." Unlike the rest of the gang, Joe had already made his toughest decisions and done his hardest labor: worked nights so he could spend his days in school; put in his military time; got a job;

got Sylvia; even got little Mikey. All he had to do now was relax and live his family life.

"True," Joe said. "I *am* an incredible human being. But some of that planning was forced by circumstances beyond my total control."

Anthony sighed. "The problem is, I think I'm seriously hung up on that girl."

"If you let her out of your sight for long, you know who's going to try to make a play for her."

"No. No, she wants nothing to do with Egan. And besides . . . a while ago Egan started parking in front of Nelson's Department Store when Cheryl got off work, trying to give her a ride even though she kept turning him down."

"You're kidding."

"She didn't want me to worry, so she didn't tell me about it until last Saturday night, when we found something strange on her front porch."

"What?"

"A red lantern—you know, the construction kind."

"Wait. A red light? Are you kidding?"

"Egan seems to have some jealous fantasy going." Or it just drives him crazy thinking Cheryl and I may be getting it on.

"Jealous fantasy? He's sick, man. The guy needs to be taught a lesson."

"No. I'm not stooping to his level, but I do intend to talk to him, face to face."

"When?"

Anthony shrugged. "Egan hangs out at Oscar's Drive-In. I'll probably just stop by there some night."

"Well, let me know if you'd like some company. I'll never forget who got me and the guys through some tough classes over the last four years."

"Thanks for the offer, but I can handle myself."

"Not to belittle your NCAA wrestling, but Egan's a gutter fighter. Plus he's got a four-inch reach advantage and must outweigh you by maybe thirty pounds."

Anthony shook his head. "Look, I only want to talk to him. That's all. I think he'll talk."

Joe grunted.

Suddenly Anthony was burning up. Nate and John were running back toward them, sand flinging off their bare feet. Anthony leaped up and raced toward them, Joe on his heels, and the four friends charged whooping into the surf. The abrupt cold zinged through Anthony as he dove over a series of incoming waves, then set off toward deeper water with powerful strokes. Far beyond the surf line he stopped, treading water and looking around for his friends.

A slimy blob slapped the back of his head. Whirling, he saw John, grinning as he reached for another bulb of giant kelp. Anthony beat him to it, whirled the brown tube over his head and let John have it across the back of the neck.

An arms raced ensued as the four friends battled over ever-larger pieces of kelp, forming first one alliance and then another. From shore they must look like a thrashing sea monster, Anthony thought.

That was when he noticed that the strip of beach had become nothing but a white line against the high sandstone cliffs. It wavered in the sun, inviting, like a mirage. *We've really drifted out.* "Last one in buys the beer!" he shouted.

He took the lead, stroking shoreward steadily and smoothly, ignoring the increasing tightening of his muscles, those of a grappler, too compact for swimming. He was relieved when he felt the first shore-bound swell pass beneath him; he'd catch the next one and body-surf the rest of the way in.

Suddenly he heard something, a faint cry. Then again: a pleading sound, not loud, but desperate. He stopped and raised his head, looking around as a wave rose beneath him. He saw John and Nate straggling along ten and fifteen yards behind him, their faces contorted, straining. And they were silent.

Where's Joe?

The cry stretched across the water again. Anthony scissored his burning legs as hard as he could and scanned the incoming swells. A hundred feet out, an arm splashed and a dark glistening head briefly broke the surface.

"Joe!" Anthony put his head down and began swimming out again, powered by a blast of adrenaline. As he passed John and Nate he shouted, "Go back out! Help him!" But they continued thrashing toward shore as if they didn't hear. Anthony realized the two weren't making much headway, and realized what was happening. They were in the grip of a rip current, a surge of water following sand channels outward against the surge, dragging everything within it toward the open ocean. This was a big one.

Traveling with the current, Anthony surged through the water like a kayak. He glimpsed a hand breaking the cresting surface several feet away, then dropping out of sight. Ducking underwater, blinking in the stinging gloom, Anthony breast-stroked downward. The surf's thunder resonated around him, and through clouds of sweeping sand suspended in green he saw Joe, his dark eyes saucered, arms outstretched, his body five feet down and sinking in a stream of bubbles.

Anthony pulled down through the roaring turbulence and grabbed Joe's arms; searched for and found a new flow of strength, and kicked hard to pull his buddy toward the surface. Into the light and air they burst, coughing and thrashing. "Just dog paddle," Anthony croaked into Joe's ear. "Don't try to swim. Just dog paddle, Joe!" Joe choked up sea water, then an eruption of vomit.

"Don't worry," Anthony said. "I have you; I won't let you go. Just relax and float."

He knew the rule about rip currents: do not fight them; go with them, or go across them. But Joe's face seemed blue and his breathing desperate. Anthony felt his own limbs tightening again as the adrenaline left his system. He could barely keep his head above water as it was; if his legs cramped they were both in big trouble. So he headed diagonally toward shore, swimming desperately with one arm dragging Joe along, lungs heaving, and salt burning inside his nose.

After a minute he cast an anxious look toward shore: was it any closer? Any closer at all? He couldn't tell. Maybe not.. .But at that moment, failing Joe frightened Anthony even more than if he drowned *with* him. He imagined the tragic face of Joe's mother.

Ignoring the shore, he kept kicking the egg-beater motion, and pulling. Kicking and pulling.

A wave crashed over them; Anthony struggled to keep his grip on his friend. Then another wave, bigger than the first. And then, to his bafflement, Joe became unaccountably light in his arms, a slight bounce up—and he felt his toes kick against hard-packed sand. The bottom; the bottom! Joe was taller. He released Joe, pushing him toward the beach but with the recoil he found himself surging back out to sea, the current stronger than ever, his body now tied up in a steel knot. His arms and legs simply no longer worked. Saltwater continuously seared his sinuses and a green translucent curtain enveloped him, closing out the sun.

Another breaker, pounding and thundering. Anthony felt trapped, caged in water. He found no up or down, just turbulence and the continuous rumbling. His body tumbled, flailed, and he felt his feet stub the bottom again. Now he thought of *his* mother. What tragedy would she bear if *he* drowned. With his last parcel of strength he bent his knees, pushed off against the sand and shot up, bursting through the surface, lungs opening in welcome relief to the air. Then down again. He pumped his arms and legs and managed to stay with the arching crest, bodysurfing or at least being propelled shoreward by the mass of incoming water. At last his feet caught the bottom again, firmly this time, and with all his muscles gathered and locked, he stood and staggered beachward. Slowly, agonizingly, he slogged the remaining fifty paces, up to warmth, and flopped onto the beach.

Joe lay coughing and gagging nearby. Farther up the beach, John and Nate did the same.

For a long time Anthony lay curled on the sand, too exhausted to talk or even think. Eventually he noticed Joe's eyes fixed on him, black slits in the sun. Through brine-caked lips Joe croaked, "You saved my—"

"Forget it," Anthony cut him off, as John and Nate were staggering toward them, faces sheepish. He had acted involuntarily, he felt. Anthony couldn't explain it. It seemed as though it all came from nature's bidding— perhaps instinctively answering a call for help.

"You would do the same for me," he told Joe in a salt-roughened voice.

Nate and John threw themselves down nearby. For a moment nobody spoke, then John blew sand out of his drooping moustache. "Well, what do you say we go get those beers? Anthony has to pay; he was the last one in."

To his astonishment, Anthony had enough strength left to laugh.

2 Valley of the Dunes

Anthony sat on top of a sand dune, one arm around Cheryl's shoulder as they watched the vibrant orange disk of the sun dip into the sea. Perhaps fifty friends had gathered in the center of a ring of such dunes. *Whoever picked that spot on the strand a few miles south of Del Coronado hotel had chosen well,* he thought. Rimming the crests were palm fronds, their shafts thrust into the sand, their curls lofting inward with the warm evening breeze. From basements and garages Joe and a few of his friends had brought bundles of tuna seine netting, which they unfolded and began to spread across the valley of sand between the dunes. Anthony knew how these families of Italian and Portuguese immigrants, fishermen all, still followed the old country traditions.

Some of the partygoers broke out beers; others opened soft drinks; and a few staggered in with hollowed-out watermelons filled with spiked fruit concoctions and decorated with straws. The sand valley became a blur of gaiety accentuated by the delighted screams of a few girls kidnapped and dunked in the surf.

The mellow strumming of a guitar and someone singing *Can't Help Falling in Love* blended with the rhythmic breath of a mildly hissing sea. *Hard to believe that's the same ocean I almost drowned in yesterday*, Anthony thought.

After the sun set he and Cheryl slid to the base of the dune and nestled together on the netting. Anthony lightly stroked her face while smoke from the fire billowed toward the brightest, fullest moon he had ever seen. "This all seems familiar somehow," he said. "Like I've been at this gathering before, maybe as a tribe member twenty-thousand years ago. Do you feel that?"

"I feel good just hugging you," she said. "Are you going into one of your Mr. Anthropologist moods?"

He laughed. "Sorry."

"It's okay. That's one of the reasons I love you." She traced his lips with her fingertip. "You know, if you had even longer hair, you'd be the best-looking Cro-Magnon man I ever saw."

"Cro-Magnon? Where did you come up with that?"

"Cave dwellers in a diorama at the Museum of Man. One day at closing time my anthropology class had just left the room and I was the only one there. I kept staring at this one Cro-Magnon man, and he looked back at me . . . and I realized he was alive. I mean he stared right at me with these blue-green eyes. He was naked and he'd just stepped back from painting a pictograph on the cave wall. In his hand the paint brush was still wet, and his hair was sun-streaked like yours. I think I fell in love with him that day, as though he were you."

Anthony felt a chill between his shoulders. "You're making this up."

"No. Then the security guard came in, kind of surprised, and said I had to leave. As I walked out something told me not to look back. I came out of there all tingling at the roots of my hair. And here you are!"

"Yep; that look in your eyes is what lured me out of the caves."

"I even thought I wouldn't mind if they locked me in the museum for the night."

The surrounding talking and strumming added to an ambiance flavored with the aroma of barbecuing steaks and hot dogs. Cheryl, clad only in her bikini, radiated the fire's warmth and glow, her blue eyes flickering with amber.

Anthony pushed the hair off her neck. "Probably no one else is looking at the party this way," he said, "but this is kind of a goodbye forever celebration."

"Why's that?"

"Well, after this summer most of us are going to leave for jobs or grad school. Someday we'll look back and wonder whatever happened to so and so and him or her. But nobody's thinking that tonight. They're all having fun, as if they'll be having the same party next year."

"Some of the guys will be going out on the tuna boats, won't they?" she said.

Anthony nodded. "Commercial tuna fishing, like I did last summer, is a lot bigger deal than you'd think. The tuna seiners are gone for months at a time and travel thousands of miles. Mexico, Central America, Costa Rica, the Republic of Costallegre, even the Galapagos and Guam. The nets alone cost half a million bucks, never mind fuel and paychecks and insurance and all the rest. That's why Joe went to college . . . to learn how to manage all that stuff better."

"Didn't someone in *your* family once own a tuna boat?"

"Yeah, my grandfather, my mother's dad, had a piece of one after he came from the old country. It's no longer the family business. They had to take huge risks, both financially and physically."

"Physically?"

"Sometimes ships sink, or a shark bites off someone's leg. Even in these modern days men sometimes have to get in the water to try and save the dolphins that get caught in the net."

"Joe told me his dad says you can go out on one of his ships again this summer, but maybe now I might worry."

Anthony shrugged. "It was a great adventure, but I'm not sure I'd have the time for the trip, especially as far as to Costallegre. Or even near it."

"I thought you were fascinated by that place. The rebellion, the politics."

He shifted uncomfortably. "Being there wasn't like watching it on the news. We put in at Puerto Nuevo for about a week for engine work and to take on stores, and everything seemed okay. Apparently Serape likes to keep Puerto Nuevo secure and the lights on because it's good for business and his family gets a little kickback from all the businesses. But that night Poncho wanted to go ashore and meet up with his brother. So I decided to go along."

"Who's Poncho?"

"One of the marine mechanics, born in Costallegre. A few years older than I; heavy accent but a smart guy, and knowledgeable about Central America. He'd been pretty highly educated both there and in the USA. So I thought it would be fun."

Cheryl touched his arm, and despite the warmth of the night he felt gooseflesh spring up all over him. "The killing happened?" she asked.

He stared up at the stars. "I'd never been close to a murder before. But there he was: Poncho's brother, right in the middle of town, crumpled up against a wall. The blood . . . They must have shot him fifty times."

"Who did it?"

"That dictator Serape did it. They found out that Poncho's brother was with the rebels. Costallegre's the reverse of the usual banana republic. Usually there's a fascist dictator on one side and communist guerillas on the other. This time it was a socialist dictator on one side and democratic rebels on the other."

"But I thought some pundit on the news said that Costallegre *was* a democracy?"

"In name only. Their constitution gives the government too much control, so General Serape's family basically runs everything. It's like the Nazis and the Fascists—despite their different names, both were actually socialist dictatorships. Which is what you get when citizens are *forced* to cooperate." He paused. "We practically had to drag Poncho back onto the boat; he wanted to steal straight into the jungle to meet up with the rebels. I think he still wishes he had."

He fell silent. Cheryl snuggled closer and slid a long leg over his thigh. She said, "I didn't really bring Costallegre up so we could talk politics."

"Sorry about that. I know I get carried away, but it bothers me that situations like Costallegre keep happening. I have theories about it and want to write about them, shine a light on them. Maybe make a difference."

"Which is exactly why you should stay in San Diego and get your Ph.D."

He turned and laid his head against her shoulder, not responding.

He felt her chest rise and fall one time to every three beats of her heart. Through the bonfire smoke he caught sight of John and his girlfriend Melissa wrapped together. The party sounds were beginning to mellow, transcended by the rhythm of the mildly rushing sea.

Cheryl gently moved him, stood and shook her giant beach towel.

Anthony watched her, heart pounding, wondering if she'd decided to simply walk away.

Instead she leaned down and took his hand, urging him up. Their arms encircled each other's bare waists and they walked away from Joe's primordial camp, through the palms at the crest of the crater and onto the pewter sand. Shadows of their near-naked forms moved with them, rippling up and down the dunes; cool sand fell cleanly away with each step.

They halted on an unspoiled peak of dune in the dry warm air above a private edge of the shore. Cheryl let the towel drop. Carefully, not too roughly or too softly, he massaged her shoulders and unhooked her top. She trembled as his hands smoothed from under her breasts the indentations left by the elastic band.

He trembled, too. More than any woman in the world, however beautiful, Cheryl was the loveliest, the dearest, and he needed to hold and cherish her. As he increased the pressure of his touch her nipples swelled, and she whispered his name. When she turned their mouths came together, tongues searching. They slipped off each other's final garments and he gathered her in his arms, gazing down the naked contours of her muted silver form.

In a small saddle of sand they spread the giant towel. As he eased her down, the arch of her back flowed with the form of the dune. He dropped to a balance, her taut thighs melting under the tender strength of his hands. Into a blurring spin of emotions he dissolved, losing all sense of time.

With the rhythm and power of the sea they moved, and she grasped him with surprising strength, her arms locked around him, her limbs encircling. Responding weakly to a sudden resolve he tried to break the hold, but knew he would fail. He wanted to fail. They rolled from the crest of the dune into the wash of the sea. A power drove him beyond his senses, his mind flying under a force that demanded he break down the gates. Through the barriers he burst and they lay entwined in a shimmering world on the apron of the sea. Overwhelming peace enveloped him, carrying him away on a flood tide of diamonds and stars.

Mild waves ebbed in ripples on the shore and lapped at his toes. He awakened, rose, tugged her hand and they stepped onto dry sand.

She shook the terrycloth and they toweled each other vigorously. He wrapped the towel robe-like around her and slipped on his bathing suit. Wet head against wet head, they began their walk back to the smoky glow in the circle of sand.

"Anthony," she murmured, "why do we have to wait? I can't take this. With me working, we'll have enough to live on."

He stopped and looked out to the moonlit sea, beyond dim silver flashes into total darkness.

"I know you're having a hard time saying it," she said, "but you've already decided to go to Berkeley. Haven't you?"

He didn't reply.

"I knew it. But you don't have to go there. You could go to law school here at night instead, or later. Don't you think?"

He sighed and leaned his face on her damp hair. "Please listen, Cheryl. The scholarship. I have to accept it. I just have to. Besides, we're still too young to get married. And while I'm away you could finish college."

She gave him a bewildered look. "School and work; that's all I ever hear from you. I know how you feel about achievement. I know how you hated the bums and weeds and railroad tracks where you grew up and you want your kids to belong to golf and riding clubs, like Susan and Melissa and John. But they're snobs."

"Hey, wait. They're my friends."

"I'm sorry. I don't really mean that. They all like *you*. You fit in. But I don't. I'm not at home with them."

"Have you considered maybe that's because they're finishing college and you dropped out?"

"No, that's not it. I felt that way in high school, too. Have you forgotten who my folks rent our apartment from? And who my mom checks bags for at the supermarket?"

"I didn't think that was such a big deal with you."

She gazed toward the glow of the bonfire, and the shine in her eyes brought back the ache in his heart. "Anthony, I don't know what you want me to do. When my parents leave next week, its permanent, and they want me with them. They don't want me to stay behind alone."

"I know, but I have a different goal, Cheryl. It's like you said: When I have kids someday, they're not going to sleep next to stinking alleys or live around winos and violence. I have to get so far ahead that no matter what, those things would never happen to a family of mine."

Like pages of an open book flipping in the breeze, her expression changed from hope to worry, back to hope, then to helplessness. "Then take me with you," she whispered, "to San Francisco."

"Let me get a year or two more school out of the way, and we'll see how it goes. Cheryl, now is not right."

"Then what should I do? Go with my folks or stay here and wait? I mean, what do you want me to do?"

He tried to think of an answer. He tucked her cheek against his neck and pressed his chest to hers. Her nipples were now cool and he could feel her heart pounding against his. Yet their interests were so different. He knew he loved her and wanted her, but just because there's love, does that mean two people are the best match for each other? Maybe it was just bad timin g: too early, too young.

"Why are things so complicated?" he lamented. She did not reply, and the silence floated on the moon-spangled surf. Then a transport ship's sad bass horn echoed in the distance.

She held him at arm's length. "Do you want to get something to eat? My stomach is aching. If we keep talking it'll only get worse."

"I'm starving, too. Oscar's?"

"Sure."

Hand in hand they walked back to the glow and laughter of the valley between the dunes.

They pulled into the restaurant parking lot at midnight. As usual Oscar's Drive-In shimmered, all lit up and jumping with its neon signs and car-hop waitresses dressed in short shorts and bobby socks. Radios blared *Do You Love Me?* from cars jammed three and four deep in a semicircular pattern facing the garishly-lighted exterior. With the windows of his shiny black '56 Chevy Bel Air hardtop rolled down, Anthony circled around looking for a parking spot, passing through aromas of hamburgers and French fries, and dodging and greeting knots of people he knew. Perhaps seventy-five customers moved about, hobnobbing in and out of their cars. Finally he parked and turned off his headlights.

"Look," Cheryl said in a low voice.

Anthony's gaze followed hers. Egan James stood on the other side of the lot, horsing around with three other guys who were drinking beer and leaning against someone's hotrod. "I see him."

She clutched his arm. "Let's leave."

"What are you talking about? We just got here. I want something to eat."

"But he's got it in for you, Anthony. Just the other day he told Mary Wills he thinks you're the one who blackballed him from your club in high school."

Anthony shook his head. "I can't believe this guy. I doubt that's what's bothering him; that was over four years ago! And I wasn't even the one." Anthony narrowed his eyes. "Look how he walks around with that sneer on his face. It's there even when he tries to act nice. Remember when he went around telling people you're his girl? They said, 'That will be a surprise to Cheryl. She says you're only a date.'"

"He didn't like that at all," Cheryl said. "He thought everyone was laughing at him. Anthony, he makes me nervous."

"I need to talk to him," Anthony said. "That's the main reason I wanted to come here tonight."

Cheryl put both hands to her cheeks. "Oh no! Don't talk to him, not tonight. Can't you see he's drinking?"

"I thought he gave that up." Anthony slid back the car's bench seat, giving them more room. "Something about that church he joined."

"Well, he's obviously off the wagon now." She shook her head. "I'm not sure what I ever saw in him."

"The guy's an enigma. Back in high school he did pretty well with grades; he could have gone on to college if he wanted to. And he did things like drive the truck for Christmas toy collection. Heard he'd even done a few years of military, But on the other hand he was always picking arguments and looking for fights. No one remembers him ever losing one. He liked to fight in the street and he fought dirty. I saw him once."

"You did?"

"Hang on a second." The car hop was approaching. Anthony gave her their order, then turned back to Cheryl. "It happened at a party at John Perkin's house. Egan had some words with 'Mr. Clean' Gleason; remember him? Then invited him to step outside. Clean never even got out the door before Egan spun around and dropped him with a roundhouse right."

Cheryl winced—then her eyes went wide.

Anthony felt fingers close roughly on his shoulder, then heard the familiar snarl of Egan James: "You here to see me, asshole? Then get out of the car. I have something to say to you, too."

Anthony jerked his shoulder free. "Bug off, Egan. I'd like to talk to you, sure—after you lighten up. Let's not start off on the wrong foot."

"Don't tell me what to do." Ridges formed on Egan's brow. Three of his friends stood behind him, smirking. Anthony could smell alcohol. "What are you afraid of? I thought you were a hot-shot wrestler."

"He ain't wrong-footed, man," one of his friends sing-songed.

"Please don't get out of the car," Cheryl whispered.

Anthony noticed some of Cheryl's friends and some of his sitting in their cars, regarding him expectantly. "Look, Egan," he said. "I'm not interested in fighting, okay? But I'd like to talk to you, man to man. Can you do that? A civilized discussion?"

Egan's scowl broadened into a smile. "Oh, collegiate style? Sure, Tony. I'm ready for that. I'd like to hear you out. Seriously, let's talk." He took a few steps back and relaxed his hands, then motioned his friends away.

Anthony turned to Cheryl. "Everything's okay. We won't fight. Don't worry."

Avoiding her restraining hand, he opened the door, swung out his knees and rose from the seat. Just as he was straightening his legs, a burning pain ripped through the center of his face with a deafening "crack." His vision flashed red, then black. He realized Egan's fist had caught him full on the nose. And now he was kneeling on the pavement, blood trickling down. That would not do. He got up unsteadily.

"Go around back," Egan's friends were saying. "Go around back. The cops will get you here."

"He doesn't want to fight me," Egan jeered. "He only wants to crawl back in his car with his little whore."

Anthony blinked his eyes and tried to find his balance. Now the blood dripped heavily onto his shirt. How could he have been so stupid? Hadn't he just told Cheryl about watching Egan sucker-punch Mr. Clean? Hadn't Joe warned him that Egan fought dirty?

Then what Egan had just said exploded in his brain. Cheryl, with her hands to her cheeks, was slowly shaking her head no, at the same time sinking low in her seat. He turned and stalked toward the dark alley behind the Drive-In. Twenty or thirty people followed. Young men, a few girls; some friends of his, others obviously siding with Egan. Cheryl remained in his car. He knew she would not want to witness this. He saw John in the group, but not Joe. Things were about to get ugly.

In the shadows behind the restaurant's corrugated iron wall a silent circle formed around Anthony and Egan. A light fog hung in the air. Anthony faced Egan and half-crouched. *His little whore?* He wanted to get the guy, to hurt him, dismember him, break all his bones. The blood trickling from Anthony's nose and soaking into his shirt and chest felt like hot molten lead.

He and Egan circled one another. Staring at Egan's smirk, Anthony unleashed what felt like a lion from his soul. Charging forward, he wrapped his arms around the bigger man, lifted him and flipped him onto his back. A heavy-winded grunt vented the air. Anthony sprang instantly onto Egan's chest, straddled him with his knees, then jackhammered one, two, three, four steel-hard punches to Egan's face. Then Egan smashed an open hand into Anthony's mouth, pushing his head back and trying to dig his fingertips into Anthony's eyes. Anthony cried out in rage and rolled away.

Eyes burning and nose clotting with blood, he circled Egan again. Their breaths steamed from mouths and nostrils. The crowd stood silent. Egan threw a fast left jab, then brought his right fist, hard and violent, into Anthony's ribs. The impact lifted Anthony to his toes but without pain; Anthony felt anesthetized. Egan's left hook came in and Anthony caught it, whipped Egan's arm over his shoulder and stooped beneath him. Strength exploded through Anthony's body. With a gut-deep growl he lifted Egan into a fireman's carry—then slammed him onto the ground as hard as he could. Dropping to his knees, he clutched Egan's head between his hands. Egan's crew-cut scalp slid against the skull beneath as Anthony, out of control, raised Egan's head, then flung it back against the dirt. Grabbed it, lifted it, threw it down—again—as if to kill a sneering giant cockroach. But he found himself easing up from a full slam. Through the red blur he knew he did not want to kill the man.

He felt punches glancing off his face; ignored them. Like him, a disintegrating Egan was now bleeding from both nose and eyes— or maybe some of that blood was Anthony's.

Egan finally stopped moving, although the sneer remained stuck on his mouth. Anthony heard blurred voices: "That's enough." "Let him go, Anthony." "He's out. He's hurt bad. Let him go!"

But Anthony wasn't ready to stop. He wanted Egan to fight back. He wanted Egan to take back what he had said about Cheryl. He wanted . . .

"The cops are coming. Let him go, Anthony!"

Headlights flooded the alley. *What am I doing*? Anthony let his friends pull him up and hustle him away.

Energy still charging through his veins, he squeezed his nose as he walked back toward his car. His once-white T-shirt looked as though he'd spent the night slaughtering chickens. The older restaurant patrons stared at him through their windshields while the younger ones made way for him between parked cars.

As he reached his Chevy the strength seemed to leave his legs, and he collapsed into the front seat. Without a word he started the engine. Cheryl pressed her face to his blood-soaked shoulder. "Anthony, are you going to be okay? When you walked around back you scared me. You looked . . . you looked like you wanted to . . ."

"I could have. But I didn't. He will feel it for a while, though."

She said nothing.

He felt his hands shaking; gripped the wheel harder as he pulled out of the lot. "One day I was happy I could help someone, the next I was trying to hurt someone."

"Just because of what Egan said? His words have no meaning. I erased them as soon as I heard them . . . He hit you first."

Anthony said nothing all the way to her street. In his hands the steering wheel felt simultaneously slippery and tacky with blood.

Finally he said, "I should have had it out with him a year ago; stopped all this before it started."

"You couldn't have known how far it would go." Then, as he pulled into her driveway, "Come in and let me get you cleaned up."

"Thanks. But all I want to do is go home and hit the sack. I'm kind of feeling it now."

"Are you sure you're okay to drive?"

He managed a smile. "It's just a mile up the hill."

"Well, be careful." She looked intently at his face, and kissed him, ignoring the dirt and dried blood. "Call me in the morning, first thing?"

"I will."

He watched her go into her house, then backed onto the street. He started up the hill, very slowly, in deep contemplation. His house was about a third of the way up the slope. The houses even higher up were larger. Many were a lot larger. Above him a pair of red taillights disappeared into a gated driveway. *Probably John.*

Anthony parked in his own drive, climbed out and pressed the car door shut behind him as silently as he could. Hoping his mother was asleep, he unlocked the front door of the house and stepped into a world of warmth and hominess. Mom had managed to keep things together since losing Dad two years before, and with Sis now working in England, she was Anthony's only family living at home. She appeared to be dozing in front of the TV, but as he crept down the hall he heard her call out: "Anthony?"

He stopped with one foot on the staircase. "It's me, Mom. Go back to sleep."

"Are you okay? You sound like you've got a cold."

"Guess the sea air stuffed me up. I'm fine."

"Well . . . maybe you shouldn't stay out so late."

He had to smile. Once a mom, always a mom. "We were celebrating. Graduation time, remember?"

"How could I forget . . . ?"

Anthony waited a minute or two then finished stealing upstairs.

In the bathroom he splashed water on the stinging at the bridge of his nose and watched the crimson swirl down the drain. In the mirror his nose looked swollen and slightly bent. No amount of pushing, grimacing or forced smiling straightened it.

He stepped into the relaxing heat of the shower and rinsed the chaos of the fight off himself. After toweling dry, he crossed the hall to his bedroom and crawled between the sheets. He wished he had Cheryl lying next to him after all. An unaccountable heaviness rose in his chest. His nose hurt. His knuckles hurt. The darkness of the room pressed down on him, filling him with foreboding, yet the reasons for his feelings seemed murky and unclear.

The moon stood a quarter full in the sky as Cheryl pulled up in front of Anthony's house in her old coupe. She had insisted on driving tonight.

"Did you notice how people keep looking at you?" she said. "Like they don't know whether to cheer for you or run away."

"It'll pass," Anthony said. "Egan's buddies took him to the ER; he'll be fine."

"Fine? Mary told me he has two black eyes, a broken cheekbone and a concussion. He could have been *blinded*. You could have been thrown in *jail*, Anthony."

"Don't forget, he took the first swing—before I was even out of my car."

"I know, but . . . now he's saying you're dead meat."

"I heard that too. Well, he'll have to take his shot before I leave for Berkeley in the fall, that's all I can say."

Silence, heavy and as dark as the night. Cheryl twisted her high school class ring.

"I'm sorry," he said. "That was a bad way to bring it up."

Cheryl twisted the ring, twisted it.

"It won't be like forever," he said. "We'll write at least once a week and see each other every summer, and after a few years we'll be together again. It will go by fast, you'll see."

She muffled a sob and leaned her head on his shoulder, close enough for him to smell the familiar fragrance of her skin. Tight and long he hugged her. They kissed, and he felt her wet eyelashes brush his healing face. "Anthony, please. Don't go. Please don't—"

"Cheryl. I have to. We've talked about it and talked about it, and . . . I have to go."

"But *why*? If you really love me, *why*?"

"Because it's important. For me, for us. For the future."

"You mean *our* future."

"Of course, our future."

He knew she had to make the decision to leave with her parents tomorrow for Kentucky. The time had come; if he didn't do it now, he never would. He opened the door and slid out. Disbelief widened Cheryl's eyes. Through the open window, bathed in the surrealistic glow of overhead street lamps, they kissed—long, tender and lingering—searching and aching for some word or feeling that would make everything all right. Nothing occurred to him. Finally he pulled away, turned and walked off.

Behind the backyard fence he stopped and waited, listening for her car to start. Silence. He peered between two slats and saw her sitting with her forehead resting on her hands while she gripped the steering wheel, the streetlight reflecting dully from her class ring. Minutes passed. Her shoulders jerked.

He blinked hard and repeated to himself that he'd made the right decision; he had to have made the right decision. . . .

But why? If you really love me, why?

At last the engine of Cheryl's little coupe rattled to life and the car lurched away.

Pain knifed into Anthony's chest. His skin turned cold. Without thinking, he sprang through the gate. "Cheryl!" But as he ran into the street her car with its one functioning taillight was already turning the far corner. He turned and dashed around the block in the opposite direction so he could head her off along the route she always took.

In darkness he flew down the sidewalk to the corner, stopped and looked down the block. No jalopy. He didn't understand it. For the first time Cheryl had not driven her usual route. Looking the other way, up the street, he saw the single taillight of her car glowing red a block away . . . two blocks . . . then it blinked out of sight.

Anthony walked home, waited several minutes, then dialed Cheryl's number. Her father answered, sounding annoyed at being awakened. No, Cheryl hadn't arrived yet, and he didn't want to be disturbed.

After a long, sleepless night Anthony called again. His jaw dropped as a taped operator's voice intoned, "*The number you have dialed is no longer in service.*"

He tried again, pressing the buttons very carefully—and got the same result.

He reached her house in ten minutes. No coupe out front; no sign of life. He knocked. No answer. Peering through the front room window he saw an empty living room: no furniture; lifeless; deserted.

He drove slowly home, banged into his room, closed and locked the door, pulled the shades, took off his shoes, and crawled back under the covers with his clothes on. Silent tears rolled down his face, and the saltiness on his lips reminded him of the taste of her tears the night before . . . a taste he knew he would never forget.

By the end of August he had received only three letters from Cheryl, mailed from the small town in Kentucky where she'd grown up. The first two were long and passionate, the last short and . . . friendly, at best. Then nothing. She never replied to his last letter.

As Anthony packed for the long drive to Berkeley, on impulse he made a long-distance phone call. Stood anxiously waiting while it rang.

A familiar middle-aged woman's voice answered, "Crawford's."

"Hello, Mrs. Crawford. This is Anthony Darren. How are you folks?"

A pause. "Hi, Anthony. Just fine, thanks. We're all just fine. How're you doing?"

"Oh . . . okay, I guess. Getting ready to go up north. May I speak to Cheryl?"

A longer pause. "She's gone on a trip, Anthony. Didn't you know?"

"No. I haven't heard from her in a while."

"Anthony, she's married. She's off on a little honeymoon. Thought surely you knew." He swallowed a thick lump. Then, "Well, tell her congratulations for me. Who did she marry?"

"Billy Burns, a boy from these parts. An Army man. I think he'll be good for her. She's really been blue since you and her broke up."

"Well, I'm sure he'll take good care of her. She's a very special girl. Please tell her I'm . . . happy for her."

"That's real nice of you, Anthony. Always thought a lot of you."

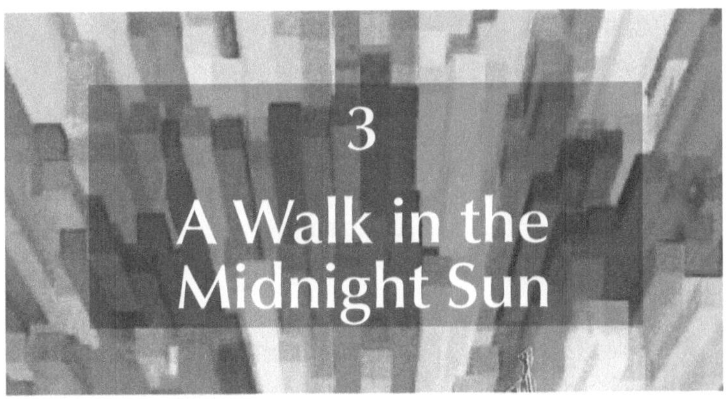

3
A Walk in the Midnight Sun

Anthony Darren sat alone at a small table in a dark back corner of the jammed bar, listening to the jukebox playing "Can't Take My Eyes Off of You." Well, what else? It seemed like "Can't Take My Eyes Off of You" was the only current song any jukebox played in 1974, but one of his favorites.

The view through the plate glass window a few feet away overlooked the rigging, masts and hulls that filled one of the most scenic yacht basins in San Diego Bay. Halfway through his second scotch, above the din of laughter and guitar riffs, Anthony heard a woman's voice: "I know you."

He looked up. "Hi, maybe so." With the dim light behind her and so much cigarette smoke in the air, he saw only her silhouette from the bosom down. But it was a terrific silhouette.

"Would you mind some company?" she asked. "I'm afraid your table has the only available chair in the place."

"No wonder you said you know me. Sure, no problem, sit down." He adjusted the chair for her. As she seated herself, a pair of black horn-rims perched on a pert nose came into view. The glasses partially hid a face he was sure he'd seen somewhere, maybe on the front page of a fashion magazine. She held what looked like a gin and tonic.

"Hi. My name is Laura Evans. I really meant it when I said I know who you are: Anthony Darren. I've seen you in the courtroom."

Anthony didn't respond. A few bars of different music filled the space: someone had discovered "Bennie and the Jets."

"Why so glum?" she said. "You look like a kid who lost his puppy."

"Lost something. It wasn't a puppy."

"Sorry . . . I don't mean to impose."

"Okay, then, *I'll* be nosy. Tell me all about you."

"Well . . . I do editing and proofreading for an educational book publisher, and also write the occasional newspaper article."

"You're a writer?"

"Not full-time. I also moonlight as a legal secretary." Her gaze intensified. "I watched you in court one afternoon about six months ago and sold a small piece about it to the *Business Daily*. Did you see it?"

"Let's see, the Archer case?"

"That's it."

He rubbed his chin. "I read that article. Factually very accurate. Well done for such a complicated matter."

"Thanks."

But he was looking out the window again. As pretty as this girl was, and as intelligent as she seemed, he wished she hadn't intruded on his solitude. *Well, that's what you get when you look for privacy in a crowded bar, you moron.*

After the silence stretched uncomfortably thin, he looked back at her, looked squarely into a pair of frankly sympathetic eyes of darkest brown. Eyes you could fall into.

"Tell me about it," she said.

And he realized he wanted to. Realized that was exactly why he'd come here—to improve the odds of talking. To anyone. About anything. He smiled. "I just left my house, and no one *there* showed any interest in talking to me."

"I'm different. I could be your secret admirer."

"You're also a journalist. This isn't going to end up in the *Business News*, is it? 'Half-Drunk Lawyer Whines Like Baby?'"

"Strictly off the record. I promise."

"In that case, I can't be rude to a possible secret admirer. But kick me or throw an ice cube at me if I talk too much."

"Deal. Go on; I'm a good listener." She shifted forward on her elbows with her chin cradled in her knuckles. He noticed her breasts jiggle beneath a thin sweater: no bra.

"Okay. My last trial. I'd been in court for a month defending these guys, Phillips, Jones & Conrad. Three partners with everything at stake. One day Conrad caught me in the hall outside the courtroom and said he was concerned about Phillips' health. Said the old guy had heart problems and was making himself sick worrying about the case. Could I do something to pep him up—give him a boost? Like, tell him we had a reasonable chance to win?"

A waitress brought the drinks. When the glasses were on the table Anthony said to Laura, "Are you with me so far?"

"Of course. Cheers." She lifted her glass and touched it to his. "So, did you?"

"Did I what?"

"Have a reasonable chance of winning the case?"

He sipped his drink; actually sucked half of it down. "You never know. It didn't look good, but you never know. The judge made some promising comments. So I was torn between wanting to ease Mr. Phillips' stress and at the same time be completely truthful. But one day I saw him standing in the hall, looking real bad. On impulse I went over, put my arm around his shoulder and told him to perk up—things would get better. We had a pretty good chance of winning, I said. He looked very happy. 'Do you really think so?' he asked. I said sure. And at the time, you know, I believed it."

She leaned farther forward. "So, did you win?"

"No. I lost. Lost big. As my secret admirer, you must have heard about it: TV cameras rolling outside the courtroom when we left, reporters cornering Phillips." He finished his scotch. "Four days later I'm at his funeral, watching his wife and kids say farewell to his casket. Heart attack. The night of the decision."

Laura reached over and placed a warm palm on Anthony's hand. Said nothing.

He stared back out at the boats. "I holed up in my house for three days reenacting the case in my head. The truth is that from the get-go I knew we were almost certain to lose. But as the case evolved I thought we had a reasonable chance. Maybe the let-down for Phillips wouldn't have been so harsh if I'd better prepared him to handle it. I don't know—I can't shake the feeling I'm partly responsible for his death."

"It wasn't your fault, Anthony. Surely you realize that." She squeezed his hand again.

He looked at her. "Isn't it funny that you're the only person I've been able to talk to about this? Maybe a stranger is exactly who I needed. I appreciate your listening." He paused. "I also broke up with my girlfriend tonight. It was a long time in coming. We both knew it."

"You're kidding."

"No. I went back to work today—for the first time since Phillips died—and when I got home she was sitting in my kitchen with all her cackling buddies—drinking, smoking and having a good ol' time. She hardly even noticed me. I felt like a renter stopping by to change clothes." He shook his head. "So I suggested that the party might be over; she knew how I still felt about the funeral. When they didn't leave, I did."

To his astonishment tears appeared in Laura's eyes, their shine almost missed behind the horn-rims. *Been through it, too*, he thought. And in that instant he was swept away. How long had it been since he'd known a woman with such an open and touchable heart? *Since Cheryl, that's how long.*

He smiled. "Will it surprise you to hear I've never been married?"

"Will it surprise you to hear I *was* married and don't want to talk about it?"

"Hey, that's not fair."

"Maybe some other time."

"Kids?" he asked.

She shook her head.

"Me neither. No wife, no girlfriend, no kids . . . only work. Am I a living cliché or what?"

"I read up on your background for that article I wrote. It didn't seem cliché to me. A full scholarship to Law School . . . and then you *volunteered* for combat in Vietnam?"

He fiddled with his empty glass. "Well, I was going over there one way or the other, right? Like everybody else. Could have opted for JAG, and soon I ended up there anyway, but . . . it sounds ridiculous when I say it."

"Go ahead."

"You know Berkeley's reputation, politically—'Moscow West.'

Well, one night I went to an event and some antiwar activists had this North Vietnamese propaganda film. It showed American soldiers getting gunned down—and the audience *applauded.* It pissed me off so much I went across the bay the next day and enlisted. I saw two other law students from my class doing the same thing; they were in the audience at the film too. Reported for duty the week after graduation."

"And saw action."

"Yes. Some. Then became a Judge-Advocate—a military lawyer—after all. They needed me more there."

"So the law is your passion."

He hesitated. "You could say it's another way to fight the good fight."

"Okay. So after your enlistment ended you came back here, served as a deputy DA for five years, and now you're a member of one of the top law firms in the city, specializing in shipping and maritime accidents."

"You *did* do your homework."

"Why that particular niche?"

He shrugged. "My best friend in high school came from a tuna fishing family, so I learned a lot about the industry and developed real admiration for the people who do it. I don't know, it just seemed natural."

"According to rumor, you're very good at it."

"I thought so, until that last trial." He spun the glass between his hands. "I don't know, maybe I'm already burning out. I've been going from trial to trial to trial for so long I'm beginning to feel like a dolphin spending too much time between resurfacings."

"Then slow down. Take a breath."

"I'm not sure I know how." He gave a laugh. "Sorry, I'm not usually so mawkish. You're very gracious to sit here listening to me whimper."

Again, the warmth of her hand pressed against his. "Maybe it's not burnout or even too much dedication. Maybe you're running away from some fundamental disappointment in your life."

Her eyes were—there was no other word for it—hypnotic. "Are you sure you're not the reincarnation of Sigmund Freud?"

"No, I told you. I'm your secret admirer."

"Not so secret now."

"No, not so secret. So 'fess up. What's *really* got you down?"

He shrugged. "I guess I feel the need for something . . . more. Graduating from college I almost went into political science. Had written some papers, got some recognition. Had some ideas. Well, those ideas are still there. In fact they keep growing, looking for a way out."

"What kind of ideas?"

"Oh no you don't. I haven't had that much to drink."

"Drat. My evil plan has failed."

He laughed, and on impulse reached out to brush a lock of her thick shiny hair behind her ear.

"That smile looks good on you," she said. "I love a deep thinker who can laugh."

"And I love a deep laugher who can think. What? Damn, I *have* had too much to drink." He threw enough crumpled money on the table to pay the tab plus a generous tip, then stood. "May I walk you to your car?"

She took his arm and they maneuvered together through the crowd and into the refreshing night.

"Where is *your* car?" she asked.

"Let's see, about two blocks away."

"C'mon; I'll give you a ride to it." She escorted him to a well- used sedan, climbed in, waited until he was buckled, and then pulled into the street.

"Right turn at the next corner," he said. His tongue felt a little thick. "I'm down about half a block."

At the corner she slowed . . . and turned *left.*

"Laura. You're going the wrong way."

"No I'm not."

She lived in a small back-lot cottage not far from the beach in Del Mar, near the famous race track. She led him through a lighted patio, landscaped as a tropical garden, and up to her front door. Once inside she told him to make himself comfortable and began brewing a pot of coffee. "You're still in no condition to drive."

He tossed his jacket onto an easy chair and looked around.

Books lay everywhere: on tables, on shelves; and where there were no books there were teetering stacks of paper. "You weren't kidding about doing a lot of reading," he said. He noticed a well-used electric typewriter on the desk against the window. "And writing."

"Always a deadline." She came to him, stood face to face and ran her fingers along his shoulders. The light brought out almost imperceptible shades of sorrow in her eyes. "You look a little frazzled in that business suit," she said. "If you'd like, the shower is through the door to your right. I could hang some fresh towels and a clean robe outside the door for you."

"Really? Thanks. I'd like that. Finishing off with a little cold water should help me out."

She arched an eyebrow. "You need a cold shower already?"

The shower stall, enclosed in clear glass, faced the tropical patio. Anthony stripped off his suit and stepped into cascading hot water. Heaven! He popped the cap off a bottle of shampoo and began shampooing his head.

"Here you are," he heard Laura say matter-of-factly, "towel and robe." Her voice came from *inside* the bathroom. "I'll put them on the towel bar." She paused. "Mind if I get in there with you?"

With soap all over his face, he couldn't open his eyes. "Um, make yourself at home. Conserving water is a public duty."

He heard the door slide open and closed, felt water spray bouncing back at him. Then her voice in his ear: "Forgive me, but you're so sad . . . and we're both so lonely . . . and life is so goddamned short."

Hard, warm nipples pressed against his chest, setting off a tingling current throughout his body. Then came her embrace; the shower massage; her arms around his waist; her warm open mouth and tongue sliding against his neck. Her touch erased the misery of the past weeks. Only Cheryl of 1962 could compare. Still dizzy and with his eyes tightly closed, he could almost believe it was Cheryl there in his arms.

Another warm whisper in his ear: "I've been thinking about you ever since I saw you in court that day."

At last he opened his eyes and thrilled to the sight of Laura's tan bronzed skin, no untanned spot anywhere evident. Her legs, smooth, glistening and hard, never seemed to stop; her curves and muscles, wizardry beneath his fingers, were the inspiration for a sculpture.

They toweled each other and she led him to her bedroom. Here he saw more books and stacks of papers, but neatly organized. Beautiful serigraphs hung on the wall, scenes of sun-drenched little children with their mothers at the edge of the sea—scenes of nostalgia for her? For an instant his appreciative eye took over. The artist's work resembled that of the Spanish painter Joaquin Sorolla.

Get out of the way, Sorolla, it's my turn now.

"So tell me more about these big ideas of yours," she said as they lay tangled together in hot, damp sheets.

"What, you couldn't get me drunk enough to talk about it, so you seduced me instead?"

"That's right; I'm only after your brain." She slid a hand down his stomach, down .

He squirmed. "Okay, okay. My big ideas? They're just . . . theoretical, I suppose. Things I started thinking about back in collage." *Are you going into one of your Mr. Anthropologist moods?*

"If you were thinking about anything other than girls then," Laura said, "I'm all ears."

"I wouldn't say that." He cupped one of her breasts. "Where was I? Oh, yeah—I was a wrestler back then, and it struck me as odd: here was this team of guys training together, helping each other out . . . by trying to crush one another, turn each other into pretzels. And then we'd go off to compete with other teams that did the same thing. The competition made us better, tougher—but so did the teamwork. Later I saw the same thing, not only on the wrestling mat but after class, studying—helping other people study, even though we might all end up competing against one another on the bell curve or in the marketplace someday. In Costallegre it was the same thing again, only amplified to the scale of murder. And in Vietnam, the same thing *again*—only amplified even further, to warfare. Hell, maybe it's even bigger than that— the principle behind the expansion of the universe, the evolution of stars, life itself."

"You're talking about balance? Yin and Yang?"

"Not balance. Balance means equilibrium, a static condition, but the universe is always changing, developing. What I'm talking about is more like . . . *synthesis*. You know, 'the whole is greater than the sum of its parts.' A dynamic synthesis between cooperative and competitive forces, just unbalanced enough to create the optimal conditions for growth. Strife is growth, but not too much of it."

"Interesting concept."

"But if perfect balance is undesirable, the question is which direction the scales should lean. I'm sure the radicals back at Berkeley would say cooperation, and that includes government-forced cooperation, for sure. Others would insist on competition, meaning full-on free market, the purer the better."

"And what do you think?"

"I think both are essential, but like I said, based on what I've seen and read, the universe seems inclined to prefer an *overall* tilt toward competition. The asymmetric lean."

She slid a long leg over his torso. "So if this synthesis is universal and natural, why worry about it? Won't each system just find its way there automatically?"

"Eventually, sure—just like ice and fire synthesize to make water. Or armies fight it out until they synthesize peace. But at what cost? We're human beings; we don't have to let things go to extremes before we find the best synthesis for a human system. As people we can always look ahead, plan, adjust—to avoid the biggest messes."

"I see what you're saying. Go on, go on."

"Did you know that James Madison and some other early Americans tried to figure out why all the previous democracies in the world had failed so they could avoid making the same mistakes when writing our Constitution?"

"No, I didn't." She dragged a slow fingertip through the sweat on his chest.

"Madison." His train of thought derailed. "Um . . . Madison even studied the political structure of the Iroquois Indians; some of our system of checks and balances came from their nation."

"Really? I didn't know that, either."

"Syn . . . synthesis. . . ." he said.

"Show me." She pulled herself on top of him. "Show me that the whole is greater than the sum of its parts."

is more like ... synthesis. You know, "The whole is greater than the sum of its parts"—dynamic synthesis between cooperative and competitive forces, just unbalanced enough to create the optimal conditions for growth [illegible]

"Interesting concept."

"This imperfect balance is fundamental, but the question is what direction the scales should favor. [illegible] would [illegible] cooperation, and that includes governance [illegible] Others would insist on competition [illegible] the purity the [illegible]."

"And what do you think?"

"I think both are essential, [illegible]

[illegible]

4 The Pinnacle

"Is this the new '78 model?" the valet asked as Anthony Darren slid out of his new black BMW sports coupe and into the shadow of the Hotel Del Coronado's Victorian turrets.

"First one in the county this year," Anthony said, handing over the keys. "So treat her carefully." His cufflinks sparked against the starched white sleeves edging his black tux as he accepted a card from the valet and turned to offer his arm to his passenger.

The glinting tiara adorning Samantha Kincaid's swept-back flaxen hair complemented the blue-white shimmer from the neckline of her indigo gown. As they stepped into the hotel Anthony slid the mink coat off her shoulders, then escorted her across the lobby toward the check room next to the carved arch that marked the entrance to the Grand Ballroom. Along the way he received at least twenty *hellos* and *congratulations*, and several judges shook his hand.

"It's like being with a rock star," Samantha said, smiling.

"Just call me Bruce."

"Who?"

"Bruce Springsteen? No? Never mind; one of these days everybody will know him. Listen, why don't you wait for me over by the ballroom where it's not so crowded?"

As he stood there in the coat check line, he spotted a familiar man several people ahead: Egan James, also dressed in formal attire, with a woman's wool wrap and dark overcoat over his arm. As if aware of Anthony's attention, he turned his head and waved. Anthony waved back. He and Egan had recently become reacquainted through their memberships in the San Diego County Bar Association. *He still has that same old sneer on his face. Maybe he just can't help it. Maybe it doesn't really reflect how he thinks or feels.*

"Hey, Anthony." A well-wisher approached, holding out his hand. "How does it feel? Youngest Bar President ever elected in the County?"

Anthony smiled. "Makes me wonder why the wise old guys ducked the job." He was being facetious, of course; he knew that leadership of the four-thousand-member association was a position from which one could later launch a political career, or join the judiciary. He respected and appreciated the responsibility that accompanied reaching such a lofty height.

He looked over at Samantha, standing like a princess by the ballroom entrance. Not since his senior year in college had he felt such satisfaction with his life. Tonight he would be installed as President of the Bar, and earlier that day he and Samantha had announced their engagement. In one sense he felt relieved. He'd held off making the commitment for so long he'd begun to wonder if it would ever happen. Yet on another level he kept asking himself if he was really making the right decision. Cheryl had loved him when he was nothing and nobody; she would have been happy married to a modest college professor teaching political science. Laura had seemed attracted to his mind as much as to his body . . . or, certainly, his future. Were the same things true of Samantha, with her blue-blood family and her aristocratic upbringing? How could he ever know for sure?

He shrugged off the doubts. Samantha was everything he wanted in a woman: level-headed, articulate, cultured, an MBA, the producer and assistant manager of a popular radio station. Not to mention a striking beauty whose family was connected to just about every judge in town. Not that that mattered to Anthony. Did it?

Up ahead Egan James checked the coat and stole, then joined a willowy blonde woman and guided her through the Grand Ballroom's huge, crown-molded double doorway.

A few minutes later Anthony walked over to Samantha and offered his arm. "Shall we?"

"Please."

As he escorted her into the ballroom he said, "Did you notice the taller man in the coat check line about six people ahead of me?"

“What about him?”

“His name is Egan James. I suspect you’ll meet him later tonight, so you ought to know he and I go back a long time. He’s been two or three years behind me each step of my career ever since high school.”

“Following in the footsteps of a good man, I’d say.”

More like tracking me, Anthony thought. “He had a few setbacks but he made it, finally. I’ve heard he’s done very well since being admitted to the bar.”

She fixed her sharp gaze on him. “Is there a reason you’re telling me this?”

“Just in case he decides to tell you any embarrassing stories about me, I guess.” He forced a smile.

They got caught up in a swirl of friends and acquaintances. Colleagues slapped him on the back and their ladies delivered pecks on the cheek. Finally Samantha eased him, with practiced social grace, to their place of honor at the head table.

During dessert Samantha said, “Anthony, that friend you told me about? Looks like he’s heading this way.”

Anthony looked up to see Egan strolling toward them across the dance floor, pausing now and then to chat with someone. He really did seem to have changed for the better. Mellowed, although from what Anthony had heard, he had a reputation for almost fanatical tenacity. On the few occasions they’d seen each other since Egan joined the bar, neither had mentioned their old fight in the alley behind Oscar’s Drive-In. Anthony hoped Egan wouldn’t choose tonight to bring it up, even light-heartedly.

Anthony stood and the two men shook hands. Anthony could never tell whether Egan’s smile was the product of sincerity, rehearsal or physiology; it always had that slight curl to it. There was an old scar over Egan’s left eye.

“Egan,” Anthony said, “let me introduce my fiancé, Samantha Kincaid. Sam, meet Egan James.”

“I hear you and Anthony have known each other since high school,” she said.

“Yes,” Egan said, still smiling, “it’s been a long time. And I don’t mind saying you've got quite a man here." He tilted his head. "Anthony, you've really made it. You're not only Bar President—and I congratulate you—but here you are with the Belle of the Ball. My congratulations on that count, too, an achievement even greater than the first!"

"Thanks very much, Egan." As so often happened, Anthony felt the pull of opposing forces inside him: the urge to compete with Egan charm for charm tugging against that cooperative behavior known as "civility." He said, "Your observation of Samantha is exactly mine, too," and pulled his fiancé closer to him.

The orchestra started up with "Just the Way You Are," by Billy Joel. Samantha smiled. "Oh, I love this song. Come on, honey, let's dance."

He sighed. "Sorry, but see those older guys over there? Looks like the other board members are waiting for me; I have to tend to some business." He turned to Egan and he felt compelled to produce a grin. "Rescued by the gavel. If Samantha had her way we'd dance to every number. Would you let her have her dance, only one. I won't be long." He laughed. Even as he spoke he wondered what the hell he was saying. Too much civility wasn't such a great idea, either. . . .

Later that night, Samantha and Anthony sipped champagne as they sat on a couch in the sunken living room of his luxurious town house on a steep hillside in La Jolla. The view through the bay windows constantly changed as the shimmering surf washed the shore hundreds of feet below.

"So," Anthony said, "what did Egan have to say about the old days?"

"A lot of nice things. He said he didn't know you as well then as he feels he does now that you're both grown up and practicing law. Why do you ask?"

"Oh, I didn't want you getting jealous if he told you about all my old girlfriends."

She laughed. "He acted as though *he* had all the girlfriends while you just studied and got straight A's."

"Mr. Studious, that was me," Anthony said. He felt his shoulders relax.

She settled against him, and the light from the homes and the beach club below sparkled off the champagne glass in her hand. But the sparkle she watched most was the one coming from the ring on the third finger of her left hand.

The phone rang. Sam picked up, and the moment the conversation began Anthony could tell the caller was her mother, Jennifer. They talked on the phone all the time, chattering more like sisters than mother and daughter. They even *looked* more like sisters than parent and child; Jennifer tended to dress and style her hair just like her daughter.

You're just upset she broke the mood, he thought while Samantha told her mother everything anybody had ever said about her engagement. But she's excited, and who would she want to share the details with more than her mother?

He sank into the cushions and half-listened with a smile on his face. Nothing could beat down his spirits tonight. Besides, he'd have plenty of time alone with Samantha tomorrow. Then, on Monday, back to work—including an appointment with someone he hadn't seen in almost fifteen years.

The intercom buzzed. "Mr. Darren, Mr. Cruz has arrived."

"Please tell him I'll be right out." Anthony cleared papers and books off his desk, then walked to the reception room. He wasn't sure what he expected to see, but when Joe stood up, tall and bronzed, he still resembled Portuguese-style bullfighter Carlos Arruza—but with a few strands of gray in his hair. His easy smile was also the same. The only real difference was that instead of the torn jeans and t-shirts he'd worn in the old days, he was now adorned in sleek dress pants and a raw silk shirt open at the throat.

Anthony held out his hand. "Mr. Cruz."

"Mr. Darren."

They shook, then Joe grinned and hauled Anthony into an embrace resembling a half-Nelson.

Back in Anthony's office, Joe dropped into the leather wing chair across from the desk and looked around. "Good taste. First rate view of the harbor, too. You a partner yet?"

"Didn't you notice my name on the door?"

"I never read the fine print."

"Good to see you still haven't found your sense of humor."

For a few minutes they brought each other up to date. Joe had scaled the ranks of the tuna fishing industry and now owned several boats. Sylvia's great, thanks. Little Mikey? Not so little anymore! No, I haven't heard anything from or about Cheryl; she seems to have dropped off the map. You're engaged? Wow, congratulations! When can I meet the unfortunate lady?

"Remember Egan James? He is a deputy DA."

"Seriously, he's prosecuting criminals instead of being one? Will wonders never cease."

Finally Anthony said, "Okay, Joe, what's up? You don't have to make an appointment to chew the fat with me."

Joe took a deep breath, let it out. "I was wondering if you'd represent me and my corporation in a little problem we're having."

"What kind of problem?"

"Basically the bank, shipyard and even the damn cannery are all trying to foreclose on my boats."

Anthony pulled a yellow pad in front of him. "Why? What exactly happened?"

With an uncharacteristic helplessness drawing his face down, Joe said, "Have you heard about the fishing boat J & D Shipyards is building for me?"

"Sure, everyone knows about it; it's been all over the financial news. The most high-tech, state of the art, among the largest tuna seiners ever built. Right?"

"Well, you're right, not *the* largest, but one of the largest. The problem is that it's not good enough for the environmentalists. You know the new laws they've passed; it's impossible to keep up. How are we supposed to save every dolphin that gets tangled in our nets? Hard as we try to prevent it, some die, especially with big boats like mine."

"Yeah, I've heard the new regs are giving you guys some grief."

"'Grief?' The government's forbidding us from setting on schools of tuna running with porpoises . . . I mean dolphins when I refer to porpoises . . . unless we cut porpoise mortality to almost zilch! Anthony, we're going broke trying to comply. Production is so far down we barely make expenses anymore. In fact, my new boat, *the Sea Diva* . . . I'm already in such serious financial trouble I can't even afford to send her on her maiden voyage! She's sitting in dry dock costing me thousands of dollars a month while they put the finishing touches on her, and I'm not even sure she'll ever get wet. On top of that, the canneries are all moving overseas where labor is cheap and they're out of reach of environmentalists."

"I read about that, too."

"But that's *still* not the whole problem." Joe became even more animated. "Fuel costs are going out of sight. Interest rates are as high as the moon. Construction costs are ridiculous. And now we're competing against foreign fisheries whose governments subsidize their boats—sometimes with money *our* government loans *them*—money from taxes *we* pay, money my government will never get back!" Joe suddenly rose to his feet, eyes ablaze. "They're killing the American tuna industry with America's help!"

Anthony waved for Joe to sit back down. "Thanks for the big picture, but what's been happening with *you*? This is all in confidence, so don't worry about that." Joe sat and stared at his hands.

"Let me guess," Anthony said in a soft voice. "You took some of the money you borrowed for building this new boat and used it to subsidize your older boats, right?"

"I couldn't help it." Joe kept his eyes down. "I had no choice. I also gave a lot of the money to my crew. They've been working like dogs on shore with no pay to get *the Sea Diva* outfitted. Some of their families have been almost starving."

Anthony stared at the top of Joe's head. "You know, I've never forgotten that summer we worked on your dad's boat. The ocean, the men, the hard work; I always thought your company was financially solid."

Joe spread his hands in a gesture that said, *so did I*. His exposed palms displayed a dichotomy: the smooth skin of a businessman crisscrossed with the old scars of someone who had once handled nets and spiky-finned fish.

"Okay," Anthony said. "Did you bring your contracts with you? Loan documents, cannery fishing agreements, shipyard contracts?"

"Here." Joe lifted a bulging old briefcase onto the gleaming desk. He seemed too preoccupied to notice the scratching sounds the bag's metal corners made against the wood.

No matter; this desk is used to battle scars. I can fix those . . . but can I fix Joe's problems?

When Joe pulled a disheveled, four-inch thick packet of papers out of the case, Anthony realized that this job was not going to be the proverbial piece of cake. "What bank is it?"

"Southern Cal Empire."

Anthony winced. "Herbert Hooks is powerful in this town."

"Yeah, tell me about it. I think he wants *the Sea Diva* for his personal yacht."

Anthony flipped through the documents, page after page, scanning and absorbing. He let Joe sit in silence.

"What do you think?" Joe finally blurted.

Anthony answered with his eyes fixed on the documents. "I think . . . we have a possibility of getting an injunction against the cannery and the bank to temporarily stop their foreclosures."

"Really? How?"

"On grounds of the violation of anti-trust regulations. There seem to be some irregularities here. I see an illegal tie-in, written between the lines of the fishing contracts and the paperwork for the cannery loan and bank loan . . . and if there's one, I suspect I'll find more."

"Anti-trust? How does that relate?"

"A little refresher." Anthony sat back. "Around the turn of the century monopolists and robber barons were taking control of industry in this country and killing off all their competition. Right?"

Joe nodded.

"Then nothing could stop them from raising prices. Congress saw the threat to the free market and enacted anti-monopoly and anti-trust laws. That forced a little cooperation on the tycoons." He leaned forward. "Karl Marx's biggest reason for advocating socialism and communism was that he didn't believe laws would ever succeed in controlling monopolies. Well, he was wrong—we *can* control monopolies with antitrust laws."

"But in my case . . . "

Anthony pointed out the intricacies of Joe's situation, including the tie-ins between the stake holder fishing contracts and the ship's mortgage, and the possibility Joe had been overcharged by the shipyard. Then he paused and gazed out the window. The sight of the harbor crisscrossed with the contrails of boat wakes sometimes helped stimulate ideas—which he could really use now, given the complexities of Joe's problem.

Finally he turned back and launched into a discussion that lasted almost an hour before culminating in the assertion that certain counterattacks could legitimately be mounted against the charges leveled at Joe. Then he added, "But I have to warn you not to get overenthusiastic, even if evidence useful to us is uncovered, because of your personal guarantee on the loans."

"What do you mean?"

Anthony flipped through the papers and stopped at the one he wanted. "Let's say I manage to stop the foreclosure on *the Sea Diva*, at least temporarily: even then I probably won't be able to stop the bank from liening your personal assets. That's a separate contract, and when you signed it you guaranteed them everything from the birth of Christ to the death of the Devil. Then there's the fact you violated the loan agreement when you spent *the Sea Diva's* loan to feed your crew and pay for your other boats. You might have violated a federal lending law there." He paused. "Joe . . . I have to tell you, that could be a felony."

Joe closed his eyes.

"But that's *still* not the end. Even if the court chooses to offset antitrust damages against the loan—you could still end up owing millions."

Eyes still closed, Joe said, "What about filing Chapter Eleven?"

"Sure, we could do that, but then we've got other problems. First, as soon as the bankruptcy judge sees how little equity there is in the ship, he might just let the bank foreclose. Second, filing Chapter Eleven probably won't keep Empire from coming after you personally on the guarantee for the difference in damages. And before you ask, no, I don't recommend you file a personal Chapter Eleven either. Believe me, you don't want the bankruptcy trustee investigating possible violation of federal lending laws."

Joe's eyes drifted open as if he were awakening from a dream. Then he snapped his head from side to side. "Well, I've got to do *something*. Sell the *Diva*? I can't just sit and wait for them to take my world apart!"

"I agree. I just wanted you to know the downside. But listen— if you can come up with more evidence supporting antitrust activities, we'll give 'em hell. Who knows, maybe, just maybe, you can make it through this and have enough wiggle room to sell the boat." He paused. "But right now I suggest you go home and try to relax. Let me see what I can do. Believe it or not, I've worked out worse problems than this."

After Joe signed a standard form retainer agreement and left, Anthony stood at the window for a while, thinking out possible paths to try, considering legal solutions. He willingly shouldered the heavy weight of responsibility. As an attorney he'd always believed that one of his functions was to take pressure off his client whenever he could.

But when he found his thoughts spiraling back in on themselves he transferred his gaze from the bay to a well-handled bundle of pages on a corner shelf of his office: the quarter-finished novel he had told Laura Evans about years earlier. Under other circumstances Anthony would have smiled at the irony: his fictional story was like a preview of Joe Cruz's current real-life troubles. Of course, the coincidence wasn't as amazing as it seemed: Anthony was a legal expert on the tuna industry; he'd grown up around tuna fishermen—including Joe and his family—and he knew that half the boats in the American fleet were currently having financial problems. He was only glad Joe had sought legal aid rather than surrendering, as Anthony's fictional boat captain did, to the urge to sink his vessel in order to collect the insurance money . . . especially since in the book, a beloved cousin died along with the boat.

Just like an Italian opera, Anthony thought with a smile.

Still, he grabbed the stack of handwritten pages and fanned through them. *Well, Laura thought it had promise; she even said she'd ask her boss to recommend it to a fiction publisher if I wanted.* Of course, that had been two years ago, before he and Laura drifted apart. Since then even the occasional friendly phone calls or lunches had become rarities. Samantha tended to get chilly whenever he mentioned other women, even friends, even professional acquaintances.

Lying on top of the manuscript was his handwritten synopsis of the story. Looking at it now, Anthony winced. He'd have to make some changes if he ever intended to complete the novel now; otherwise someone would surely assume he'd plagiarized the story from Joe's reality!

After a moment's consideration he scribbled the current date—November 18, 1978—on the synopsis, then attached a separate transmittal letter previously dated October 26, 1978 that he hadn't yet mailed.

October, 26, 1978

Dear Laura:

I know it's been a while, but I thought you might still want to have a peek at the novel I've been working on forever. This synopsis is already out of date, but will give you a general idea of what I have in mind. What do you think?

Sincerely,
Anthony

He laid the papers on his secretary's desk for mailing, then tucked a copy of the October 26 transmittal letter inside a personal file in his credenza and pushed the whole idea of the novel to the back of his mind. The time had come to roll up his sleeves and do a great job for Joe. If he could get the injunctions he was hoping for, *the Sea Diva* might get to leave dry dock after all. If so, and if Joe Cruz was still anything like the man Anthony remembered, that ship would be the focus of one hell of a maiden voyage party.

5 The Maiden and the Black Widow

In the damp darkness of the shipyards Anthony and Samantha stepped over railroad tracks embedded in pavement on the pier. Ahead, the glare of *the Sea Diva's* masthead lights galvanized a blend of fresh marine air amid the aroma of creosote-coated pilings. The beat of a rock band playing The Who's *Who Are You?* echoed off the unlit warehouse buildings in counterpoint to the clicks of Samantha's high heels. Bursts of laughter punctuated the rhythm.

Such goings-on, thought Anthony, you could almost believe Joe will get out of his mess and be able to send this monster out to sea. If the partiers only knew the truth.

At close range the boat's size was astounding. Though Anthony knew her precise measurements, he hadn't been able to visualize what they really represented. With all her lights and fixtures *the Sea Diva* looked like a giant pier next to the real pier. Down low, curved tubes of water, pumped from somewhere in the ship's internal organs, splashed into the bay.

Anthony followed Samantha up the boarding ramp to the main deck, where they were ushered through a crowd of cocktailing guests to the bar. Finally, drink in hand, Anthony heard Joe's voice, and the squeeze of a bear hug greeted both him and Samantha.

"God, it's great to have you on board! Samantha, without my buddy's knock-out lawyering we wouldn't even be here. Some heavyweights around this town are still holding their poor kicked butts, thanks to him."

Samantha smiled and squeezed Anthony's arm. "Anthony kept me posted on the courtroom motions. He smiled like a fool for days after he stopped the foreclosures."

"Well, let me show you some of what he saved." Joe threw an arm around their shoulders and steered them toward a group of young men. "Anthony, let me introduce you to someone you might vaguely remember—my son Michael."

"Mikey?" Anthony said as a handsome college-aged man stepped over and shook his hand. Anthony frowned at Joe. "How come he's so good-looking and you're so ugly?"

"Ahhh, he takes after his mother." Joe put his face next to Michael's, obviously trying to prove the opposite. "Son, please irritate my friend and his fiancé for a few minutes; I see some people without drinks in their hands I have to take care of."

Anthony watched him swagger off then smiled at Michael. "I remember when you were drawing pictures on your dad's term papers."

"I'm sure they improved his grades." Michael grinned. "Mr. Darren, I can't say I remember you, but I do feel like I know you; Dad talked about you all the time. And of course now." he waved a hand around, just as Joe had done. "We really appreciate what you've done for us."

"Thanks for the vote of confidence, but we still have a long way to go before—"

"This son of mine," Joe interrupted, "is the guy who discovered all the shipyard cover-ups you were so sure we'd find." He turned to Samantha. "Anthony warned us exactly what might have happened. Michael, tell her."

As Michael went on about the lawsuit, Anthony felt a dread tie a knot in his gut. *This kid really believes his dad will fight off the bank and save the* Diva. Yet he couldn't bring himself to tell Michael the true odds. Besides, miracles could happen.

"All this legal talk makes me feel like I'm at work," he said. "Let's talk about you, Michael. You're doing graduate work?"

"Do you mind if I excuse myself again?" interrupted Joe. "Some more people I want to thank."

"At the bar, no doubt," Anthony said.

"How did you guess?"

As Joe walked off Michael said, "I'm in the second year of my Master's at UCSD. Oceanography at Scripps Institute."

"Good field, good school," said Anthony. "Will your thesis relate to the tuna industry?"

"Yes, experimenting on reducing dolphin, or the fishermen say porpoise, mortality."

"Wonderful. The business, including your Dad, could use a breakthrough in that area."

"I'm hoping to get approval from the Department to go out on *the Sea Diva's* first trip"—he glanced around—"but I want to keep that as a surprise for my dad, if you don't mind."

Anthony crossed his heart. "Top secret."

"My lips are sealed," Samantha said. Anthony thought she was beginning to look a little bored. *I'd better—*

Just then a huge man in his late twenties, with curly rust-colored hair and a wildly gleeful expression on his face, strode up and threw an arm around Michael. The newcomer looked like an NFL number-one draft choice: six-six or so, and all muscle.

"Our helicopter pilot," Michael said by way of introduction. "Moby' Jack Callucci."

"Nice to meet you," Anthony said. "I noticed the helipad behind the bridge. Would you mind telling Samantha what a chopper is doing on a tuna boat?"

"Sure." Moby Jack released Michael and straightened, his size a startling contrast to his boyish smile. "When we get out on the fishing grounds, I take the bird up and circle out to a distance of maybe ten or twenty miles looking for schools of tuna."

"Or dolphins," Michael said. "Their relationship seems symbiotic.

We don't know for sure which one needs the other, but lots of times dolphins and tuna run together."

"Don't get him started on the Flippers," Moby Jack said. "Where was I? Oh, yeah: when we spot fish we radio back and the ship comes around to corral them."

"Corral them?" Samantha said.

"The tuna boat drops off a gang of speedboats that go around the school like cowboys riding herd on cattle to keep them from scattering. At the same time a big skiff pulls the net out opposite the tuna boat and starts making a huge circle. When the tuna boat and skiff meet up again, the net might be a full mile or more around."

"A *mile*?"

"Yep. Then they draw the bottom of the net into a giant purse, pull it in with a power winch and start brailing aboard the compressed fish."

"Along with any dolphins hanging around," Michael said.

Samantha sipped her wine. "I remember reading about that."

"Many said it was wholesale slaughter," Michael said, "but not anymore. And Flipper, the dolphin you see on TV, is not the species that gets caught in the nets. We use different operations to try and help the dolphins escape before the net is closed. Unfortunately they aren't completely effective."

"What operations?"

"Well, one fishing captain invented a panel of small mesh we submerge near the surface near the stern to give the dolphins a chance to escape before we completely draw the tuna in. It helps, but for some reason if the kinds of dolphin we're dealing with miss the panel, they won't jump over the flotation barriers. They *could* jump over, but they won't. We don't know why."

"So, what happens to the ones that don't escape?"

"We send men into the net, sometimes with scuba gear, to physically slide the porpoises out over the flotation barrier. Sometimes guys have to stand up to their chests in the water on top of stacks of dying tuna to do this. It's dangerous."

"But I thought dolphins were intelligent animals. You see them doing tricks at Sea World. And they can jump like crazy!"

"Good point, ma'am," Moby Jack said. "But those trained dolphins are bottlenose dolphins. They're a coastal species and don't come out where we are and get caught in the nets, so we don't know if they'd jump out or not. But they're so smart; we think they'd just jump out. The kinds that run with tuna are spotted, spinner, striped and common dolphins—and for whatever reason including that they are dumber than the bottlenose, they won't jump out of the nets. And yup, their populations have been cut, but not to the point that they're endangered."

As always, Anthony found the subject complex and interesting. The relationship between tuna and dolphins—was it cooperative or competitive? Symbiotic, as Michael seemed to think, or parasitic? If the latter, were the mammals taking advantage of the fish, or the other way around?

He looked at Michael. "If you find a better method for saving dolphins, will the fleet implement it?"

"I think so. First we'll try it with our code boats, then expand to the entire industry. Maybe we'll even get cooperation from foreign fishing fleets for a change."

"Code boats?" Samantha asked.

Anthony laughed. "I should hire her as a cross-examiner."

Once again Moby Jack took the helm. "Ma'am, when we're fishing, most of the time we work in small competing teams. For example, when the *Diva* goes out she'll work with some of Joe's and his cousin's other boats. So let's say the *Diva* finds a nice school. She'll fish it, of course, but maybe also find other schools around. So she'll radio her location by secret code to her team boats—we call them code boats—so they can come in without tipping off the whole fleet. If everyone knew the location there'd be wall-to-wall boats at the hot spot within hours."

"In other words," Anthony said, "you cooperate with each other and compete against each other at the same time."

"So we can beat up on the rest of the fleet," Moby Jack said. "Yup."

"Where did you play college ball?" Anthony asked.

Moby Jack raised one red eyebrow. "How did you know?"

Michael laughed. "Are you kidding, Tiny?" Then, to Anthony: "Notre Dame. Engineering major, but he would've turned pro except for his ROTC obligation."

"ROTC where you learned to fly choppers?" Anthony asked.

Moby Jack nodded. "Marines."

Samantha gave him a sympathetic look. "Were you in Vietnam too?"

"Saw my share, ma'am." Then he forced Michael into a headlock and said, "Pardon me, folks, but I'm taking this boy over to his pals before they throw me off the ship."

In the pilothouse high above the deck, Joe Cruz stood gripping the wheel and staring out through the windows. From this perspective the bow of his ship extended so far it made him proud. He could sense the generators running even though no vibration came through the wheel. His soul felt the power idling within the bowels of his ship.

All she wants to do is go to sea and fish.

He looked around the pilothouse with the same feeling he got at home in his den. His skipper's license hung on the port bulkhead next to his college diploma and above his navigator's license. He'd come a long way.

The Sea Diva was the culmination of his dreams. Because of her, all his friends in the industry showed him respect. Of course, they didn't know the depths of trouble this same boat had sunk him into. Joe didn't like to show it, but he doubted that even Anthony Darren could save him in the long run.

Yet he still hoped for a miracle.

The door opened behind him, delivering the full impact of the rock music along with a rush of cool night air, then clicked shut again. Joe didn't turn around.

"Thanks for inviting me to the party," came the dry voice of Herbert Hooks. "That was quite diplomatic of you."

Joe turned then, but couldn't bring himself to speak.

"I presume you accepted my explanation for the foreclosure,"

said the banker. His half-smile was rueful, even apologetic. "It truly is out of my hands. Just business."

"Yeah, but apparently even foreclosing isn't enough for your Board."

Hooks shrugged. "You should have let us put you out of your misery when the opportunity first arose. I've run the projections, and it's obvious you're in too deep to get out. There's no way this boat is going to make a profit no matter what your big-time lawyer argues or even how many fish you bring in. Not that you'll ever get untied from this dock."

"Interest rates can always come down," Joe said. "Fuel costs can drop. Or we might solve the dolphin thing. Those can still happen."

Hooks shook his head. "It's not just you. This entire industry is dying, at least in the United States. It's going the way the sardine business did in Monterey. I'm sorry, but if you expect this boat to save you you're looking in the wrong place."

"Do you have a better idea, Herbert?"

Hooks gazed out the nearest window. "You're carrying eight million dollars of insurance on this vessel."

"So?"

Hooks shrugged. "Surely the answer is obvious."

"I don't . . . *what?*"

"Oh, don't be such a Boy Scout. My bank is going to have serious problems if you don't pay this loan off soon. I stuck my neck out for you, Joe. I got you the eight million you—"

"Bullshit!" Joe exploded. "What you got is loan points up the butt and outrageous interest rates. You stood to make a nice profit on me, Herbert. As for your . . . suggestion . . . I know what you're talking about. I've been around the block. And the answer is no. I wouldn't do it. To me this boat is a living being."

Hooks turned toward him. "One of the big lessons of business that you've clearly forgotten is *don't get emotionally attached.* Money and profits: that's all you need to think about. But so be it. If you insist on going down with the ship I'll be damned if you're taking my bank with you."

"What's the matter, Herbert? Afraid that if my loan goes unpaid, Pandora's box might open up? The feds might find out about the 'sweetheart' loans your bank made to certain lucky borrowers?"

"Don't let your imagination get you into more trouble than you're already in."

"Payments under the table that left some crumbs you can't clean up? Am I right? You want my boat to drown so your house of cards won't fall—right, Hooks?"

The banker wiped his brow with a handkerchief. "Speculate all you wish, but the fact remains: one way or another we're going to get our loan money back. Mr. 'Smooth' Darren might have temporarily stopped our foreclosure, but he can't stop us from attacking your personal guarantee. Do you know what that means? We'll take everything you've got, including your home and your wife's nice car and jewelry. You won't be able to pay for the rest of your kids' education. How would you like to see your daughters drop out of their sororities and those expensive colleges you've got them in? A total has-been, that's what you'll end up." He tucked the handkerchief into his jacket pocket. "Be smart, Joe. Get out of Sunday school and play ball in the street where you grew up."

Joe's fists clenched at his sides. "Get your slimy ass out of here before I slide you off the chute like a frozen tuna."

Hooks smiled and straightened his tie. "I'll see you, Joe. Probably in court, unless you think about what I said."

Joe turned away. A moment later, waves of rock music resonated past the back of his head as the door opened . . . then dropped to almost nothing as the door closed again.

But the memory of Hooks' smug face remained clear.

From the deck Anthony watched Herbert Hooks descend the steps from the pilot house and stride away, coat flapping. After he was out of sight Anthony climbed up the steps himself. It was like scaling a mountain. *This boat is* huge.

As he approached the pilothouse he saw Joe Cruz standing inside, shoulders hunched, clearly trying to calm down. So much for *bon voyage*.

Anthony stepped into the pilothouse. As Joe turned toward him, Anthony faked a right hook to Joe's jaw, then a straight left to the chin. "Hey, Buddy, come back to the party. What's all this hermit in the pilot house stuff?"

Joe put his hands on the wheel. "Just thinking what it would be like to take this baby out myself. I miss that."

"Generals don't fly the plane. And John Di Santi's the best skipper there is."

"I know. Speaking of the best, see Poncho down there?" Joe pointed through the forward windows.

Peering through the glass, Anthony spotted a blocky figure moving toward a cluster of crewmen huddled around the embers of lighted cigarettes at the bow. "Glad he's still with you. He's the chief engineer now, right?"

"Been with us ever since Pop found him scrounging around on the docks in Costallegre," Joe said. "Turned out to be a mechanical genius, you know, came back here, went to school—and now, yeah, he's my chief engineer." He paused, smiled fondly. "Still speaks English like a Costalegran, bur much more erudition."

Anthony watched Poncho and his group for a while. Even from this distance he could see the respect the men had for the engineer.

"Hey, you two have something in common," Joe said. "You know what subjects Poncho liked best when he was in engineering school? Diesel mechanics? No: civics, history and political science, and he was at the top in his classes."

Anthony nodded. "I'm sure what happened to his brother had something to do with that."

Joe's face sagged. "Man, that was a rough summer. If it hadn't been for Pop, the whole crew—including you and me—would probably have gone after those Serape sons-of-bitches and gotten ourselves killed too."

"Probably. From what I see on the news, Serape's government doesn't look like it will last much longer."

"I hope not. I just hope Poncho doesn't decide to stay down there next time the fleet's in the neighborhood."

The muffled beat of the band started up again, and Anthony clapped Joe on the shoulder. "Forget politics; let's get below. You've got a great party going. People wonder where you went."

"Go ahead," Joe said. "I'll be down in a minute. Have to think a little more, just a little more. Thanks for the company, though. I mean it."

Anthony stepped out and pulled the pilot house door shut behind him.

Joe watched Anthony disappear down the ladder. What if Hooks and Anthony were both right? What if the bank came after him, personally, and wiped him out? Maybe his feelings for this ship were like being mated to a black widow spider—love her, then die. Still, his heart told him to ignore logic and pray for that miracle.

Surely the answer is obvious.

No. No. To do "the obvious" he would need the assistance of his Chief Engineer, Poncho, a man who owed Joe's family almost everything. But Joe would never ask such a thing of Poncho, or of anyone else, including himself. He would never, under any circumstances or for any purpose, deliberately drown his ship.

6 The Code

Tucked high on a hill—on Point Loma—the Cruz house overlooked thousands of multicolored lights: Christmas lights on his neighbor's houses; harbor lights; boat lights on the water. Joe had traveled to many places in the world, but he never got tired of this view from his back porch. It was one of the most spectacular vistas he had ever seen.

Yet tonight as he sat and talked with Poncho, he was not encouraged by the scenery. He dragged his upholstered rattan chair closer to his chief engineer. "So . . . the *Diva* will be ready to sail next week?"

"She'll be ready."

"Poncho, this has to be a perfect trip, quick and efficient. If her fish wells aren't loaded up fast and full, we won't make it . . . financially, I mean." He lowered his voice. "In fact, the bank says we won't make it anyway."

"I heard." Poncho's eyes were downcast. "Well, we'll give this trip everythin' we got—but you know we'll have problems settin' nets without killin' dolphins, especially with that government observer on board."

"Anthony Darren says that might be unconstitutional, the government putting an observer on the boat. He says it's like stationing troops in your house."

"But for now they're doin' it. And what about all the countries south of here extendin' their fishin' limits to two hundred miles offshore? That sure cuts down the water we can work."

"I know." Joe offered Poncho a cigar, lit it and one for himself. They sat for a moment in a net of smoke.

"Remember when we lost the old man?" Joe said.

"A terrible day. I swear, if I'd been on board then I would never have let the storm take him."

Joe exhaled a gray cloud. "I wonder what he'd do now. In my situation."

Poncho shifted. "The right thing."

"The right thing for who? The bank? The business? The family?"

For a long moment Poncho was silent. Then he said, "When that bastard Serape took control of my country, my father told my mother, 'We can make it'—in Italian. When my brother was killed, my mother told my father, 'We can make it'—in Spanish. They tell me the same thing in both languages every time I visit. Joseph, if my mother and father can make it through what they've been through, we can make it through this."

The smoke curled in the night air around them. It was a good way to make sure Sylvia stayed well out of earshot. "The bank isn't letting up on me," Joe said.

"What do you mean?"

"Hooks keeps reminding me about 'the way out.'"

"Joseph . . . "

"I keep thinking there has to be a way to play his game and win. All I need is time, Poncho. The *Diva's* a great boat, and we've got a great crew. I know we can make money. At least we'd have a fighting chance. That's all I ask for. But Hooks won't let the *Diva* leave the pier unless he's convinced she'll never return again."

Poncho squashed out his cigar. "Joe."

"I'd never actually go through with it, Poncho. Not in a million years. But if Hooks *thinks* I might do it, he'll back off long enough for me to get the *Diva* out there and fish and, in his mind, have time to reconsider doing it. And after that . . . well, anything can happen. Right?"

Poncho shook his head. "He won' fall for it, Joe. If he knows you for even ten minutes he'll know you would never sink your own boat."

"I've thought this through. I didn't tell him I'd do it for sure. I told him I needed to think about it. I'd think about it while *the Sea Diva* was fishing. You know what he did? He laughed. He said, 'You think you're going to catch enough fish to pay off your loan, but you're wrong. The interest is accruing so fast you couldn't catch up if tuna were made out of gold.'

Poncho scowled and shook his head.

"But then he told me to go ahead and catch some fish anyway. Know why? Because it would look more convincing if the *Diva* sank with full holds."

Poncho crossed himself, face knotted in anger.

Joe lowered his voice. "You're wrong that Hooks won't give me time to think about it, Poncho. Know why? Because in the end he's sure I'll do what he wants. Men like Hooks think everyone's as crooked as they are."

Poncho puffed on the cigar. "I got to ask you somethin' Joe: why did you even tell me about this? Even *talkin'* about sinking your own boat is bad luck, the worst kind of luck. So if you're not plannin' to go through with it, why tell me?"

"I'm sorry about that, my friend. But I had to. I'm not a captain or fisherman anymore; all I do is pilot a desk. So obviously, if I were really going to go along with Hooks' plan, I'd need an accomplice on the *Diva*—someone loyal to me and with the knowhow to scuttle a ship."

"Like your Chief Engineer."

"Exactly. Look, I understand if you're too uncomfortable to go along with this, but I couldn't tell Hooks you were involved if you didn't even know about it. He might ask you questions. And besides, he'll be waiting for me to send you a signal."

"Signal?"

"When the time comes to . . . you know . . . I'm supposed to radio you with a coded signal."

Poncho looked puzzled.

"You know how I've got all the shells and sharks' jaws in my den?" Joe asked.

"Sure. What about it?"

"I told Hooks that when the time seemed right, I'd radio you and say, 'Poncho, try to find me a *sea* turtle shell.' Because sea turtles, you know . . . dive."

"Ah, *mierde*."

"But if I decided *not* to scuttle the *Diva*, I'd radio and say 'Poncho, try to find me a *tortoise* shell.'"

"Because tortoises stay dry."

"Right."

Poncho let out a long, hissing sigh. "Let me think." A handful of interminable minutes passed, punctuated by the roar of a navy jet climbing out of North Island.

Poncho looked up. "Okay, I'll help you. I'll preten' to be part of this plan. But please, do me a favor, brother to brother."

"Of course."

"Try findin' another answer to your problems before we leave. Because I don' trust Hooks, and if somethin' goes wrong out there and anyone gets hurt or if the ship is harmed, it's gonna break both our hearts. That beautiful ship . . . You'll have a hate against yourself you won't ever get rid of the rest of your life."

Joe nodded with no enthusiasm . . .

"Who else knows about this idea?" asked Poncho. "Anthony?"

"Are you crazy? Jesus, if he knew what I'm doing he'd drop my case so fast my file would hit the floor before the door hit my ass. No, the only people who know about this are me and you. Hooks will think he knows, of course, but he'll be wrong."

Poncho examined the stump of his cigar. "You sure we're the only ones?"

"Don't worry, Poncho. Hooks is in this too deep himself to tell anyone else about it."

Shortly after eight p.m. Herbert Hooks left the SCE Bank Building and walked three blocks to a garishly lighted café. In its window hung a small, B-rated sign, courtesy of city health inspectors. Hooks stepped in and selected a booth. Within a few minutes he was joined by a wiry-muscled man with straight black hair pulled back into a small pigtail.

"Alfonso Martin," the man said, and held out his hand. ..They looked around; huddled toward each other. . . . Oblique discussion then quietly followed . . .

" . . . you're in luck: I'm willing to grant you an extension on your loan . . . ."

A waitress took their orders for coffee.

. . . More discussion . . .

Alfonso stared into his eyes. Then: "Are you sayin' what I think you're sayin'?"

. . . More discussion . . . Then, for a few moments the silence hung like a blanket.

Alfonso rotated his coffee cup on the table exactly four times . . .

. . . Hooks struggled to keep the anger off his face. He couldn't believe this. Instead of falling to his knees in gratitude, this little rodent was trying to *negotiate*? Well, so be it; there was no time to search elsewhere.

More discussion . . . Alfonso was silent again for a moment, staring into his coffee. "You say the engineer is in on this whole thing? Poncho Pascalle knows about this?"

"Yes."

"Man, that's hard to picture. I think he loves *the Sea Diva* as much as Joe Cruz does."

"Well, that's the problem right there. These men are romantics, not realists. They want to believe some miracle will save the day. So instead of fully committing to the only plan that can actually keep his company solvent, Cruz wants to pretend he has the option to back out."

Their talk continued . . .

. . . "He and Pascalle have worked out radio codes for when the time comes to make the decision. One of the codes means 'sink the boat'; the other one means 'leave her alone.' But it doesn't really matter what they are," said Hooks.

". . . So no matter what the signal is, you have a job to do. I hope you don't need me to explain . . . "

Joe and Poncho stood on the old wood-and-concrete pier beneath the white cliff of *the Sea Diva's* spot-lit bow. The air was damp with a mixed bouquet romantic to certain kinds of people: creosote from pilings encrusted with mussels, oily brine splashing into the bay from the ship's bilge, the lingering aroma of fish from a freshly unloaded boat farther up the bay.

Joe waited for the sense of excitement he knew should be enveloping him right now, but he felt only doubt and dread. "I hear the revolution is getting close to Puerto Nuevo," he said. "Take care of yourself when the *Diva* gets down there, Poncho, and keep an eye on my crew. Don't let them get caught up in the trouble."

"My friends will see that we're okay," Poncho said. "Try not to worry about it, Joe."

"I'm not." Joe had to laugh. "The least of my worries is a civil war. What does that say about my priorities?"

Poncho did not reply. This close to *the Sea Diva*, the air smelled powerfully of diesel vapor. The boat lay low in the water, burdened by what seemed like a thousand tons of fuel. Joe felt the burden himself; he'd paid for the gas. Between shifting clouds of mist the bulbous white bow loomed overhead like the bust of a proud opera singer awaiting the final act.

Joe glanced at his watch: 11:54 p.m. Although the *Diva* had been ready to depart since that morning, by tradition it was bad luck for a tuna boat to leave port on a Friday. Joe wasn't about to tempt fate on this boat's maiden voyage, even though interest alone was costing him fifty thousand dollars a month. This trip was already too burdened with foreboding.

He lowered his voice, even though no one was within earshot. "Remember, I'll radio you with the code shortly after the boat turns for home. And Poncho, I want you to make sure someone overhears us talking about it. The radio operator, the skipper, someone."

"Why?"

"Because when *the Sea Diva doesn't* go down, Hooks is going to put pressure on me. He'll start bugging me. I want him to know I made my final decision. When he hears I gave a 'tortoise shell' code, he will know The Diva is not going down, and I do not want any further contact from him on the subject. We achieved *our* objective we made the maiden voyage.

"Sure. Okay." Poncho held out his hand. "We'll bring you back a full load of yellowfin, Joe, and maybe some bluefin."

They shook, then clasped one another in a brief, powerful hug.

Poncho walked to the boarding ramp, picked up a huge duffel bag, climbed the incline and stepped aboard *the Sea Diva.* Joe watched him, the dampness of the air permeating his cotton sweater like a film of slime spreading across his skin. He felt . . . contaminated.

Headlights from an approaching vehicle slid across the pier buildings, then a familiar pickup truck rolled at excessive speed toward him along the pier.

What the hell is Michael doing here? Joe stepped forward as his son braked so hard the tires screeched. "Hi, Dad," Michael said as he leaped from the truck. "I've been trying to reach you from school for two days."

"Well, you know," Joe gestured vaguely at *the Sea Diva.* "Michael, what are you doing here? I thought you had a paper to finish."

"Great news!" Michael wrestled a beat-up duffel bag out of the front seat. "I just got approval to do an experiment on the dolphin problem. It's a sabbatical for the spring semester; I'll get class credit and everything. Can you believe it? An opportunity to do direct research on my thesis!"

"You're not going on this trip."

Michael drew back. "Why not? It's perfect. I can really help out. And besides, Moby Jack already took most of my equipment on—"

"Michael . . . listen . . . you just can't go. I'm serious."

"I don't know what the big problem is. Why are you so uptight?"

"I'm not uptight."

"Yes you are. I can tell you're uptight when you start sounding like Uncle Ramon."

"There's nothing anybody can do about the damn dolphins, all right?"

A battle of respect versus determination drew lines across his son's face. "Dad, I've got a good chance. The dolphin's big enemy is the killer whale. With this new underwater sound system I've got, I can broadcast killer whale hunting calls and scare the dolphins out of the net."

"Son, it won't work. That experiment was tried."

"I know, but they were doing it wrong. Dr. Robinson, Professor Borgini and I have it all worked out."

Joe couldn't think of a logical argument, so he reverted to the father's prerogative: "You're not going," he said. "That's it. Find another boat to do your experiments on."

He forced himself to avoid his son's face, and to evade the punishment of seeing the mangled expression of confusion, betrayal, anger there. Then he looked at his watch, turned and signaled to the skipper and waiting deck hands. Immediately the heavy dock lines released, splashing into the bay, and the crew hauled them dripping and snaking onto the ship. He watched *the Sea Diva* back slowly away from the pier, foaming white whirlpools playing tag with each other near her stern. When he finally turned away, Michael and his pickup truck were gone.

Only after the *Diva* shrank to a cluster of stars did Joe walk to his car. Halfway there he heard the consecutive chiming of bells tolling through the fog. One. Two. Three. It sounded like the reliable old clock tower in Balboa Park, but the sound was too faint to be sure about. Besides, the chiming went on and on, counting all the way up to midnight. Which was absurd.

Joe climbed into his car and began the drive home. When he stopped for gas he glanced at the clock above the cashier's booth. 12:12.

His own watch showed 12:22.

He stood there, jaw hanging. He had begun *the Sea Diva's* maiden voyage on a Friday after all. Ten minutes too early! Damn.

"This is motor vessel *Sea Diva*, Whiskey Zulu Yankee 1468, USA. We hear ya. This is Sparks. Over."

"Sparks, Joe here. How you guys doing?"

"Doin' fine, Joe. Only been out two days; not enough time for things to start happening yet. Hold, I'll get the skipper. Over."

Momentarily the radio squawked again. "Di Santi here. Over."

"John . . . I hear things are going okay?" Joe couldn't help making it a question.

"Everything's working slick as a tuna slide, but we got a week or two more motoring before we can expect to spot schools and really see what this beautiful clipper is made of. Over."

Joe twisted comfortably in his chair. "I'm calling from my house radio. Took a while to raise you guys."

"I guess Sparks didn't expect you to call so soon." A pause. "How's the lawsuit going, Joe? Hate to ask, but . . . we gonna still have a boat when we get back?"

"Anthony Darren's got everyone off my back for now, so I can concentrate on managing the ship, shore side. Over."

"That's great." The skipper let out a small cough. "Um . . . aren't you going to ask about your boy?"

"My boy?"

"You forgot to tell me Mikey was coming on this trip. A fine young man he is, glad to have him aboard, but . . . do you want me to get him?"

"You say . . . Michael's aboard?"

"You mean you don't know? He met us at the harbor entrance in one of our speedboats. Richie had it out for repairs; Mike flagged him down at the Point Loma pier. Told me you said it was okay."

For a few seconds Joe's mind spun so fast he couldn't say anything.

"Joe?"

"Yeah—yeah, I did talk to him about it. Look, just tell him, tell Michael, everything is okay here. I'll tune in with him next time. Call me in a few days."

"Roger and out."

Joe leaned back in his chair and rubbed his face with his hands. He dared not focus on the fleeting thought: *Poncho could not be right, that even a game played with the bank might bring bad luck!*

"Five more months," Samantha said, holding up her plastic champagne glass, "and we'll be Mr. and Mrs. Anthony Darren."

"May they pass quickly," Anthony said, clicking his glass off hers. "The five months, I mean."

She laughed. "You're drunk."

"On you." He nuzzled her neck. The seawall of the Pacific Beach boardwalk curved away into hazy darkness on either side; ahead, the ocean thumped against an unseen beach. In syncopation with the sound a pulse of intense blue light jumped out of the darkness, thinned to a horizontal line and unraveled swiftly to left and right.

"That was a good one," Anthony said as it faded away.

"And it's uncommon?"

"I've only seen it once myself."

She ran a palm across his face. "It's a sign. Great things are going to happen for us, my dear."

He smiled. "How could it be otherwise?"

7
A Turn in the Storm

"So," Joe said into the radio phone, "to repeat: Your location is 9 degrees six minutes three seconds north and 90 degrees 22 minutes 15 seconds west? Over."

"You got it," replied Di Santi. "What time do you have there, Joe?"

"8:02 p.m., over."

"Roger, over."

The announced coordinates were completely incorrect but, properly adjusted by the secret codes. They contained the actual location data for *the Sea Diva*. She floated some two hundred miles south of the stated location, over one of the deepest areas the fleet would fish the entire trip. "You did a great job today, John," he said.

"Thanks, but tomorrow might be a different matter. Costallegre weather radio says there's a pretty big storm brewing up."

"You'll handle it fine, John. Listen . . . would you call Poncho to the phone?"

"Poncho? Sure. Hold on." Joe heard the skipper call out on the ship's P.A. a few times. Then Di Santi returned his attention to the radio and told Joe how delighted he was with *the Sea Diva's* performance, both at sea and in harbor. Joe grinned. By God no matter what, he had built one hell of a ship.

Almost fifteen minutes passed before he realized Poncho had apparently not responded to the summons.

"I don't know what's up," Di Santi said. "Unless he's too busy in the engine room to respond. Listen, do you want me to give him a message?"

Joe hesitated. "Well, okay. Tell him to bring me back a tortoise shell. He'll know what you mean. Just make sure he understands I want a *tortoise* shell, a land tortoise, not a *turtle* shell; not a sea turtle."

"Are you talking about a Galapagos tortoise shell?" the skipper asked. "We aren't going back to those waters."

"I know."

"Well, okay, Joe, sure. I'll give him the message."

The moment Joe signed off he felt he'd just made a mistake. He should have insisted on having Poncho found and brought to the radio shack. But no, that was paranoid. Di Santi would pass on the message, and then Poncho could relax for the rest of the trip. Also, Poncho would never have to explain what was so goddamned important about bringing back one type of shell over another. Poncho Pascalle was the Chief Engineer, after all, not some gopher charged with purchasing cheesy souvenirs for the boss.

Still, as Joe got ready for bed he couldn't shake the chilly feeling that had somehow taken root between his shoulder blades.

Although not as devoutly religious as many other crewmen on *the Sea Diva*, Poncho had become a devotee of the boat's tiny chapel. To him, Joe's misinformation plot to play like intending to sink the boat was little better than the real thing. Even thinking about deliberately scuttling your own vessel carried a *maldición*, a curse. True, the voyage had so far been unusually free of trouble— but that worried him too. Like overpressure in an air tank, bad luck could easily accumulate in secret . . . and then erupt without warning.

So he came regularly to the chapel, a closet of a room cut off from the rest of the boat, to try to build up good credit with God. Tonight as every other night he knelt before an effigy of the Blessed Virgin, crossed himself, and prayed. Swinging and rocking with the growing seas, the candles flickered in random directions, casting light and shadows in unpredictable patterns across the walls. Mary's eyes and face changed: one moment sublime, then sad, but never accusatory.

Poncho closed his eyes and prayed to be forgiven for sins he had not committed, even in his heart.

⚓

"Motor Vessel *Equator Queen* calling Joe Cruz . . . Come in . . . In the darkness, Joe's eyes snapped wide open.

Motor Vessel *Equator Queen* calling Joe Cruz, over."

"What is it?" Sylvia muttered.

"Radio. I'll check." Dawn light framed the edges of the drawn blinds in the window. Joe rolled out of bed and stumbled to the next room, where a shortwave radio sat casting its own patterned light. He grabbed the mike. "This is Joe Cruz. This is Joe Cruz, over."

"Joe, thank God. This is Charlie on *Equator Queen*. Joe . . . I hate to tell you this, but . . . *the Sea Diva* . . . she had big problems last night."

Joe was aware of Sylvia's shape standing motionless in the doorway. "What happened?" he said. "Was it the storm?"

"I don't know, but . . . she's down, Joe. She's down. *The Sea Diva* sank. We're standing by."

Joe was vaguely aware of Sylvia pressing her face against his bare back, wrapping her arms around his waist.

This can't be happening. . . .

"The crew?" Joe said. "The crew? Are they okay?"

A pause. "We picked up most everybody; most everybody made it to the rafts or the net skiff. We picked them up. But . . . Joe, I don't. I . . ."

"Say it, goddamn it!" Joe shouted. "Just say it!"

"Poncho Pascalle is missing. Some of the men say they saw him in the water, but that was last night and nobody's seen him since. And . . . Joe. . . ." Charlie's voice broke. "We found Michael. We think he was trying to gather his papers when the *Diva* went down. We found him, but he . . . he didn't . . . he didn't make it. I'm so sorry."

A pause filled with radio static came over the air.

"Joe, did you hear me? Joe, answer, over."

Locked together, Joe and Sylvia sagged to their knees on the carpeted floor. She pounded on his back, crying, "No, no. Oh, God, save us! Oh, Mother of God, don't let my Michael go. Don't take my Michael."

Joe dropped the mike and huddled on the floor with his wife, rocking with her back and forth, back and forth, their faces sliding together in wetness as salty as the sea.

BOOK II

8
Omen

The previous day, Anthony had been golfing with clients in Palm Springs; today he stood in a secure VIP room graciously provided to him by the Los Angeles International Airport administration. The room smelled of tired fishermen who had just flown a long way only to be whisked here before they even saw their families. They had not been mollified when Anthony assured them he would only hold them for fifteen minutes or so. As the legal representative of the ship's owner, Cruz Enterprises, on an insurance claim of several million dollars, it was his job to learn as much as he could about what happened to *the Sea Diva* before the media or, God forbid, the insurance companies got involved.

Although he knew he'd have to eventually interview or depose each man individually, he believed that it would be most efficient to speak to them first in small groups. Even in clusters the men responded to questions mostly with mutters containing little substance; with turned away faces; with a general tendency to edge toward the door. Clearly they wanted nothing more than to get the hell out of there and go home, and who could blame them?

But then came a change. The *Diva's* navigator said, "Talk to the chief engineer's assistant. He's got something to say."

Anthony consulted his list of the crew. "Alfonso Martin?"

"He told me . . ."

"What?"

The navigator glanced at the four other crewmen with him, then stared at the floor. "He told me Poncho Pascalle sank the *Diva*."

"I beg your pardon?"

"He saw it with his own eyes, he says. Even tried to stop it. I told him he was full of shit, that's what I told him."

"Wait. He says the Chief Engineer sank his own ship?"

A nod. "That's what he said. That's all I know. I think he's full of shit."

The rest of the men shuffled their feet.

Anthony had Alfonso Martin brought in next . . . alone. Martin was a wiry man with a wispy ponytail and a face that looked as if it had been caught in one of *the Sea Diva's* spinning props.

"What happened to your face, Mr. Martin?" Anthony asked.

"I ain't talking until I get a lawyer. I know you're a lawyer. But I mean my own counsel."

"You already talked to the navigator, who says you made some pretty strong accusations about the Chief Engineer, Poncho Pascalle. Is that correct?"

"Didn't you hear me, man? I said I'm not talking until I have my own lawyer."

And that was all he would say.

The next group Anthony interviewed included a gigantic copper-haired man who spoke little, but lingered when the other men left. Then he quickly approached Anthony. "I'm Jack Callucci. Remember me, Moby Jack, from the maiden voyage party? Helicopter pilot and fishing crew member?"

"Yes, I remember you very well." Anthony held out his hand and had it briefly disappear from view inside Moby Jack's paw. Anthony felt an irregular vibration, and looking into Moby's face, realized the big man was struggling to keep his composure. Then he remembered how, at the party, Moby had horsed around with Michael Cruz like a frat boy at a kegger.

But now Moby looked anything but frivolous. "Serious problems are coming down, Mr. Darren. I mean *serious.*"

"Problems with how *the Sea Diva* sank?"

"Yeah. I was lying in my bunk that night when I heard an explosion. Not a fuel tank cooking off; that came later. What I heard was like a satchel charge, a controlled charge of high explosive. I've heard it enough times. So I go running out on deck, and there's

Michael. . . ." He faltered, swallowed heavily. "I guess I'm the last person who saw him alive. He tells me, he tells me everybody has to get to the skiffs; the *Diva* is sinking. Then he says he saw the Chief, and the Chief told him it was Alfonso Martin who did it. Him and the banker."

Anthony looked up from his notepad. "The banker?"

"That's what Michael said Poncho told him. Then Michael says he has to get his dolphin papers, and he runs off before I can stop him." Another pause to swallow. "And that's the last time I saw him until we pulled his body out of the sea."

Anthony pushed a glass of water toward Moby and waited while he drank it dry. Then Anthony said, "Apparently Alfonso tells a different version of the story."

"I know he does. But he's a friggin' liar, Mr. Darren. Ask anyone."

"'Anyone' hasn't been talking to me much, actually," Anthony said.

"Maybe not, but these men will talk to their wives and girlfriends, and before long. . . ."

Anthony suppressed a wince. "That's what I'm afraid of. What about you? Have you told anyone else what Michael said to you?"

"No."

"Good. Unless authorities question you, please keep it that way, , at least for the time being."

Moby's eyes tightened. "Mr. Darren, you've got to get whoever did this. There has to be some justice come out of this."

"I understand. And I agree. I'll do my best."

"If you ever need me for anything, I'm there. Just ask."

"Thanks. In my business one never knows when the need for help will come. But for now. . . ." He looked at his watch. "They should be unloading Michael's casket soon. I need to help Joe and Sylvia deal with that."

Moby covered his eyes with one hand. "Ah, Christ."

Laura Evans was getting ready to take a shower when her doorbell rang. She frowned at the clock—11:37 p.m.—pulled on her favorite silk robe, and hurried to the door.

She squinted through the peephole. Blinked in surprise, then opened the door. "Anthony?"

Even in the darkness and without her glasses on she could tell he looked terrible: his fashionable suit a web of wrinkles, his hair knotted, his eyes red-lined.

"Come in," she said.

"Anthony, it's been a long time."

He nodded, and recognized the robe he'd bought her for her birthday. That was two years ago.

"What's happened? It's going on midnight."

"Did I wake you?"

"No, but what's wrong? What happened." Please don't tell me you had a fight with Samantha.

She had never seen him like this.

She led him to the living room and sat him down on the couch. For herself she selected a low-backed chair by the fireplace. Then she waited.

He hunched forward over his knees as if about to throw up. "Did you read about the tuna boat that sank out in the Pacific three or four nights ago?"

"Sure."

"It belonged to one of my clients, an old friend named Joe Cruz. Today I was up in L.A. interviewing the surviving crew members."

"Most of them made it, right?"

"Most. Two men were lost: the chief engineer . . . and the owner's son."

"The owner's. . . ." She put a hand to her mouth. "Your old friend."

"He lost his only child, Michael."

"Oh, God, that's *terrible*."

"You can't believe the tragedy the family is suffering. Michael—he was just one of those all-time super people. And the other man, too. He—they never even found his body."

"Are you sure you wouldn't like some coffee, or a drink or something?"

"You're very kind, but I have to prepare for the insurance adjusters tomorrow." He raised his face. "I do have a favor to ask of you, though."

"Sure, Anthony. Of course."

"When you read about the sinking, did it remind you of anything?"

"Remind me?"

"Remember the novel I was working on back when we first met? Then about six months ago or so I sent you some sample chapters and a synopsis."

"Sure, I remember. It was about the owner of a fishing boat who. . . ." She blinked. "Oh, he lost his son too, or was it cousin that's—"

"Weird. I know. Well, that book will never be finished now. In fact I wish I'd never started it. It was based on an extremely unlikely plot anyway." When I get home tonight I'm going to destroy every page I've got. I'd like you to do the same: take every piece of paper associated with that book I sent you, and destroy it. Burn it in your fireplace. Tonight, please?"

"*Burn* it?"

"I know. Maybe I'm getting as superstitious as a fisherman. It just seems . . . like a bad omen to have any of it around. I'm sure the crew would agree."

Laura started to lean toward Anthony, the pull automatic and powerful, but then forced herself to settle back. "All right, I'll burn the manuscript. Would you like to stay and watch?"

"No. I believe you. Just make sure you destroy it all—the letters I wrote you about the book, the synopsis, everything. Exorcise it. Do it now, please."

"I will."

He stood, gave her a distracted hug, said good-bye, and walked out without a backward glance.

After she heard his car depart, Laura searched for and found the chapters, the transmittal letter, and the synopsis. She prepared kindling and logs in the hearth and started a fire. At first she fed the flames page by page. Then she tossed in handfuls of paper until she was sure that every scrap having to do with Anthony's novel, his source of omen, had been consumed.

All that remained was ashes.

Kind of like me and Anthony, she thought.

In their dwindling heat she sat and cried.

Was that really necessary? Anthony thought as he drove away. Surely I could have waited until tomorrow to ask Laura to do that. Or waited forever. I'm not ordinarily so superstitious. Or I could have just called her.

The truth was, he'd wanted to see her. At his moment of greatest darkness, she was the person he had most wanted to see and speak to. That's just because Samantha's going to grill me about what happened up in L.A., even though she knows I can't talk about it. She won't mean to or try to, but she'll do it. Because part of her will be thinking how great it would be to give her radio station a scoop on every news service in the country.

Laura, on the other hand, had thought only of . . . *him*.

He shook his head hard. His history with Laura was . . . confused. After a torrid year as lovers, she had become his—what, exactly? Acquaintance, confidante, friend? Of course their relationship had stalled before he met Samantha . . . but why? Perhaps they had both been too protective of their separate spaces; perhaps they had both thought they had all the time in the world, like a pair of Galapagos tortoises or Bristlecone Pine trees.

Or perhaps the problem was all his. He had to admit, after all these years, Cheryl was still on his mind. Still.

I could have just called Laura . . .

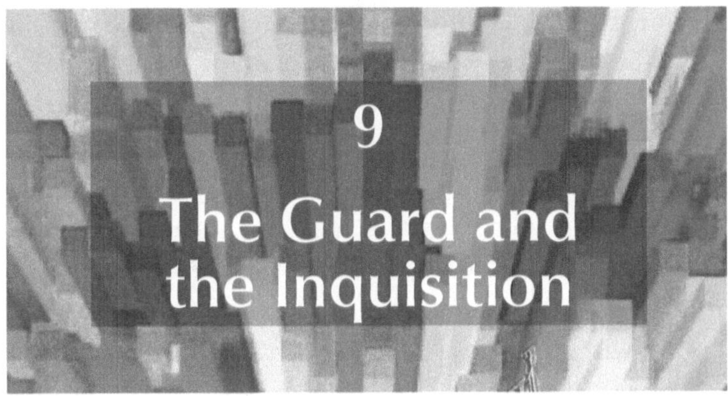

9
The Guard and the Inquisition

A week and a half later, Anthony was standing at his desk flipping through his mail when he spotted an envelope bearing the logo and return address of the United States Coast Guard. It was addressed to *the Sea Diva Corporate Counsel.*

For a moment he just held it in his hand. Then he thought *Here it is*, and slit the envelope open. He extracted a letter serving notice that an inquiry into the sinking of *the Sea Diva* was scheduled to take place at the Coast Guard station located along the edge of San Diego Bay.

Feel that suction pulling us out to sea, Joe? Anthony thought. That's the rip tide. And all we can do is swim with it.

He reached for the phone.

The morning of the hearing could have been selected by a filmmaker: overcast sky, a blustery wind, gray chop hacking at the surface of San Diego Bay.

The hearing room filled quickly with witnesses, reporters— obviously, spectators and several lawyers—obviously, all taking seats on gray metal folding chairs arranged in neat rows facing a witness chair and a newly-varnished, eight-foot oak table backed by three more folding chairs.

Anthony followed Joe into the room. Joe looked pale and withdrawn, his slacks ironed and his shirt wrinkled, his eyes covered by dark glasses despite the relative gloom outside. Anthony had dressed carefully in a natural-shoulder, dark blue suit with a red and blue striped tie. They sat three rows back, facing the witness chair.

Looking around, Anthony noticed that the U.S. Department of Justice was being represented by John Woods, a big, bristly-looking Assistant United States Attorney. Even in his suit and tie Woods could have been cast in a John Wayne role in a war movie, and he had a similar reputation for adherence to honor and duty. Next to him sat a Deputy District Attorney for the people of the State of California, a familiar man with an almost imperceptible sneer on his face.

Shit. It's Egan James.

Egan turned and glanced at Anthony, nodded once, then faced forward again.

At precisely 0900 the military guards braced to attention and a trio of high-ranking Coast Guard officers, wearing crisply starched white uniforms trimmed with gold braid and festooned with ribbons and medals, stepped in and took the three chairs at the head table. Two of the guards stationed themselves alongside the closed door.

A gavel rapped sharply, and Anthony focused on the man in the center chair: acting Judge Advocate Captain Theodore Dowdy. "This inquiry on the sinking of motor vessel *the Sea Diva*, with the loss of two of her crew, will come to order," Dowdy said in a loud, clear voice.

Although Anthony was sure he appeared calm, he felt his heart galloping. The questions *the Sea Diva's* crew had refused to answer at the airport would be asked again here—and this time, the answers *would* come. Although newspaper stories had dripped with innuendo, no one had officially mentioned the conflicting statements of Alfonso Martin and Moby Jack Callucci. Whatever the rest of the crew had heard or believed, they had apparently kept silent about it—so one would think that as far as this board knew, the sinking had been nothing but an accident.

But then why were John Woods and Egan James here?

Joe stared at the table. Anthony hadn't been able to get him to talk with any interest about the *Diva's* sinking, or to show concern about anything much. In fact Joe had come here only because he'd been subpoenaed. He was almost catatonic.

The first witness called to the stand was skipper John Di Santi, who stood tall in suit and tie as he raised his hand to be sworn in. He sat just as tall as he calmly answered a series of preliminary questions.

Then Captain Dowdy asked about the night of the accident, and the entire audience trained its attention on Di Santi's lean, weathered face.

The skipper cleared his throat. "Manuel Ramos had the deck watch. He woke me at about 0400, yelling that my ship was going down fast. The first thing I did was make sure that Sparks, our radio man, had our correct location. The navigator had given him false coordinates when we hauled in a school earlier that day."

The hearing officers looked at each other. "False coordinates?" Dowdy said. "Why?"

"It's normal procedure, to keep other fishing boats from knowing where we are and cutting in on the school we're working."

Dowdy frowned. "Were there any other radio communications that evening?"

"Well, an hour or so before that I'd gotten a call from Joe Cruz, *the Sea Diva's* owner. He wanted to speak to the Chief Engineer."

"That would be Poncho Pascalle, one of the deceased?"

"Yes, sir. It turned out Poncho was in the ship's chapel right then and didn't hear me on the P.A., so I told Joe I'd give him the message when I could find him. Joe said fine."

"And did you give Mr. Pascalle the message?"

"No, sir. His assistant, Alfonso Martin, happened to be in the radio shack right then, and he said he'd take the message down to Poncho."

"And what was this message?"

"Nothing important. Just something personal about a souvenir Mr. Cruz wanted Poncho to pick up for him."

After the skipper stepped down, other members of the crew were questioned one by one. They all recited a variation of the same story they had told Anthony at LAX: they had awakened to find the boat sinking, and headed for the big net skiff. A few remembered seeing flames and smoke coming from the lower decks. And that was all.

Next the Board called Alfonso Martin to the stand. Instantly Anthony's attention sharpened.

After swearing Alfonso in and asking few preliminary questions, the officers straightened in their chairs and leaned forward. "Mr. Martin," Dowdy quizzed, "Tell us—if you know—what caused *the Sea Diva* to sink."

Alfonso hesitated. His hair was pulled back so hard it gleamed. He glanced at the three officers, then vaguely around the room. "Poncho came on watch early, like about 0340. Said he couldn't sleep. I gave him the message from the radio shack. He looked upset for some reason, and relieved me. I left the engine room and went up. About ten minutes later I go back down because I forgot my thermos. I come down at, like, about 0350, and the first thing I saw was Poncho hammerin' a chisel into the fuel line on the day tank, cuttin' it open. Fuel started pouring out. Then I saw something else taped to a fitting right by the leak: a hand grenade."

A wave of whispering surged through the room. The Judge Advocate slammed his gavel down with a *crack* like a gunshot.

"Go on, Mr. Martin."

"There was one more thing: the top was off the sea chest, and I saw all this sort of rope-looking stuff wrapped around the valves and hoses. I wasn't sure what it was, but it didn't belong in there."

"Did you speak to Chief Engineer Pascalle at that time?"

Shifting his hips, Alfonso replied, "Yes. I asked him what he was doing, and he said Joe Cruz had ordered him to sink the boat."

Gasps buffeted the room. Again the gavel slammed down.

Somehow Anthony kept his face locked in the semblance of calm. He knew that although Alfonso's statement was hearsay, it fell under an exception to the Hearsay Rule. In the very likely event of a criminal trial later on, the statement would be admissible in court as a declaration against Poncho, and deliver a devastating blow to Joe.

But Joe did not react. He kept his head bowed as if he heard nothing, as if he were not even in the room.

"What happened next, Mr. Martin?" Dowdy asked.

"Well, I tried to stop Poncho, and he started swinging the chisel at me. We fought, and I knocked him down. But then he reached into his pocket, and the next thing I knew there was an explosion and sea water started pouring in through the sea chest. That wasn't the grenade, though, because the grenade went off next— real bright; I think it was one of those incendiary kind. Phosphorus. And the day tank started burning."

"Was anyone else around at this time?"

"Right about then Michael Cruz come down the ladder, as I was heading the other way. I told him what happened and said he better run. Later I heard him and Poncho both come back up, people saw them on deck, but they didn't make it. That's all I know."

Joe's shoulders jerked a single time and again went still.

"One last question, Mr. Martin. You say Mr. Pascalle used a hand grenade and some other sort of explosive material to sabotage the engine room. Were such materials commonly available on *the Sea Diva*?"

"Not usually, sir, no. But, Poncho's from Costallegre, and they're havin' a revolution down there. I heard he had a big stash of munitions and weapons in the engine room storeroom on the voyage down. He must have been running munitions."

Next Moby Jack Callucci was called to the stand. Anthony had already discussed the red-headed giant's testimony with him in considerable detail.

After a series of preliminary questions, Dowdy said, "Did you talk to anyone after you learned the ship was sinking?"

"Yes, sir. I talked to Michael Cruz briefly. He's the one who told me the boat was sinking."

"What else did he say to you at that time?"

A man in the audience stood up, an electric blue tie hanging from a slightly unbuttoned white collar. "I object to the question. My name is Morton Smith, and I am an attorney representing Alfonso Martin. I beg the court's indulgence. The question calls for the grossest form of hearsay."

Captain Dowdy shifted his attention to Smith. "This is an investigation, an administrative proceeding. The statement might lead to admissible evidence. The witness is instructed to answer the question. However, your objection is preserved. Mr. Callucci, would you please proceed with your answer."

"Yes, sir." Moby Jack gripped the mike with one hand and turned his head to train his glare on Alfonso. "What Michael Cruz told *me* was that he saw Poncho Pascalle fighting with Alfonso trying to stop *Alfonso* from sinking the boat."

"Objection!" Morton Smith roared, shooting back to his feet.

The crowd erupted.

The gavel slammed everyone to silence yet again. "I will ask the guards to escort out anyone who violates my demand for order!"

"This is hearsay on top of hearsay." Smith's face flushed red in contrast to the snowy hair curling over the back of his collar. "And the statement can't come in as a 'Dying Declaration' exception, because Poncho Pascalle didn't know he was about to die— assuming he even made such a statement."

"Overruled."

Anthony's shoulders seemed to melt with relief.

"Proceed, Mr. Callucci. What else, if anything, did Michael Cruz say?"

"He said Poncho told him that Joe would never sink his ship; that it was one of the bankers who loaned money for *the Sea Diva* who set everything up, along with Alfonso. That's all I know. That's all that was said."

Noon recess was called. As the room emptied, Anthony was relieved to see a wiry man of forty-five years in a well-tailored, dark blue suit and vest walk in against the human tide. Anthony had not handled a criminal case for years, so he had contacted Dirk Miller, one of the most prominent criminal defense lawyers in the city, to advise Joe on these proceedings.

"Sorry I'm late," he said. "So many trials, so little time. Shall we have lunch?"

Anthony drove down Harbor Drive toward Farrentino's Restaurant on the edge of the bay. On the left passed the yacht basin, filled with hundreds of masts and riggings looking like broken bristles of giant curry combs brushing the melancholy sky. As they traveled past the basin the bay changed aspect from naval ships, yachts and sailboats beating into the wind, to tuna boats and an occasional seaplane landing or taking off above scows and barges. To the right, the frequent roar of passenger jets at Lindbergh Field shattered the sky. *At least there's some scenic diversion after that hearing room*, Anthony thought sardonically. He passed the Naval Training Center, and the Sonar and Submarine Training base, and pulled into Farrentino's parking lot.

During lunch Dirk and Anthony talked over the morning's testimony. Joe sat silently, ignoring the hors d'oeuvres Anthony had ordered for him. He didn't even react when Anthony brought up his biggest concern: "Dirk, am I right that Alfonso's statements against Joe would probably be admissible in a criminal trial, but Moby Jack's version might *not* be admissible?"

"A lot depends on the flexibility of the judge we get. Some courts have admitted such statements; stretching them into the spontaneous, excited declaration exceptions to the hearsay rule. They'll probably have a hearing on an offer of proof on the credibility or reliability of Moby's statements."

Anthony suppressed a shudder. In a handful of words Dirk had turned the possibility of a criminal trial into the certainty of one.

For once Joe seemed to notice. Still staring out the window, he said, "It's true, you know. I did tell Hooks I wanted the option to have the *Diva* sunk. But I never said I would go ahead and do it. I didn't intend to do it. I just told him I wanted the option."

Dirk stared at him. Anthony stared at him. Then Dirk shook his head and turned to Anthony. "Well, Joe obviously has to plead the Fifth Amendment."

"I don't want to take the Fifth," Joe said. "I want to take what I got coming to me."

"What about the people who might suffer if you say something that's not exactly correct?" Dirk demanded. "Something that might just be how you *think* it is?"

"Think about your family," Anthony added. "What about Michael's memory and reputation?"

Joe's sunglasses reflected Anthony's face in distorted cameos. "What do you mean?"

"Someone might conclude that Michael was *in* on some kind of plot with you."

"That's ridiculous. He never—"

"The point is, we need time to investigate before you testify," Dirk said. "For God's sake, Joe, just plead the Fifth Amendment for today; after we get to the bottom of this you can always change your mind."

Joe fell silent again. Anthony called for the check.

The moment the hearing reconvened, the Captain called Joe to the stand. For the first time in Anthony's memory, his friend looked frail despite his stature. He took off his dark glasses, revealing eyes almost as dark, and was sworn in.

"You have the right to remain silent. Anything you say can and will be used against you. You have the right to have an attorney . . ."

The officer asked Joe if he was willing to waive his rights and talk to the panel. Anthony fought not to shout: *Take the Fifth!*

"I have an attorney present," Joe said. "So I want to hear the questions."

Anthony heard Dirk grunt as if punched in the stomach.

After a few preliminaries the panel's interrogation turned to the boat's financial status on the date she sank. Joe glanced at his lawyers.

Anthony stiffened. *He's going to blow it.* But Joe said, "I refuse to answer on the grounds—on the advice of my attorney, I take the Fifth Amendment."

Anthony closed his mouth to trap a sigh of relief.

"You mean you invoke the Fifth Amendment of the US Constitution?" Dowdy asked.

"Yes, sir."

"Do you refuse to answer further questions on those grounds?"

"Yes."

The officers looked at each other. "In that case this inquiry is adjourned until further notice," the captain said, "or until a report and determination are issued concerning whether or not maritime regulations have been violated."

Everyone filed out of the room. Anthony watched Egan James and John Woods as they walked together to their cars, heads collected in deep discussion.

A week later, Anthony stepped into his office after a morning spent in court on other matters. When he looked into his incoming mail tray, a fist formed in his stomach: on top lay another envelope from the United States Coast Guard. He tore it open and skipped to the last paragraph:

The Board rules that the fishing vessel the Sea Diva was intentionally sunk. Joseph Cruz and the deceased Poncho Pascalle are the leading suspects. Their licenses have been suspended, Pascalle's posthumously, because of illegal citizenship papers and prima facie evidence of illegally exporting arms.

Anthony sank slowly into his chair. *Well, what else did you expect?*

He recovered quickly. No one ever got convicted of a felony in an administrative Coast Guard hearing; this was only the first round of what was certain to be a long fight to come. Still, Anthony had hoped that the Coast Guard would believe Moby over Alfonso.

Round One to the opposition.

His secretary informed him Samantha was on line one. Anthony punched the button. "Hi, sweetheart."

"Looks like you've been keeping secrets from your beloved fiancé."

"Secrets?"

"It's in the local paper and on the news wires: the Coast Guard has accused Joe Cruz of sinking his own boat and killing his own son."

Anthony rubbed his eyes. "That didn't take long."

"Any details you'd like to share with your loving spouse-to-be, the intrepid radio producer?"

He managed to chuckle. "You know I can't do that. I'll tell you, it's been hell not talking about this with you. But I still can't."

"Spoilsport. So, dinner at Croce's tonight?"

Herbert Hooks, denizen of the 32nd floor of his own skyscraper, was annoyed by the rumble of traffic intruding into Morton Smith's ground floor office. But he pushed the distraction aside while he listened to Smith's analysis of the Coast Guard proceedings.

Ignoring the disarray in the room was more difficult. The desktop was littered with open law books, piles of papers in disarray, phone messages and an ashtray filled with cigarette butts. How could any professional function in such conditions? But being distracted by details at the moment was not a good idea. Smith was speaking about Moby Jack's reference to the nameless banker who had supposedly ordered the sinking of *the Sea Diva*; the attorney even speculated on the possibility that federal indictments might be sought.

"Federal indictments?" Hooks asked.

"The reports indicate that counts will be based on fraud for attempting to obtain insurance proceeds illegally, as well as indictments for possible murder charges under. . . ." Smith leaned forward. "I looked it up: 18 USC 1111."

"So you're talking about indictments against Cruz and his chief engineer."

"Yes, although it would be well to remember that this Callucci says the banker for the Cruz interests conspired to sink the ship. And the identity of the banker who he is referring to is obvious.

"Sorry I am late," someone behind him said. "I did not hear that, Mr. Hooks."

Hooks turned as Alfonso Martin stepped into the room, led by Smith's secretary.

"Sit down, Alfonso," Smith said. "Actually, I was just about to tell Mr. Hooks here that Poncho's statements, as reported by Jack Callucci, I feel should never come into evidence. Under the constitution an accused has the right to cross-examine his accuser. And Poncho is dead. And so far that's the only testimony that could link you Alfonso and"—he looked pointedly at Hooks— "any *third parties* with the sinking."

"Sounds good," Alfonso said, dropping into a seat.

Smith leaned back. "Herbert. Of course I have no knowledge that you had anything to do with the sinking, but even so, don't say anything specific on that issue in my presence. Officially I represent only Alfonso, and I don't want to hear anything that might put me into a conflict of interest. In fact, I think it best if I not even ask why you're paying Alfonso's attorney's fees."

Hooks bit a fingernail and peeled it back.

Smith went on: "Assuming there are no other witnesses or statements from other parties that could link Alfonso to the sinking, he'll probably avoid prosecution. Especially since the prosecutor needs Alfonso on his side in order to convict Cruz, which is who he's really after."

"But what if Cruz told Anthony Darren that someone else was involved *with* him?" Hooks blurted. "I mean, I don't know if that's the case, but what if?"

"It's not likely. If Joe Cruz implicates you—strike that—if he implicates some *third party*, he's cooking his own goose. It could point to a conspiracy charge against him. Also, so far the only evidence that any third party exists is the unproved, inadmissible statement by Jack Callucci, who says he received the information from Michael Cruz, who got it from the deceased Poncho Pascalle. Alfonso's statements, on the other hand, implicate only Joe Cruz and Pascalle."

Smith lit his cigarette with a flourish, and smoke poured from his mouth and nose. "Joe Cruz's best defense would be to deny he knows anything about the incident, and simply hope he's not convicted. On the other hand—and this is an intriguing possibility—if he *did* confess to Anthony Darren that a third party was involved in the plot, then Darren and Dirk Miller might go to the US Attorney and try to make a deal for Cruz. They might offer to have him plea bargain to a lesser offense in exchange for putting the finger on this alleged third party."

Hooks took his fingertip out of his mouth. "And what should the alleged third party do?"

Smith raised one hand in a *stop* gesture. "There's a potential conflict of interest between the third party and Alfonso here, so the third party should seek out other criminal defense counsel. But I will say that if I was representing him and he were implicated, I'd tell him to strike first: go to the US Attorney and turn state's evidence against Cruz before Miller and Darren beat him to it."

"That's kind of drastic, isn't it?" said Hooks.

"Maybe, but it might be the person's only option. It all depends on whether Cruz is dumb enough to conceal the third party implication from his lawyer." Smith shrugged. "And how can anyone find out something like that until it's too late, and the other side beats them to the punch and turns states' evidence first?"

Hooks walked out of Smith's office so wrapped in worrisome thought he forgot where he had parked his car. For a quarter hour he wandered around the multi-story parking garage until he finally spotted his taupe Mercedes sedan—and realized he had already passed it twice.

How much did Darren know? What had Cruz told him? Everything hinged on the answer to those questions. Without that information it would be impossible for Hooks to strategize, plan, maneuver. He might actually have to follow Smith's advice and turn state's evidence just to keep Cruz from doing so first. But he hated the idea. It reeked of surrender. A *reaction*, not an action. And Herbert Hooks had made his name, reputation and fortune by planning and striking first.

What he needed was more information.

As he climbed into the Mercedes and began driving back toward the Empire Bank building, his nail-bitten hands gradually became steadier on the wheel. He knew what his next step would be. He would go up to his office and call a certain phone number; a number given to him by a friend who had recently gone through a nasty divorce.

10 Out of Nowhere

"Excuse me, Mr. Darren, you have messages."

Anthony had walked in from a morning meeting so preoccupied with Joe's worsening situation he had passed the reception desk without checking his phone slips. "Thanks, Julie."

As he walked along the hallway and its walls of law books, he flipped through the messages. One made him hesitate: *Call Cheryl Burns*, followed by a phone number he did not recognize. Cheryl Burns? Cheryl . . . No, it couldn't be. There were a thousand Cheryls in the world, and he hadn't heard from *her* since . . . well, since that graduation summer.

Also, the area code on the number was local, not out of state. Not Kentucky. *But she could be back in town.*

He sat at his desk, thought for a moment, then shrugged and punched in the number. Eight or ten rings went unanswered. He realized his heart was racing. *Samantha would love to know that.* Fifteen rings. Twenty.

He hung up.

Several times over the next few hours he dialed the number again. Finally he heard a clatter as someone picked up. "Who is this?" a male voice demanded.

"This is Anthony Darren. Someone from this number called me earlier today."

"Well, this is a payphone outside a Speedy-Mart. Only drug dealers use this goddamned phone."

"Sorry to bother you." Anthony hung up and smiled wryly at himself. Serves you right for getting excited about someone from your past. Get your head back in the present—there's more than enough for you here.

Smitty Epstein had been cleaning the offices on the 20th floor of the Wells Fargo Bank Building five nights a week for eighteen years. By now he had a system: start in the northeast corner suite, then work clockwise around the building. There were four businesses up there, each with its own suite of rooms anchored by a corner office with a nice view of one quadrant of the city. To clean each suite he had to do two complete passes: one for dusting and emptying trash cans, and the other for vacuuming.

The law offices on the southwest corner took the most time, not because they were so big but because the woman who managed them was anal-retentive, or OCD, or something. She insisted that the carpets be vacuumed in such a way that a scalloped pattern was visible in the nap. If she came in in the morning and saw no such pattern, or a fractured one, she would call the company and complain.

Bitch.

Still, by now Smitty had the system worked out so well that if he followed it just right, he would have an extra fifteen minutes for dinner.

Which was why he was pissed off one Monday night when he unlocked the door to the Law Offices of Anthony Darren, pushed his cart in—and realized somebody was still there. Even Darren himself was usually gone by the time Smitty started his shift at 11 p.m., but tonight the light was on in the corner office, from which came the thumping sound of a desk or credenza drawer closing.

Smitty sighed. Damn it, now he'd have to leave and start his cleaning cycle in a different suite. Which would mess up the whole—

Just then a guy walked out of Mr. Darren's office . . . and it wasn't Mr. Darren. It was another custodian, a middle-aged guy wearing the same coveralls as Smitty. His name patch read "Carlos," even though he didn't look Hispanic.

"Who are you?" Smitty demanded.

"Carlos," the man said, spreading his hands. One clutched a sagging trash bag. "I'm new. This is the twenty-first floor, right?"

"Twentieth," Smitty said.

"What? Well, Christ. I just wasted a half-hour then."

Smitty shook his head. "Better learn to count, man."

"Yeah. Well, guess I'd better get to the twenty-first then. At least you won't have to vacuum the corner office."

Oh yes I will, Smitty thought.

Then, a minute or two after Carlos left, something else occurred to him: *I wonder where his cart was.*

Just before noon the next day Anthony spotted another message from Cheryl Burns. The area code was the same as before, but the rest of the number different. Scowling, he stepped into his office and kicked the door closed. Punched the buttons.

After six rings he was about to hang up. Then a male voice said, "Auto repair."

Not quite a Speedy Mart, but still. Again he started to disconnect—then heard himself say, "Hi, is Cheryl Burns there?"

"Hold on a minute. I'll get her daughter."

A young voice answered. "Hello?"

"Hi. I'm returning a call to Cheryl Burns. Is she there?"

"I'll get her. Hold, okay?" Above a background of machinery noise, the girl said, "Mom . . . Mom, you're wanted on the phone." Was there a hint of the South in her voice?

Then: "Hello . . . Anthony?" And it was Cheryl, as surely as if he had spoken with her only the day before. "Do you re-re-remember me—Cheryl C-C-Crawford?"

"Do I remember you? Are you crazy? It's so good to hear from you. How did you know it was me?"

"What other m-m-man would be c-c-calling me here?" Although he was puzzled by the halting stutter in her voice, her laugh was the same happy chiming he remembered from his youth. "We're waiting here for our c-c-car. Andrea, my daughter, is out in shop checking with the mechanic."

"This is such a great surprise."

"It's been a long t-t-time, hasn't it? You sound great. Just the s-s-same."

He made no comment on how she sounded. He tried to push the thought away.

But that became increasingly hard to do as they chatted. He had so many questions. What had she been doing all these years? Had she moved back to San Diego? Was her family with her? At first she rushed her answers with the stutter and slurring so pronounced he could barely understand her; then her voice grew spacey, as though floating out of a dream state. But he got the basics: she was back in town permanently, along with her two children, Andrea and Johnny. Andrea was sixteen, Johnny eleven. Cheryl conveyed the idea that she was still married, although she was less clear about where the husband was now. She was surprised Anthony had remained a bachelor all this time, but was pleased to know he was now happily engaged.

Then she repeated everything she had just said, almost word for word. She sounded not exactly like someone on drugs; more like a punch-drunk prize fighter. Regardless, something was very wrong. "Cheryl," Anthony said. "Where are you living, exactly?"

No response. Then she said, "Where are you g-g-going to be next Saturday m-m-morning?"

"Probably in my office, like most Saturdays. Why?"

"I'll be over at the ice . . . ice . . . ice skating r-rink at Huntingwood Shopping C-C-Center from ten thirty to noon. I'd l-l-l-like you . . . like you to come sit in the stands with me to watch someone sk-sk-skate."

"Your children?"

"Well, one of them. My d-d-daughter Andrea."

"That would be great; I'd love to meet her."

"Good. Y-y-you two have a lot in c-common."

"Really? How's that?"

"S-S-Simple. You're her f-f-father."

"Wait. What?"

"She l-l-looks just like you. So b-b-beautiful, and so s-s-smart. You'll be very p-p-p-p-proud of her."

The telephone receiver slipped from his hand as if it were suddenly coated in ice. He caught it. "Cheryl, you must be kidding. You're kidding, right? You got married only a few months after you moved."

No response. "Cheryl?"

"A-a-all this time I've been trying to get m-m-myself together to . . . to tell you. Her f-f . . . stepfather doesn't know. But I . . . I finally decided you would never forgive me if you f-f-f-found out about the precious ch . . . child you gave me but d-d-d-didn't get the chance to meet."

"Does she . . . Does Andrea . . . know? About me?"

"Yes. But she doesn't know I've f-f-f-found you. Anthony . . . d-d-do you want to see her?"

"Well, of course I do. It's just . . . this is a lot to take in all at once. And there's my fiancé to consider. I don't know how . . . how . . ."

"M-m-m-maybe I shouldn't have c-c-called."

"No, no, of course I'm glad you called. I'm thrilled you called. And yes, I want to see my daughter. I just hope she wants to see *me*."

"Oh, she does. I've t-t-told her all about you. You're her h-h-hero."

"God. Don't say that."

"W-w-why not?"

"Remember Joe Cruz? I'm acting as his attorney in a matter right now, and things are not going great. I'm no hero."

Silence.

"Cheryl? Are you still there? Cheryl?"

"Who is th . . . th . . . this?"

"This is Anthony. Are you okay?"

"Anthony?"

"Anthony Darren. You asked me to call you. Cheryl, what's wrong?"

"I th . . . think I'm ti . . . tired now. C-c-can we hang up now?"

"Sure, of course. Will I still see you Saturday morning?"

"S-S-Saturday morning?

"At the ice skating rink."

"Oh. Yes. P-P-Please just . . . b-be in the stands. Get a look at us fr . . . from th . . . there before you decide. Okay? I d-d-don't want Andrea to kno . . . kno . . . know you're there until you d-d-decide."

"I've already decided, Cheryl. I'm dying to see you both."

A long pause. "I . . . I'm not the same, Anthony. I-I-I've been in hos . . . hos . . . hospitals."

"Don't cry, Cheryl. Don't worry. Don't be sad."

"I'm not s-s-s-sad," she whispered. "I'm happy. That's why I'm c-c-crying. I'd better g-g-go."

"Okay. Thanks so much for calling, Cheryl. I'll be there Saturday for sure. But at least give me your real phone num—"

Click.

⚓

If Herbert Hooks felt completely out of place at the fast food restaurant, the man he was sitting with seemed designed for the place: middle-aged, paunchy, balding, dressed in JC Penney rejects.

"To be honest, Mr. Hooks," the man said, "I don't know what to make of it. I didn't find anything in the Cruz file that implicates anyone except possibly Mr. Cruz . . . certainly not you. Doesn't look like Joe Cruz pointed his finger at you. I photographed it all for you anyway, of course."

Hooks nodded. "Good. That's very good, Mr. Steele."

"On the other hand . . . I did find some things in a personal file I found stashed in back of one of Darren's credenza drawers that you might find interesting."

"'Interesting' in what way?"

Steele placed a manila envelope on the table, unfolded a blade from a Swiss Army knife and slit the flap open. With pudgy fingers he drew out a photo blow-up of a single sheet of paper.

Hooks looked at it. A handwritten page dated November 18th, 1978. Businessman owns tuna seiner, is in great financial difficulty. A lifelong friend works on the boat. Businessman decides to scuttle the seiner to collect a huge insurance payoff. Boat is sunk by a trusted employee off the coast of Central America in very deep water. . . .

The text went on like that for the length of the page. It provided no specific names, of either ships or people. When Hooks finished reading, he gave the investigator a confused frown.

"Sounds like a summary of *the Sea Diva* matter, doesn't it?" Steele said.

"So? It tells us nothing new, nothing I can use."

The PI held out a palm. "There's more. While I was there I real quick compared the handwriting on that with a sample from Darren's legal pads. I'm no expert, but they obviously matched."

"I still don't—"

"Look at the date on there, Mr. Hooks. November 18, 1978. That was *about five months* before *the Sea Diva* went down."

Hooks frowned. Then his cheeks flushed. "Jesus. Darren was talking to Cruz about sinking the boat clear back before the party."

"What party?"

"Never mind. Did you bring me everything?"

"Everything I found. That's what you paid for."

"You made no copies?"

"Come on, Mr. Hooks, I'm a professional. You think I keep files labeled 'Evidence of criminal activity on behalf of clients?' I damn near got busted as it was."

"What do you mean?"

"Janitor came in while I was going through Darren's personal file; I didn't get a chance to photograph the last page so I just grabbed it. But it's in there with the rest."

"What if he notices it's gone?"

"I don't know. Hey, if you want to pay extra I'd be happy to sneak it back in for you."

Hooks curled his lip. "Was Darren's office neat or disorderly?"

"A little of both. You want me to return the page or not?"

"Forget it. People lose papers all the time."

"Your call. Well, I've got other clients to take care of. Here you go." Steele slid an oversized envelope across the tabletop.

The banker pushed a smaller envelope back. "And here you go."

That envelope vanished. "Pleasure doing business with you."

Hooks lived in the old, beautifully-landscaped neighborhood of Mission Hills. Many of the homes rimming the mesas and canyons offered spectacular vistas of the harbor and airport. His was no exception.

He entered the grounds through the side door of the garage, then walked through his back yard. The leaves and flowers of the patios and the tiles of the decks and swimming pool reflected the sky, throwing differing hues of color onto the surrounding stucco walls and windows. But Hooks did not notice. He seldom noticed. Why bother? He lived alone save for the groundskeeper and housekeeper . . . and they stayed out of his way.

In his den he sat in his favorite chair and thought things over. As he had suspected, information was what he'd needed. Now, thanks to the bombshell the private investigator had found in Anthony Darren's personal file, Hooks had options. Scenarios, possibilities.

He reached for an outdated copy of *The San Diego Union* and scanned an article about *the Sea Diva* disaster until he found the name "Egan James." According to the article, James was one of the men in charge of the *Diva* investigation, a DA, . . . and therefore, potentially, a mortal enemy of Herbert Hooks.

Unless . . .

After another half-hour of thought, Hooks used a handkerchief to wipe down the envelope Steele had given him. He had no idea what sorts of materials the police could pull fingerprints off of these days.

Holding the envelope with the handkerchief, he went to his desk, sat and shook the envelope's contents onto the desk. Photos of a dozen or so documents. Not photo*copies*; actual photographs; apparently Steele had himself a nice little camera. Hooks pushed the prints around until he found one depicting a document written in longhand rather than being typed. Since he'd handled that one already, he wiped it carefully with the handkerchief, then read it again:

Businessman owns tuna seiner,

is in great financial difficulty . . .

Perfect. Just perfect.

Hooks turned to his typewriter and began to laboriously peck out a letter. When it was finished he slid it into the original envelope along with the photo of Anthony Darren's handwritten plan to sink a tuna boat, and taped the slit closed.

Tomorrow he would mail it from a post office across town.

Meanwhile he collected the remainder of Darren's documents, none of which interested him in the slightest, and ran them through his shredder.

Now he was disconnected from anything that might otherwise associate him with Anthony Darren in one direction, or Egan James in the other.

Now he was safer.

⚓

The mail room girl for the DA's office wheeled her little cart to Egan James' door and placed his stack on the desk in front of him.

Without thanking or even glancing at her, he reached out and began sorting through the material. A manila envelope designated "Confidential" drew his immediate attention. He noticed that its gummed end had been either re-fastened or reinforced with Scotch tape. He tore open the opposite end and tipped the contents—two sheets of white paper—onto his desktop.

One sheet proved to be on thick, expensive bond, with a couple of paragraphs of typed text in the center, written obviously a few days ago:

July 21, 1979

Dear Mr. James:

Enclosed find a copy of notes in the handwriting of Mr. Anthony Darren that detail a plan for sinking a fishing vessel to profit from the insurance. As you can see, the notes are dated well before the Sea Diva was sunk.

I hope this helps with your investigation.

There was no signature.

Egan stared at the words for several seconds, his face darkening. This was ridiculous; a joke. And he hated nothing more than being made the butt of a joke.

Still, he picked up the second sheet of paper. This one was stiff and, on one side, glossy: a black-and-white photograph. It depicted a handwritten document detailing precisely what the letter indicated: the tale of a tuna boat owner who decided to sink one of his vessels in order to collect the insurance.

Then he read the date, and his eyes widened: November 18, 1978. About five months *before the Sea Diva* dove to the bottom of the Pacific. . . .

Egan's pulse thumped in his ears. If this is really Anthony Darren's handwriting?

He read the synopsis two more times. Three times. Finally he put the photo carefully on his desk, face down. He thought, *Anonymous tips can lead to successful prosecutions . . . or to lots of egg on your face.*

He examined the envelope the documents had come in. No return address, a San Diego postmark. He tore it the rest of the way open . . . and a sheet of standard yellow legal paper, folded in half, dropped onto his desk. He unfolded it and saw more scrawled handwriting resembling that in the photographed document, but this time in the form of a transmittal letter:

October 26, 1978

Dear Laura,

At last I am enclosing the first three draft chapters of the high seas crime novel I told you about. Anxious to hear what you think. After all, you are the best editor I know.

Love ya',
Anthony

The eager drumbeat of blood faded from Egan's ears. *Novel*? That was what the photographed outline or synopsis referred to, then? An unfinished *story* about sinking a tuna boat? Fuck!

So someone was yanking Egan's chain after all.

Still . . . he didn't throw the material stuff away. In fact, the more he thought about it, the less it seemed like a practical joke. For one thing, why send this stuff to *him*? Nobody outside his own head knew of the resentment he still carried for Anthony Darren, or for how long, or why. No; more likely Mr. "Anonymous." had mailed the documents to Egan James simply because Egan was known to be a lead attorney in the *Sea Diva* investigation..

He considered the three items again. An anonymous cover letter typed on expensive bond, dated July 21st, 1979. A black-and-white photo of a handwritten plan to sink a tuna boat, dated November, 18, 1978. And some sort of transmittal letter written in the same hand, dated October 26, 1978, referring to three chapters of a novel, but *what* novel? The letter mentioned no title and described no plot or characters. It could be about some other high seas crime story entirely. Whoever sent it might have included it as nothing more than a corroborative handwriting sample.

Yes. That made sense; in fact, it was the only thing that *did* make sense. The transmittal letter was an outlier, insignificant document. What mattered here was the plan to sink a tuna boat, which showed clear foreknowledge of what would occur in the middle of the Pacific Ocean five months later.

And if Anthony Darren wrote it . . .

Egan heard his pulse rising again. But he had to think about this. The documents had been sent to *him*, after all. No need to rush straight to his boss with them. Much better to think things over first. Think them over carefully.

He slipped all three pages into a "safe" file and locked it in the untidy credenza behind his desk. He began flipping into the air the silver credenza key. Then he stared out his window at the surrounding buildings and slid one fingertip slowly down the length of the scar above his left eye, over and over again.

Samantha was talking with her mother on the phone again, discussing one of the DJs at her radio station.

Anthony wished she would hang up.

Sam, there's something I need to tell you about.

No, no, not something.

There's someone I need to tell you about.

Someone I want to tell you about.

But Samantha just kept chattering away with her mother. Maybe I should get on the extension, he thought. Tell both of them at the same time that I've discovered I have an illegitimate daughter I've never met. "How's that for inappropriate, ladies?"

But he didn't. He naturally needed to talk to Samantha first. Still, he had to admit that he felt a bit relieved that they were still on the phone when he decided to try some other night to bring it up.

Egan James followed a secretary into the office of Assistant U.S. Attorney John Woods. Woods glanced up, jacket off, tie loosened, pen in hand. His gaze lingered a half-second on the manila envelope in Egan's hand.

"Sit down, Egan," he said. "Hope you don't mind me working while we talk. I've got to review this damned brief—has to be filed today."

"I'll only be a few minutes." Egan sat on the opposite side of the desk and took in a slow, deep breath. He felt like a gold prospector getting ready to present an assayer with bags from the Mother Lode.

Finally Woods looked up again. "Well, what's so important you had to come over and tell me in person?"

Egan opened the envelope and passed Woods the photo he'd been sent. "Take a look at this."

Woods read the paper. Slowly, the corners of his mouth turned down. "What is this? It reads like a description of the *Sea Diva* sinking. Why did you—"

"Look at the date. November 18. Five months before the sinking."

"I see that. What about it?"

"Notice the handwriting. Care to guess whose it is?"

"No, I don't. Didn't you hear me say I have—"

"Anthony Darren's."

A pause. "What?"

"The handwriting is Anthony Darren's. I had it analyzed and confirmed. It's his, no question about it. Which means he wrote down the idea of sinking a tuna boat for the insurance five months before it actually happened to his client."

Woods turned the photo over in his hands, then back. "Where did you get this?"

"It arrived in the mail along with an anonymous letter." Egan fished inside the envelope. "Here."

Woods read the cover letter. "That's it? These two documents?"

"Yes. That's all. I have no idea who sent them."

Woods eased back in his chair, face grave. "Ah, it *kills* me to find out a respected lawyer might be mixed up in something so . . . underhanded. But I have no choice—I've got to subpoena Darren to testify before the Grand Jury. Egan, talk to my paralegal Joyce on your way out and she'll have the subpoena served this afternoon."

"That's just what I was going to suggest," Egan said, ignoring thoughts of that awkward second letter, that irrelevant transmittal by Darren of parts of a novel. He'd left it in his personal folder. Judging by John Wood's expression, the assayer liked the color of the gold Egan had brought him.

Anthony was speed-reading a case in an old hardback *Federal Reporter* when he heard his name. He looked up and saw the receptionist's puzzled face poking around the door frame of the office library.

"There's a man wearing a badge in the reception area who wants to see you about serving papers, Mr. Darren. You still have clients waiting, too."

11
On a Cliff in the Fog

The clients had just left Anthony's office when Julie called to say that Dirk Miller had arrived.

"I got here as soon as I could," said Dirk, as he walked in. "What's this about a subpoena?"

Anthony shrugged. "I don't know; it's screwy." He handed over the papers. "What do you think the Assistant US Attorney is up to?"

"I don't know. Hell, let's just call him and ask."

Dirk got John Woods on the speaker phone. "Why the subpoena of Anthony Darren, John? The Attorney-Client Privilege prevents you from delving into anything Cruz and Darren might have told each other, so why are you wasting everyone's time with a subpoena? Is Darren some kind of target of the investigation? By the way," he added, "I hope you don't mind. You're on the speaker phone and Anthony is right here."

"No problem," said Woods. "Hi, Anthony."

"Hello, John."

"Dirk, you know very well Grand Jury proceedings are secret. I couldn't tell you one way or the other if Darren is a target."

"Okay, but I'd like to be present in the Grand Jury room when he's questioned. Would you make an exception?"

"Sorry, Dirk. You'll have to wait outside the room. If a witness needs to talk to a lawyer, a recess can be called. And Darren can always leave the jury room for a conference."

"Just asking."

"It's okay. See you there?"

"We'll be there." Dirk hung up and turned to Anthony. "I don't like the way this sounds, Anthony. But it's too early to jump to conclusions."

That's easy for you to say, Anthony thought.

All the rest of that day the subpoena hung on his mind, and for the rest of the week he caught himself imagining various scenarios about what the US Attorney's Office might be up to.

The only way he could distract himself from this untargeted dread was to think about an entirely different surprise: seeing Cheryl again—and her daughter. *Their* daughter.

Tomorrow.

The giant digital clock at the end of the hockey rink showed 10:40 AM. Anthony found a seat on the benches about fifteen rows up, and tried to relax. Having dressed in comfortable jeans and a light sports jacket over a white golf shirt, he hoped the past sixteen years wouldn't be too hard on Cheryl's memory of him.

People, mostly young, came and went in every direction. He watched the skaters through the protective hockey netting. A few skilled young women circled in the center, going through their exercises with a coach standing by. Leaning forward, forearms on his knees, Anthony scrutinized every female skating across his field of vision, as well as those walking up and down the aisles to the locker room. None looked the way he imagined Cheryl might after sixteen years. Nor did he see any teenaged girls who looked "just like." him.

At eleven he was still there, waiting.

At noon he finally got up, deflated, bewildered.

They weren't coming.

The following morning hung like a painting, bright and cool, but its beauty gave Anthony no comfort as he and Dirk Miller walked up the steps of the old gray Federal Court House. Its pillars and Washingtonian architecture always reminded Anthony of buildings around the Mall in the US Capitol.

Half way up the steps a gaggle of newspaper reporters crowded around. Cameras flashed and voices riddled him with questions.

"No comment," he said several times before he and Dirk managed to break away. Under his breath Anthony muttered, "I thought Grand Jury proceedings are supposed to be secret. Who tipped them off?"

Dirk shrugged. "Who knows? John Woods is a pretty straight shooter." They went through the revolving brass-framed glass doors and into the subdued lighted and echoing halls of the building. A side door led to the Grand Jury room.

Woods came up and shook hands with them both. "Are you ready, Anthony?"

"I'm ready."

"I'll be right out here if you need me," Dirk said.

Woods escorted Anthony into the Grand Jury room, where twenty or so average-looking men and women of various races sat in neat rows and looked stoically at him. To Anthony the people looked as though they were sitting in an adult education class and their teacher was escorting in a visiting professor.

But rather than a teacher's lectern, a witness stand dominated the front of this room. On it stood several paper cups and a small pitcher of water. There was no judge's bench or, for that matter, judge—just the Assistant US Attorney, a court reporter, and the Secretary of the Jury at her separate table.

As Anthony took the stand he gave the jurors a confident, professional smile. They did not smile back. A fast count confirmed that twenty of the twenty-three members of the jury were present. It took only twelve "yes" votes to get an indictment.

The jury's grim air told him that Woods had already given his opening statement, summarizing what he expected to show and what evidence he intended to elicit from Anthony. Anthony couldn't help but be a bit annoyed by this waste of his time, but he felt no fear. He had nothing to hide and nothing to do with any alleged crime. Besides, a Federal Grand Jury does not convict. If it decides to take action against a suspect, it can only indict; then the defendant must stand trial before a separate jury where he or she is presumed innocent until proven guilty beyond a reasonable doubt.

As directed, Anthony raised his hand and swore to tell the truth.

John Woods' preliminary questions brought out the fact that Anthony was himself an attorney, and disclosed some of his background. Along the way Woods asked a question Anthony believed violated the attorney-client privilege—so Anthony, strongly asserting his privilege on Joe Cruz's behalf, refused to answer.

Woods seemed unconcerned. He skipped a few pages of notes on his yellow legal tablet, then asked the clerk to mark as Exhibit "A" a document he described as "A paper containing handwritten notes dated November 18, 1978, last year."

While Anthony was trying to recall what the document might possibly be, the US Attorney approached him holding up a single sheet of paper. "Before I hand this document to you, Mr. Darren, I must state your rights. You have the right to remain silent. You have the right to have an attorney present outside the jury room, with whom you may consult before you answer any particular questions. Mr. Darren, you have an attorney available outside this courtroom, do you not?"

Anthony realized he felt as light-headed as he did after a particularly long run. Woods wouldn't have read him his rights unless he, Anthony, was himself a target. *What kind of circus play is Woods up to?*

"Mr. Darren?"

"Yes, there is an attorney present outside the courtroom."

"Do you wish to consult with him?"

"No." Anthony made his voice curt and disdainful, as befitted the President of the County Bar Association. "I have nothing to hide from the Grand Jury panel. Get on with it, Counsel."

Woods shrugged and finished stating Anthony's rights. Then he said, "All right, counsel, I hand you Exhibit 'A', a document containing handwritten notes dated November 18 of last year. Have you ever seen the original of this document?"

Anthony looked at the paper. Although he did not telegraph even the slightest reaction, on the inside he felt the settling of frozen mist. "Yes, I recognize it. But I can explain."

"Mr. Darren, you will have full opportunity to explain; however, first let me ask a few more questions. You are aware, are you not, that *the Sea Diva*, owned by Joseph Cruz Enterprises, sank on or about April 25 of this year, 1979?"

"Yes."

"And you are aware that the owner's son, Michael Cruz, who was aboard the vessel at the time of the sinking, drowned in connection with that incident?"

"Yes."

"And that Chief Engineer Poncho Pascalle was lost also?"

"Yes."

"You have been a close friend of Joe Cruz since college days, correct?"

"I would say *friend* rather than a *close friend*," Anthony replied with care.

"Well, didn't you save him from drowning back then?"

"I helped him to shore, yes; but I'd like to think I would have done that if I'd never met Mr. Cruz before."

Woods waved a hand as if at an errant mosquito. "He is currently your client, though, is he not?"

"Yes."

"Referring again to Exhibit 'A', are you familiar with the handwriting on that document?"

"Yes," I asked Laura to burn this synopsis and everything else associated with my novel. How did Woods get a copy?

"That handwriting is yours, isn't it, Mr. Darren?" Woods asked.

"Certainly."

"So it won't be necessary for us to bring in a handwriting expert to prove you wrote this, correct?"

"Counsel, you know that's an objectionable question. Your sarcasm is unnecessary. I said the notes are mine."

"Did you date this document on the day it was written— November 18 of last year?"

"I don't remember, but I presume so."

"Do you know the approximate date the tuna fishing vessel *the Sea Diva* departed on its one and only voyage?"

"I don't remember the exact date."

Woods' tone became condescending. "It was on or about January 15 of this year, wasn't it?"

"That sounds about right."

"Which was almost three months after you wrote these notes—correct?"

"Yes, but . . . wait . . . I can explain."

"Just a few more questions, Mr. Darren." Woods turned, "Now, ladies and gentlemen of the jury, I'm going to read from these notes." He proceeded to read the synopsis, line by line, as it described the owner of a tuna vessel entering into a conspiracy to sink his own boat in order to collect insurance proceeds. When he finished, the room was so quiet Anthony heard the blurry scratch of pens and pencils on notepads.

"Now, Mr. Darren, I wanted to give you as much time as possible before you presented the explanation you promised. Have you had enough time to think?"

"I don't need time to think up an explanation, counsel."

"Then tell us: how do you explain these notes?"

"They're the outline or synopsis of a fictional story, a novel I was writing back then."

"A novel. Fiction." John Woods turned to look over his shoulder at the Grand Jury and roll his eyes. "So you're saying it's a *coincidence* that *the Sea Diva* sank under circumstances almost identical to those you wrote about in this document."

"That's right."

"I suppose, Mr. Darren, that you have the manuscript of the story itself, preferably dated to show that it was written before the *Diva* departed on its fishing voyage? You can give us a manuscript whose characters have different names than the people involved in *the Sea Diva* matter?"

Anthony poured himself a cup of water.

"Mr. Darren—Did you hear the question?"

"Yes, I did."

"Well?"

"No, I don't have a manuscript."

"Why not?"

"I only wrote three chapters, and I destroyed them. In fact, I destroyed everything I had on the story, or thought I did. Burned it all, or had it burned, in a fireplace."

Woods frowned. "Did this happen before or after *the Sea Diva* sank?"

"Well . . . after."

"Was the story you wrote that bad? Is that why you burned it?"

"No."

"Then why *did* you destroy it?"

"I felt . . . after what happened with *the Sea Diva* I felt my story might have been a bad omen, or that the fisherman would think it was. Besides, I was certainly no longer interested in finishing it."

"It never crossed your mind that someone might compare your story to the sinking of a real tuna boat, and accuse you of arranging the actual sinking?"

"Not at all."

"But you have no shred of evidence—no photocopies or letters—to back up this claim about a novel."

"I believe I wrote a cover letter showing I sent the first few chapters of the manuscript to an editor before Mr. Cruz came to me. I might still have a copy of that somewhere."

"Perhaps stored on one of these new floppy disks on the IBM computer devices?"

"At that time, I don't think we had converted to the IBMs."

Woods flipped through a few more pages then took off his reading glasses. "Mr. Darren, I'm requesting a continuance of this hearing for one week to give you the opportunity to bring that letter, that transmittal letter you speak of, here to the Grand Jury. You keep an office calendar of appointments, correct?"

"I do."

Woods turned to a gray-haired gentleman in slacks and a cardigan who sat at the end of the first row near the secretary. "Mr. Jury Foreman, I request a one week continuance and request you subpoena that calendar and the alleged transmittal letter, and have Mr. Darren also bring it with him next week."

"Mr. Darren," the foreman said, "this matter is continued for a week and you are subpoenaed to bring that calendar and the letter with you."

"Certainly I will."

"Do any members of the jury have questions?" asked Woods.

A man in the second row, who appeared to be in his early thirties and wore a tie and shirtsleeves, raised his hand. "Mr. Darren, assuming you really did have a story like the one you describe before Mr. Cruz came to you, how do we know that you didn't tell *him* about the plot? And then both of you went ahead and sank the boat?"

"Because I didn't," Anthony said.

A middle-aged woman raised her hand. "Mr. Darren, is it possible that you burned the manuscript because you feared Mr. Cruz was actually *following* your story, and it was you who gave him the idea in the first place?"

"I never gave him the idea—assuming he ever had one—to sink the boat," Anthony said. "I never discussed my novel idea with Joe Cruz."

Several more questions in the same vein followed, each stinging him with a clear sense of bias.

"Ladies and gentlemen of the jury," Woods said at last, "Unless your foreman has objections or further questions, I request this hearing be recessed. Remember, all these proceedings must be kept strictly confidential." He turned to Anthony. "That is also true for you, Mr. Darren."

As the jurors filed out, Anthony stood slowly. His legs wobbled. He felt as if he'd been walking along a mountain path in a fog and stepped off a cliff. As he shuffled out the side door Dirk Miller's face floated toward him.

"That was rough," Anthony said.

"I heard." Dirk tugged on his arm. "Come on; nobody ever uses this back hallway."

"You heard? How—"

"Oh, I had my ear planted against the keyhole the entire time. Sounds like old John Woods hasn't mellowed a bit; he's just as tough a son-of-a-gun as he always was. What I don't understand is that he's generally an honorable guy—it sounded as though he really *believes* you're guilty. Where did he get that handwritten synopsis?"

"I have no idea . . . but I do have a bad feeling. Woods is working with Egan James and the D.A.'s office . . . I don't know how you feel about James, but I'd rather trust a rattlesnake."

Dirk had no response to that. As they started down the back

steps, he said, "Okay, we'd better get over to your office and find the original of that transmittal letter, then find you a good criminal defense lawyer. I obviously can't represent both you and Joe Cruz." He paused. "Anthony, this is very serious business. Two people died in that sinking. I believe that under 18 USC 1111, there is a charge of murder if anyone dies during an act of arson. And I think dynamiting is arson."

Anthony swallowed. *Murder?*

"You're sure you didn't destroy whatever copies of that letter you may have had?" Dirk asked after they had searched Anthony's office for two hours. "You just maybe threw them out?"

Anthony collapsed into his chair. In his hand he held the folder marked PERSONAL. "No way," he said. "I shredded my manuscript, but not the transmittal letter. It was in this folder, along with the outline. But now, there's just the synopsis."

"Unfortunately, it's the transmittal letter we need most. Maybe your secretary has an idea where it is."

"I'll ask her." Anthony squeezed the bridge of his nose. "And I'll call Laura, too; see if she still has a copy. Christ, now I hope she *didn't* do what she promised."

"We never checked your calendar," Dirk said. "There might be something there."

"Good idea." Anthony leaned over his desk and flipped back the pages of his appointment book to the previous November. Then he sat back. "Christ, how much worse can it get? I have Joe Cruz penciled as coming in on the 18th of November 1978, the *exact same day* as the date on the synopsis. But I actually wrote the synopsis long before then; I must have just written in the current date when I decided to mail it to Laura."

Dirk gave him a long stare. "I believe you, Anthony . . . but will *Woods* believe you?"

The moment Dirk left, Anthony telephoned Laura and told her about the Grand Jury and the papers they had demanded he produce.

"Laura . . . is there any chance you saved a copy of that transmittal letter I sent you?"

"I'm so sorry, Anthony, but I burned everything. In my fireplace. Just like you asked."

He sighed wistfully. "And here I thought keeping that stuff around was bad luck. Perhaps you recollect the date I put on the transmittal letter?"

"No, I'm sorry. I can't say I do."

"Okay, Laura. I appreciate your efforts. Thanks anyway."

He hung up and stared at his blotter. He wondered if, rather than writing a proper transmittal letter to accompany the synopsis he'd sent to Laura, he had simply scribbled a note and paper-clipped it to the synopsis or something. That wasn't what he recalled doing, but . . . at least it would explain why there was no copy of the transmittal letter.

His secretary announced that Samantha was holding on line two. Anthony stared at the handset for a long time before he picked it up.

At Dirk's recommendation, Anthony contacted a well-known defense attorney named Hal Goldman to assist him for the duration of the Grand Jury. Hal invited Anthony to have a seat in his law firm's conference room then dropped into a chair directly across the polished walnut table. Anthony looked around. Three walls were lined with the inevitable bulk of law books; the fourth was glass and looked out over the sparkling waters of San Diego Bay.

As for Hal Goldman himself, someone had long ago given him the moniker "the Gray Eagle," an apt title. Hal kept his steel-toned hair close-cropped, crisply set off by steel-rimmed glasses through which sharp eyes suggested he either knew all the answers to all the questions, or soon would. He wore a well-tailored gray suit in a shade only slightly darker than his blue-granite eyes.

From beneath grizzled brows he stared at Anthony, but did not speak until Anthony finished telling the entire story again. Then Hal sat back and said, "Well, this is certainly a bizarre set of events. Unique, even. But before we go any further we've got to both be satisfied I'm the right guy to take on your defense." He held up a hand as Anthony began to speak. "Hear me out. As you should know, lawyers are sometimes the worst people to defend, even if they're innocent. One or more jurors might have had painful experiences with lawyers. Then there are our fees; as I'm sure you know people often don't realize how expensive it is for a lawyer to complete a complex legal task. What I'm saying is, finding a jury that doesn't automatically harbor resentment toward you can be a problem."

Anthony nodded glumly.

"On the other hand, I have to admit this case intrigues me. How did Woods get his hands on that synopsis? Who's responsible for trying to set you up? I'm *interested*. I'd like to try to break this case. And I can't think of a more competent lawyer to have working with me than you, Anthony."

"Thank you. That means a lot to me." As though tethered to a thousand rising helium balloons, Anthony felt weight lifting off him.

Then the Gray Eagle raised a finger. "But—and I'm sure this is something you fully realize—we have a tough battle ahead. Herbert Hooks has a ton of clout in this city, which means the political pressure against you will likely become intense. If he teams up with the DA's office, we'll have added dimensions to deal with. Not to mention that the newspapers and the good ol' boys are bound to poison the water."

Despite this warning, as Anthony discussed the case with Hal in increasing detail, he realized he liked the Gray Eagle. He liked Hal's humanity, and the perceptiveness glinting behind his blue-gray eyes. Surely if Hal could make Anthony like and trust him in these circumstances, he would have the same effect on a jury.

As Anthony signed Hal's retainer agreement, he felt sure he'd drawn the best doubles partner available.

Anthony and Hal climbed the steps for Anthony's second Grand Jury appearance while once again reporters rushed at them out of nowhere. Both lawyers "No commented" their way through the questions and camera flashes.

Inside, at the side door to the Grand Jury room, Hal rested a hand on Anthony's shoulder. "Hopefully this will all end with the Grand Jury, and you won't have to put up with that kind of thing again."

"That would suit me just fine."

John Woods opened the door, greeted them—always a gentleman outside of battle—and then took Anthony in.

The questioning resumed as if no time had elapsed. "Mr. Darren," Woods said, "during your last appearance here you referred to a transmittal letter that supposedly showed you sent the synopsis of a novel you were writing to an assistant literary agent or reader. Is that correct?"

"Yes, it is."

"You were supposed to find the letter. Did you?"

"No, I didn't, but I know it was there . . . before."

"Before what?"

"Before this."

"You mean it's missing now?"

"Yes."

There was a pause. "Did you find any other pertinent materials dated prior to when Mr. Cruz first came to your office?"

"No, I couldn't find any."

He noticed one juror raise an eyebrow.

"Did you at least bring your office calendar with you?"

"Yes." Anthony extended it to Wood's outstretched hand. It was marked as an exhibit and handed back.

"Please find the date you first met with Mr. Cruz."

"I've already looked it up." He paused. "It was November 18, 1978, last year."

Woods eyes glittered. "Is that not the exact same date written— in your handwriting—on the plan for sinking the ship?"

"Counsel, it was a synopsis for a story. Yes, it's the same date, but—"

"You've answered the question, Mr. Darren: The synopsis is dated the same day that you initially met with Joe Cruz. Now, is there something you want to add?"

"Yes. This may sound strange, but my recollection is that I wrote the synopsis well *before* that day; I only dated it the eighteenth because that was when I sent it to Ms. Evans for review."

"What do you mean 'this may sound strange'? Do you mean sound *contrived*?"

Anthony hesitated.

"You know what the word 'contrived' means, don't you?"

"Of course. I don't mean *contrived*, I mean *coincidental*."

"Oh, I see. So you're telling us there was another coincidence, on top of the spectacular one that your supposed synopsis so precisely mirrored, of the actual sinking of *the Sea Diva*?"

"If you want to put it that way."

Woods turned away. "No further questions."

As Anthony and Hal stood in the antique paneled hall outside the Grand Jury room, Laura appeared, walking briskly. She wore a trim business suit, her black-rimmed glasses, and a brave expression. She smiled at Anthony and entered the Grand Jury room.

The moment the door closed, Hal bent and put his ear to the keyhole.

"Ms. Evans," Woods said, "when did you first meet Anthony Darren?"

"About three years ago."

"Where?"

"At the Mariner Restaurant."

"That's a bar, right?"

"It's a restaurant, but yes, there is a bar there also."

"You met in the bar?"

"Yes."

"Had drinks together?"

"Well . . . yes."

"Have you ever been sexually intimate with Mr. Darren?"

Laura sat back hard in the chair. She thought she saw both scowls and smirks amongst the jurors' faces. "Do I have to answer that? Don't I have a right to privacy?"

"You must answer," Woods said. "If you wish to check with Mr. Darren's lawyer, who is standing by outside, you may."

She set her shoulders. "No, go ahead. Let's get this over with."

"I repeat: have you ever been sexually intimate with Mr. Darren?"

"Yes, I had a loving relationship with him for a period of time."

"When was the first time, and when was the last time, you went to bed together?"

"The first time . . . the first time was the night we . . . we. . . ."

"The night you met?"

"Yes."

"The night you picked him up at the bar?"

"Mr. Woods, he was not a 'pick up.'"

"You took him home with you, correct?"

"How do you want me to answer that?" she snapped, and glanced at the jury. *What are they looking at*, she wondered, unable to ignore the avid light she saw in some of the eyes there.

"When was the last time you were sexually intimate with Mr. Darren?" Woods asked.

"I can't remember. I think a year and some months ago."

"How many months?"

"As I said, I don't remember. Must you be so callous, Mr. Woods?"

"I'm sorry, Ms. Evans." Woods spoke sincerely. "I have to ask these questions. The dates of your relationship, and your biases, are important. But let me ask something else: is it true that you were requested by Mr. Darren to burn all evidence of this story he says he wrote?"

"Yes."

"And he had you do this for him only a few days after *the Sea Diva* sank, correct?"

"Yes."

"Did he tell you he was concerned that those papers might be a danger to him, possibly linking him to a conspiracy to sink the ship?"

"No. He said he believed his story had stirred up a bad omen, or at least the fishing community would think that. He mentioned how superstitious they are, and wanted to respect that tradition."

"But did he not also tell you he didn't want anyone to get the . . . *incorrect impression* from his outline, otherwise sometimes referred to as the synopsis?"

"I don't remember."

"You wanted to help him, right?"

"Yes."

"And you want to help him now—at this moment?"

"Yes, but honestly."

Hal stepped back from the door to the Grand Jury room as Laura exited. She stepped up to Anthony and hugged him hard.

"It was awful. I did the best I could, but when I finally got the opportunity to explain what happened, some of the jurors looked like they were *sneering*."

Hal caught John Woods as he came out the main door of the Grand Jury room. Under the high echoing ceiling of the courthouse hall they talked.

"You know Anthony's a brilliant lawyer and a superb County Bar President," Hal said. "An indictment will surely ruin his professional life, even if he's later acquitted."

Woods raised his shoulders in an almost Gallic shrug. "Hal, if you have any evidence that would help demonstrate Anthony's innocence, I'm willing to listen. In fact, I hope you *do* have something. But to my thinking, the absence of this supposed transmittal letter is pivotal. That and the fact that the boat sinking plan—or synopsis, as you call it—is dated the same day as Anthony's first meeting with Cruz. Then consider the huge contingency fee Anthony would have made off the insurance company if the sinking had gone off better. Hal, I don't relish what I have to do, but it's my job."

"Come on, John; I've told you that that contingency fee is a standard part of all attorneys' printed fee agreements. You know there's no way he would have charged Cruz one-third of the insurance proceeds. In fact he'd agreed with Cruz to work by the hour—at his usual rate of one-fifty per."

"Yes, but they reached that agreement only *after* the ship sank, *after* the supposed manuscript got burned, and *after* the Coast Guard hearing. At that point Joe wasn't going to get any insurance proceeds anyway. Look Hal; if I don't press this investigation it will look like a damn palliation. If you want this to stop, you've got to come up with something better than you have so far."

"This is so awful," Samantha cried to Anthony as they had dinner at his townhouse. He had grilled a nice steak, made a nice salad, but neither of them could eat.

Joe Cruz had been federally indicted earlier that day on charges of arson, criminal fraud, and murder under the felony murder rule.

"Can you imagine?" Samantha said, her hair perfectly shaped around her beautiful face. "I had to sit at the station and help prepare the news release. I could *feel* my crew pretending not to look at me. Everybody's wondering, Anthony. Everybody's wondering . . . *is her future husband next?*"

Anthony said nothing. Of course he could imagine it. He felt those same stares every day, in every situation. He read the newspapers, listened to the news, and watched TV. Above all, he felt the currents in the legal community and knew the undertow was pulling him away from shore, just as it had already taken Joe.

But right now, that wasn't what bothered him. What bothered him right now was the fact that Samantha had sat there dry-eyed while he described what Joe must be going through right now, and Sylvia. Sam had sat sadly but, he felt, only ostensibly. When she brought up how it all affected her, real tears began to show.

12
Edge of Revenge

Egan James sat in a straight-backed wooden chair at a small oak table in the center of the room. Across the table an identical chair stood empty. The room was a little bigger than Egan's clothes closet at home and had no windows. Two closed doors, one at each end, were the only openings to the outside world.

While he waited for his guest to arrive, he thought about the room he had been sitting in forty minutes ago: the somewhat more plush office of Assistant U.S Attorney, John Woods. That time he had not been alone. Woods had been there, of course, along with the banker Herbert Hooks.

A quirky man, Hooks. Publicly tight-fisted, but politically charitable when he thought no one was looking, and it might do him some good. He'll never know that good fund-raisers like me trace anonymous checks. Got to know who to tap the next time.

He was there to give a statement: at the bon voyage party for the Sea Diva, he had reminded Anthony Darren that Joe Cruz was vulnerable on his personal guarantee on the loan. And Darren had replied, "Relax. Joe has a contingency planned for getting you paid off."

Ladies and gentlemen of the jury, we now know what that plan was, don't we? Send the Sea Diva down!

So far all the media reports were painting Southern California Empire Bank as a victim. The newspapers in particular regularly pumped out sensationalized stories about Cruz's indictment, often including sly innuendoes about his attorney Anthony Darren, the

Youngest President Ever of the County Bar Association. Blah, blah, blah. They had also printed excellent photos of Joe Cruz being arrested and driven off to jail.

And there he still sat. Obstinate Joe Cruz; clearly he had not cooperated with his lawyer. Ordinarily a man in his situation would have been booked and released immediately with his bail already set. But not in this case. Cruz was stuck behind bars until he got bail review, which could take a while.

Word was, Cruz didn't care. Word was he just sat in his cell, fingering his rosary beads and staring at the floor. Martyr or masochist, who cares? He probably just wants to die and join his son.

But now Egan itched with anticipation, like when he watched a kill shot loop toward him during a racquetball match.

A single knock at the door broke the silence.

Egan raised his head. "Come in."

A burly US investigative marshal entered with an inmate dressed in an orange jumpsuit. Egan motioned toward the chair. The inmate seated himself, all the while combing his hair using both hands. Trim, of average height, the prisoner had a convivial face like that of the preverbal door-to-door salesman. Just enough clean-cut gray hair to give him some distinction. Egan approved. Wearing an orange jumpsuit the man looked like the prisoner he was, but in a suit and tie he would come across well.

"Do you want me to wait here?" the marshal asked.

Egan shook his head. "Not necessary. Get yourself some coffee. We'll be finished in fifteen or twenty minutes."

"Do you at least want me to shackle his ankles?" "I'm told he is not in here for a violent offence."

"Nah, he's just a con man who defrauds old folks."

Williams flicked an imaginary particle from his sleeve.

"I can handle him," said Egan. "If it makes you more comfortable, lock us in."

"Okay," said the marshal, "I'll be back in fifteen." He walked out, and Egan heard the external bolt slide into place.

Egan slouched in the chair. "How's it going, Steve?"

"I'm in jail, Mr. James. It could be better." Williams smiled. "Did you really ask if I was violent?"

Egan smiled. "Listen, Steve: you did well on the last matter, so I'm checking to see if you'd do another investigation for me."

"Hey, I'd like to help, but I've already taken a lot of risks for you and no one's even told me how many points I got for the last time."

"Don't worry about that. Have your attorney call me so we can work out a plea bargain. If you do a good job on this one . . . well, no promises, but there's an excellent chance you'll be out in four or five months rather than five years. What do you say?"

Williams shrugged as if he didn't care much one way or the other. "Tell me what you want to know and I'll see if I can get it."

"Joe Cruz and the sinking of *the Sea Diva*, you've been reading about it in the papers?"

"Yeah; I understand he's now a guest in this very establishment."

"That's right, and he's stuck here until he has bail review."

"Four or five days."

"For a man like him that's an eternity. The thing is, he's been seriously depressed ever since his son died. I need someone on the inside to keep an eye on him in case he tries to commit suicide. I've arranged for you to have the other bunk in his cell."

"My job is to keep him from killing himself?"

"That, and get him talking. We understand he was going to church every night before he was arrested, and he's been asking to go to the chapel here. That give you any ideas?"

Williams smiled. "I can think of an angle or two. What do you want me to find out?"

"We suspect that his lawyer, Anthony Darren, was part of the conspiracy to sink *the Sea Diva; that it was his idea*, but the evidence isn't as strong as we'd like. See if Joe will give you any leads."

"No problem."

"Don't be so sure. According to rumor, Darren saved Joe's life back in college, so you can expect Joe to protect his friend."

Williams nodded. "Temporary lapse of Darren's true character. All right. I have it."

"We're not going to put a wire on you, not in that place. So don't forget: any statements you get from Joe have to be either very believable or backed up in some way in case he later denies he spoke to you."

Williams waved a hand. "I've been through that drill before. All I have to do is get him to tell me the kind of details you fellows like to keep confidential, and that will corroborate that he talked to me."

"Do you think you can do that?"

"If I couldn't, you wouldn't have brought me in here for this little conversation, now would you?"

Egan signed the marshal's return form, not aware that Steve Williams had a penchant for reading and remembering I D's and passwords upside down.

That evening Williams was sitting on his newly-assigned bunk when Joe returned from the eating hall. Williams put aside a Knights of Columbus magazine he'd been pretending to read and introduced himself.

Joe's response was a grunt.

That set the pattern. Over the next couple of hours Steve tried several times to start a conversation, but he was about as significant to Joe as the gray paint on the concrete-block walls.

Later the watch commander gave Joe permission to make a twenty minute visit to the chapel. When he returned Steve was kneeling beside his bunk with a string of rosary beads in his hand, mumbling under his breath. After fifteen minutes he didn't think his knees could take much more, so he glanced out the corner of his eye. Joe was looking at him.

Williams finished and staggered to his feet, but still Joe said nothing.

This process continued over the next two days: Williams pretending to pray, Joe watching him, Williams attempting to draw Joe into conversation, Joe not saying a word. Then he heard scuttlebutt that Joe would be released on bail soon—possibly even the following day.

Williams began to panic. His future was slipping away. *Better switch gears.*

One thing he had learned in his illicit career was that if one scam wasn't working, all you had to do was change gears. Giving up on the rosaries, he saved his knees and went to the library to read newspapers instead. There he found the names of the county investigators in the pools for the District Attorney's office who had been assigned to the Cruz's case. None of the names was familiar.

At noon break he made a call from the inmate's phones near the guard station. "Hello," he said in a low voice with an official-sounding tone. "Is this the exhibit storerooms section? This is Deputy D.A. Egan James. May I speak to an archive clerk?" After a pause: "Hello, Mr. Robbins, did you say? This is Deputy D.A. Egan James. I am assigned to the case of U.S v. Cruz et al. US6361980. Oh, my I.D. is #12864.Could you take a peek at the exhibit list? I need the items added in the last two weeks . . . ? I'll wait. . . . Not since last week . . . ? And that was the *hundred garage door openers*?" Williams nodded, playing the part even to himself. He had to admit, *the mimicry wasn't bad, even though it wasn't necessary.* "Thanks . . . No, let's save that. Reminder, no leaks to the press. Thank you very much Robbins."

Back in the interrogation room, Egan James slid a yellow legal tablet onto the table and poised his pen above it. "So you've got something for me?"

Williams slouched in his chair as if this were *his* office, *his* desk. "I had a hard time getting Cruz to warm up, but you were right about the religion thing. After I showed him some rosary beads a few times, he finally opened up."

Egan made a brushing motion with his hand. "Go on."

"He told me he ordered, like a hundred garage door openers and piano wire to put on board *the Sea Diva*. Look for receipts with the signature or co- signature of the ship's chief engineer, Poncho Paqualle, on them."

Egan was taking notes. "Go on."

"You wanted me to pump him about Anthony Darren. That turned out to not be so tough after all. Joe sort of thinks his son's death won't be set right until everyone involved pays a price. And Anthony Darren isn't paying yet. But he should, Joe said, because he was the one who came up with the plan to sink the ship in the first place."

Egan's pen hesitated. Went back to work. "Anything else?"

"No, that's it."

Egan looked up. "You did okay, Steve. We knew about the invoices for the chisel, garage door openers, but nobody else does. I can't understand how you get these people to talk to you."

"I'm like a priest," Williams said. "Everybody's guilty of something, and everybody likes to get it off their chest. Now, about that plea bargain."

Samantha Kincaid closed and locked the door of her office at the radio station and stood looking out a second story window at the heavy freeway traffic on I-5 near the Mission Valley flood control channel. Beyond the freeway she saw slots of blue broken by patches of sand and an eclectic assortment of motels, Sea World, palm trees and more traffic. She remembered her father telling her that when he grew up there had been nothing out there except marshes and estuaries surrounded by reed grass. He'd even gone camping there. Personally, she was glad the city had cleaned the place up, dredged it and constructed landfills and hotels. It would have been awful to sleep out in a smelly marsh. Camping! That was one of the things Anthony liked to do that she couldn't stand. She dialed the District Attorney's office and asked for Mr. James. When the receptionist insisted on knowing her identity she snapped, "Please just get him. It's very important."

Finally she heard his voice: "Egan James here."

"Hello, Egan. This is Samantha Kincaid. Do you remember me?"

"Why, of course. How could I forget the Belle of the Ball? How may I be of service?"

"I'd like to make an appointment to see you right away. Is that possible?"

"Certainly. May I ask what it's about?"

"Well . . . do you mind if we meet away from your office?"

There was a pause. "Why don't we meet at the restaurant at my club for lunch? Say—day after tomorrow?"

"That would be fine."

The sight of Samantha sitting by a garden window in the afternoon light stopped Egan momentarily. When she looked at him and smiled, the bouquet of irises on the table perfectly matched her deep blue eyes.

Egan shook her hand, then sat across from her. "You look well."

"Thank you. This is a beautiful place."

"Yes; it—"

"Egan, I'm sorry; I'll get right to the point. Anthony and I need help."

He leaned toward her. "I hope I can help both of you."

"The US Attorney's office is laboring under a misimpression that has to be straightened out." She also leaned forward, her hands squeezed together on top of the table. "Anthony has done nothing wrong. I can confirm what he says. I know you're assisting Mr. Woods; please ask him to drop his investigation." Tears welled in her eyes. "The strain is beginning to take a toll on our relationship. My mother told me the other day that she's hearing little jokes at the country club about Anthony. It's reflecting poorly on me and my family."

Egan resisted the urge to reach over and cup her hands in his. "Samantha, God knows I don't want to see bad things happen to Anthony, and it's a shame you have to suffer because of something someone else d . . . might have done. I'd truly like to help. So if you have anything concrete to offer, please tell me, and I'll tell Mr. Woods."

She gazed out toward the golf course. "Before we go on, there's something I have to ask of you. You seem to be a gentleman, so—I need your promise you'll never let Anthony know we spoke."

"If that is important to you."

"The other day I hinted that perhaps I could get my dad to approach you about this, and he became extremely upset. He said John Woods is running the case; not you, and furthermore, ethically, you have to go by the book."

"Actually, he's right on that. But I'm still willing to do what I can—and as I said, I'll gladly honor your wishes for confidentiality."

"Thank you." She paused, let out a breath. "The truth is that the similarities between the story Anthony had created a synopsis for, and the actual sinking of the Sea Diva *are* purely coincidental."

Egan sipped his Dubonnet. "Do you have evidence of that?"

"Anthony sent a transmittal letter about the story to a reader friend of his *before* Joe became his client. Isn't that evidence?"

"It is if someone can produce a copy of this letter, including the date."

"He had one, but he can't find it."

"So I've heard. I also heard he asked the reader friend to burn her copy, along with everything else pertaining to this story." He spread his hands. "You see the problem."

"I do, but—"

"What about you? Did he ever tell *you* about this novel?"

"Not until all this happened. It was his private hobby; he wouldn't share it with anyone else unless he felt he was good enough."

"Not even his fiancé?—I'm sorry, forget I said that." Egan arranged his features into an expression of compassion. "Samantha, I'll do what I can, but John Woods is lead counsel and he has a mind of his own."

"What if you tell him that this reader will back up what Anthony says?"

"He's already aware of that. The problem is she's not really a good witness for him. She can't even remember the date she received the transmittal. And then, well, there's that affair she and Anthony had. Since it happened so recently, the jury will undoubtedly assume she's just trying to protect—"

"Recently?" Samantha's eyes flashed. "What are you talking about? They were intimate more than a year ago, but—"

"I'm sorry, Samantha. Forget what I said. It's probably nothing."

"Are you saying that Laura and Anthony have been—"

"Please forget it, Samantha."

She stared out the window again. "I will."

Anthony pushed open the driftwood-planked door and escorted Samantha out of the World Famous Bar in Pacific Beach. On the boardwalk he drew in a deep breath of briny night air. Waves crashed on the sand about a half block west of the low seawall. Columns of lights flanking the walk dully illuminated the beach stretching away, pocked by thousands of shadowed footprints. They saw no people out on the sand; even the windy boardwalk was almost deserted. So was their mood as they walked side by side, bundled in heavy wool sweaters.

"Samantha," Anthony said, "suppose things . . . interfere with our plans? You didn't expect to be engaged to a man who's being investigated for a serious crime."

"You won't be charged. You're innocent."

"I'm glad you sound so confident, but . . . what if I *am* charged?"

"You won't be."

He sighed. "All right. Tell me this: would you still want to marry me if, say, I found out I was going blind? Or broke? Or if some child came out of nowhere and claimed to be mine?"

"Anthony, that's silly." She looked at him with strangely wild eyes, her hair thrashing around her face. "Don't you dare disrupt my plans."

"I wouldn't think of it. But sometimes life disrupts things for you. Seriously, what would you do if you found out—if we both found out—I had a child from a relationship a long time ago?"

"Anthony, I don't like to waste time on fairy stories. Especially bad ones. Rumors, even ridiculous ones, can affect your image in the community. And I hate to think what my parents would say!"

Anthony didn't respond.

After a few more paces Samantha said, "By the way, when was the last time you saw that reader person? Laura?"

"Why would you bring her up?"

"Just wondering."

He looked at her profile. "Sam, that relationship ended over a year ago; you know that. In fact, I hardly ever see her at all anymore." He picked up a broken skateboard lying in their path and set it on the seawall. "Besides, you've never had problems with her being my friend."

"Not at all," she said. "We all need as many *friends* as we can get."

Some of the secretaries were just returning from their morning coffee breaks. In an hour Anthony had to be in court on the Cruz receivership status conference. "There is a Cheryl Burns on line two," said the receptionist.

Anthony swiveled and punched the blinking button.

"Hi, Anthony." Chimes rang again in his head.

"Hi. Cheryl, I waited for you at the rink for almost two hours a couple of weeks ago. What happened?"

"It . . . It was awful. Just when w-w-we were about to l-l-l-leave, a m-m-man from the finance c-c-company showed up and t-t-t-took away our van. M-M-My husband stopped payment on our l-l-l-last check."

Anthony rubbed his eyes. "Why didn't you call me? At least let me know you wouldn't be coming?"

"I-I-I-I-I was so upset I couldn't f-f-f-find your n-n-n-number."

"I was afraid you didn't show up because of the troubles I've been having. I don't want to be a problem in your life. Or Andrea's. I wouldn't blame her if she didn't want to claim being related to me."

"What are . . . are . . . y-y-y-you saying, Anthony?"

"Haven't you been reading about me in the papers?"

"N-n-n-no. . . ."

"Oh. Well, I'm suspected of doing something illegal, something I had no part of. But so far I'm having trouble convincing people I'm innocent, and this could all get a lot worse for me before it gets better."

"I k-k-know how s-s-s-successful you've been, Anthony. M-M-Mary kept me informed all these years. So don't worry; you'll always be Andrea's hero, and mine too. No problem . . . problem . . . c-c-c-c-can be bigger than the feelings I still have for you to this d-d-day . . . day."

He closed his eyes, guilt and happiness churning into embarrassment. "Could we try meeting again, Cheryl? Just you and me this time, so we can talk. And not in some crowded public place."

"O-o-okay, Anthony."

They arranged to meet him at his office at six the next evening.

The following afternoon he walked the few blocks to the shopping mall. The gaiety of the department stores, the lit displays, all brilliant

Tivoli lights draped inside and out, and the sounds and aromas of Christmas and the holidays filled his head. Waves of emotion rolled through him as he walked. His office phone had all but stopped ringing lately, except for clients asking to come in and pick up their files. In the store-front windows his reflection revealed a man in shadow, a man who wanted to crawl into a dark cavern until the storm outside subsided. In the window he saw images of other people crossing behind him, some of them teenagers. Most smiled or laughed, full of plans and hope.

On he walked, his spirits lifting a little.

At a department store convenience counter he ate a quick and tasteless lunch. Then he shopped a little. Soon he was carrying two small packages, light and precious, back out through the music and the aromas, and down the street to his office. There he sat and waited.

Six o'clock came and went, and Cheryl did not come. Finally Anthony took his feet off his desk, unfolded his hands from his chest and looked at his watch. The minute hand pointed to 6:30 PM. No one else remained in the offices.

Still he waited.

"Hello?" The voice carried from the reception area.

Instantly Anthony was on his feet. Stepping out of his office, he peered up the hall. There she stood, several pounds heavier than he remembered, but with the same sparkling smile and captivating eyes.

And behind her stood someone else: a teenaged girl with big hazel eyes.

For a moment Anthony couldn't move. Cheryl came toward him down the hall, her gait not quite steady but not quite a limp; the girl followed a step behind, looking affirmatively into Anthony's face. Anthony rushed forward. He swept Cheryl into a hug and felt her warm tears on his cheek. Then she stood back and said, "Anthony, I'd like you to meet Andi."

Those eyes! Anthony immediately saw in them, his mother, the beauty of his sister. The girl—his daughter—hugged him too, damp eyelashes brushing his face. For a while the three of them clung to one another, and an upheaval Anthony couldn't choke off misted his eyes.

As if in salute to memory, he took them to dinner at Murphy's Place, after all these years still loud and happy with college people. Cheryl and Andrea opened their gifts: an unpretentious diamond-crested locket for Andrea, and a modest gold bracelet for Cheryl. At first he couldn't tell whether Cheryl was laughing or crying, then she embraced Andrea, whose presence, mannerisms, looks, voice—everything—astonished Anthony so much he could hardly look at her.

They began to speak about the things they had gone through for the past several years. From long experience in courtrooms, Anthony knew they were withholding quite a bit, and questioned them gently but persistently. Finally the women looked at each other as if in silent communication . . . and the full story burst out in a flood.

Through a darkening depth of blue Anthony sank. Cheryl spoke as if immersed in a halting dream. As he listened to her he filtered out the stutters, gaps and slurs in her speech and heard her as she used to be.

Cheryl said that Billy never seemed suspicious about the early arrival of his daughter; he proudly distributed cigars when Andi was born, and simply grinned when his buddies ribbed him about having a shotgun wedding. But his friends were also a problem: Billy liked going out with them more than he liked staying home. Pretty soon he was drunk so much that he got into trouble with his commanding officer at Fort Knox. He lost a stripe . . . and was never again the same.

One night during a drunken tirade about money and freedom, Billy whipped his fist around and slammed his knuckles across Cheryl's cheek. Cheryl cried out and fell to the floor. Across the room in her highchair, little Andi wailed. Billy reared over her and roared, "Shut up! Shut up, you *little bitch*!"

Terrified of what her husband might do next, Cheryl gathered Andi up, took her to her tiny room and cuddled the baby's wet little mouth and face against her bruised cheek.

The next day Billy was contrite and white-faced, presenting gifts and promises: *never again*. And that became the pattern: a savage blow, a night apart, a slobbering apology and oath. It went on and on, seemingly the same each time but actually trending, over the years, toward greater violence and weaker apologies. Even after Billy finally got his boy child, his behavior grew worse.

At that point Cheryl lowered her head and stared silently at her plate. Andrea touched her on the hand and picked up the conversation.

From Andrea's perspective, her parents' relationship consisted of closed doors, muffled shouting, things breaking, sobs. Until one night when Andrea was eight, when her father's drunken curses and her mother's wails suddenly ended in a series of heavy, repetitive thuds "like someone beating a rug." Andrea huddled under the covers in her room, put her hands over her ears and closed her eyes until she heard the front door open and slam shut . . . then she raised her head and heard her mother moan. "Not like she had before. This sounded so faint."

Andi tip-toed to her parents' bedroom door and listened. From the other side came a strange, bubbling noise. Terrified, she twisted the knob and pushed. The door opened part way then stopped against her mother's slumped form. "I'm okay, sweetheart," Cheryl sputtered between bloody lips. More blood matted her hair and flowed across the floor. "M-m-m-momma's okay."

Three nights later Andrea was alone in the apartment with her little brother Johnny. Billy was gone—out with his friends, of course—and Cheryl working at her waitress job at Leo's Palace several blocks away. Cheryl had promised to bring dinner home when her shift was over. But the hours passed and nobody came; Andi finally had to rummage in the refrigerator for food. Eventually she and Johnny fell asleep on the couch, huddled together cold and hungry.

Later she awoke to hard knocking on the door. She opened it and saw one of her mother's bosses from the restaurant, Mrs. Dawson, standing there, wringing her hands. She said that Cheryl was in the hospital, unconscious. "She just passed out in the middle of the restaurant."

The Dawsons took Andrea and little Johnny in to live with them for a while. Billy was fine with that arrangement, especially after the

Dawsons discouraged Andrea from telling anyone about what went on privately between her mother and father. . . .

Through hypnotic darkness Anthony heard a man's voice. He blinked, looked up. "Excuse me?" he said to the waiter. "Would you repeat that?"

"Sorry to interrupt. Would any of you like dessert, coffee or an after-dinner drink?"

"Nothing for me, thank you," Andrea said. "Mom, do you want anything?"

Cheryl, face pointed at her plate, shook her head.

Hoping to cleanse the ashes from his mouth, Anthony took a swallow of water. "Nothing for me, either, thanks."

But no amount of water could cleanse his mouth; no regret could cleanse his soul. The environment he had always visualized providing for his future children had been secreted from his control. And he'd known nothing about it.

Suddenly a new thought struck him: if he ended up behind bars, how could he ever give Andi the support she so much deserved?

His daughter clasped Cheryl's hands between her own and went on with the story, which rolled over Anthony like the wheels of a train.

For Cheryl the next few years had loomed gray and dark blue. Diagnosed with traumatic brain injury due to an accidental fall, Cheryl was committed to a VA convalescent hospital, and Billy took Johnny and Andi away from the Dawsons and back to their old apartment.

Although Cheryl soon regained consciousness she remained impaired, almost unrecognizable, and recovering very slowly. Meanwhile Billy drank more than ever and took to beating Johnny and threatening to beat Andrea. She tried to escape the hurt and closeted herself with books, achieving the highest grades in school.

It was while studying Mendel and his genetics experiments in ninth grade biology that Andrea began to wonder about herself. Small-boned and auburn-haired, she seemed to have little in common with her big-boned, pasty-faced, blond-haired father.

But it was the eyes that got to her. The thing about the eyes.

One day, Mrs. Dawson drove her to the VA hospital, and they took Cheryl outside to a bench in the courtyard warmed by the sun. By then Cheryl was able to walk with the aid of a cane, and could use many more words than when she first awoke from her coma. Andrea helped her mother sit down amongst the box hedges and stands of early summer flowers, and settled beside her. Mrs. Dawson left to speak to the head nurse.

After several minutes of sun-washed silence Andrea said, "Mom, what color eyes did your mother and father have?"

"B-b-blue. B-B-B-Both of them."

"I thought so, from the pictures. And Dad's parents' eyes are blue, too."

Cheryl nodded vaguely.

Andrea took a deep breath. "Mom, am I adopted?"

Cheryl's eyes—blue, yes, although no longer as intense as they used to be—moved to track a yellow and brown butterfly fluttering an ever-changing course past them. "Adopted?"

Andrea shifted forward to intercept her mother's line of vision. "Mom. Please. Tell me."

Cheryl gradually returned her focus to her daughter. "Adopted? No, honey. You're not adopted. You're m-m-my ch . . . child."

"But my eyes are hazel, which is really just a version of brown. Everyone else in the family has blue eyes, going back at least two generations. We've been studying this. The chances of me having brown eyes are almost zero. Do you understand?"

Cheryl blinked at her then looked around as if searching for assistance. Only the sounds of bees and chirping of birds filled the pause.

"Mom."

Cheryl sighed, shuddered. "B-B-Billy doesn't know. P-P-P-Promise me you'll never tell him."

"Tell him what?"

"Promise."

"Of course. I promise."

"And p-p-p-p-promise you'll be understanding."

"Mom, please. Of course I'll understand."

"You're such a s-s-s-smart girl." Cheryl touched her hair, took a deep breath. "I'm not lying. I *am* your mother . . . but B-B-Billy . . . Billy is not your father."

Andrea sat there in silence, waiting for the shock to strike her. Instead, she felt . . . relieved. As if she'd known the truth all along. "So who *is* my father?"

"His n-n-n-name is Anthony Darren. He was my b-b-boyfriend b-b-back in Calif-f-f-fornia."

"Is that where he is now?"

Cheryl nodded. "Honey, please understand. I-I-I didn't know what to do. I w-w-was already married to B-B-Billy when I f-f-f-found out I was p-p-pregnant. I couldn't hurt him, or A-A-Anthony. So I just let things b-be."

"You mean my real father doesn't even know I exist?"

"I-I-I'm so sorry. H-He had such big plans f-f-for his life, and he was j-j-just getting started . . . I didn't want to ruin it."

Anthony clenched his fists on the tabletop. I made her think that. I wove the web these two women got caught in. I caused them sorrow while I was preparing my life to protect my future family from ever suffering sorrow.

Andrea picked the story up again. Within a year Billy gave up beating on his son and turned his attention to Andrea, who avoided him as much as possible by becoming involved in every extracurricular activity her school offered. Still, she had to return home eventually, if only to make sure Johnny ate and did his homework. On one of those evenings she heard her father stumble into the house, drunk and snarling—the two ingredients that always signaled a beating to come.

Until she found herself stealing into Billy's bedroom, she had no complete idea what she was about to do. But she did not stop herself as she slid open his bedside drawer and pulled out his .38 revolver. Then she went to her room, closed the door and locked it.

She heard him colliding with furniture, doors, appliances. "Where's my fuckin' dinner? You're worthless you know, *where's my dinner?*" She did not reply. She knew Johnny was lying on his bed in his own room, earphones clamped to his head, heavy-metal music probably turned up to deafening volume.

Her door bounced to pounding thunder. "Get out of there and get that food going, now! You're as bad as your worthless mother!"

"I don't feel good," she said. "I'm in bed."

"Bullshit! I've heard that before. Now get out here, and I mean *now*!"

She pulled the covers over her head and drew back the hammer of the .38 in the blackness. "I'm sick. Please leave me be."

The door crashed open, shooting splinters of wood everywhere, and Billy's shadow loomed over her covers, his muffled panting, like a wolf. The light struck her eyes as he ripped off the covers. The stench of liquor filled her nose. He glared down with his eyes—blue irises in pools of red—and reached for her. Then froze, eyes almost crossing as he took in the bore of the revolver pointing at the bridge of his nose.

He drew slowly back, gaze shifting from the .38 to Andi's face, which contained no more humanity or warmth.

"If you touch me," she said, "I'll blow your head off."

"Hey, now, you—"

"I won't even feel sad about it. I don't care about you, Billy. You're not even my real father."

His watery pink eyes momentarily cleared. He stared into her face, then turned and stumbled out of the room. A moment later she heard his old pickup start up and drive away.

She immediately packed and hustled the suitcases and a bewildered Johnny into her mother's old VW. Then she drove to the convalescent hospital and wheedled the attendant into letting her take her mother "for a little ride." They walked out the front door and, supplied with the precious little money she had hoarded— amplified by what she pilfered from Billy's dresser—left for California.

Anthony glanced around Murphy's restaurant, now almost empty. Busboys wiped off the tables. "Didn't realize it got so late," he said.

He and Andrea helped Cheryl to her feet. Anthony put an arm around each of the women, each of whom slid an arm around him, and all three put their heads together. "Everything will be okay now," he said, even though he couldn't smother the uncertainty.

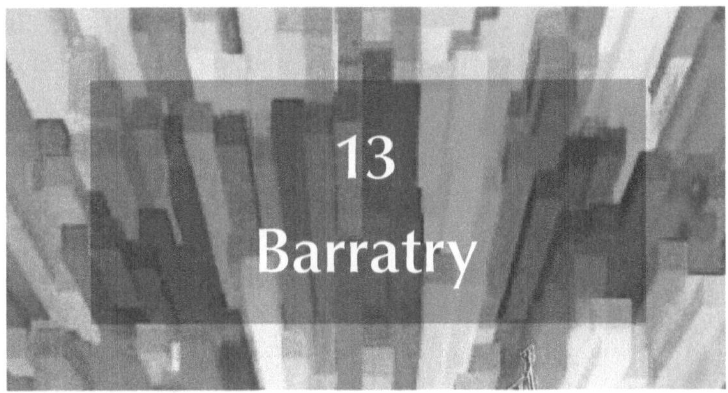

13 Barratry

John Woods capped his pen and looked at Egan James across the desk. "I'm getting to where I have to make a decision whether or not to indict Darren. Right now I'm on the borderline. Everything hinges on this transmittal letter Darren says would clear him. He's a careful lawyer; I find it incredible he happened to lose the one thing he happens to need most."

"Me, too," Egan said, tossing a small silver key into the air and catching it again. "That's why I doubt it ever even existed."

"If we proceed against him and that letter turns up, it would be devastating. I'm willing to be embarrassed, but not because I was trying to convict an innocent man."

Egan flipped the key. "There's no letter," he said. "I promise you. But if it will make you feel better, I recently got a pretty devastating statement from an informant."

"What informant?"

"Steve Williams. He's an inmate at MCC who bunked with Cruz for a while. He says Cruz told him Darren came up with the plan for sinking the tuna boat."

"Egan, you know those slimy jailhouse snitches will say anything to shorten their time. I have to be convinced his testimony is sincere or I'd never put him on the stand."

Egan shrugged. "Williams had details the public doesn't know. Things he couldn't have gotten from anyone but Cruz."

"Like what?"

"Like that Poncho Pascalle ordered a hundred garage door openers and piano wire for *the Sea Diva*. He was mixed up in smuggling munitions and remote control detonators to the rebels in Costallegre."

"What's that got to do with Anthony Darren?"

"I'm just saying, Williams proved he's legit. So that makes him believable when he says Darren came up with the plan to sink the ship in the first place."

"According to Joe Cruz?"

"Apparently the more Cruz thinks about what happened, the more convinced he is that Darren should take responsibility for his son's death."

Woods shook his head. "I don't know . . . jailhouse snitches just aren't—"

"Let the jury decide."

"Don't lecture me, Egan. We have to be responsible and selective about who and what we put before a jury. Like I said, if we use Williams' testimony and we're wrong, we'd lose credibility— maybe even the case. Or even worse, get an innocent man convicted. Egan, I don't win cases on bullshit."

"I know. But John, I've put a lot of work into this. You owe it to the people not to ease up on Darren just because he's Bar President."

Woods stiffened. "I consider that an affront."

"I'm sorry. You're right. But listen, we've got some heavy guns behind us on this. You heard Morton Smith in here, and Herbert Hooks. That banker has a lot of power in this city. Just listen to Williams for yourself."

Woods drummed the desktop with the butt end of his pen. "I'll think about it."

As soon as Egan got back to his office he called Samantha Kincaid.

The Maitre d' of the upscale rooftop restaurant Mr. A's guided Samantha toward the table where Egan James sat gazing at the view of the harbor and airport. As soon as she sat, the wine steward appeared and began pouring a selection Egan had obviously made earlier. Through the window behind Egan a jet airliner came gliding down on the runway approach, crossing in front of the city high-rises almost level with her line of vision.

They clinked glasses, she holding hers by the stem, he cupping his in his palm.

"You look absolutely stunning," he said. "You should be on television, not the radio."

"Thank you. But I'm a producer, not actually *on* the radio. And I'm afraid my worry lines are showing anyway."

"I am just trying to confidentially help you and Anthony, if I can."

As they looked over the menu she talked about the work she was doing at the station, and Egan talked about his lead counsel going for re-appointment. The waiter interrupted artfully to take their orders.

When he left Samantha said, "So how do you think it's going?"

"John Wood's campaign-appointment?"

"No. Anthony's situation."

He straightened the knife and fork next to his plate. "I hate to say this, but it's frustrating. No matter what I say, John Woods is convinced that because nobody can find this transmittal letter Anthony keeps talking about, it never existed. And remember, the date on the plan for sinking the tuna boat matches the day Cruz first went in to see Anthony."

"It's the synopsis of a *story*, not a *plan.*"

Egan leaned forward. "Samantha, I shouldn't tell you this, but . . . Woods says he's got a witness who's willing to testify that Anthony masterminded the whole plot."

"I refuse to believe that."

"On top of that, Woods is prepared to show that Anthony stood to receive a very substantial contingency fee—millions of dollars—from the sinking, if it had gone as planned."

This time Samantha said nothing.

"And there's one more thing. I don't know if I should say anything about this, either; or if you're prepared to hear it. But maybe you already know about it."

"Please continue."

"Well, we've received a tip from a man in Kentucky that Anthony . . ."

"Go on."

". . . that Anthony has a daughter. A sixteen-year-old he abandoned even before she was born."

Alarms clanged in her chest. "What are you saying? He has a daughter? In Kentucky?"

"Don't be surprised you didn't know. Anthony has apparently never acknowledged her to anyone, never supported her, never married her mother . . . in fact, he concealed his paternity from the man who *did* raise her."

The blood draining from her face, Samantha turned to stare out the window.

"I know this is a shock," Egan said, "but I wanted to make sure you knew before it came out in the media. You should also know it's also going to be an issue in the trial, because it reflects on Anthony's character."

"Will you excuse me, please?" Samantha said in a strained voice.

"Of course."

In the ladies' lounge Samantha crumpled onto a crimson-upholstered love seat. She ignored passing quizzical looks and piped-in Christmas music. A hundred thoughts flew through her mind, each one bleaker than the one before. Her plans for the future were coming apart in every respect. Likely criminal proceedings against him? And now an illegitimate daughter? An *abandoned* daughter? How would she ever explain this to her family, or to her friends? To *herself*? She'd knocked herself out being the best person she could be for Anthony, and now *this*?

She struggled to her feet and freshened herself in the mirror until she was satisfied she appeared composed. Then she went back to the man with the compassionate face.

The idea was Anthony's. Though Samantha knew the event was one of his favorites, she insisted they watch from inside the crowded bar rather than outside in the damp and cold.

Soon the first boat came into view out on the bay, strings of colored lights wound through its rigging, sending shimmering across the black surface of the water. Then more boats—some yachts, some fishing boats—slid out into the bay until a seemingly endless line of differently-patterned holiday lights glided by.

Inside Rudy's Harbor Bar, customers sometimes blocked Anthony's view. Occasionally he raised his head to let the sight of the bay transcend his grim thoughts.

Samantha sat with her back to both boats and water, gazing in composure at her hands. He was amazed and pleased. He had expected her to be shocked when he told her about his daughter, but she seemed oddly calm.

Then she said, "Do you realize what this will do to us in the community?" And she got to her feet and walked out. By the time he realized what had happened, she was climbing into a taxi. By the time he got outside, the taxi was gone.

"Mary, I'll help bring in the groceries," Andrea said, grabbing a sack of potatoes and a half gallon of milk from Mary's arms. As Mary tried holding open the back door with her hip, Andrea dragged two large brown bags through the kitchen doorway. The TV blared from the living room. Andrea set the groceries down in the kitchen and went to adjust the volume.

She froze with her fingers on the button.

"Today's indictment of Anthony Darren, President of the County Bar Association, has rocked the legal community. Deputy District Attorney Egan James said that sinking a vessel for personal gain is comparable to the old crime of 'barratry' in the law of admiralty. Most shockingly, Mr. Darren is also technically charged with the murders of Michael Cruz and Poncho Pascalle. . . ."

Several days later Andrea sat in the reception room outside the law office of Harold Goldman, her true father's attorney, waiting to be interviewed. She focused her attention on the obviously expensive reproduction of a French Impressionist painting on the wall across from her. She recognized it as a Monet. In a high school art appreciation class the year before, his work had been her favorite. From her seat she could also see the door where the secretary had gone to announce her. It was open, and above the clatter and ringing of typing she could just hear a man on the other side talking, apparently on the phone. She paid no attention until she heard her father's name—then everything vanished except her sense of hearing.

"Anthony up and left his firm, Dirk. He's opened a solo office, although his practice is down to odds and ends. Even the clients who believe in him have too much at stake to . . . what? Yeah, he resigned the Bar Presidency yesterday. It's like it never ends. His fiancée dumped him, too. Yeah. Wait; just a second Jane, would you please close my door?"

After that Andrea heard only typewriters and phones.

Finally she was summoned into the office with its panoramic view of the harbor from 20 stories high. Goldman—Anthony had referred to him as "The Gray Eagle"—introduced himself and invited her to sit at a small marble-top coffee table. His tone seemed genuinely friendly, and she thought he didn't look at all like an eagle.

"Anthony told me you're a gift from heaven," he said as they sat. "I believe him."

"Thank you." Andrea looked at the toes of her shoes. "He's innocent, Mr. Goldman. I know he is."

"Good. That's what I want to hear, and what Anthony *needs* to hear. We have to keep the fires going in him."

She nodded.

"The reason I asked you to come here today is so I can explain something to you. I wanted to do it face-to-face."

"Yes. . . ?"

"I hope you understand . . . as far as your father's defense is concerned, it would be better if we did *not* reveal your identity right now."

"Why not? I'm proud to be his daughter."

"And you should be. The fact that you're his daughter is not the problem. In fact I think it's wonderful, could even help him with the jury. But certain persons on the prosecution side seem to enjoy attacking your father's character and reputation. If they found out about you, they would undoubtedly argue that Anthony not only abandoned you—his own daughter!—but helped fool your stepfather about your identity just to avoid paying child support."

"But that's—"

"Then there's your mother. I know a little about her health problems. I'm sorry to ask this, but . . . how do you think she would fare on the stand?"

Andrea nipped at a fingernail. "Mom's seeing a new specialist today. Maybe he'll be able to help her, and—"

"Andrea, the trial starts in less than a month."

Andrea sighed. "Then . . . no. She wouldn't do too well on the stand. She gets easily confused and vague."

"Thank you for your honesty. We don't have much time, and we have to prepare for every contingency. For example, if someone makes your paternity an issue, it won't really matter if I manage to keep it out of the courtroom, or prove your father is not responsible—the newspapers will still have a field day with the innuendoes."

"Which would make it hard to get an unbiased jury?" she asked.

"Anthony said you were quick. Yes, that's it exactly."

"So you want me to keep it a secret that I'm his daughter."

"Not forever; only as long as necessary. Just so you know, Anthony's not fond of the idea even though he knows it's the best strategy. I haven't convinced him yet."

Again she considered then offered, "Of course I'll go along with it. I've already lived over sixteen years without even knowing Anthony Darren existed—I guess I can keep the secret a while longer if you think it's best."

Hal smiled. "Excellent."

Maybe he did look a little like an eagle after all.

A few hours later she heard her mother and Mary coming through the back door. She jumped up from the desk where she had been doing homework and ran to the hall.

Mary was smiling. "There's a risk, but the doctor believes he can help your mother."

"Tell me!"

They all went into the living room where Andrea sat on the couch next to her mother, holding her hand.

Mary sat in the recliner across from them. "The doctor says that by now, eight years after the accident your mother should be showing a lot more progress in recovering than she has been. But he thinks he knows what the problem is. He says a cyst has developed near the point of concussion from the original injury. In fact, the injury is probably what got the tumor started in the first place."

"And. . . ?"

"And her condition will most likely keep getting worse unless the cyst is removed."

Andrea briefly closed her eyes. "Okay. What are the risks?"

"He wasn't specific, but they're bad enough the doctor recommended we get a second opinion."

Andrea turned toward her mother. "Mom, do you understand what Mary's saying?"

"Y-Y-Yes. I w-w-want the operation, sweetie. I w-w-want to be able to spend time with Anthony and you."

"Mom, you haven't had a relationship with Anthony for sixteen years. He's probably totally different than what you remember."

"N-N-No. Not Anthony."

"He's also in a lot of trouble right now. He might even go to prison."

"That doesn't mean w-w-we can't spend t-t-time with him. I w-w-want to see the t-t-two of you t-t-together, every m-minute I can."

Andrea leaned over and wrapped her mother in her arms.

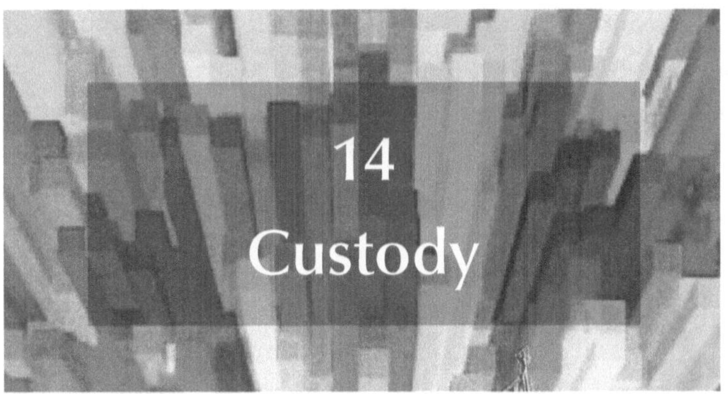

14 Custody

Three weeks later Anthony returned to his office after lunch to find Hal Goldman stepping out of the elevator across from him. The expression on the Gray Eagle's face stopped Anthony in his place.

"What is it?"

"We have a new witness to contend with. Let's get into your office and figure this out."

As they stepped into Anthony's office his receptionist handed him a phone message: *Need your legal advice. Please call soon. —Andrea.*

Anthony frowned. Legal advice for his daughter? Sounded important . . . but he had other things to deal with first.

"So," he said as he closed his door. "Who's this witness?"

"A man from the Midwest the prosecution is bringing in to try to sully your character. They're planning to use him on rebuttal."

"The Midwest? Who the devil would that be?"

Hal stared into his eyes. "William Burns. Andrea's father—or rather, her step father, the man who claims he raised her."

"How can he be a character witness? He doesn't even know me."

"That's more or less the point. From what I've heard, he's saying that you and the mother tricked him into supporting Andrea so you could avoid your fatherly obligations." Hal rapped his knuckles on Anthony's desk and cocked his head like a raptor tracking prey. "Look, Anthony. We always knew something like this might happen. I even warned your daughter about it, remember?"

"Yes, but. . . ." Anthony sagged in his chair. "It doesn't make sense. They'd have to prove I've known about Andrea for years, and they can't do that because it's not true."

"The truth is beside the point. You should know that. When it comes to undermining your reputation and integrity, all Egan James has to do is make the right insinuations. The press will happily do the rest."

Anthony felt his jaw muscles crack. He forced them to relax. "Then let's counterpunch the same way. William Burns is a monster. He caused Cheryl's brain damage by beating her.. Then he started in on Andrea and Johnny. Frankly, I'd like to take him behind a building somewhere and show him what it's like to be on the receiving—"

"You can't touch him." Hal jerked a chair around and sat. "You can't even *threaten* him, Anthony. Not a word. That would be tampering with a government witness. That would be another felony."

"I know, I know. But can't we make a motion to stop Burns from testifying? Surely what the prosecution is trying to do would be both irrelevant and highly prejudicial."

"I've already started the paperwork on such a motion. But the judge probably won't hear it for a few days—and in the meantime, if the media picks up on this. . . ."

"Right, right."

"The first thing I'm going to do is try to have all the court papers sealed. Meanwhile, Anthony, start preparing a declaration for me to attach to the moving papers."

The moment Hal left, Anthony returned Andrea's call.

"Anthony, my fa . . . I mean, my *step*father, Bill Burns, is in San Diego."

"I heard he was going to come."

"Well, he's not just here; he says he's going to take Mom, Johnny and me back to Kentucky."

It was, apparently, all about money. Billy was used to receiving dependents' checks from the V.A., but those had stopped when Mary applied to the V.A. San Diego for help for Cheryl. Now Billy wanted to get Cheryl put back in the institution so the flow of funds would resume. "And he says I have to listen to him, because I'm underage and still legally his daughter," Andrea concluded. "Can he do that? I'm afraid of him. Johnny doesn't want to go, either. He's made new friends here, and he's happy. And Mom's about to get the medical help she needs."

"Try not to worry," Anthony said. "Billy won't get away with this, not if I can help it."

Three days later, papers in hand and Mary Wills at his side, Anthony sat waiting in Judge Judith Meyerson's empty courtroom. He could barely keep his eyes open. For the past two days he had basically worked two jobs: helping Hal prepare motions in federal court to prevent Billy's testimony and seal the information about Andrea's birth; and filing a petition in State Court on behalf of Mary to try to gain custody of Andrea and Johnny and set up a guardianship for Cheryl. Andrea and Cheryl were waiting in a snack lounge down the county courthouse hall.

He looked up as three men strode into the family law courtroom. One was Egan James; the other two were strangers to Anthony.

Mary stiffened. "That's Billy Burns—the man who looks like he slept in his clothes."

Anthony noted him then shifted his attention to the second stranger, who wore a suit and tie and carried a briefcase. He walked over, Egan James beside him, and extended his hand. "Are you Anthony Darren?"

"Yes." Anthony shook hands.

"I'm Luke Peterson from the Family Law Enforcement Division

of the D.A.'s office. We're representing Mr. Burns here. Seems as though he has slam dunk credentials—a birth certificate saying he's the father of Andrea, and a marriage certificate saying he's the husband of Cheryl Burns. And, of course, there's no question as to who the boy belongs to."

Anthony glanced at Egan James.

"I'm just here as an observer, Mr. Darren," said Egan with his usual crooked smile. Then he leaned closer and lowered his voice. "But I'll see you in Winchester's courtroom this afternoon. My friend, your ass is going to be kicked on both these motions."

"When you try to kick my ass," Anthony muttered back, "you'd better hold on to your balls."

Then he turned away and focused all his attention on Billy Burns—a big, barrel-shaped man with sunburned arms and a reddened nose on a pale face. His watery glare tried to hold Anthony's, then shifted away. He was the only one in the room dressed in casual clothes— as Mary had said, so casual it looked as though he had slept in them.

Avoiding Anthony's glare, he spoke to the empty seat to Anthony's left: "You ain't got no right to keep my wife and kids here."

Before Anthony could reply, the clerk called the attorneys into chambers. Mary and Billy remained in the courtroom, sitting on opposite sides of the aisle.

"Please be seated, gentlemen," said Judge Meyerson. She looked to be in her early forties, attractive and pleasant.

The lawyers took seats in the cushioned chairs around the judge's desk as she sat in her executive chair. A court reporter appeared and set up her machine.

Anthony opened by giving a history of the physical abuse suffered by Andrea and her mother, backed by affidavits and declarations from Cheryl, Andrea and Mary, as well as by letters Cheryl had written Mary over the years. He also presented letters from doctors he had called in Kentucky, who, by overnight mail, had sent out separate affidavits.

Luke Peterson presented the hard evidence of the birth certificates and marriage license.

For a while Anthony and Peterson argued back and forth, then the judge interrupted. "I've heard enough at this point. Let's bring in Mr. Burns."

When William Burns stood before her she looked him up and down slowly. Then she asked him to sit and to explain why he wanted to take Cheryl and the children back to Kentucky.

Billy went into the inevitable recitation: he was the Cheryl's legal husband and the legal father of their children. He wanted to give "their kids." a proper upbringing. He had the right to have his wife with him.

Judge Meyerson looked at him down her nose. "Mr. Burns, where have you been for the last four months?"

"Huh?"

"You've known all this time your wife and children were here with Mary, have you not? Yet as I understand it, you've never called or written or in fact made any attempt to contact them."

"Yeah. Well, you see, Miss . . . I mean, Your Honor. I've been helpin' a friend work on some trucks, and I've been real busy."

The judge tilted reading glasses onto her nose. "According to these affidavits from the City Attorneys' office in Louisville, you've been arrested five times over the past few years for public drunkenness, disorderly conduct and driving under the influence." She lifted the glasses. "Have you been drinking already this morning?"

"No, Judge. Honest."

Anthony wished Billy would hiccup and burp at the same time.

"Hmm. Let's discuss these doctors' affidavits. They indicate that your daughter suffered bruises and contusions due to physical beatings—and she says you were responsible. Were you?"

He gave lame excuses and she continued with questions; and he made more excuses.

Meyerson flipped through a file. "Tell me, when did you find out why your dependent checks were being held up?"

"About two weeks ago."

"Which was only a few days before you started proceedings to get these children and your wife back to Kentucky, is that correct?"

"Yeah, Miss Judge."

She closed the file. "You're excused, Mr. Burns."

Mary Wills was brought in next. Dressed in the nicely-pressed pink floral suit Anthony knew she had worn to her niece's high school graduation, she presented a pleasing contrast to the man who had just left.

The judge asked her why she felt she should be a conservator and have custody of the two children.

Mary replied in a soft, clear voice. "Over the years Cheryl wrote to me many times about the things her husband was doing to her and the children, so I asked her to come out. When they got here Andrea still had a fresh scar on her ear from where Billy split it with his fist." She handed a pile of letters to the judge. "These are the letters Cheryl wrote. She's afraid to go back, and Andrea and Johnny don't want to go either. I enjoy having them with me. I want them to stay here, and they want to stay."

After ten more minutes of questioning, the judge asked Mary to wait outside, then requested the lawyers to bring in the girl and her mother, one at a time. She would speak to them separately..

Anthony walked down the hall and rounded a corner. Through the glass wall of the snack room he saw Andrea and Cheryl sitting at a table with the sunlight falling through a floor-to-ceiling window, looking admiringly out at a rooftop planter ablaze with poinsettias.

Andrea spotted him and waved. Cheryl turned to follow the gesture, her features slack and confused. Anthony walked up and gently took the handles of Cheryl's wheelchair. "The judge wants to see you lovely ladies," he said, and headed back to the courtroom. As they entered, Cheryl didn't seem to notice Billy sitting in the gallery off to one side. But Andrea gave him such a glowering stare that he looked away.

A bailiff took control of the wheelchair and rolled it into the judge's chambers. And she did her interviews, which confirmed what Anthon had stated in his papers, and then she called a recess.

Twenty minutes later they were all called back to the courtroom. As Anthony and the others filed back in, he saw the judge already sitting on the bench reading what he hoped were some of his papers.

She waved them all to the counsel tables. "Anything further, gentlemen?"

"No, your Honor," they all said.

She put the papers aside. "All right then. The gag and seal orders are *temporarily* in effect." She went on to explain that whoever prevailed with Judge Winchester's ruling later that afternoon should call her clerk immediately; her final decision would be rendered promptly after that. She pointed out that the burden on Mary Wills would be a heavy one to carry, so no matter how she ruled the situation should be considered temporary until she got an opinion from a psychologist at County Social Services.

As Anthony left the room he almost dared to smile: for once, Egan James' smirk looked just a little flat.

There was no smiling whatsoever that afternoon in Federal Court, two blocks away, as he and Hal waited Judge Winchester's decision. Except for Woods and Egan sitting on the other side of the aisle, the courtroom loomed empty around them—the proceedings had been ordered to be kept secret, and two federal marshals guarded the corridor entrance.

Minutes ticked past on the wall clock. Hal flipped through some legal briefs he had filed earlier while Woods methodically examined the papers he had filed in opposition to Hal's motion. Egan scrutinized his fingernails.

Finally Jenny, the judge's clerk, entered from the door nearest the jury box, while Judge Winchester, black robe flapping, strode in through the opposing door. At once Hal and Woods rose and moved past the swinging gate of the bar to take seats at their respective counsel tables.

After the customary greetings, Winchester sifted through some notes and looked down at the attorneys. "Counsel, I have read the papers of both sides—well-written, I must say. I am ready to rule. Does anyone have anything further?"

Hal Goldman stood. "Nothing, Your Honor."

"Mr. Woods?"

"Nothing, your Honor, unless the court has any questions."

"I have no questions." Winchester looked directly at the assistant US Attorney. "Mr. Woods, the issue of Ms. Andrea Burns' paternity as it bears on Mr. Darren's character is outweighed by the emotionally charged prejudice it could cause to Mr. Darren's defense. I find that if evidence is allowed on this issue, it could be so highly explosive for some jurors we wouldn't get a fair trial here. Therefore I agree with the defendant's motion to exclude such evidence."

Anthony felt his muscles quiver with the release of tension, but held himself still.

Woods approached the lectern. "Your Honor, if I could be heard for a moment?"

"Mr. Woods, if you have something new to add I will continue to listen, but from what I see here you've got an uphill battle. You are a highly respected advocate for the Government, and you have been in my courtroom many times; however, I am of the belief that your attempt to present the evidence in question approaches overzealousness . . . something I don't recall ever coming from you before."

His words brought everything to a stop. Woods looked down at his notes, then up. He took off his reading glasses. "Your Honor, there have been a few times in my career when I lost on a ruling, yet felt okay about it afterwards. This is one of those occasions. The United States voluntarily withdraws its opposition to the motion. I'm afraid I let myself get carried away by suggestions from others." He looked at Egan James.

Winchester thanked him and ruled that the papers remain sealed and the motion and Andrea Burns identity shall not be leaked to the media. The gag order is granted. "Now," he said, "we have a jury to select."

In the corridor, Anthony hurried to the nearest pay phone and called Judge Meyerson's clerk. He recited Winchester's ruling, then dialed Mary's number. At least ten rings sounded as he waited.

Finally Mary answered, sounding breathless. "Anthony?"

"We got what we wanted, Mary. The judge—"

"Billy is here."

"What?"

"He's got Cheryl and Johnny in his car. They were sitting out front on the porch, and he told them to get in. Now he's ordering Andrea to get in, too."

"Jeez. Don't let her get in that car, Mary! I'll be there in fifteen minutes."

"You'd better hurry. Andrea says she *has* to go; she's afraid that Billy won't give the proper medications."

"No . . . Mary, tell her to stall. I'm coming. Tell her not to go near that car!"

"She's already packing their things, even Cheryl's medicine. . . ."

Anthony heard no more. He sprinted down the hall past Hal, shouting, "I'm going to Mary's! Billy's trying to take off with everybody. Call Meyerson's clerk!"

Outside, he leaped into his car and raced out of the parking garage, leaving burned rubber smoking in the air. Streaking through the streets, he double-clutched the turns, and on straightaways his speedometer registered eighty-five and climbing. He had time for only a fleeting sarcastic thought: *All I need now is to get pulled over by the Highway Patrol.*

He almost lost control taking the corner onto Mary's street. A beat-up brown sedan with Kentucky plates was just pulling away from the curb. Mary stood on her front lawn, frantically pointing at it.

As Anthony roared up behind the sedan he counted the silhouettes of four heads through the dusty back window. He swerved left and came up alongside the sedan, where his gaze momentarily locked with Billy's furious, carrot-colored eyes. Then he jerked the steering wheel hard to the right, forcing Billy to veer. A jolt, a bang, and Billy's sedan bounced up over the curb and onto a neighbor's lawn. It tore through the grass and sank partway into a Eugenia hedge before stopping.

Anthony was right behind it, wedging the front bumper of his car under Billy's trailer hitch. The sedan powered up in reverse, spewing grass and dirt beneath its own frame, but Anthony revved forward, throwing a rooster tail of turf in the opposite direction, holding both cars in stasis.

For a moment it was a wrestling match, the vehicles pushing and rocking, banging, engines screaming, rear wheels sinking into the moist turf.

Then white smoke erupted from the old sedan's tailpipe, and its engine shut down with a clatter. The driver's door flew open.

Anthony yanked the hand brake and got out of his car as Billy was extracting himself from the sedan, an ax handle clutched in one hand. He stalked toward Anthony, red faced and grinning. "Hey, you! Shyster! You just committed another felony: tampering with a government witness! Now I'm gonna break your head and give the judge what's left." Dirty white T-shirt protruding over his jeans, arms extended and locked, he swung the ax handle like a baseball bat toward the side of Anthony's head.

Wind buffeted Anthony's chin as he jumped back. "You got that wrong, fat man," he said. "You aren't a government witness anymore."

Billy hesitated with the ax handle twisted behind his left ear.

"Come on," Anthony said. "Let's see you beat me like you beat wives and children."

Billy did not move.

"Come on, Jelly Belly. That was strike one. Take another swing."

Billy clubbed the air in front of him, but at the same time eased back a step. "There ain't no court order says I can't take my family. And you just ran my car off the road, asshole. You're goin' to jail for that, shyster boy!"

"By now there *could* be a court order," Anthony said. "And if it says you're enjoined from taking anyone anywhere, well, I'm only carrying out the court order by stopping you now. On the other hand, if it says I have to let you take them, I guess I'll do that—after I give you some of your own medicine."

By then Billy had backed up as far as his open car door. Abruptly he turned and reached into the side panel of the door with his left hand. Blue steel glinted as he pulled out a revolver. The ax handle still in his right hand, he immediately began to switch weapons to get the revolver into his primary hand. In that moment Anthony dove forward with his hands out. Billy instinctively swung the gun away, but Anthony was going for the ax handle. He grabbed it and yanked it free without effort, then delivered a short, smashing blow to Billy's left wrist. Billy shrieked and dropped to one knee; the revolver flew back inside the car as if trying to return to its hiding place.

Anthony hurled the handle aside. Clenching his hands into a two-fisted, two-armed human ax handle, he twisted and swung from the side. His fused fists slammed against Billy's quivering jaw, snapping his head around. His second knee thumped into the wet grass.

Without stopping his momentum, Anthony changed the direction of his swing into a giant uppercut. The two-fisted knot of bone caught Billy under the chin and flipped him backward so violently he almost landed on his head. He groaned, rolled and sprawled on his face in a muddy pile of sod.

Anthony realized Andrea was helping Johnny and her mother get out of the car. Adrenaline still charged inside him. He grabbed the ignition keys, strode around to the trunk, unlocked it, and began tossing suitcases out onto the lawn.

In the distance a siren began its baleful wail, and a minute later a patrol car squealed around the corner. At the same moment a civilian car approached at high speed from the opposite direction. Both vehicles skidded to a stop in front of Mary's house. Hal got out of the civilian car; two police officers spilled from the cruiser and ran up on the lawn toward Anthony and Billy. One pulled his revolver. "Freeze! Don't move!"

Billy groaned and rolled over. The right side of his face was already ballooning. He opened his eyes and pointed a shaky finger at Anthony. "This here man run my car off the road and attacked me, officer. I'm a government witness, and I'm pressing charges against him!"

The second officer pulled the handcuffs off his belt and stepped toward Anthony.

"No!" yelled Hal. "You have the wrong man! Judge Judy Meyerson enjoined this man, Bill Burns, from taking these people away." He pointed from Billy to Cheryl, Andrea and Johnny. "Mr. Darren is using a citizen's rightful means to carry out the court order!"

Now the officers looked confused.

"Also, Federal Judge Winchester ruled that this man, Billy Burns, *can't* be a government witness."

The officer with the gun did not seem inclined to holster his weapon. "Are you a lawyer?"

"Yes, and so is Mr. Darren. Look, call the judge's clerk. Here's the number."

Mary had joined Andrea in enclosing Cheryl in protective arms. "Go right across the street to my house," she said. "The phone's near the front door."

"Hennings," the first officer said, "go make that call. I'll take care of things out here."

"Roger that. You two lawyers or whatever you are, come with me." The officer who had tried to handcuff Anthony escorted him and Hal inside Mary's house and got on the phone.

The officer introduced himself to Judge Meyerson's clerk, then said, "Hope you can help me with some information. There's a fight going on here and someone claims the judge made some kind of ruling. What's the case number?" He turned to Hal.

Hal pulled a folded sheet of paper from his pocket.

The officer read the information over the phone then waited a minute, keeping a steely eye on Anthony and Hal. Finally he said, "Yes, go ahead. Okay . . . so that means William Burns can't lay a hand on these kids or the mother at this stage, right?"

Anthony waited for the reply he couldn't hear.

"Okay, thank you very much." The officer hung up and gestured for Anthony and Hal to follow him outside. "All right," he called to his partner as he walked down the porch steps, "we can let this Darren guy go." He strode over to Billy, who stood swaying a bit on his feet, his face now grotesquely distorted. "As for you, Mr. Burns, you don't look too good but you appear able to drive. You'd better be getting on your way or I'll take you in for a breach of the peace."

Billy blinked at him with the one eye that was not swollen to a slit. "What? *Me*? Are you shittin' me?"

"Mr. Burns. . . ."

With a heavy sigh, Anthony turned away from the argument, got into his car, released the hand brake and shifted into neutral. Then he walked up to the front of his coupe and jumped on the bumper until it sprang loose from under Billy's trailer hitch. Back in his car, Anthony started the engine and with a steady, easy foot, backed up and off the curb, and parked.

The officers were still talking to Billy as Anthony got out again, crossed the chewed-up lawn and put his arms around Cheryl and Andrea. Mary held Johnny. Silently Anthony walked them all across the street to Mary's house, up the steps and inside.

As the adrenaline drained out of his system he thought, *Maybe this is a good sign.*

With his collar unbuttoned and his tie loosened, Dirk Miller looked at his client across his paper-strewn desk.

"Joe, it's great to see you come back to life again . . . but listen to me. This is our last night before the trial. I've been trying to nail down my strategy and I need your cooperation. You *have* to listen to me. Are you listening? I'm telling you: If I keep you off the witness stand, I believe I can get you acquitted. Is that sinking in? *I think I can get you acquitted.*"

"It's not just about me." Joe raised his chin. "If Anthony needs my help, I'll get up there and speak."

Dirk waved his hands in the air. "I appreciate your feelings, Joe—but I'm *your* attorney, not Anthony's; I have to do what I think is best for you, not him. Look. For the prosecution to convict you, their own case has to stand on its own two feet. They don't get to question you unless you agree to let them. But if you do that, if you testify, they'll go for your throat with every weapon at their disposal. This is a conspiracy case. They can come at you from out of the woodworks. Just one misstatement or even a misunderstanding from you could cost us the whole trial!"

Joe clenched his fists. "They've got Anthony on the ropes. I'm telling you I won't plead the Fifth again. The jury . . . I have to explain to them that Anthony had nothing to do with sinking *the Sea Diva*, that Michael had nothing to do with it. It was my idea— mine and Hooks.'"

"See, that's what I mean; that's exactly how you'll get into trouble on the stand. You *didn't* plan to sink *the Sea Diva*. That's the whole point; you only wanted Herbert Hooks to *believe* you were going to retain the option to sink her, so Hooks would release her from the receivership. This was the only way you could get the Diva on her maiden voyage. You were putting on a game to delay the bank, period. There's no crime there. Do you understand me? *There is no crime there.* But I'm afraid you'll say whatever it takes to get Anthony acquitted, even if it's not in your own best interests. Even if it means getting *yourself* convicted."

"You have to put me on the stand. Anthony is a good man, and he's *completely* innocent; even more than I am. And I owe him my life. So I've got to tell my story, my son's story, the way it really happened."

Dirk stared at him, then shook his head, "All right. I'll consider it, but only on one condition: you answer my questions and don't volunteer *anything*. Don't answer beyond the scope of *any* question, whether it comes from me or the prosecution. Agreed?"

Joe nodded.

Dirk got up, walked around the desk and draped his arm over Joe's shoulder. "You have a thin line to walk, you stubborn son of a gun. I like you, and I think the jury will like you. I just hope they'll see the subtlety of what you intend to say. . . ."

15 Buzzing Red Blur

On the morning of the trial Anthony tried to understand the quality of the tension he felt. It took him a while to realize that although there was much more at stake for him personally this time, the added sense of responsibility he always felt for a client was not there. In this case he *was* the client.

Then he thought about Andrea, and instantly the other dimension kicked in. His daughter needed him more than any client ever had.

He looked around, and suddenly felt dwarfed by the courtroom. Never before had he really considered how large and imposing the oak paneled space really was, with its ceilings almost two stories high.

Every seat was occupied. He had looked around earlier for Samantha and not seen her—no surprise there—but Laura and Andrea sat together near the front of the audience. Laura caught him looking and shot him a reassuring wink. He realized he got more of a lift from that than he would have from the sight of ten Samanthas. Why had he ever let Laura drift away?

He realized that Samantha aside, there were a lot of good friends still in his life: Cheryl, Mary, Andrea, Laura, even his lawyer, Hal, and not the least, his sister. He'd had a hard time talking her into remaining in London with her family and her job. She was desperately needed there.

The clerk handed the list of jury panel names to the attorneys on both sides. Conferences took place at each counsel table. Finally Hal sat back in his chair. Projecting an image of calm enhanced by his steel gray hair, steel-rimmed glasses and dark gray suit, he seemed to be almost in pleasant meditation. But from his own experience as a trial lawyer Anthony knew that Hal was shielding the anticipation hammering in his chest.

"All rise," called the bailiff. Judge Winchester appeared at the entrance of his chambers and strode into the courtroom, his black robe in sharp contrast with his sandy gray hair. "By the authority of the United States of America and under the flag of our country, this court will come to order, the Honorable Roger Winchester, Judge presiding. Please be seated." The slap of the gavel cracked across the room.

The solemn atmosphere of Federal Court settled around Anthony . . . and the long, meticulous preliminaries began. For hours the lawyers jockeyed for the dominant position as they selected the jurors they wanted and excused those they believed would have a bias against their client. More often than not they canceled out each other's choices.

The trial had reached the middle of the third day before they finally swore in the panel and prepared to deliver opening statements.

Now it begins, Anthony thought: the court procedures where movements and progress were as strictly defined as in a baseball game or complicated dance. On the imaginary clock face that was the courtroom, the judge sat at twelve o'clock. Anthony was at six, the jurors at three and the opposing wall of books at nine. In the center was the "well," a space no one entered without the judge's permission. Evidence would be presented and witnesses questioned around the perimeter of the well.

Finally John Woods rose, yellow pad in hand. "Your Honor, may I step into the well to set up the lectern?"

"You may."

The bailiff helped Woods slide a lectern, like a symphony conductor's stand, to a spot eight feet from and directly in front of the jury. Although this territory was almost sacred, its use was generally permitted for opening statements and final arguments. In some courts this could be done even without asking, but Woods, always respectful, played by the book.

Off came the prosecutor's reading glasses. Looking at the jury, he began to explain what he expected the evidence to show. As Anthony listened a red blur began to buzz in his brain; he fought the urge to jump up and shout *no!* after almost every sentence the prosecutor uttered.

Woods' long index finger swung around and pointed at Anthony. He said, "The evidence will show that this man—this person who had been given the trust of the people to be licensed as an attorney at law, and the trust of his own profession to be elected President of the County Bar Association—this man did, willfully and with knowledge, conspire to sink *the Sea Diva* for the purpose of fraudulently collecting millions of dollars in insurance proceeds. The government will show that Mr. Darren met with his co-conspirator Joseph Cruz and recorded their plan on paper. The evidence will show that on that same day Mr. Darren entered into a fee agreement with his client that would procure him more than a million dollars in fees out of those same insurance proceeds."

Anthony tried hard not to stare at the jurors, but he couldn't help notice some winces, some hostile stares.

"The evidence will further show that both the beautiful new ship, *the Sea Diva*, and Cruz Enterprises itself were hopelessly in debt, and there was virtually no way that debt could be paid without resorting to crime—heinous crime—to a crime that resulted in the deaths of two people. Mr. Cruz and Mr. Darren were both well aware of this serious and uncontainable financial problem; they knew that Mr. Cruz's creditors would come to claim all of his assets unless they received payment very soon."

Anthony found himself slumping in his seat as if to melt out of sight. Several jurors were eyeballing him. He straightened up.

"You will be instructed on the law by the court," Woods continued. "One of those instructions will speak of the crime of murder, should a death occur during the commission of arson. The evidence will show that Mr. Cruz's own young son of twenty-two years, just entering the prime of his life, drowned as a result of exactly that: arson."

The agonized stare of Joe Cruz followed each gesture of Woods' hands. Hal jotted notes on his yellow pad, seemingly unconcerned. For his part, Anthony now understood why no accused person should try to represent himself in court. His brain felt inflamed, Woods' words shooting through it like incendiary bullets.

The first witness to take the stand was Alfonso Martin, who looked like a ferret in a suit that Anthony suspected had been picked out for him by Egan James. Still, he performed well, sticking steadfastly to the story he'd given at the Coast Guard inquiry and before the Federal Grand Jury. Hal's and Dirk's blistering cross-examinations did not shift Alfonso's stance one inch.

Feeling an irresistible compulsion to assist, Anthony started to whisper a few witness questions to Hal. He welcomed the participation.

Two weeks into the trial, Egan James caught up with Woods outside the courtroom as recess began. "John, you know Joe wants to try to clear Anthony Darren. He's going to want to take the stand."

"I'm prepared for that," Woods responded as they continued down the hall. "You might even say I'm *waiting* for the opportunity."

"Well, be careful. He's so anxious to get Darren off he'll say almost anything." Egan paused. "Don't forget about Steve Williams; his testimony would be perfect to rebut anything Cruz might say."

Woods shook his head. "I've still got mixed feelings about Williams. However, if the right opportunity comes up, you might be right—I might have to put him on."

The next morning as the attorneys finished with a crew member's testimony, Anthony sensed the coming of a vital moment. "Call your next witness, counsel," the judge told Dirk Miller.

Dirk looked at Joe, and hesitated. Joe stared back fixedly with his dark eyes.

"Counsel?" said the judge.

"Yes, Your Honor, the defense calls Mr. Joseph Cruz to the stand."

A murmur rose from the gallery.

Direct examination began with Joe's background, starting with his teenage years. Anthony caught himself repeatedly holding his breath, even though things were going well. Questioning brought out how he and Joe had met, and how Joe had worked his way up in the tuna fishing business. Skillfully Dirk Miller brought out the history of *the Sea Diva*, its financial problems, and the events that led up to the hiring of Anthony as counsel.

Looking good, Anthony thought. Joe seemed confident; his demeanor was almost infectious.

A full hour and a half into questioning, Dirk looked up from his notes and calmly took off his glasses. "Joe, at any time did you have any conversation or communication with Mr. Darren regarding the idea of sinking *the Sea Diva* or any other ship?"

"No. Anthony Darren had nothing to do with the sinking of the ship."

Anthony saw Dirk conceal a flinch behind a brush of his hand. Joe had violated his instructions, stating a conclusion instead of stopping at a simple answer of "No."

But surprisingly, Woods let the answer lie with no objection.

When it was time for cross-examination, John Woods rose slowly to his feet. "Mr. Cruz, you said on direct examination that Mr. Darren had nothing to do with the sinking of *the Sea Diva*. What facts can you give us that make you so sure of that?"

"He just didn't do it."

"But how do you *know* that? Do you know who *did* sink the *Diva*?"

"Objection," said Hal. "Calls for a conclusion."

"Overruled."

"Do you know who did it, Mr. Cruz?" Woods asked again.

"Yes. I do know."

"Who?"

"My banker, Herbert Hooks, and a worm named Alfonso Martin—that's who!"

Woods' expression remained unchanged. "Please tell us . . . on what facts do you base that statement?"

This time Dirk Miller objected, asserting that the question called for all kinds of hearsay and conclusions.

"That can hardly be determined unless Cruz answers, now can it, Counsel?" Winchester said. "Overruled.

Woods turned back to Joe. "Do you remember the last question?"

"Yes."

"All right. Please tell us on what facts you base your accusation against Herbert Hooks and Alfonso Martin."

Cruz fidgeted in the chair. "Herbert Hooks suggested to me that the *Diva* could be sunk to collect the insurance."

The eyes of a few jurors widened.

"When did you and Mr. Hooks have that conversation?"

"At *the Sea Diva's* maiden voyage party."

"Which obviously took place before the boat sank."

"Obviously."

"Isn't it true you yourself *also* suggested a plan for sinking the vessel?"

Cruz flushed. "Well, I . . . I . . . It wasn't for real."

Woods leaned forward slightly, hands squeezing the lectern. "Just answer the question, Mr. Cruz. Yes or No. Isn't it a fact that *you* came up with a plan to sink *the Sea Diva* in order to collect on insurance?"

"Well, yes, but—"

"You've answered the question, Mr. Cruz," Woods said.

"Objection!" Hal shouted, gray eyes flashing. "Let him answer!"

"Overruled," said the judge. "You will have your opportunity to cross-examine, Counsel."

Hal sat down with an almost imperceptible shake of the head.

"Mr. Darren was also at that maiden voyage party, wasn't he?" asked Woods.

"Yes."

"Did you tell *him* about the conversation you claim to have had with Mr. Hooks?"

"Objection," Dirk snapped. "Attorney-client privilege."

Winchester shook his head. "There is nothing before me that shows Anthony Darren was acting as counsel with regard to that specific statement at that time."

"Your honor," said Dirk, "may I *voir dire* the witness before you rule?"

"You may."

Dirk faced Joe. "Prior to having this conversation with Mr. Hooks, had you already hired Mr. Darren to act as your attorney?"

"Yes."

Dirk turned back to the judge. "I renew my objection."

"May I ask additional questions on *voir dire* before you rule, your honor?" said Woods.

"That's somewhat unusual," the judge replied, "to *voir dire* your own witness. But you may proceed."

Woods laced his fingers together. "Mr. Cruz, did you hire Mr. Darren at that time to advise you regarding the bank's threatened foreclosure of *the Sea Diva*?"

Dirk and Hal both leaped up. "Objection, objection, attorney-client privilege."

"Overruled," said the Judge. "I can't know if the question is objectionable unless I know *for what purpose* Mr. Darren was hired to represent Mr. Cruz."

"Mr. Cruz . . . you may answer," said Woods. "by the time your conversation with Mr. Hooks occurred, had you already hired Mr. Darren to act as your attorney in connection with the threat of foreclosure of *the Sea Diva*?"

"Yes."

"How many weeks or months before the maiden voyage party did you hire Mr. Darren?"

"About one month."

"And did you ever tell Mr. Darren about your conversation with Mr. Hooks?"

"Same objection!" Goldman cut in.

"Sustained," said the Judge.

"Your Honor, may we approach the bench?" asked Woods.

"Certainly you may."

Woods, Dirk and Goldman all walked to the side of the bench opposite the jury box. The court reporter moved her stenographic machine closer.

Woods whispered to Judge Winchester, "I won't argue too hard about a ruling sustaining the objection as far as Cruz's defense is concerned—however, the testimony should be allowed with regard to the charges against Mr. Darren. After all, we *are* talking about a conspiracy case here."

"Perhaps," the judge whispered back. "But I have no way of separating the two without prejudice to one party or the other, and I don't think a jury could separate them even if I should so instruct them." He looked at each counsel, then raised his voice enough for the jury to hear. "The objection is sustained." He reseated himself on the bench, and the attorneys returned to their tables.

Leaning over the rail, Egan James whispered to Woods, "What do you think?"

"The objection's okay with me," Woods muttered. "The jury's got to be wondering why Joe's own lawyer won't let him say whether or not he told Darren about this supposed conversation."

"Ready to proceed?" the judge asked.

"Yes, your Honor." Woods reached for a document and turned to Joe Cruz. "In your retainer agreement with Mr. Darren, isn't it true that if insurance money was collected for the sinking of *the Sea Diva,* Mr. Darren was to receive one-third of the recovery as his contingency fee?"

Once again Dirk and Hal jumped to their feet in unison. "Objection!"

"If such a document exists," Dirk said, "it would speak for itself, your Honor."

"I'll sustain the objection on those grounds," replied Judge Winchester.

Woods handed a paper to the clerk. "I'd like to have marked next in order Exhibit H, being a document entitled 'Retainer Agreement' and dated the 18th day of November of last year." The clerk marked the document and handed it back.

Woods handed Exhibit H to Joe, who identified it as the retainer agreement he had entered into with Anthony Darren shortly before the maiden voyage party. After the judge admitted it into evidence, Woods put his reading glasses on.

"Mr. Cruz, in a clause from page 2, second paragraph, it states, 'Should attorney perform services in connection with any tort or negligence claim on behalf of the vessel, client agrees that attorney shall be entitled to a fee of 33 1/3 per cent of any recovery resulting from such services.'"

Joe didn't reply.

"Mr. Cruz, did you read this document before you signed it?"

"Yes."

"So you were aware of that clause before you signed?"

"Vaguely."

"What is the total insurance claim for the loss of the vessel *the Sea Diva*, together with the catch of fish on board?"

"Seven million."

"Seven million what?"

"Seven million dollars."

"Have you calculated how much money Mr. Darren would make under that clause if he had succeeded in recovering the full seven million dollars?"

Joe's eyes shifted. "You figure it out."

"Just answer the question, if you can, Mr. Cruz."

"Two million, three hundred thirty-three thousand—but he would have taken much less."

Woods turned to the judge. "Move to strike starting with the word 'but' as being non-responsive."

"Objection to the motion," said Hal.

"Your time to re-direct will come, Counsel," the judge told him. "It shall be stricken. The jury is to disregard the last part of Mr. Cruz' answer."

Anthony noticed a few jurors raising their eyebrows as they jotted in their notebooks.

"Mr. Cruz, previous testimony from other witnesses established that boxes labeled 'spare parts' were delivered to *the Sea Diva* a few days before the voyage began. The truth is that those boxes actually contained firearms, hand grenades, about one-hundred garage door openers and other munitions. Isn't that so?"

"I found that out eventually," Joe said.

"But . . . in the meantime you signed the invoices and receipts for those boxes, didn't you?"

A pause. "Yes, along with my chief engineer's signature."

"And did you not also set up a secret code communication with Poncho Pascalle so that he would know whether to sink the boat on your command?"

"Not really."

"Yes or no, Mr. Cruz."

"Yes, but like I said, it was just a game for the bank."

"Do you also admit that *the Sea Diva* was in great financial difficulty?"

"Yes."

"And that the bank—Herbert Hooks' bank—had threatened to go against your personal guarantee?"

"Yes."

"Was it your understanding that the court injunction alone may not have held off the bank from going against your personal guarantee?"

"That was my understanding."

"Do you admit that if those personal guarantees had been executed upon, you could have lost essentially everything you own?"

"I guess so."

"Mr. Cruz, at any time either before or after the sinking, did Anthony Darren ever tell you he had coincidentally written a synopsis or story about a boat sinking incident?"

Several long seconds passed. "Not really."

"Does that mean no?"

"That means no."

Anthony sensed the jurors storing each question and answer with disheartening intensity.

"Mr. Cruz, I hand you Exhibit E, previously identified as a synopsis about a scheme or story describing the sinking of a ship to collect insurance. You were in court, were you not, when this document was shown to be in the handwriting of Anthony Darren?"

"Yes."

"And the date on it—also in Darren's handwriting—is November 18; you see that?"

"Yes." Joe's voice was slightly softer.

"Tell me, what was the date of your first meeting with Mr. Darren in his law office? Would you like to refer to your desk calendar, exhibit P, on the stand with you?"

Joe began slowly flipping through the pages, then stopped. "Okay. It looks like we met on November 18."

"Which is the same date as found on the synopsis, right?"

"Objection," said Hal. "The document speaks for itself."

"The answer is obvious, Your Honor," Woods replied. "I'll withdraw the question."

Despite Joe's efforts to add further explanations, Anthony saw devastation on his face. This was not what Joe had expected to happen when he told the truth on the stand.

Fortunately an excellent rehabilitating examination by Hal, and an equally fine redirect examination by Dirk, brought Joe a long way back from disaster. Among other things, the defense attorneys established that Anthony's retainer fee clause was "boilerplate," not written especially for this occasion. They also brought out that Anthony had orally agreed to pursue the insurance claim at his usual hourly rate.

Still, during the evening recess, Anthony walked down the darkened underground parking ramp to his car thinking that the jury had left the courtroom favoring the prosecution.

The trial went on, and on. He never saw Cheryl in the gallery, which was a relief in many ways; hopefully she was concentrating on her own progress. But Laura and Andrea came to court every day . . . Laura, even though she was working full-time and making up for it at night. He had the feeling she would be standing beside him even if she weren't the one person in the world who knew for a fact he was not lying about the strange coincidence of the novel synopsis.

16 Whispering Pines

The wind fought them every inch of the way as they peddled furiously uphill in single file on their ten-speed bikes, slowing them even when the steep grade up the Torrey Pines bluff began to flatten out. Anthony realized that Laura and Andrea were actually working to beat him. Only when the ranger station entrance swung into view did they whip around him, sprinting hard. By the time he got up to full speed Andrea had already crossed the imaginary finish line, with Laura right behind, both of them with arms upraised in triumph.

"Cheaters," he gasped as he stopped. "Nobody told me we were racing."

"Competition," Laura said. "The life's blood of growth and development. Or so somebody once told me."

"You forgot about the importance of synergy," he said. "So show some cooperation and help find a place to lock up these bikes."

They walked to a protected location at a sunny wooden table isolated within the limbs of the scraggly forest. Rare Torrey pine trees surrounded them, a thousand boughs twisted and sculpted by thousands of years of ocean wind. Between the trunks spread a spectacular view of the Pacific Ocean. Anthony tried to let the beauty fight his lingering feeling of disconnection.

Tomorrow, Monday, would be the last day of testimony in the trial. After that, his fate would be left in the hands of what? Twelve men and women, a jury of his peers? Fate? God?

Laura and Andrea had suggested the ride up here. Had he ever told them this was one of his favorite spots in the world?

"How's Cheryl doing, Andrea?" he asked. "Any news about Billy?"

She cut a grim smile. "Nobody's seen him since you beat the crap out of him."

"I hope I didn't get too . . . carried away. I just couldn't believe he was trying to run off with you guys."

"It worked out fine," Laura said. "He never even showed up for the custody hearing, so now Andrea and Johnny don't have to worry about being taken away again."

"And mom's doing much better," Andrea said. She focused her hazel eyes on Anthony. "I'm sure you've noticed she hasn't ever come to the trial."

"Actually, I'm glad about that."

"It's just that we're trying to keep her from getting upset. When they say 'Anthony Darren is not guilty,' that's when we'll go into detail about everything that happened."

Anthony stared at the ocean. "In my experience it's best to prepare people up front for the worst that might happen—so they'll be ready to handle it if it comes." He glanced at Laura.

Laura rested a hand on his.

"Mom's in a different situation," Andrea said. "She's not a client, and she's about to have a delicate medical procedure—so our job is to keep her calm right now, no matter what."

Anthony raised his eyebrows. "Delicate medical procedure?"

"Brain surgery." Andrea swapped glances with Laura. "Mom asked us to keep it a secret, but."

"Cheryl's going to have *brain surgery*?"

"Her doctor is a top neurosurgeon. He says if she has the

procedure, she has a chance of improvement, maybe significant improvement. Without it, she'll just keep getting worse."

"But. . . ."

"There's risk, yes. Of course. But Mom wants it. She says she doesn't want to go on living this way."

Anthony rubbed his forehead. "My God."

"We thought you ought to know. I know the timing is terrible, but her surgery is in two days."

"I'm glad. I'm glad you told me, Andi." A mockingbird fluttered to a nearby branch, and clung there trilling. From far below the wind brought the sound of the sea over cliffs and trees. Finally Anthony rose. Laura and Andrea followed him to a small grassy clearing on the edge of the bluff, where they stood staring out at the endless blue.

"I want to be at the hospital with you when she's in surgery, Andrea," he said at last.

"Me, too, if that's all right," Laura said.

"Thank you both. That would be great." Andrea blinked and held out her hands, one on each side. "For the first time in my life, I feel like I've got a complete family."

The three of them held hands amongst sandstone crags crowned by wreaths of trees shaped to forms of art beyond the capabilities of mortal man.

From its perch the mockingbird squawked and flapped away. The branch sprang up, flipping pine needles into the breeze.

Andrea jarred them with a question from out of the blue: "Dad, would you object if I decided to go to law school some day?"

Surprised, his mouth quirked in one corner. "I'm probably not in the best frame of mind to encourage anyone to go into law, Andrea. But then you've got at least four years before you have to decide; you haven't even started college yet."

"True." Andrea reached into her canvas pack and pulled out an envelope with a ripped flap. She held it out to Anthony.

Frowning, he withdrew a letter and held it flapping in the wind. Read it. Blinked. Looked from Andrea to Laura. "Did you know about this? She's been awarded a full scholarship to Stanford University."

"It must have slipped her mind until just now," Laura said.

They threw their arms around one another and did a little dance on the edge of the cliff.

"Speaking from recent experience," Anthony said after they seated themselves on a patch of bent grass, "it can be easy for people to forget there's a noble and uplifting side to the practice of law. Not only do you get to help people, but you get involved in so many different fields. I've worked cases dealing with just about everything imaginable, which required me to study the works of professors of those diverse subjects. You have to get ready to do a proper examination on the stand, you know. It's a constant education."

"And you really enjoy that." Laura said.

He nodded. "But to me, all that knowledge doesn't do any good unless it's put to use in a productive way. I once had a very successful businessman client—let's call him Richard—who was about to close a deal with tons of dollars at stake. I told him he was leaving a lot on the table for Larry, the other guy. Richard said that he was aware of that, but he wanted Larry to be successful on his side of the bargain, too. For one thing, he wanted him to make enough to pay the balance of the note. To Richard, *mutual* success was the glue that makes a deal stick."

"Which is knowledge used productively," Andrea said.

"Exactly. Since then I've noticed that most of my successful clients have that same attitude. On the practical side, overkill does not lead to repeat business, trust, confidence and good will. But I think there's even more to it than that. I believe these men and women have discovered intuitively that there's something special about synthesizing cooperating and competing."

"Like when we rode our bikes here?" Andrea said. "Most of the way, we swapped being in the lead and took turns drafting off each other—that was cooperation. But when we started sprinting it was pure competition. Right?"

"Not to mention cheating on your part," Anthony said, and they all laughed. Then he turned serious. He realized he had missed this sort of discussion, this sort of thinking, during the long weeks of his trial. "If you look for it," he said, "you see that kind of synthesis all over the place, all the time. I think it's a fundamental principle of the universe."

"You were talking about this when we first met," Laura said.

"I only wish I had more time to explore the idea and develop it." He paused. "Well, not too much time. Like, say, fifteen to twenty."

No one laughed. The silence between them filled with the endless rumble of the surf.

"Do you rest, Mr. Miller?" Judge Winchester asked.

"Yes, Your Honor," Dirk replied.

"And do you rest, Mr. Goldman?"

"I do, Your Honor."

The judge turned and looked at John Wood's counsel table. "Does the prosecution have rebuttal?"

"The prosecution has a rebuttal witness," Woods said.

"You may proceed."

"The United States calls Mr. Stephen Williams to the stand."

Anthony watched as a distinguished-looking man in his forties walked forward. He wore a suit and tie as if used to it and Anthony had trouble visualizing him in a jail cell. Still, as he stood at the bar and swore to tell the truth, the whole truth and nothing but the truth, so help him God, Anthony knew the man intended to lie the moment he opened his mouth.

How could a reputable lawyer like John Woods allow such a man on the stand?

"Mr. Williams," said Woods. "You are an inmate at the Federal Correction Center?"

"Yes, I am, sir."

Every juror stared at him.

"And you were previously convicted of a felony."

"Yes, sir."

"What offense?"

"Writing bad checks."

"No violent crime convictions?"

"No, sir."

Woods swung around and pointed at Joe Cruz, whose expression remained impassive.

"Mr. Williams, have you ever met this person?"

"Yes, sir. His name is Joseph Cruz."

"Where did you meet him?"

"At the Correctional Center while he was waiting for bail release, about four months ago."

"Were you cellmates for a time?"

"Yes. For about a week."

"Did you get to know him, in the sense of having conversations with him, during that period?"

"Yes."

"Please describe the circumstance of your meeting him and getting to know him."

"Since my conviction I've gone back to the flock of my shepherd the Lord, and Joe and I prayed together every day. One day we talked about confessing our sins as a way of cleansing our souls."

Anthony watched Joe's mouth sag open.

"When did that communication take place?"

"The day before Joe was released on bail."

"Where did the conversation take place?"

"In our cell, right after each of us got back from the chapel."

"Was anyone else present?"

"No, sir."

"Tell us what Mr. Cruz said, and what else you said at that time."

"Objection, Your Honor!" Goldman and Dirk shot to their feet so fast and in such perfect harmony that some of the jurors jumped.

"Your Honor," Dirk said, "I know you've already ruled on this issue at our motion *in limine*; however, I wish to renew my objection for the record."

"I, also, for the same reason," said Hal Goldman. "I further request instructions that the testimony this man is about to give, if admissible as against Cruz, should be disregarded as against Anthony Darren."

Anthony's hands tightened in his lap.

"I understand," said the judge. "Both objections are overruled. You may proceed with your answer, Mr. Williams."

"Joe said he hoped God would punish *him*, but forgive Anthony Darren. I asked him, what do you mean? He said it was Mr. Darren's idea to sink the ship; that it could be done in a way that no one would ever find out. But then things went wrong, and Joe lost his son, and couldn't forgive himself."

Jurors began writing in their notebooks.

"Did he say why he wanted Mr. Darren to be forgiven?" asked Woods.

"Yes. He said Darren was only trying to help him. Told Joe the only way out of the financial mess he was in was to sink the boat, collect the insurance money and pay off the loan. He obviously didn't know Joe's son would die."

Anthony felt himself sinking deeper in his chair. When he caught sight of jurors looking over at him he sat back up.

"Did Mr. Cruz say anything about the retainer agreement that provided Mr. Darren would make over two million dollars in fees off the insurance?" Woods asked.

"Objection!" Hal yelled. "Document speaks for itself."

Winchester pondered. "The part about what the retainer agreement *said* is stricken, and the jury is to disregard it." He leaned forward. "But whether Cruz *talked about* the retainer agreement stands. You may answer that question, Mr. Williams."

"Which one?"

"If Mr. Cruz said anything to you about a retainer agreement."

"No, he didn't. I don't believe he was even thinking about that at the time."

"Objection!" Hal said again. "Beyond the scope of the question, and speculation; move to strike."

Again Winchester thought a moment. "Everything after the word 'No, he didn't' is stricken. Mr. Williams," he continued, peering over his reading glasses at the witness, "please just answer the question."

"I'm sorry, Your Honor." Williams folded his hands in his lap.

"Mr. Williams, did Mr. Cruz say anything else at that time?" asked Woods.

"Yes, he did. He told me he'd signed invoices for boxes of diesel parts even though he knew they contained illegal weapons and garage door openers, because he wanted to help his chief engineer, Poncho Pascalle, smuggle arms to his rebel friends down in Costallegre."

The jurors wrote faster. Anthony glanced at Joe and saw his friend's face darkening.

"Now, Mr. Williams," Woods said. "There has been testimony from the District Attorneys' office that they had previously found evidence indicating that Mr. Cruz and his chief engineer, Poncho Pascalle, signed those invoices . . . but they kept the evidence confidential. Such information had never been leaked to the media or appeared in any newspapers. So I'm asking you, Mr. Williams— do you know of any facts showing that this information was *not* kept confidential?"

"No." Williams turned to look straight at the jury. "Mr. Cruz told me about signing those invoices while we were in the cell together."

"Let's be clear about this: Did you get that information from any other source?"

"No, I did not. I got it from Joe Cruz himself, and that's all."

This man missed his calling, thought Anthony bitterly. In Hollywood he'd probably have a few Oscars on his mantle.

"I have no further questions, Your Honor." Woods returned to his counsel table.

Hal Goldman rose, his gray eyes sparking. "Mr. Williams, how many felony convictions have you had?"

"Three."

"All for writing bad checks?"

"Yes. Sir."

"And on all occasions the victims of your crimes were little old ladies. Isn't that correct?"

"I wouldn't say that."

"Let me be more specific. These ladies were each in their seventies and of less than average height, were they not?"

A few jurors smiled.

"Well, maybe they were elderly, but I don't remember how tall they were," said Williams.

More jurors smiled.

"And each bad check was for over five thousand dollars. Correct?"

The smiles vanished.

"Maybe so. . . ." Williams bowed his head and clasped his hands as if in prayer.

"How well did you get to know Mr. Cruz during the time you were cellmates?"

"I think pretty well."

"Did you consider him a friend?"

"Yes. I still do."

"Yet you just now ratted on your so-called friend, didn't you?" Hal's voice rang off the mahogany ceiling.

"Objection!" Woods jumped to his feet. "Argumentative, unintelligible, ambiguous."

"Your Honor," said Hal, contempt on his face, "the witness knows what the colloquial term 'rat on your friend' means. He should answer the question."

"Do you know what the phrase means, Mr. Williams?" asked the judge.

"Yes, Your Honor."

"Objection overruled. You may answer the question."

"I didn't *want* to tell on Joe. But it seems to me it's Mr. Darren who should pay for his sins, not Joe. Joe has paid and suffered, and I believe the Lord will forgive him."

"Mr. Williams. Isn't it a fact that you face a potential sentence of up to five years for your last conviction?"

"Yes, sir."

"And isn't it a fact that Mr. Egan James of the District Attorneys' office promised that if you testified at this trial, he would recommend the least sentence possible at your hearing?"

"Not really."

"You had a conversation with Mr. James shortly before you were put into the cell with Mr. Cruz, correct?"

"Yes."

"When was that?"

"I guess about the time Mr. Cruz was arrested."

"And where did the conversation with Mr. James take place?"

"At the Federal Correctional Center."

"Who all was present?"

"Just Mr. James and me."

"What did you say, and what did he say at that time?"

"Mr. James told me that Joe was depressed and maybe suicidal. He asked if I'd keep an eye on him."

Some jurors began writing again.

Hal pressed on. "You also made a deal with Mr. James that he would recommend a lighter sentence for you if you cooperated and got evidence against either Mr. Cruz or Mr. Darren. Isn't that so?"

"He never promised a deal like that."

"But he made the *suggestion*, didn't he, Mr. Williams?"

"He . . . he reminded me that a good citizen who cooperates would be treated fairly by the judge. That's all."

"Mr. Williams, you have yet to be sentenced for your own crime, is that correct?"

"Yes."

"Isn't it true that your sentencing has been put off—that is, continued—at the request of the DA's office?"

"No, it's been delayed because the probation department hasn't finished its report yet."

"Your Honor, move to strike the unsolicited reason he gave for the delay," said Hal.

"Overruled. The answer may stand."

Hal scratched his cheek. "Mr. Williams, do you consider yourself a religious person?"

"I do now, sir. I study the Bible every night."

The Gray Eagle took off his steel-rimmed glasses and curled his fingers over the edge of the lectern. He seemed to rise as though readying to fly at the witness stand. "Mr. Williams, would you recite for us the Ten Commandments?"

The witness looked startled. So did the jury.

"Objection, Your Honor," Woods cried. "Counsel is going far afield. His request is totally irrelevant."

Winchester hesitated; "overruled."

"Mr. Williams, state the Ten Commandments."

"Well, Thou shalt not kill another human. Thou shalt not steal.

Thou shalt not covet thy neighbor's wife. Thou shalt not say God's name in vain. Thou shalt not . . . not . . . that's all I can remember at the moment."

"How about, 'Thou shalt not bear false witness against thy neighbor?' Do you remember that one?" Hal stared down his nose at the witness.

"Oh, yes. I'm sorry."

"You should be." Goldman's fingers clenched the lectern like talons. "No further questions to this false witness."

"Objection!" Woods roared. "Move to strike and I ask that counsel be admonished for his last two comments."

"You don't have to ask," said the judge. "The last phrases by counsel were argumentative, and shall be disregarded and stricken. I am calling a fifteen minute recess at this time. Counsel, please remain in the courtroom."

The jurors filed out, some looking confused, some thoughtful.

The moment the bailiff shut the door behind the last juror, the judge turned a deeply furrowed brow toward Hal Goldman. "Mr. Goldman, you know better. I won't put up with any more obviously inappropriate comments. This trial is almost over, but I'm holding you in contempt and sanctioning you four hundred dollars. If you intrude again, I will hold you in further contempt and impose a more severe sanction. Do you understand?"

"I do, Your Honor. I apologize to the court and counsel. I got carried away." Hal stood erect, respectful, and sincere. Even though he knew he was entitled to a hearing on the citation, this was one he wouldn't quibble with.

"All right. You are all excused for the recess." The judge's face relaxed. "I intend to instruct the jury and send them out for deliberation before this day ends."

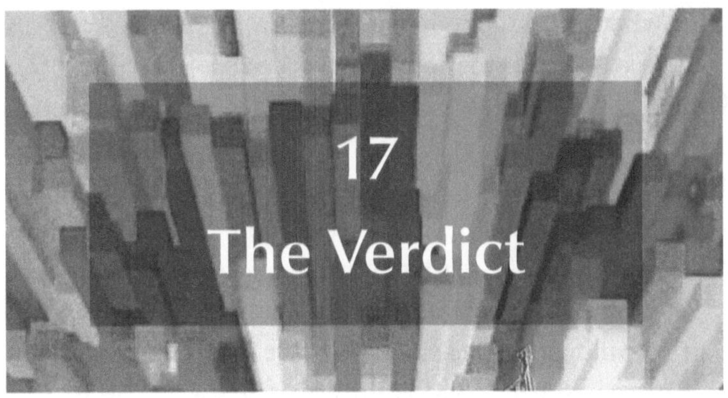

17
The Verdict

The gallery was packed.

The clock above the jury box read 1:27.

It finally moved, Anthony thought. In three more minutes, after six days of deliberation, the jury will finally tell me what my future is going to be.

He looked around one last time. The attorneys sat quietly at their tables—all except Hal Goldman, who paced slowly with his hands in his pockets. In the gallery, Laura and Andrea were almost hidden by the other spectators. Reporters had their pads and pencils ready.

Finally Hal put a hand on Anthony's shoulder and sat down next to him. Joe Cruz stepped past the bar and took a seat beside Dirk Miller. The bailiff, her gold badge shimmering, took her position behind Cruz and Anthony.

The mahogany door to chambers opened, revealing Judge Winchester standing partially in shadow. A second uniformed bailiff walked across the courtroom and stood behind Anthony and Joe. The throbbing rush in Anthony's ears grew louder and faster . . . incessant, escalating.

"Please stand," said the clerk, and announced the judge.

Black robe flowing, Winchester took the bench. Everyone sat.

The judge asked the bailiff to bring in the jury. One by one they filed in. Following the habit of a trial lawyer, Anthony tried to make eye contact with each of them. None looked at him.

His heartbeat quickened further.

When the jurors were all settled, the judge requested the foreman to declare whether the jury had reached a verdict. A crew-cut man in his sixties rose from the lower left section of the jury box. "Yes, Your Honor . . . Tom MacNamara, foreman. The jury has reached a verdict."

"Mr. Foreman, please hand the written verdict to the clerk."

The paper was passed up to the bench, and Anthony counted fifteen seconds as the judge read it. With no expression he had it passed back to the foreman, who was asked to state its contents aloud.

The first bailiff positioned herself more squarely behind Anthony and Joe. Anthony started to look down at the surface of the varnished oak table, then forced himself to lift his gaze to Mr. MacNamara.

The foreman spoke in a firm, clear voice: "We, the jury, find the defendant, Joe Cruz—guilty as charged on all counts . . . We, the jury, find the defendant, Anthony Darren—guilty as charged on all counts."

Shackles on his ankles and steel cuffs around his wrists, Anthony stood in line in steel grated anterooms, waiting as buzzers sounded, guards talked through intercoms and steel-barred doors electronically slid open and closed. The guards took him into a blur of yells, clangs, curses, coughs, urinating, farting, and sarcastic laughter, all under a dull smear of fluorescent light. When he heard the jangling of keys and saw the green uniforms and shiny brass badges of the jailers—*his* jailers—he flinched.

A camera strobe flashed in his eyes: full face, profile. Mug shots. His thumb was pushed onto a black ink pad, then a white card. Fingerprinted. Finally he was ordered to strip naked, bend over and pull apart his buttocks. Cavity search.

Now he understood: The moment he walked out of that court room he had become an object, an animal—a trapped animal. As a Deputy District Attorney, he had visited jails many times to interview witnesses, and later he had done occasional free defense work for accused men and women who could not afford an attorney. Back then, the thought of what it would be like to be an inmate had made him cringe. Now it made him deeply nauseous. *Oh God, now—at this prime time—now I am here. I can't help Andrea and Cheryl from here.*

All through that night he lay in a cell enveloped in a cloud of noise, anxiety, claustrophobia and insomnia. When morning came he counted every minute that went past, unable to think about anything except what was happening with Cheryl and what the bail decision might be. Finally, at ten-thirty he was called out to meet his attorney.

Through wire mesh-reinforced glass Hal spoke to him by phone. "Bad news on bail release, at least for now. How are you doing? You hanging okay?"

Anthony struggled to reply. "I was holding together till right now. What's the release problem? I've got to be with Andrea and Laura for Cheryl's surgery, Hal."

Hal's gray eyes were soft. "I tried everything, Anthony. The court is convinced you're a high risk to skip to another country; that you might even have a nest egg stashed somewhere. Even if you were granted temporary release, the bail would be astronomical. And you'd never raise it in time anyway."

Anthony felt his grip on . . . everything . . . slipping. "I know you did all you could, Hal. Thanks. Would you tell Andrea why I can't be with her? Tell her . . . tell her and Laura . . . that my prayers and thoughts are with them every second. And please have someone call me as soon as there's word on Cheryl's condition."

"I'll make sure."

Anthony returned to his cell and waited. He didn't answer the call for noon meal. Then he began pacing. Hour after hour he walked the same three steps back and forth. By mid-afternoon no word about Cheryl had come. Through vertical bars he watched the clock on the block wall stutter forward minute by minute until it pointed to five o'clock.

A guard came to his cell and inserted a key into the lock. The latch clanged open. "Darren, your attorney's outside."

Anthony tightened his lips. Why was Hal here rather than Andrea or Laura?

In the visiting area he once again saw Hal looking at him through the reinforced glass. No longer exemplifying the Gray Eagle, Hal wore the expression Anthony remembered seeing on his father's face in the rain when Dad told him his dog had been run over. Anthony sat and picked up the receiver on his side of the partition.

"She's dead," he said.

Hal's lips moved. "I'm sorry to be the one to tell you. There were . . . they did everything they could."

Anthony pressed his forehead to the glass. It felt cold, but not as cold as the shiver running through him. "Give Andrea my deepest love and sympathy," he murmured. "And tell Laura I miss her already, and I hope she'll keep an eye on Andi for me. And Hal . . . thanks to you for being so kind."

In a daze he stood up. Sitting on the free side of the glass, Hal looked helpless, his wings clipped.

Anthony turned and walked away, his dad holding a rain-dripping black umbrella over him.

BOOK III

18 A Touch of Family

George Hartford sat in the upstairs study of his country home and watched his son's convertible speed off back toward the entrance gate. The sports car's tiny back seat bulged with luggage and the handles of tennis rackets. In the front sat two figures in shorts and t-shirts, each flashing a smile and raising a hand to wave farewell. Stuart was driving, of course, with his girlfriend of almost three years in the passenger seat.

On the edge of the Spanish-tiled turnaround in front of the house, Marsha waved farewell to her only son. She always acted like he would never return . . . and the way Stuart drove, she carried the natural proclivities of any mother.

The car vanished way down the lined willow-shaded drive, but Martha kept standing there waving.

George took a deep breath and reached out for the telephone. Hesitated. Took another breath. *Better get this over with before she comes up here.*

In less than a minute he was speaking with his personal attorney in San Francisco.

"Have you got anything for me, Bryant?" *Please say no . . .*

"But I do."

George sighed. "Okay, go ahead."

"Where did you say you got this name again? From your daughter?"

"Cynthia, our youngest. She saw it on an envelope that fell out of her friend's backpack. The friend and Cynthia are sisters at the same sorority at Stanford. Cynthia said she started to put the envelope back, but noticed the mail had a post mark from Brockton Penitentiary. So Cynthia jotted down the sender's name."

"Right George. I actually thought I recognized that name when you gave it to me yesterday—and I should have. Anthony Darren is rather famous or I should say infamous—in my profession. Some years ago he was a stalwart highly respected young lawyer in the Southern California area—President of the County Bar there, in fact. Then he got convicted of fraud and murder under the federal code for masterminding the sinking of a ship to collect on insurance. Two of the crew died."

George swiveled his chair to face the photos adorning the opposite wall. Some showed the interiors of various Hartford Electronics plants around the world; high-tech facilities photographed in nostalgic sepia. The others, in full color, depicted eight prize-winning Hartford Farms thoroughbred racehorses.

By the time he swiveled back toward the window Marsha was walking back toward the house. "What's Darren's current situation?" George asked. "Andi's always talking about the law; any chance she's interviewing him for a class paper or something? We're really impressed by her. She seemed awed by the family, talked about the cooperation of bonding between us and the cousins we had up here, and that it added to the fun of the competition at tennis and crochet, and even in the pool. Besides being off-the-charts bright, she's a good little athlete. Yet I don't think she's had much of a family upbringing. Avoids the subject."

"Andi?" Bryant responded, "You're still talking about your son's girlfriend, Andrea, of course. You said she's studying quite a bit of philosophy and anthropology, so I suppose it's possible. I understand Darren's working on some kind of philosophy or social science project himself down there at Brockton, along with running the prison library and teaching college classes to his fellow inmates. Of course, all that is probably helpful, makes him look good for the parole board." Bryant paused. "I don't know how much you want to know, before I summarize this report, but there's some old society gossip about him as well."

"I'd better have it all."

"All right. Apparently Darren once had a fiancé—a Samantha Kincaid—I've heard of her father, Richard T. Kincaid. Anyway, after the trial she started dating the Deputy D.A. who worked on the case against Darren—and married him last year. His name is Egan James. I talked to him, too. He says Darren has never been married and basically has no family, except for a sister in Europe and a daughter born out of wedlock twenty or so years back."

George's fingers tightened so hard the handset creaked. "Daughter? What's her name?"

"It doesn't seem like a coincidence. The name I was given was Andrea . . . damn. Jesus, George, I'm sorry. Andrea Burns. At least the last name doesn't match."

"Right. Thanks, Bryant. . . . Listen, let's keep this whole inquiry confidential, okay?"

"As always. George . . . I hope none of this causes your family any problems."

"Oh, it won't." Oh, it will. Marsha will be fine; she's always favored Stuart marrying the Thornton girl anyway. And Cynthia was put off by Andrea's secrecy. But Stuart . . . well, he's plain crazy for the girl. Damn it, he planned to marry her the moment they graduated.

He thought he heard Martha's tread on the boards of the upstairs landing. "One more question, Bryant, if you don't mind. When is Anthony Darren supposed to get out of prison?"

"That was actually pretty harsh. The judge who sentenced him called him a disgrace to his profession and said he should be held to a higher standard than ordinary citizens, so he got fifteen to twenty years. By way of comparison, his co-conspirator only got seven years because there was testimony he wasn't the one who came up with the overall plan. Plus his son died in the sinking, so the judge said he'd had already received maximum punishment."

George nodded. "I agree. Nothing could be worse than losing a son to a single bad decision. And naturally, we wouldn't want our son and our families to be affected by any bizarre ramification of that unfortunate decision,"

⚓

Anthony waited in the visitor's area, embarrassed, as always, by his orange jumpsuit. He squared his shoulders and tried to appear crisp and fit on this cool March day.

His daughter's smile warmed him as she came through the gate. They walked out to a grassy area and sat at the concrete table where they'd visited together before.

"How was your drive down?" he asked.

"Nice . . . It's such a beautiful day."

"How's school?"

"Okay. Fine."

He tilted his head. "What's wrong?"

"Stuart and I broke up, Dad. I don't understand. I thought he was *the* guy."

"I know you did." Anthony placed his pale hand over hers. "What happened?"

"I have no clue. I did go up and spend a weekend with his family at their summer house—I mean mansion—a couple of weeks ago, but that all seemed to go fine. His mom's a little mother-hennish, but basically nice, and I really like his father. And of course one of his sisters is in my sorority. It all seemed great. I really liked the ambiance and warmth of their family life. We didn't have anything like that with Billy you know. And I am not talking about the lack of money. That has no bearing whatsoever. But after we'd been back at school a couple of days, Stuart stopped returning my calls. Until then, we had seen each other almost every day. Then he sent me a letter saying essentially that 'It's over between us.' No way could that relationship ever be resurrected, nor would I ever consider that thought after his note. It is over."

"As if I didn't know about your determination streak, Andi." Anthony's intuition told him that his notoriety had become a factor, but it would do no good to commiserate over that spilled milk. She knew, but she certainly wouldn't bring it up. He felt his guts wrench.

"Not only that, it is over with the sorority also. The girls became somewhat cool. I don't know why and I don't care." She set her jaw and shrugged one shoulder. "So I moved out, too. It's just as well. The sorority was too expensive anyway even with the grants, and I never really felt like I fit in. So now I'm rooming with a girl who goes to a junior college nearby. It's working out. We don't get in each other's way."

Anthony studied her expression. "I'd hoped you'd have a fuller, happier life once you got to college."

"Oh, it's full all right. Forget Stuart, I've got another dilemma. I've been offered scholarships in two different fields and have to choose between them."

Anthony grinned. "That's just terrible. I once faced that same dilemma, actually—choosing between two fields, I mean, not two scholarships. So tell me."

"One's law school; the other is the Philosophy Ph.D. program."

The drug of pride surged through him. "That's amazing."

"But what do you *think*?"

"Andrea . . . I'm not the right person to ask. I've got certain biases here."

"C'mon, just be honest. I'm not saying I'll agree."

"Okay, then, for whatever it's worth. It's obvious to me that you have a flair for the human behavior field, and you're gifted in anthropology. So why go into law, where you'll probably end up in litigation and burn out in a few years?"

"That's easy: because someday I'd like to get you out of this place. You were framed, and I want to be in the position to find out who did it and cut off his—"

"Ouch! Don't say it." Anthony shook his head. "I know exactly how you feel, Andrea, believe me—but obsession for revenge can eat away at you, do more damage psychologically than any punishment you'd ever give."

She produced the half-smile that Laura told him was just like his when he heard an argument he considered weak. "Dad, you're forgetting your own theory: always find the best synthesis point between competition and cooperation . . . with the edge given to competition. Well, getting *revenge* means getting *justice*, which is the ultimate form of competition, right? But to roll over and ignore what was done to you—surely that's the weakest form of cooperation."

"That's not the point. This is my battle, Andrea, not yours. You're young, with your whole life ahead. I don't want you to devote it to avenging the destruction of *my* life."

"But what about what *I* want?"

He rubbed his face with his hands. "Don't you see? That's just it: You're talking about going into law for my benefit, not yours. But sweetheart, you can't give me back my life no matter what. Even if I get pardoned someday I'll still walk out of here a convicted murderer. Nobody's going to forget that. The stigma will hang around my neck until the day I die." *And yours too, as you just experienced, he thought.*

"No. There has to be some way your record could be wiped clean, for you to be exonerated and redeemed."

"Like what? Hal pushed my appeals and petitions all the way to the US Supreme Court, and they were turned down every step of the way. That route's closed. At this point the only way I could even come close to exoneration would be by a full pardon—but that would require evidence so convincing even a Missouri farmer would believe it. A pardon no one considers justified wouldn't do me much good. What I need is *exculpation*—and that's an impossible goal for you to set yourself up for."

"You want me to be happy in life, don't you?"

"Of course."

"Well, I won't be happy until we've brought whoever framed you to justice, and they pay for what they did, and you're released from this place with full apologies and respect."

He straddled the bench, noting the much greater length of the tower's shadows over them, and leaned toward her. "Do you mind if I go into what your mother used to call me?"

She laughed. "Your Mr. Anthropologist moods. Of course not."

"Okay. On a case I worked on long ago, an opposing lawyer pulled a trick on me. The exact details don't matter, but he refused to correct his trickery. It took me some time and effort to get the trick reversed. Years later this same lawyer made a professional error on a different case we had against each other. He had a huge malpractice claim staring at him. He'd forgotten what he'd done to me back in the old case, didn't remember me at all in fact. So when he asked a favor from me to get him out of his dilemma, I said, "Do you remember who I am?" He almost passed out when I refreshed his memory. He actually came into my office, closed the door and got on his knees. The point is, justice has a way of coming back at people on its own. We humans intuitively know that. So we *cooperate, even as we compete* against each other. He was the rare one who did not follow nature's rules in those old days. When my turn came, for the benefit of my client, I was compelled to give him some cooperation. But I exacted a justifiable penalty from him."

"But the opportunity to vindicate you isn't going to fall into my lap if I'm a philosophy professor, now is it? Besides, no offense, but you're wrong to assume the only reason I want to help you is to get you out of here. I *do* want that, of course—but only as the first step toward righting some of the other wrongs I see in society." She paused. "Also, frankly, I think I'd be a really good lawyer. It's in my blood, after all."

He shook his head. "I'll bet when you were a child you were the one who didn't stop searching for Easter eggs until you found the last one. And you probably found the most, too."

"Every time, so stop resisting me. Besides, there might be a third way for me to finish out my college career."

"What's that?"

"I could get a double graduate degree—J.D. *and* Ph.D. They do it in med school all the time, giving MD's and Ph.D.'s to the same graduate."

Anthony had to shake his head. "Stuart's going to rue the day he let you go."

"Stuart who?"

"So, for the next few years you'll be in a monastery of education while I'm here doing my prison monkhood, is that it?"

"Dad, monks were volunteers; you're not. But that doesn't mean you can't take advantage of your situation as long as you're stuck in this place."

"Take advantage?"

She spread her hands. "What's a prison except a gigantic social science experiment? So use it. Apply and test your theories; see how they fly. I'll help you. Laura will help you. Any research you need, any information you can't get from here, we'll get it for you. In return, you help me earn two advanced degrees."

"And Laura? What's she get out of it?"

"First dibs on editing your book. Also, personal satisfaction. She loves you, Dad."

"What?"

Andrea rolled her eyes. "Men are such idiots. Look. A wise man once told me that combining efforts produces a force greater than the sum of its parts."

"Wait. I thought you said I was an idiot."

"Not when you said *that*."

He gazed at the guard tower. *She loves you, Dad.* He cleared his throat. "The authorities here won't like the idea of one of their lab rats running the lab."

"So don't tell them. Compete with them by pretending to cooperate or something."

He raised his eyebrows. "Actually, I *could* get permission to teach some classes in philosophy."

"On your theories, by any chance?"

"Well, I might sneak some of that in, see how it flies with men in here who have never been near an ivory tower." He focused on her again. "You're awfully persuasive, young lady. Maybe you *would* make a good lawyer."

She grinned and held out a hand, palm up. "So we're in agreement? We help you, you help us?"

"It's a pact."

Several guards raised their heads at the sharp *buzzer* that echoed off the walls.

19 The Protégé

What a fine-looking group of struggling intellectuals, Anthony thought as he stepped out front to face his first class. Seven cons . . . more than he'd expected, actually . . . plus two guards standing to one side. He'd deliberately chosen the topic "Differences between Major Political Systems" because he figured it would minimize attendance at this first session, giving him a chance to ease into his new role as prison professor, teaching watered down political science, economics and philosophy.

If he had been wrong about attendance, he was even more wrong about thinking his audience members had only come here to make disparaging comments. In fact, after he had spoken for a while about democracy vs. monarchism and communism vs. fascism, the men began to ask questions. Admittedly, most of the inquiries were about the relative "fairness" of one political system versus another, a sort of fumbling search for utopian options in which men like them would never need to be incarcerated.

With a wary glance at the guards, Anthony said that any government had to find a way to welcome and embrace ex-cons who truly wanted to rejoin the team and behave as responsible citizens. "There's no cooperative balance if responsible ex-cons and society continue to regard each other as enemies," he said. "The main reason the same people tend to keep recycling through a prison system is that the moment they get out they start fighting with a society they're programmed to regard as their adversary but in nature should be their teammates."

"Amen, brother," said one of the cons.

"Shut up, Lester," snapped a guard.

Later, an inmate who had sat in a dimly lit corner of the library stacks without speaking raised a muscular arm. He asked a well thought-out question about socialism verses a free market—a broad question, but insightful and lacking in any obvious self-interest. The man's English was excellent with a slight Hispanic accent. Anthony had never seen the man before.

Later, as the inmates filed out, the muscular man hung back: he was much shorter than Anthony, but with forearms and shoulders resembling those of a home-run hitting outfielder for Oakland Anthony had seen on TV.

Anthony faced him, gripping one of his fat reference books in both hands. Even the guards had left. "Can I help you?" said Anthony.

"I was wondering what you think about this: If a country relies on corruption and bribery as a way of life, can it still have democracy or a free market?"

Anthony took his time answering. "If you're wondering whether democracy can survive rampant, systemic corruption, the answer is no. Or a free market either. In a truly corrupt society the people in power hoard it at the expense of everyone else. They tend to illegally kill the competition necessary for free enterprise and democracy to thrive."

"So a system that's been based on bribery and corruption for centuries can't be changed into an honest one?"

"Maybe, but it would take extraordinary effort."

"Like what?"

"Seems to me the government would have to institute some kind of high court that enforces a charter or constitution that's supreme to any man or group. This court would have to be absolutely honest and free from outside influences, and be backed-up by the force of the law. The highest judges should be appointed for life so no one can remove them except for reasons of personal dishonesty or serious permanent illness—that way their decisions won't be influenced by the threat of losing their livelihoods. This threat against them could happen if they make rulings against the powerful or the popular, or even the majority view. They are supposed to just follow the law, the charter, and the constitution."

The inmate mulled this over for a moment. "What if a system like that can't be made because of the 'old ways' and powerful families or strongmen, or if the judges don't have enough power to make their decisions stick? What then? Is revolution a valid way to change things?"

"As a last resort? If everything else fails? History says 'yes.'"

The man's face broke into a grin. "Good, because that's what we did. What we're still doing."

"Where?"

"The Republic of Costallegre. The problem is, every time we change things, sooner or later the system falls back to the old corrupt ways. Like Serape giving way to Bramoso. Hey, you need help carrying those books?"

Anthony hesitated, then willingly handed over a twelve-hundred page *World History* volume. "What's your name?"

"Hector Lopez."

"You're Costalegran?"

"By birth, but now I am a US citizen. If I can hang onto it."

"What are you in for?"

"Gunrunning."

"To Costallegre?"

Hector nodded. "For the revolution."

"For which side?" Anthony asked bluntly.

"The Democratic RF?, against Bramoso. You keep up with Central American affairs?"

Anthony hesitated. He had been in prison long enough to know better than to explain how he knew anything about anything— especially a crime like gunrunning. So all he said was, "I was in Costallegre for a week once when Serape still ran the country, that's all. I understand Bramoso's even worse."

"Far worse. Calls himself a Communist so he can take everything away from the people who worked for it. Then he redistributes it . . . mostly to himself and his cronies."

Anthony nodded. "So how long are you in for?"

"Four more years . . . plus three hundred and twenty-five days."

"For gun-running? That's pretty harsh, especially since the U.S. government probably doesn't even support Bramoso."

"That's what you would think, but there's some bleeding hearts in our government who blindly believe Bomoso's bullshit. I am writing my appeal now."

They walked a ways without talking. Then Anthony surprised himself. "Do you need any help on it? I'm an attorney, or used to be. If you'd like, I could look your brief over for you."

"Really? I don't want to put you out."

"No problem. Just don't tell anyone else, or everyone in here will want me writing their briefs . . . and that would interfere with other things I'm already working on."

"I can keep a secret," said Hector. "And thank you in advance for your help. If you ever need *me* for anything, I will help you, no matter what."

Anthony knew better than to accept such a pledge, too. "I haven't practiced criminal law for years," he said. "I warn you I'll be rusty, but bring what you've got to the next class and we'll look it over."

Hector missed the following week's lecture on "History and Malcontents," but showed up for the talk after that, along with a full dozen other cons. Afterward Hector ambled to the front of the room carrying a thick handwritten document and some transcripts.

He and Anthony drew chairs up to the lecture table and sat. Anthony shuffled through the papers. "Okay, let me find the clerk's transcript. Got it. Let's see, yeah, they charged you with illegally exporting firearms. No permits, no clearances—and it was your second conviction for that offense. Right, Hector?"

Hector shrugged. "At least under that name."

"Hm. I wonder why they didn't charge you with plain, garden-variety smuggling at the same time? Maybe they didn't want to give the jury the option of convicting you of that possibly lessor offence, which could include a misdemeanor, instead of the much more severe charge of gunrunning."

He read on, felt his pulse begin to accelerate. "The weapons," he said. "How were they stored when you saw them."

"In boxes."

"Did you ever actually look *inside* the boxes?"

"No; they were not labeled and sealed up tighter than scared turtles. Why?"

"Because you were charged with gunrunning, not just smuggling. That means the government needed to prove you *knew* what was in those boxes at the time of your arrest. Did the prosecution present any evidence that you knew what was in the boxes?"

"I don't remember."

"Did you take the stand in your own defense?"

"No."

"Good. Okay, let me read the trial transcript to see if there's any evidence showing your specific intent. If not . . . Hector, you might have a shot at the appeal."

A week later Hector attended "Economic Disparities and Who's Responsible." Afterward he came up and again asked if he could help carry Anthony's books.

"Does this mean we're going steady?" Anthony asked.

"Don't say that kind of thing in here, man."

"Sorry. Sure, give me a hand."

They started packing books into boxes to return to the library.

"Well?" Hector said.

Anthony smiled. "Okay. I read the transcript from cover to cover. Nowhere, *nowhere*, does anyone say or present any evidence that you knew what was in those boxes. The instructions the court gave the jury forced the jurors to presume you knew what was in the boxes just because you drove the truck. But logically that doesn't follow. Do you understand? Sure, you knew you were doing something illegal, helping smuggle something or other. But it could have been plumbing parts or firecrackers for all you knew. To convict you of gunrunning it's not enough for the government to prove you smuggled *something*; they have to prove you knew for a fact you were smuggling *firearms*. They didn't do that—yet like I said, the jury instruction left no alternative but to convict."

"So . . . you think you can get me out of here?"

"I think we can try," said Anthony.

A guard stuck his head into the classroom. "Hey! This ain't no social club. Class is over. Get your asses back in your houses!"

A few days later Anthony and Hector sat together in the raucous eating hall during the midday meal. One unexpected advantage of being "The Prof," Anthony had discovered, was the unusual latitude he had to move unmolested through the rigid, self-imposed racial layers of the prison population. "Thanks again for working on my brief," Hector hoarsely whispered. "I couldn't have done it without you—I know because I tried."

"I'm just glad we got it done in time. You sent it to the US Court of Appeals for the Ninth Circuit, right?"

"Like you said. Now, how long do I have to wait?"

"It'll be about six months before they come down with a decision." As he spoke Anthony automatically glanced around to make sure no one was listening. For a moment his gaze locked with that of a man sitting at a crowded corner table across the room. The con was giving him a flat stare, and Anthony looked calmly away. So far he had managed to avoid becoming part of the inmate hierarchy or any of its territorial cliques, and he didn't want to. . . ."

His gaze shot back to the man across the room.

"You know that guy?" Hector asked.

"Yes," Anthony said. What he didn't say was, His name is Steve Williams. He used to be the cellmate of a friend of mine. He's also the lying asshole who's half-responsible for me being in here. . . .

But he didn't say any of that. Instead he said, "He's one of those guys I talk about, one of those outliers who never seem to learn and keep falling off the fringes." He paused. "Must have run out of favors with the U.S. Attorney."

Hector gave a piece of cornbread a suspicious sniff. "Doing better in here; that table he's at is home of the king cons who really run this joint."

"I know. They're the guys I try most to avoid."

"Good idea. Is he signaling you? Don't do it, man; don't go over there."

"I don't intend to." Anthony looked down at his tray.

"Now I remember where I saw that guy before—in the post office. He's the one who mailed off my brief."

Anthony fixed a look on him. "Did he see it? Your brief?"

"He sort of flipped through it when he weighed it. He says, 'You didn't write this, did you?'"

"Great. Listen, Hector—if he pressures you, tell him the truth. Don't worry about me. I wouldn't help that man if my life depended on it."

"Hope it never comes to that," Hector said, and popped the cornbread into his mouth.

As Anthony followed Hector out of the dining room a voice behind him said, "Hey, Darren."

He stopped, and turned slowly to face Steve Williams. "I guess you missed my sign back there."

"Was that what it was? Then I must suffer from a genetic defect. The communication center in my brain has difficulty responding to garbage—especially garbage that hooks a finger at me like I'm some sort of servant."

Williams smiled and shook his head. "Man, you're just as dumb in here as you were on the outside. Didn't you see me signaling you to come sit with the big boys? Those are the people who can make your life livable in here or not. You wrote Hector's brief; I know you did. Well, all you have to do is look at a few other appeals, starting with mine, and—"

"Sorry, Williams, I can't help you. You're garbage, and that substance offends my sense of smell. I can't write legal briefs when my sense of smell is screwed up."

Anthony strode away and caught up to Hector. "Either you're very dumb," Hector said, shaking his head, "or very pissed off at that dude. I guess you're pissed because you sure ain't dumb. So what did he do to get you so mad you want to commit suicide?"

"He was a witness in my trial," Anthony said. "He was already in prison and lied to get early release."

Hector seemed to consider this as they walked across the yard. Finally he said, "The boys at the corner table might be badasses, but they're not stupid. This guy must be conning them, too. Nobody likes snitches." He grinned and clapped Anthony on the back. "My friend, it looks like you're not the only one trying to commit suicide in here."

The closing-time buzzers went off. Anthony walked out of the library and across the yard toward his cell block. He entered a dark stairwell and started climbing. Half a flight up, movement above him drew his gaze. Two thick-necked prisoners stood looking down at him with their weight-pumped arms crossed over chests the size of steamer trunks.

A red buzz shot through Anthony, and without thought he grabbed the handrail and vaulted up and over, dropping to the landing several feet below. The moment he hit the floor a steel door slammed shut in front of him with a flat echo. A shadow stood with his back pressed to the door.

Anthony had seen his share of fights in the yard; they tended to be swift, bloody and completely one-sided. This—here in an enclosed stairwell—might be different.

Again he didn't hesitate. He flung himself toward the door, head down, and drove the full weight of his body through his shoulder and into the solar plexus of the shadowy man. A shocked cry and belch burst out and the inmate plummeted to the floor, eyes bulging, mouth gaping, quivering body blocking the door.

Anthony managed to drag the door open about a foot when a calm voice behind him said, "Don't break his writing hand—the right one."

Everything went red and purple; then Anthony's brain registered nothing but flashes of light and explosions of pain. Neck. Ribs. Crotch. He fell and rolled into a ball, arms over his head. Kidneys. Thighs. Skull.

Then he felt a vise catch his left hand and compress it until the fingers rolled helplessly open.

Shock spurted up his arm like electricity, and everything faded to black.

When Anthony woke, the clock on the block wall showed 11:30 and the windows were dark, but there was no calendar to inform him of what day it might be. Must be he was in the infirmary. His head hurt so deeply it made him want to vomit.

He did vomit. And welcomed the return of swirling darkness.

A prison medic approached him through fog and told him he had a concussion. When Anthony tried to move, spears seemed to plunge into every quarter of his body. He noticed that his left hand was in a cast, with the two middle fingers splinted straight out. The medic told him someone had bent them back until they snapped.

For the next few days Anthony lived in that fog. On the morning he was to be released back to his cell a guard came and questioned him about “the incident.” Anthony told him the truth: he had not recognized and couldn’t hope to identify his assailants. Then he lied: No, he had no idea why anyone would want to work him over.

“Well,” the guard said, “whoever did this had a reason. Otherwise they would have just killed you.”

Anthony waited through a week of ferocious headaches before he gathered himself enough to get back to his evening lectures. Just walking over to the hall again made him feel a bit better.

Hector the Costalegran was sitting in the rear of the room when Anthony entered. With unusually impassive eyes he looked at Anthony’s swaddled hand, and after the lecture he walked out without speaking a word.

“Hey, Darren!”

Anthony looked up from the book he was trying to read. He still got headaches very easily, and his hand hurt like hell.

The guard they called Sluggo stood at the bars of his “house.” “C’mon. We got some questions for you.”

“Who has questions for me?”

“I said *get up*.”

As Anthony preceded Sluggo toward the guard station at the end of the corridor he noticed that the cell block was quieter than usual. Sluggo shoved him into a room enclosed with thick glass windows.

The Captain of the Guard told him to stand at the counter. “Darren, we hear you and Steve Williams had words the other day. “

“That’s right.”

"What about?"

"He wanted me to help with his appeal, and I told him no."

"You told him 'no?' That's it?"

"Well, I might have said something like 'I don't write briefs when my sense of smell is fouled by garbage,' or something like that."

The captain half-smiled before his lips flat-lined. "It was right after that you got beat up, right?"

"Yes."

"Didn't Williams testify against you at your trial?"

"Yes."

"So it's fair to say you two didn't like each other."

"You could say that."

"You were in the library all day today, correct?"

"Yes. Why?"

"You don't know?"

"Know what?"

"This afternoon we found Steve Williams stuffed in a canvas bin behind the postal station. His neck was broken."

Anthony's eyes widened. "Dead?"

"As a canceled stamp. Darren, do you know anyone who might have been interested in killing him, besides you?"

"I wasn't interested in killing him. As far as I'm concerned garbage is already dead and decomposing."

"That kind of attitude isn't going to help you any."

"Help me what? I was in the library all day; I've got witnesses."

"You could have had an accomplice." The captain pointed a finger. "Look, I know you think you're smarter than everybody else, but you're wrong. And now you're on our scope. Go back to your cell, but keep in mind this investigation is just getting started."

Anthony was always pleased to receive mail. Most of it came from either Andrea or Laura, with a letter from his sister every month or so and an occasional "I am praying for you." missive and religious tract from someone he had never met.

But it had been a while since he'd heard from Hal Goldman.

Dear Anthony,

I've got news. I've been working on an application for early parole. Don't get your hopes up too high, but so far things are looking good. Your prison record is exemplary—don't let up on that.

Here's a surprise: Egan James recently left the DA's office and went into private practice, specializing in securities work. Sounds like he's once again attempting to walk in your footsteps. The difference is he's working with Herbert Hooks' companies, advising on the securities laws and helping to put together investment syndications.

I guess you could have gone all day without hearing either of those names, but I thought you'd be interested; it sounds to me like another case of the fox guarding the henhouse.

Another painfully familiar name will be John Woods; he is now in charge of the US Attorney's office. I hope you hold him no animosity for your conviction; I still believe he was doing his job as best he could under political pressure and undoubtedly using bad evidence. I don't think you need fear any further trouble from him but be wary of Hooks and James; they have the power to screw up your parole application.

Very Truly Yours,

Hal

Anthony folded the letter shut, placed it on the little folding desk and lay back. He stared at the ceiling. *And now you're on our scope*, he thought.

Terrific timing, Darren.

One night after Anthony excused his class, Hector surprised him by finally approaching. "Tony the Professor," he said. "How you been? You're getting so good at your talks, I'm going to be sorry in a way that I won't be hearing 'em anymore."

"Hi, Hector," Anthony said. He looked around. Almost everyone had left. "It's been months. Long time, no talk, eh? Why now? Are they transferring you?"

"No." Hector smiled broadly. "I just got the word from the Court of Appeal, Professor. They liked your brief—I'm a free man."

"All right, Hector!" Anthony slapped fives with him, low and high. "When do you leave?"

"Two weeks."

"Wow," Anthony replied, trying not to think about his own parole application.

"I'll stop by on my way out." Happily, Hector turned and quickly walked out the classroom door.

Sluggo, wearing his slightly tarnished badge, was just coming in. His glance followed Hector. Then he turned and raised his eyebrows at Anthony.

"Okay. I'm going," said Anthony as he picked up his books.

"How long has it been since we made our pact?" Andrea asked as they sat on their usual little grassy mound under the triangulated gazes of the guards.

"I guess about a year and a half."

"And you've been teaching your classes all that time, right? Testing your theories?"

"I haven't missed a week." Not quite true, but he had no intention of telling her about the beating he had taken, or about Steve Williams' death. Fortunately she hadn't noticed how little he was using his recently-freed left hand, or how withered it was.

"So . . . ?" Andrea said.

"So what?"

"So when are you going to say 'enough's enough' and send your manuscript to Laura so she can start trying to get it published?"

Anthony plucked a dandelion out of the half-dead grass and fluffed its underappreciated petals. "It's not really a manuscript. Really just a bunch of notes."

"Don't believe you."

He had to smile as he looked at his daughter, who on every visit reminded him more and more of Cheryl . . . except for her eyes, which were so like his, and her poise, which were all her own.

"Okay, okay," he said. "The truth is I just don't think it's good enough yet. And since Laura's just getting started as a literary agent, I don't want to saddle her with a loser."

"She's only doing the agenting part-time so far," Andrea said.

"It's not like she depends on you. But have you ever considered that your book might be the thing to *launch* her career?"

He rotated the dandelion blossom between his fingers. It looked like a tiny yellow sun, spinning. "I'm trying to be realistic. The truth is I have no credentials to write a book like this. I'm not a trained philosopher, sociologist, economist, historian, or anything else that qualifies. What I am is a disbarred lawyer convicted of fraud and murder. Which looks *really* good on the dust jacket of a book about how to build better societies and live happier, more productive lives."

Andrea startled him by laughing then made him proud by not apologizing. "Okay, I see your point . . . but that doesn't mean I concede. I still think your ideas need to get out there, one way or another, and sooner rather than later. And you think so too, or you wouldn't have come up with a tentative title. What was it? *The Law of* . . . something."

"*Fusing Order and Chaos,* changed titles, remember."

"That's right. Which I assume is a combination—or maybe I should say *synthesis*—of 'cooperative' behavior and 'competitive conduct.'"

"Very good."

"Okay. But what makes it a *law*?"

He put the dandelion on the ground. Now he regretted plucking it. "Years ago I told you I believed there's a common theme in human behavior on this idea, a thread that runs through everything we do.

"Your favorite theme?"

"Yes, but I'm not the first person to flirt with it. In fact, the more research I do, the more thinkers I find who have at least come close."

"Such as . . . ?"

"In the early 1960's a writer on economic philosophy named Joan Robinson almost hit the nail on the head. She said that a society of unmitigated egoists would knock itself to pieces while its members fought over food and mates, while a perfectly altruistic society could never exist because each individual would starve to death. Both egoism and altruism are necessary for social existence. That makes sense, but doesn't go far enough for me; I say there has to be a set of rules that reconciles the conflict between the extremes. Everyone knows that subconsciously; it's why mankind adopted laws by which to govern itself."

Andrea raised her brows and rotated her eyes theatrically from side to side, drawing attention to their surroundings.

Anthony smiled. "Okay, no, not everybody follows all the rules. But that's part of the synthesis, too. In any society governed by law you'll find a whole spectrum of adherence in the population, from anarchy at one end to ultra-conformity at the other."

"Okay. Go on."

Imagine a primitive society. An overly-competitive individual would drive everyone else off and find himself alone without a team to help him survive. On the other hand, a too-cooperative individual would have trouble catching or keeping a mate, so those genes would tend to fade out of a population. What's needed—what's *natural*—is a synthesis of the two. Only when that ideal unification point is approached will there be real success in the system. And I argue that's true for *any* system."

"Any?"

"I've applied it to everything I can think of: social science, economics, politics, even art and music."

"Really?"

"Biology, psychology, religion, astrophysics. . . ."

"Dad." She looked directly into his eyes. "The world is wallowing in crime, pollution, terrorism, poverty, disease, loneliness, the proliferation of nuclear and chemical weapons, and overpopulation." She took a breath. "We need all the new ideas we can get. Besides, possibly some recognition of your thoughts could someday play a part on getting you out of here."

He smiled sadly. "Who's going to listen to a convict?"

An amplified voice shivered off the walls: "Visiting hours are over in five minutes. Five minutes."

With a sigh, Anthony got to his feet. Andrea joined him and they started walking toward the exit gate. "Dad . . . are you going to be okay?"

"Sure. I'm hanging on."

"Still giving the lectures?"

"For the moment, but apparently I've said some things that the powers that be don't appreciate. So much for keeping a low profile."

She tucked a hand under his elbow. "Have you heard about getting a new parole review?"

"No. I should have heard something by now . . . I don't know; maybe my evil lectures are the problem, or maybe Hooks and Egan James are still working against me behind the scenes." He stared speculatively toward the gate. "After Socrates was condemned, his friends arranged for him to escape, but he turned them down. Remember that?"

"What about it?"

"For him martyrdom was a way of competing; his final protest. Of course, he was already famous by then so it was more than just a gesture. But me? After all these years, I'm not even *infamous*. No one knows of me or my ideas. So perhaps I'll have to take the other course—the one Socrates did *not* choose."

"Shhhhhhh." Andrea looked around. "Dad, if you try what you're thinking you'll be caught and locked in here the rest of your life. Just hang in there. I'm close to getting my law degree."

"*And* your Ph.D. too. I'm so proud of you."

Her eyes narrowed into hazel slits. "I wouldn't be getting *either* of them if it weren't for my collaboration with you. Not to mention that if it weren't for you I'd probably have gone back to Kentucky years ago and gotten beaten to death by that unspeakable monstrous bully."

Anthony leaned away from her, eyes wide.

"So don't you dare take away my chance to repay you," she growled. "I'm going to pass the bar, and then I'm going to jump into battle and find a way to get you out of here legally and in one piece. Do you understand?"

He stared at her for a moment, then smiled. "I almost feel sorry for Hooks and James. Those two have no idea what's heading their way."

Stayed well [illegible] toward the exit gate. "Dad? [illegible] are you going to be okay?"

[illegible]

"Still [illegible]"

"[illegible] apparently [illegible] said something that the power [illegible] keeping [illegible]"

She [illegible] hand under his elbow. "Have you heard about [illegible] new [illegible]?"

"No. I should have [illegible] something [illegible] now. [illegible] I don't know; maybe [illegible] or maybe [illegible] and [illegible] are still working against me behind the scenes. [illegible] toward the gate. "After Socrates was condemned, his friends arranged for him to escape. But he turned them down. Remember that?"

"[illegible]"

"[illegible] was [illegible] by them, so it was more than just [illegible] all these years, I'm not even [illegible] perhaps I'll have to take the other [illegible]"

"[illegible] But if you try [illegible] and [illegible] the rest of your life [illegible]"

[illegible] you."

[illegible]

[illegible]

[illegible] smiled. "[illegible] almost [illegible] those we [illegible] way."

20 Debate with Pomposity

"My goodness," Laura said as Andrea opened the door of Mary's house, "every time we get together you look more beautiful."

"Look who's talking." Andrea led her into the living room where Mary had set out a tray of coffee and cups. "When I first saw you I thought you looked like Wonder Woman. And you still do." She touched Laura's sleeve. "What a darling French rag."

"You like it?" Laura seated herself at the coffee table. "I did some promotional writing for a store in Mission Valley selling the craziest knits. Got it in trade, mutual benefit, in keeping with Anthony's theories."

Andrea sat beside her on the couch. "Mutual benefit sounds like a good approach to being a literary agent, too."

"We'll see . . . I've only made a couple of deals so far. But how about *you*? A few more months and you'll have the big double, Ph.D. *and* J.D. Incredible."

"I can't wait to put them to use."

Laura laughed. "Maybe you should take some time off first, Andrea. Go to Paris. Go to Rome. Hell, go to *Fresno*. Go anyplace where you won't have your face in a book."

"I can't. I am on the magnificent mission."

"Oh, he'd hate to hear you say that. 'Find the synthesis,' he'd say."

"He's already said it to me . . . several times. The thing is, his own thesis seems to take too long to work for *him*."

"Too long?

"The last time I saw him he looked . . . I don't know, *desperate*. But not in a frantic way; sort of detached. It's hard to explain."

"I don't like the sound of that. He's not going to try anything crazy, is he?"

"I honestly don't know. When I left he was talking about Socrates." Andrea shook her head. "It's like a shadow's fallen over him the last few months. Before that he seemed to be getting enough satisfaction from working on his book and giving classes at the prison, but all of a sudden . . . what? Laura, what?"

Laura was staring down at her intertwined hands. "It's my fault."

"What's your fault?"

"His change of heart. It's my fault." She wiped her eyes with the back of her hand.

"What do you mean?"

"I didn't do it on purpose. You know how he's been sending me pages, his best-developed ideas, for me to look over? Well, a few weeks ago I got so excited I asked if I could show them to a sociology professor I know, Dr. Randy Parsons."

"And . . . ?"

"Your dad said yes. But Randy was *brutal.* I didn't know the extent until after I'd already mailed off his comments to Anthony; your dad insisted on having it that way. When I read what Randy wrote . . . I couldn't believe it."

"Did he know about Dad's . . . situation? Could that have colored—"

"No, he didn't know. Which is kind of ironic; one reason I thought of Dr. Parsons in the first place is that he often gives lectures at prisons. I even imagined him wanting to go up to Brockton to discuss Anthony's theories with him. Or writing an endorsement for the book if it gets published someday. I was so sure he'd be impressed."

"But he wasn't."

"There's nothing uglier than an academic in full scorn. He tore into Anthony's thesis, his writing style . . . everything." Laura sighed. "The thing is, I should have seen it coming. Dr. Parsons is one of those academics who believes everyone's character is determined almost entirely by their environment—the way they're brought up. He's scornful of the socio-biologists who believe genetics plays a significant role along with environment in human development, which your father also believes, of course." She hesitated. "On top of that, I think he is biased. He's aware of my past relationship with your dad."

"Oh."

"That's strictly a one-way street, Andrea. Always was."

"All the more reason for him to resent Dad, then."

Laura put down her cup. "Okay, I've got fences to mend. When I get back to my office the first thing I'll do is start looking for a publisher brave enough to take an honest look at *Fusing Order and Chaos* and give us an unbiased opinion."

"No, that's the second thing you should do. First we have to convince Dad it's worth finishing the book at all. I'm not sure how to do that. We changed titles. Seems he lost all his fight."

Laura stared down at the coffee table. "Fight. . . ."

"What?"

"You're right; that's exactly what Anthony needs. A good fight."

"He needs a good fight?"

"Yes. Andrea, you're brilliant."

"I must be, because even I don't understand what I said."

"We are going to arrange an academic fight."

LECTURE proclaimed the announcement on the cafeteria bulletin board. Anthony paused and read the rest:

Renowned Philosopher and Professor of Sociology

Dr. Randolph Parsons, Author of

To Mock a Killing Bird

TO SPEAK NEXT WEDNESDAY NIGHT ON

"PENOLOGY AND ITS ERRORS."

Penology and Its Errors? Anthony thought. Well, that should be better attended than any lecture I ever gave.

Then he reread the speaker's name: Parsons. Dr. Randolph Parsons.

"What the fuck . . . ," he said out loud, not even thinking about it, like any good inmate.

That's the same jerk Laura sent my manuscript to!

At first he wasn't going to attend, but on the appointed date and time he followed a line of prisoners into the hall and took a bench near the back. Perhaps twenty-five inmates sat ahead of him—more than he got at some of his own lectures; fewer than at others. He recognized the broad back of Hector Lopez in the second row.

A prison counselor introduced Parsons, a tan-faced man, sporting well-coiffured combed-back hair. He wore a tan corduroy sport jacket with leather elbow patches and a slightly crooked bow tie. As he stepped to the lectern he held his arms out Christ-like to a smattering of applause, his preacher's smile confident. This was clearly a man who knew more than anyone here, more than anyone just about anywhere . . .

As Parsons began addressing his flock Anthony tried to listen past his growing anger but soon enough he realized he was hearing nothing new: just the same old sociological, penologist drivel, or maybe he'd elevate it to drudgery, he had listened to years before in college. Anthony noticed that many of his fellow audience members nodded throughout the monologue, well pleased with the direction the professor was taking. Meanwhile Anthony pondered escaping out the back door.

Then Parsons accepted a question from Hector Lopez.

"Professor, don't you think humans are born wanting to both compete and get along at the same time, and when they can't put the two things together that's when they get into trouble?"

Parsons looked at the ceiling—not quite an eye-roll, but close. "I'm sorry, I don't follow you."

"Maybe I'm not saying it right," Hector said. "We've got a professor here, one of our own inmates; maybe he can put it better."

"A professor? Really? Does he possess a Ph.D. degree in sociology or philosophy?"

"I don't know. He's a lawyer."

"Well, I'm sure a license to practice law suffices in a courtroom, but we're talking about academic matters. If ever any of you gentlemen further your education, you'll discover that a scholar must always proportion his or her acceptance of information to the qualifications of the teacher. Otherwise he can be led down any sort of odd path."

Hector interjected, "Nobody leads me down no—"

Another voice from the back of the room asked: "Have you ever acted as an expert witness in court?"

"As a matter of fact I have," said Parsons with a triumphant smile.

"Did you always prevail with your theory?"

"Well, not always. I appeared only a few times as an expert."

"On those occasions that the judge or jury rejected your theories, did not a lawyer cross examine you as he questioned your theory in front of the jury?"

Parson's mouth fell open.

"Of course one did," said the voice from the back. "Obviously the lawyer surely must have become as much an expert on your rejected theory as you? Isn't that true?"

"Who are you back there?" demanded Dr, Parsons as he turned the shade of squashed pomegranate. Anthony rose to his feet. "Darren is the name. Excuse me. Dr. Parsons, perhaps I can help explain what this man meant a few minutes ago.. The essence of his comment is that humans are born with drives to both cooperate with their brothers and at the same time compete against them. Neither aspect should be ignored; the solution is to find a synthesis that proportions those two drives to reach the optimum level of behavior."

'"The optimum level of behavior.' How droll." Parsons' eyebrows rose. "Would you happen to be the inmate-professor previously referred to?"

"I am, but a professor only by nickname."

"I compliment you on your charming uniform. However, your understanding of both psychology and philosophy leave a great deal to be desired. As does your timing. This discourse is far beyond what is appropriate for this gathering, but now that the other gentleman brought it up I'll enjoy putting it to bed if you will all bear with us."

The cons glanced back and forth between the speakers. They looked a lot more interested in this discussion than any ordinary usual lecture; probably they were hoping it would devolve into an all-out riot. Anthony held his peace.

Parsons took a deep, long-suffering breath. "Now then; it should be obvious that it is impossible to synthesize behavior patterns that are diametrically opposed to one another. If you mix fire and ice you do not get cold fire or hot ice; you get lukewarm water."

"Or enough steam to power a train," Said Anthony.

The cons looked back at Parsons, who waved a hand as if erasing a chalkboard. "Let us dispense with the vague metaphors, shall we? What human behaviors are you specifically talking about synthesizing?"

"Competition and cooperation."

"From a philosophical point of view, what is the meaning of each of these terms? Or is that too abstract for this discussion?"

"By my definition, competition is akin to chaos/separation/ repulsion; it's something taken away from something else; it's separation and division. You could say it's similar to dissonance. On the other hand, cooperation is a form of giving, akin to uniting. It's order/ attraction. It unites and combines . . . it is consonance. In physics, the forces that separate and repulse are chaotic, so they are, to coin a word, competitionistic. On the other hand, the forces that combine, such as gravity, are cooperative and tend toward the orderly. The forces of particles which resist being combined or drawn together are competitionistic. My point is that, paradoxically, each of these basic drives *needs* the opposing drive against which to brace, or stand, in order for the total system to thrive. In that respect they are not diametrically opposed at all."

Parsons shook his head. "Even after all that I can't say you make clear sense."

"To Who?" an inmate in the back piped up.

Ignoring the comment, Parsons continued, "However, you did mention human behavior and subatomic particles in the same sentence, which implies that the rule you propose must apply to *any* dynamic system."

"Yes. I believe it does."

"So then in your view everything in physics can be reduced to a synthesis of competition and cooperation? Or in music? Tennis? Origami? In any subject whatsoever?"

"Yes. I believe this principle is universal, and in fact I'm fascinated you related it to music. Surely you're familiar with the music of Tchaikovsky?"

"I've moved on to more challenging composers, but yes, who does not know *Dance of the Sugarpum Fairies?*"

"Or how about the overture to *Romeo and Juliet?*" piped up another inmate.

"Pick any composer," Anthony continued. "In fact pick any music. Any composition that stands the test of time includes both contrast and cooperation—surprise and harmony. Musical sounds and chords often have both contrast *and* order within them. Many chords have dissonant notes when they are paired separately."

One of Parson's eyebrows rose.

"For example," Anthony went on, "monotones should be balanced by changes or even dissonance, or they would become boring, or even become noise, like a constant horn blast on a car alarm. But too much dissonance is too disorderly, to noisy—*too competitive.* Similarly, if you combine orderly, cooperative rhythm with a spice of competitive counter beats—such as syncopation in a four-four time signature—you have achieved musical co-opetition."

"'Co-opetition?' I have never heard the word."

"That's because it was only recently coined," Anthony said.

"Why does that not surprise me? You realize, I hope, that the term is an oxymoron? Do you even know what an 'oxymoron' is?"

"It's a self-contradicting figure of speech. But that's not what the word is—which you would understand if you'd really heard me. The seemingly apposed behaviors can be melded together into a win-win, or a sweet spot, balance. "

"Go, Professor Anthony!" an inmate cawed. "School the dude!" The rough laughter of the yard erupted through the room.

The guards shifted forward, and after a moment expectant quiet returned.

"Were you again just called 'Professor?'" Parsons asked.

"A nickname—I'll accept that," said Anthony.

"May we return to the discussion?"

"Picture a game of chess," Anthony said. "When two people play chess, they agree to cooperate with the rules and with each other, yet at the same time they compete against one another. Where is the self-contradiction there? Or if two competing auto manufactures decide to engineer an engine together that they will each independently put into their competing cars, where is the self-contradiction there? The manufacturers have found the sweet spot within *the synthesis of opposites*-between cooperating and competing."

Parson's neck had turned scarlet. "It's easy to hide behind metaphors and rhetorical examples. But let me test if I'm hearing you correctly. You are trying to convince these poor fellows that *music* and chess explain why they are in prison?"

"Discordant music is an abstract example, yes. I think humans like and appreciate music because they subconsciously feel that it's a signature, a code signal, of the synthesis we seek in the universe. Emotionaly moving music kicks off endorphins that act like opiates in the brain. When the sounds and rhythms of music feel right, our subconscious tells us something *is* right. So, yes. There is a synthesis of order and chaos in good music—music that moves us. And yes, finding that balance in life generally can help keep people away from crime, away from disorder."

A slender black inmate rose to his feet. "I was an artist before I came in here, and what the Prof Anthony says makes sense. When you're doing a painting, you don't want total disorder, but on the other hand, you don't make everything one color, too orderly. It's boring. You need contrast. Variation."

Anthony added . . . "A few hundred years ago or so the philosopher Frances Hutcheson backs up what this man says, using the words 'uniformity' for cooperation and 'variety' for competition."

"Same thing with movies," said another inmate, tattooed to his earlobes. "Gotta change things up."

"Yeah," said a third inmate. "Tits *and* ass!"

This time the guards stepped forward before the laughter even got started. "You dirt-bags want us to clear this room?" one asked.

The cons fell silent, but their grins remained in place.

Parsons tried to straighten his bow tie, but it ended up even more askew. His eyes narrowed. "This gentleman seems to fancy himself a philosopher, yet if his theory had any validity outside his own imagination, surely someone before him would have discussed it. So, Mr.—what is your name?" He stretched his neck to get a better look at Anthony.

"Anthony Darren."

"Perhaps you'll thrill us with your depth of philosophical insight by revealing what the great thinkers of the past have said about this theory of yours."

The cons looked at Anthony. He realized more and more orange jumpsuits were squeezing into the room. He shrugged. "I believe you'll find that from Socrates right up to the present day, each major philosopher had a different point of view along a spectrum ranging from egoistic, greedy, competitive behavior on one end to total cooperation and submission at the other. Using their own words, they all effectively explained where they believed human behavior falls on the continuum between competitive and cooperative."

"That's—"

"For example, Hobbes was pessimistic, believing the nature of man to be greedy and competitionistic. John Locke, on the other hand, believed man to be basically good, which he defined as cooperative. But many other philosophies take a more centrist view; they speak of a need for both elements to exist in balance. The Yin/Yang of Taoism is one; Hegel's description of a synthesis of opposites is another."

"Hegel was—"

Although the preferred organized sports of most of the inmates were boxing and football, they turned their heads the other direction in unison like spectators at Wimbledon.

Parsons was shaking his head. "Mr. Darren, where on your spectrum would you place such dissimilar thinkers as, say, Voltaire, who described the human as a 'Noble Savage,' and Friedrich Nietzsche, who believed in the development of the superman?"

"Actually, it was Rousseau, not Voltaire, who spoke of the native human as a 'Noble Savage,'" commented Anthony.

Parsons opened his mouth, closed it. Now, his neck was the color of a blood orange.

"Regardless," Anthony went on, "in my interpretation, 'noble' means cooperative; 'savage' means competitive. Friedrich Nietzsche argued that the dominant force of history is the 'will to power,' but that there should be a 'transvaluation of values' wherein 'feminine virtues'—he meant compassion, cooperation, submissiveness—would merge with 'masculine virtues', which he considered to be bravery, strength, and competition—to achieve 'greatness rather than mere goodness.'"

Parsons fumbled through his notes. The captain of the guards strode up, cleared his throat and turned toward the audience. "Dr. Parsons appreciates this opportunity to have spoken to you, but the lecture is now over. You are excused back to your blocks."

As the men began leaving, the professor raised his voice. "I have a new book coming out next month. I'll leave my address with the captain if you want to purchase one."

The men ignored him.

He did not even look at Anthony, who was one of the last to leave.

Later that day he saw Hector walking down the corridor of the cellblock in a prison-issue suit, carrying the complementary suitcase in one hand, the other hand waving to the hooting inmates he passed. At the locked door of Anthony's house he stopped and waited until the whistles and catcalls subsided. Then he let the suitcase drop, and using two hands gave Anthony a handshake through the bars. "Professor, if there's anything I can ever do for you, let me know. One day when I get some money, I intend to pay you for the legal services you gave me. By the way, thanks for helpin me out with Dr Parsons today too. You sent him away thinking, and I hope *re-thinking.*"

"Ah, forget all that, Hector." Anthony tried to smile. "Helping you on the brief took me out of my own misery for a while. Besides, if I'm not mistaken, you already *did* pay me."

"Why, Professor, I have no idea what you're talking about."

Anthony's mouth quirked up in the corner. "So where are you going now? I mean, other than out the front gate?"

"Can't say . . . but I wouldn't be surprised if I migrate south for the winter. Down near the Equator, if you get that."

"Got it."

Hector glanced around, his smile fading. "Anthony, if you ever want to reach me, here's my sister's address." He held a scribbled-on scrap of paper through the bars. "She lives in LA and will be able to find me wherever I am."

"Thanks." Anthony folded the scrap into his shirt pocket.

"Hang tough, *amigo.*" Hector turned and walked away.

"I will." Anthony said, but couldn't hear himself above the renewed roar of whistles, catcalls and clattering metal.

Several weeks later the clang of a steel door echoed in the air. "Attorney coming through!" a guard called.

"Who gives a shit?" a solitary inmate shouted, but the usual cacophony of jeers and bangs dimed measurably, as it usually did when someone was there on a mission for a prisoner. Still, Anthony could tell the approaching footsteps and jangle of keys was heading his way.

He started to sit up on his bunk. *Hal?* Then he lay back down. *Don't get your hopes up.*

But the footsteps and keys fell silent at the door of his house. "Darren, you lucky shit, your attorney is here."

Anthony looked up as the door rumbled open and Hal stepped in. "How are you doing, Anthony?" he asked with a smile. Then he turned to the guard. "Thank you; I'll let you know when I need my paralegal brought in."

"I exist to serve you," the guard said, and sauntered away.

Anthony waited a few seconds then said, "I'm hanging in there, Hal. It's good to see you." They shook hands and Anthony motioned Hal to sit on his bunk. He drew up a stool for himself.

Hal looked around as if mesmerized by the décor of the cell.

"Okay," Anthony said. "So it's bad news."

Hal sighed, shrugged. "They turned you down. I'm so sorry."

"It was good of you to come in person," Anthony said over a high-pitched ringing tone that cascaded through the entire prison. His next opportunity to appeal would not come for years.

"Are you okay?" asked Hal.

"I'll make it," Anthony whispered. Then he raised his chin. "One of these days I'll stroll down that catwalk with you, Hal. I swear it." He clenched his fists. "All right, what happened? What am I up against?"

"It's political, basically. A mob of good ol' boys led by your old friends Hooks and James are pulling strings against you all over the state. Also, you'll have to explain this one to me, Anthony, but somehow word got to the hearing board that you might have had an inmate killed in here—Steve Williams, the man who testified against you."

Anthony leaned back in the chair. "It's true that he was in here, and it's true he was killed—but I had nothing to do with it."

"Another unfortunate coincidence, then."

"The story of my recent life." Anthony pulled a sour face. "But let's face facts, Hal. You and I both knew they weren't going to let me out this time around, no matter what. I'm still too hot."

"You're probably right." Hal looked around the cell again. "Where do you do your writing?"

"In the library."

"Is that where you wrote your article about prison reform? The one that got published in *Social Science*?"

Anthony's eyebrows rose. "You know about that?"

"The better question is, 'Does the warden know about that?' Because the answer could have had an effect on your parole consideration, you know."

"I knew it was a possibility, but . . . I had a few things to say."

"Yes, that was clear from the article." Hal shook his head. "Anthony, how did you manage to even get it out for submission? It couldn't possibly have gone through the prison censors."

Anthony smiled. "Being a model prisoner means keeping your nose clean, following the rules, cooperating all the time. But you know I don't believe in total cooperation, so whenever possible I manage to work in a little competition . . . at the system's expense."

"And their embarrassment, no doubt."

"More like anger. Last week the warden called me in and implied I might find myself cleaning toilets and loading the trash truck if I don't get smart. Basically he was threatening my library job."

"Are you no longer lecturing to the inmates?"

"Ah. Well, no . . . there was a bit of a fracas in the lecture hall a few months ago. Some embarrassment concerning a visiting scholar. Afterward I was disinvited from participating further in prisoner education."

"That's a shame."

"Not really. It gives me more time to work on my next book."

"Your *next* book?"

"About the 'hidden hand' of *the synthesis* in major historical events."

"But what about your *first* book?"

"My agent has been submitting it for several months now; I completed it in record time right after the fracas in the lecture hall. Smuggling it all out a few pages at a time took a lot longer."

"Its status?"

"No response. Presumably it's being read. I told my agent I've got nothing *but* time."

Hal looked at his watch. "Speaking of time, I have an appointment with your prison counselor in a few minutes. While I'm gone my paralegal will come in to get information for your parole reconsideration."

Anthony gritted. "Great. Tell him if he works all night I can still catch my flight to the French Riviera in the morning."

"I'll do that."

A few minutes later Anthony heard the guard's shout: "Attorney paralegal coming through!" The whistling and hooting started up in its usual automatic fashion, but swiftly escalated to a deafening pitch. When the door rattled open Anthony looked up to see Laura, briefcase in hand, beaming at him. Even in a business skirt and jacket she looked like a mirage from the Moulin Rouge.

Anthony waited until the guard was gone, then opened his arms and backed up against the wall behind his double bunk, out of sight of most of the other cells. Laura came toward him and he drew her close. The intoxication of her fragrance, her smooth skin on his cheek, her silky lips wetting his mouth . . .

"Why did I ever let you go?" he whispered in her ear.

"Because you were an idiot."

"Now you sound like my daughter."

"That's okay; I was an idiot back then too."

"Thanks for taking some of the blame." Anthony slid his hands up her sides . . .

Down the catwalk rattled the jangle of keys and the staccato beat of a baton dragging across the bars. Anthony pushed Laura gently onto the stool and sat on his bunk, hoping their disarranged clothing would not give them away.

The guard peered in. "Darren, is your shyster coming back soon? Time's getting short . . . Well, not for you." He sauntered off.

Anthony shook his head. "Welcome to Hotel Graybar. Are you really Hal's paralegal?"

"For today, sure. Listen, I've got a few things to report."

"About my book?"

"Anthony. . . ."

"I know; patience, patience. So, what, then?"

"I found out several of Herbert Hooks' investors have filed civil suits against him, charging him with carving out extraordinary fees disguised as expenses and salaries for himself and Egan James."

"Really."

"Yes. Egan is an officer, director, *and* corporate counsel for Hooks' companies. Right now, from what my sources say, he's especially busy with the lawyering part. Not that any of the lawsuits are getting anywhere."

"Hooks still has his political clout?"

"And tons of money to back it up; he's made jumbo-sized campaign contributions to everyone from state legislators to U.S. Senators. But. . . ."

"Yes?"

"Well, there's one guy—a young Congressman named Richard Morrison, from the thirty-second district—who actually must have turned Hooks' money down. Turns out this guy, Morrison, knows about finances and markets, so he's become a real thorn in the sides of people who prey on unsophisticated investors. Even better, he just became a candidate for the U.S. Senate."

"He's honest, knowledgeable *and* refuses shady money? Can't win."

"Don't be so cynical. He's very charismatic. Even though his own party isn't terribly fond of him because they can't control him; he keeps winning elections."

"Sounds like my kind of politician."

"I thought so too."

Anthony sighed. "Unfortunately whether he wins or not won't do *me* much good, except for the satisfaction I'd get having Hooks and James sharing the next cell over."

She didn't smile. "I wish I could do more for you, Anthony. But I do have a bit of news I think you'll like."

"Tell me."

"Joe got an early release. He's already out."

"You're kidding! Oh, man, that's great!" And he meant it, despite the despair that he was still here. "I'm glad he finally got a little mercy."

"He wishes he could visit you, but he's not allowed to contact you at all—a condition of his parole."

"Yes, we mustn't have felons plotting new crimes together."

She rested a hand on his knee for a moment, then removed it.

"He got a job mending nets on the docks, but he spends the rest of his time working to get you released. Sylvia says he's a fanatic: he writes letters to judges, congressmen, senators, the U.S. Attorney's office, even the President of the United States. Not to mention good ol' Judge Winchester and every newspaper and magazine in town—over and over again."

"Oh, boy, now Sylvia's going to hate me."

"She's *helping* him."

"I won't ask if they've gotten anywhere; I'd already know if they had."

The guard reappeared at the bars. "Lady, step away from the prisoner. Time's up."

Anthony rose to his feet, his eyes locked on Laura's. "One last thing. Andrea graduates from law school on June 16th. Please ask Hal if he can get me a furlough for that one day."

The guard snorted. "Good luck with that."

Several days later Anthony gripped a telephone handset still warm and sweaty from the last inmate. "So what did you find out, Hal?"

"Once again I have to apologize, Anthony."

Hal said they wouldn't furlough him for even half a day; that Andrea wasn't a close enough relative; that maybe Anthony should come out and disclose his true relationship with her.

Anthony clenched a fist so hard his entire body trembled. "No. All I've ever been for her, from the day she was born, is trouble. Now that she's job hunting my situation could really harm her, especially if she goes with one of the big firms."

"Is that her preference?"

Anthony couldn't disguise his sudden enthusiasm. "She's got the pick of the litter, Hal; just about every firm she's applied to has offered her a position. I've tried to convince her to go into a big private firm and stay away from litigation, but she's interested in the courtroom."

"Like father, like daughter."

"Oh, let's hope not. But you know where she's most interested in working? The US Attorney's office in the Southern District."

"What? You mean John Woods would be her boss?"

"Ironic, isn't it?"

"Is it?

"That said, I assume John doesn't know who her real father is."

"He doesn't even know *her*. It's been too long since he saw her sitting in the courtroom, and her last name is Burns, so that won't ring any bells. If they ask her who her father is, she certainly won't hide the truth."

"Well, she'll certainly get the best training and experience in Woods' office. What a gutsy move. Listen, if she gets the job, tell her congratulations for me. And also congratulations on graduating. Will she have anyone with her there to celebrate?"

"Mary and Laura will be there, and her half-brother Johnny if they can find him."

"What do you mean?"

"He's the outdoors type; moved to Mammoth where he can ski. He attends community college up there and works construction in the summer."

"That reminds me. Whatever happened to *his* father?"

Anthony shook his head. "Apparently when John turned seventeen he went back to Kentucky to find that out for himself. He found Billy in a VA Hospital, dying of cirrhosis of the liver. Johnny stayed with him during his last week of life."

"Sound like they reconciled."

"He's a good kid. I hope he got some closure." Anthony paused, and the words just popped out of his mouth: "And I wish I could visit him in Mammoth."

21 Snow Flake and Political Ache

"This is good work, Andi, "Brian Churchill said. "Very impressive."

Andrea smiled. Even though her office was the smallest in the US Attorney's suite, any boost she got from big gun trial lawyers like Brian sparked her pride. She was playing in the major leagues, window or no window.

Brian's comment referred to the draft of an opening statement she had prepared for his trial starting in a few days. As he read, sitting across from her steel desk with his feet propped up on the blotter and his tie loosened, she watched him for any other reaction. During her first few months here she'd helped several veteran Assistant US Attorneys get ready for their trials. Often she also sat at the counsel table in court with them, handling exhibits, lining up and interviewing witnesses, digesting transcripts of depositions. All good experience.

It didn't hurt that she also had a secret weapon: her father, confidentially providing invaluable instruction on the nuances of trial work.

What a fine surprise it had been when Brian asked her to write him an opening statement for this trial. For one thing he wanted her to get the experience; for another, he had limited time and wanted a second legal mind to cross-check his work. Still, it was an honor to be chosen for these tasks. Brian's previous assistant, Sarah Billings, now went out every morning loaded with briefcases and exhibits to try cases on her own.

That will be me some day, Andrea thought.

Brian dragged his feet off her desk. "Andrea, this is perfect. We're going with it."

On the morning of trial, the judge wanted a preliminary conference with the attorneys. Brian let Andrea accompany him into chambers. Defense attorney Kelly had just arrived. A graying, curly-haired, wiry, close cropped Judge Thomas Marshall sat at his large dark oak desk with his suit jacket off and sleeves rolled up. From what Andrea had heard, this man was a glutton for work. The pent-up energy in his body seemed about to pop his chest buttons.

Brian introduced Andrea as his associate counsel. The judge rose and gave her a warm and vigorous handshake. After they all settled in their chairs Judge Marshall said, "Give me a little overview from your side, Mr. Churchill."

Each counsel in turn gave a brief synopsis—basically about the Secretary of Labor's action to shut down a shipyard until safety regulations were met. Three workers had died in separate accidents. They'd refused to follow regs because they believed the cure was more dangerous than the disease—their life jackets made their welding extra difficult and dangerous as they hung outside the ship.

"Are you both ready?"

"Yes, Your Honor," Churchill and Kelly said almost together.

"Very well, then. Be prepared to start in five minutes."

Back outside, Brian and Andrea had no sooner taken their seats at the counsel table than the clerk announced a ten-minute delay.

Brian got right back to his feet. "I've got to make a phone call," he said, pressing a hand against his stomach as if to make sure his shirt was tucked in. "Andi, if the judge is ready to take the bench before I get back, please ask for a few minutes' delay." He walked off, leaving the synopsis of his opening statement and notes on the counsel table.

Ten minutes later the clerk announced the judge ready to proceed, and Brian had not returned. The judge stood in the open doorway in his black robe, looking at his wristwatch.

"Mr. Johnson," Andrea said to the clerk, "would you ask the court if we can have three more minutes? I'll try to find Mr. Churchill. He said he would be right back."

The judge overheard her request. "Three minutes," he said impatiently.

Andrea ran into the hall. No sign of Brian. She ran to the hall phone and called the office. They hadn't heard from him.

When she returned to the courtroom the judge sat at the bench.

"Ready to proceed, counsel?" he asked. "Or should the government's case be dismissed?"

Andrea gulped. "Ready, Your Honor." She stepped to the lectern and, Brian's yellow pad in hand, commenced the opening statement.

Five days later Andrea found herself wrapping up the trial, having argued and submitted the entire matter to the judge. Brian Churchill had spent those five days in a hospital bed following surgery for a ruptured appendix. The "phone call." he had made had actually been a trip across the street to buy antacids for his stomach pain.

To Andrea's shock she won her first trial, as well as the respect of Brian Churchill, John Woods and all the other big guns in the office.

At the end of the day she phoned Anthony, hoping the news would give him a lift. "Mr. Woods asked me to think about which I'd prefer: trial work on the civil side—mainly corporate securities enforcement—or prosecuting drug cases. I'd get a lot more trial experience, faster, if I did the drug cases. What do you think?"

"Did he say if you'd have to work yourself up the ladder in the securities field?"

"He said I'd be the office securities specialist almost from the start; I'd be the only U.S. Attorney here doing it. Sarah Billings, who's two years my senior, told John she wants to continue trying drug cases."

There was a pause; she could almost hear her father thinking. Then he said, "My recommendation is that you go into securities enforcement. You'll gain broader experience in the civil area, which will be useful if you ever go into private practice."

She smiled. "I was leaning that way myself. We're thinking more and more alike every day."

"I hope not too much; don't forget to have a life. Don't burn yourself out. Speaking of which, I haven't heard much about your social life for a while."

"That's because I don't have one. My mind has been on other things. Besides, I haven't met any guys who go around in shining armor, carrying lances and riding mighty steeds, which are my minimum requirements in a boyfriend."

She was pleased to hear her father laugh. "That'll change, if I know my girl."

Then someone in the background snarled that his time was up.

"You should get out and circulate," Sarah Billings told Andrea. "All you do is work, work, work. Now that you've won five good-sized trials in a row they're starting to call you 'Mad Dog' Andi around here."

"They are?"

"Could be worse. As the Queen of Drug Law, my nickname is 'Doperina.' C'mon, go with me tonight. You'll get to see the hottest candidate for U.S. Senator."

"Hot? Are you talking about Richard Morrison?"

"He's the man. I'm one of his volunteers. But hey; if good-looking, intelligent, charming Congressmen aren't your thing, it's okay; there'll be all kinds of other guys there. You do remember *guys*, don't you?"

"I have a vague recollection." Andrea shrugged. "What the heck. Okay, let's go. This office is turning me into a dreary mole."

"Glad *you* said it."

At dusk they stepped out of Sarah's sports car in a self-parking lot in the downtown area. Andrea took in Sarah's green eyes and white flashing smile, which contrasted strikingly with her black satin skin and cascade of relaxed curls. Andrea looked down at herself. "I got ready in such a hurry I must look awful."

Sarah raised one eyebrow. "Yes, indeed. Big hazel eyes, auburn hair, sexy dress . . . yep, I'm ashamed to be seen with you." She tossed her head. "Come on, you're going to knock 'em dead."

Their spiked heels clicked over the Spanish-tiled street leading to the outdoor rally in the historical, and increasingly trendy, Gaslamp Quarter. A zinging beat and the blare of brass from a Dixieland band reverberated off the buildings, and red, white and blue bunting adorned the barricades cordoning off the street. Strings of Tivoli lights and multitudes of colored balloons laced the trees. Laughing people moved everywhere as Andi stepped into the crowd. *Oh, how good it feels to be with people having fun for a change.*

A drumroll drew everyone's attention to the platform decorated with more bunting as the candidate, Richard Morrison, stepped up to the microphone.

"I see that look on your face," Sarah said into Andrea's ear,

although the roar of the crowd still almost drowned her out. "Told you he was a hunk."

Morrison gave a short but intelligent talk that Andrea thought contained far more substance and sincerity than the usual political speech, but was at the same time delivered with the charisma that made people want to line up and vote.

The next thing she knew Sarah was pulling her by the hand toward the platform. Up ahead, the young candidate for the US Senate leaned down from amongst the red, white and blue decorations to shake hands with his supporters.

He glanced over the crowd and waved at Sarah—then, for half-a-second, locked eyes with Andi. In that heartbeat she felt him take her in, and thanked her intuition for her carefully chosen high-waisted navy blue summer jacket, opened to a red and white polka dot blouse. It had enough plunge to reveal the modest diamond crested locket necklace her father had given her when she was sixteen.

As the line moved her closer to Morrison, she thought he glanced toward her several more times. A thrill rushed in at the thought. Even with the distraction of hundreds of enthusiastic well-wishers, he kept looking back at *her*. When she was within twenty feet of the stage she was absolutely sure she was right: she caught and held his eyes for a full second.

Haven't flirted like this since college. Better be careful. This guy has some chemistry. . . .

Sarah leaned toward her ear. "Don't look now, Snow Flake, but you've got a man staring at you. Isn't he beautiful? Give me your honest evaluation in ten words or more."

"Face: tan, well-sculptured. Body: looks like he plays tennis regularly. Tall, relaxed, confident but not cocky. Face just craggy enough to show some experience and wisdom." Andi laughed. "Okay, that was more than ten words."

"You sure you're not a casting agent?" Sarah said.

Then they were face to face with him. As Sarah introduced Andi, she again made direct contact with Morrison's clear blue, smiling eyes. The three chatted for half a minute above the cacophony of music and voices; later Andi would not be able to remember a word of the conversation; for her everything disappeared in a crystalline light.

As she and Sarah walked away she said, "He *is* single?"

"Where have you been? Those lines of women you see? They're all waiting to try on the glass slipper." She shook her head. "Just long relationships with a special girlfriend or two. Actually, it's almost unheard of for a Senatorial candidate, being single. But he sure had eyes for you."

"That just shows how intelligent and perceptive he is."

Sarah laughed. "I told you."

On Monday morning Andrea dawdled over the paperwork on her desk and wondered why she couldn't seem to concentrate. She'd had the same problem all weekend, actually, and it was completely unlike her. Could her father's prediction about burnout already be coming true? That was ridiculous; she'd barely gotten started as a—

She jumped at the buzz of her intercom. "Andi, would you believe it?" Millie said. "Congressman Morrison is on the line!"

"Wait. Congressman Morrison is calling *me*?"

"It's him, all right. No prank. I've fantasized over his voice enough times to know the real thing when I hear it. Do me a favor and ask him if he has any brothers."

"Don't get so excited, Millie; he's probably calling to ask about the Federal Election Code." She took a quick breath. "Put him through."

The next Friday at noon the maître d at the Executive Club led Andrea to a cozy corner table where Congressman Rich Morrison waited. She hoped her excitement wasn't showing too much.

The conversation began over hors d'oeuvres and continued through lunch. Andi was only vaguely aware of the other diners in the room and the hail of curious glances that fell on her and her . . . date.

When he asked about her background and education, and then listened with what appeared to be every shred of his attention, she tried to remind herself that coming across as sincere and fascinated was something politicians do for a living . . . but she answered nonetheless—skimming the bare essentials of her midwestern childhood: enlisted army brat, born only eight months or so after the stepfather marriage, *so she wasn't going there, if he didn't mind*; mother and stepfather passing long ago. She basically began the story with college . . .

He was delighted that she had attended law school, which he'd known, and they talked about that for quite a while. That gave her the opportunity to swing the questions around on him.

"Ivy League undergrad," he said. "Major in Political Science, minor in Economics, then Law School."

"Private, Eastern, patrician," she said.

"I know what you're thinking, but it wasn't that way at all. In fact, for me the best part of going to school back there was developing friendships with students with scattered political and cultural views—from very liberal to very conservative. If I'm fortunate enough to win this campaign, I hope to adopt the best points each has to offer and synthesize them into a coherent policy."

"Synthesize them?" Andi said.

"What?"

"Nothing . . . it's just that I know someone who loves that word, 'synthesize.' Maybe we can talk about that later—but for now, please go on."

"Okay, let me give you an example. One of my college acquaintances was Rudy Bramoso."

"Rodolfo Bramoso? Now the Communist leader of Costallegre?"

"Back then he was just an international law student on a scholarship. As for being a Communist, he's adopted that label . . . but I'm not sure it fits."

"No offense, but politically speaking, isn't it dangerous to be buddies with a man like that? Hasn't he been accused of all kinds of civil rights abuses?"

"Acquaintance, not buddy. He knows I categorically disagree with his political and economic views, but I don't want to lose contact with him. Apart from friendship, I don't see the sense in closing off contact with a political opponent just because it makes for bad PR."

"What about the President? He's about as conservative as they come, but he endorsed you. What does he think about your knowing Bramoso?"

"I told him I don't mix my political views with my choice of acquaintances, and he said he wished he could afford to do the same thing. So I've managed to keep a good relationship with both him and Bramoso, which would be great if they need a mediator in the future."

"Do you see that happening?"

He looked at her with luminous intensity. "As long as the lines of communication stay open, anything is possible."

The moment she walked back into the office, Sarah and Millie pounced.

"The lunch was wonderful," Andrea said. "Oh, and before you ask—Rich has two brothers. One is already married, though, and the other is back in Connecticut."

"Bummer," Millie said.

"Did he ask you out again?" Sarah demanded.

"He did."

"An evening date?" This time from Millie.

"Yes. *Yes* . . ." And Andi fought the adolescent urge to dance around the room with her friends.

Sarah held her at arm's length. "Don't blow it," she said with mock seriousness. "Don't make him think you're too anxious."

"But I'm *not* anxious—just excited. So far I think he's great . . . but don't forget, I don't really know him, and he must have a hundred other women friends."

"Five hundred," Millie said. "Maybe six."

"And there's also the fact that he doesn't really know *me*," Andi added.

Seven months later, she could no longer say that. After 28 weeks of intermittent but exclusive dating, she had told Rich Morrison more about herself than she had ever told anyone else.

But not everything. Using every evasive skill she had learned in the last eight years, she had managed to not reveal any details about her real father. She knew that it could not last forever. She and Rich spent every break he'd had from Washington together. Long ago her vulnerability had passed beyond the point of no return. And this night, from the moment they stepped into the taxi that took them to the La Jolla Playhouse, until now, as they rode another taxi to his place, he had dropped more than a few hints about a certain subject . . .

She just hoped he wouldn't bring it into the open just yet. Not until she had the answer; until she had solved the problem.

"The play was great," he said, pulling her against him.

"I agree," she said, inhaling the scent of his aftershave. No matter whether Rich wore black tie attire as he did this evening, or sweats for a late night jog, when she was near him all her senses turned on. Her heart raced to him, drawn by a warm light, a very sensitive human light. She lay quietly against him, the movement of the taxi adding to the vibrations their bodies exchanged.

The multicolored lights of the street flickered by and he raised her head, his fingertips under her chin, and gazed at her. "Andi, some important things will be happening in my life soon, whether I win the election or not. Either way, I don't want to go through it alone. I want you by my side. I want to share the rest of my life with you. Will you share your life with me? Will you marry me. . . ? Now, right away?"

She had dreamt of this moment. Framed it in her mind . . . and feared it. A few seconds of hesitation shattered the night.

"Rich . . . I love you more than I ever knew was possible . . . but your political career is . . . is . . . so important, not only for you but for all of us. Don't you think it's best if we . . . wait until after the election before we decide?"

She felt him sag. "No. I don't see why."

"It's just that . . . I worry that if you marry during the campaign it might distract your constituency and hurt your chances."

In the slight cooling of his hands she felt the effects of rejection.

"Rich, please don't press me on this now," she said. "I want you more than anything in the world, but for *your* sake we have to wait. Please tell me you'll wait and . . . and . . . after the election, things will be better. The time will be right."

He shook his head. "Andi, you're a complete mystery to me." He looked out the window, the lights and street scenes flashing past. Finally he sighed. "Okay. I'm devastated, but I do think you love me, so I'll wait. But listen: no matter what, on election night you'll hear me ask the same question again, and this time you'd better be ready to answer . . . or I'll get a monk's robe, find me a cave and never come out."

She lay her head back on his chest and reflected on what she had just done. Surely it was the right thing. During her father's trial, his lawyer had successfully kept the facts of her true parentage away from the jury. But no such motion existed in politics. She could imagine the headline: *MORRISON MARRIES MURDERER'S DAUGHTER*. Forget about being invited to a presidential cocktail party then; the Washington crowd would rather be burned by lava-hot cheese hors d'oeuvres stuck to the roofs of their mouths than be seen talking to the young Congressman's wife. Or, worse, the Congressman himself.

Despite what she had told Rich, she wasn't sure she could subject him to the political risk of marrying her even after the election, and even if he won. The skeleton in her closet would become the skeleton in *his* closet; it could destroy his career, his brilliant future. More than that, if Andi ever managed to get her father a federal pardon, people would naturally assume she had benefited—perhaps even improperly—from Rich's political influence.

So she tried to relax, tried to convince herself she was doing the best thing, even though Rich's words kept looping through her mind: *Andi, you're a complete mystery to me. . . .*

22 Fusing Order and Chaos

After waiting his turn for the cell block phone, Anthony returned to his solitary cell and lay prone on his bunk. Hands behind his head, he fixed his gaze on the bottom of the mattress above.

Andi had asked his opinion; he had given it even though he didn't think he deserved the confidence she had in him. They agreed that her biggest threat was the familiar duo of Hooks and James and their business associates, all of whom had opposed Morrison in the primaries. The more details Anthony had given Andrea about them, the more concerned she had become.

But she was worried about the wrong thing, of course. *I'm the real problem.*

He was so tired of that. Why was he the problem? Not because he was a liar, a thief and a murderer . . . but because people *believed* him to be those things. And why did people believe them? Because of a missing piece of paper and the testimony of a false witness.

What is the opposite of lies and deceit? Where is the point of synthesis between them?

Abruptly he rolled out of his bunk, blood coursing through his cramped arteries. He put on his reading glasses—a recently developed necessity, and from the drawer of a small steel cabinet next to his bunk took out the letters he had received from Hal Goldman. He reread the parts dealing with the Hooks Company and its transactions, pondered for a moment how those comments dovetailed with the things Laura had recently told him . . . then set his beat-up portable typewriter on the cabinet, sat on the edge of the open toilet bowl and began typing.

To the Enforcement Division of the Securities Exchange Commission,Washington DC.

Reference: Possible violations of the 1933 Federal Securities act of the United States by Southern California Empire Bank Corp. and its related Herbert Hooks corporations and their General Counsel. . . .

Three hours later, after looking up federal securities code sections in the law books he kept in his cell, he finished the letter and folded the pages. For whatever it was worth, he had released a jaguar back into the jungle. The letter's last words had given him particular satisfaction:

Many thanks for your consideration.

Sincerely yours,
Anonymous

Whistles, horns, shouts, songs, blaring bands, smiles, hugs, lights, placards, balloons, a fusillade of lights and colors and enthusiasm cascaded down on Richard Morrison as the latest returns on the election came in over the monitor in the convention hall of the Beverly Wilshire Hotel in L.A. Smiling dizzily, Rich walked down a crowded aisle toward the center of a large stage where a prominent sign congratulated the youngest senator in the United States. Another read *36 To Get Ready, 36 To Go.*

With over a thousand supporters shouting congratulations and encouragement, Rich Morrison stood on the rostrum and raised his hands. But banners kept waving and songs thundered through the room. Finally he just began speaking, and quiet quickly followed. The words flowed from him with an eloquence that surprised him because they were not from the victory speech he had prepared. He felt as though he'd floated into the audience and was watching himself talk, like an out-of-body experience, as if he was drifting above the hall looking into people's faces—and he saw Andrea's, radiating excitement, beauty, intelligence. . . .

The inner circle of the senator-elect crowded into his hotel suite. Milling people shouldered their way through the rooms, drinks in hand. Rich escorted Andrea into the bathroom, the only available privacy, and closed the door. In the mirror he saw his hair partly fallen across his forehead, but didn't care.

"Andi, I'm thrilled we won of course . . . but you know what I'm most happy about? You said I should ask you again after the election." He took both her hands; pulled her into an embrace. "So I'm asking . . . I'm asking you now."

She clung to him, her fingers pressing hard, and buried her face against his neck. In the mirror he saw tears streaming from her closed eyes, but she said nothing.

"Andi—look at me. Why are you crying? Just say *yes*."

"I can't," she said, her chin trembling. "I can't say anything."

"What's wrong? What the hell is standing between us? Without you this whole thing, the election, means nothing! Don't you understand? If you're telling me no again, I might as well flush this night down this toilet."

"Forgive me, Rich." She pulled away. "I have to go."

She opened the door, stepped into the anteroom, picked up her coat and pushed her way through the crowd toward the door. She thought she heard Rich call after her, but it might have just been the excited thunder of the crowd.

"So . . . how is he doing?" Laura asked.

"Are you asking about Rich or Dad?" Andi spoke into the telephone receiver trapped between her shoulder and ear while she shrugged out of her jacket. She'd just returned from Brockton.

"Either one, I guess," Laura said. "I think we're both feeling like we've failed our men."

Andi dropped a clot of unopened mail on the coffee table and threw herself onto the couch. "Yeah. Well, I don't see too much of Rich these days; he's busy slipping into his new role, you know. Although last week he said, 'At least you know where I'm going when I disappear for days on end.'"

"Ah, sweetie. . . ."

"I wish I could go public about who I am, announce Dad's identity and innocence to the world, get it all over with. But I can't do that unless I break up with Rich first. It's terrible; a conundrum."

"And you talked to your father about it?"

"He told me not to put my mind ahead of my heart. He said that when he was young he made that mistake—he didn't follow his heart. Well, actually what he said was that he forgot everything he'd learned from Rousseau." She couldn't help laughing.

Laura laughed, too. "At least he didn't tell you he's finally learned to synthesize intellect and emotion. That's what he said to me."

"Such a romantic." Andrea wiped her eyes. "So . . . what's the latest on his manuscript?"

There was a pause. "I hate to say it, but I've pretty much run through my list of publishers—and still no takers. That's why I feel like I'm failing your father."

"Damn." Andi poked at the pile of mail. Bills, sales flyers . . . same old stuff. "I just have a feeling it's crucial we get that book to press. It's important to Dad, of course, but it's more than that. I think it's an important work."

"The problem isn't with its content or even style," Laura said. "The publishers all like the book itself. What bothers them is that I won't give them the author's name or credentials. They want evidence he's qualified to write such a work. Of course there's nothing I can say about that . . . so they just give it a pass." She exhaled. "I wish we could say *you* wrote it; your Ph.D. and J.D. would impress them."

Andi was barely listening. She had reached the bottom of the mail pile and found an envelope addressed in Rich's impatient scrawl: *Ms. Andrea Burns.* Not *Andi.* Fingers shaking slightly, she struggled to tear the flap open.

"Wait a minute. . . ." Laura was saying into her ear. "Wait. Andi, I just had an idea. Andi . . . are you there?"

Andi managed to open the envelope and pulled out a single folded sheet of paper. Held it, still folded, between wilting fingers. "Yes. I'm here."

"Listen. You contributed a lot to *Fusing Order and Chaos.* Researched some of the concepts, even, right?"

Ms. Andrea Burns. He addressed it to Ms. Andrea Burns. . . .

I can't read this. I don't want to read this. "Yes," she said. "I did research; I even adapted the main theme for my Philosophy thesis. Why?"

"What I just said about your degrees . . . I was joking, but think about it. What if we try this again, only this time we list you and Anthony co-authors? Except we'll have him use a pen name. The two of you could even revise the manuscript together to incorporate your ideas. Do you think Anthony would agree to that?"

Andi's fingers began to unfold the letter; she ordered them to close it again. "I . . . I think he wants to get his ideas out to the world. That's all that matters to him. So yeah, I think he'd jump at whatever might work. He'd probably even consider what you're suggesting as an example of *the synthesis* at work."

"And you? Would you be all right with it?"

"Are you kidding? If it would help get Dad's work published . . ." She realized her treacherous fingers had unfolded the letter.

"The more I think about this, the better it sounds. And I'll bet Anthony would be thrilled. He's so proud of you. . . . Andi? Hello? Are you—"

"I'm here. Laura . . . I have to go. But I like your idea. I like it a lot. I'll talk to Dad about it. Soon, okay?"

She disconnected and set the receiver down, rattling, next to Rich's open letter.

Dearest Andrea,

I hate to say this, but considering the way things have been going, I think it would be best if we not see each other until we have both figured out if we can ever have a future together . . .

"I don't know, honey. . . ." Anthony said, his voice almost lost in the usual background clamor of shouts and clangs.

Andi sat straight in her chair. She in the office alone, having arrived long before anyone else, as had become her custom—along with being the last to leave. "What do you mean, you don't know?

Dad, it's your best bet for getting *published.* I thought that's what you wanted more than anything."

"Not at the expense of tainting your career if my identity gets out."

Jeez, I'm getting sick of hearing that. Don't you know what I'm going through because of your background, your ideas, your needs, your . . . ?

She took a deep breath. Let it out slowly. "My name would be on the copyright. Nobody could trace your pseudonym back to you."

"Pseudonym. . . ."

"Lots of authors have used them—everyone from Mark Twain to Adolph Hitler."

"Ah, the best of company. Come to think of it, Hitler even wrote his opus while he was in prison."

"Dad, you know what I mean."

"Yes, I do." He paused. "Is everything all right, Andi? You don't sound like yourself."

That's because I'm not even sure who I am. "I'm fine. I'm just . . . I want something to happen, Dad. For you, for me, for Laura, for somebody."

"Your Mr. Morrison seems to have had some good times lately."

"Yes. Yes, he has."

There was a long pause. Then Anthony said, "Okay, let's discuss pen names. . . ."

Eight weeks later Laura successfully placed *Fusing Order and Chaos* with a small, maverick publishing house specializing in New Age philosophy. Most of the publisher's books had cardboard covers and contained no bibliographies. *Fusing Order and Chaos* was different. Although a paperback, it carried both an extensive bibliography and a few pre-review citations by editors and prominent professionals.

Its authors were Andrea Burns, Ph.D., J.D. and a man named Bric Locket.

"Bric Locket." was a little joke by Anthony, *locked* in the Federal pen surrounded by *brick* walls.

Anthony pressed the receiver of the payphone tight against one ear and screwed a fingertip into the other ear. "It comes out in six months? You don't sound very excited."

A beat passed. Then: "Of course I'm excited, Dad. I'm just a little tired, that's all. Been working a lot."

"I should believe that excuse, given my own history," he said, "but I don't. One thing about living in prison: if you want to survive you have to learn subtext, instantly reading what people are really thinking. Andi, I haven't heard you mention Rich in two months. What's going on?"

"Rich and I aren't seeing each other anymore."

Anthony let his forehead press against the steel-lined wall next to the phone.

"He thinks something mysterious is holding me back," she said.

"Which it is. I thought . . . perhaps you were going to tell him the truth."

A brittle laugh—not Andi-like at all—clattered down the line. "Dad, I can't tell him the truth for the same reason you're calling yourself 'Bric Locket' on the cover of your own book: I have to protect a loved one from scandal."

"Shouldn't that be a decision you both make?"

"I told him about Billy's alcoholism. So he thinks I must have been abused as a child. You know, a while back I made a comment about how much he—Rich—was drinking, and he said he didn't have a problem; he said maybe my fears from my childhood were affecting our relationship. How's that for irony?"

Anthony pressed his head harder against the wall.

Andi sighed. "Anyway, he's dating another woman now."

Back in his cell, Anthony grabbed his heavy prison pillow, tossed it into the air and slugged it, slamming it into the wall across the tiny space. He wanted to punch the wall in the same spot. Punch through the wall, through all the walls that kept him separate from the world where he could *make things happen*.

He had to make something happen. But what? And how?

That letter he'd written to the SEC had apparently done no good. No cooperation there. No consilience.

He picked the pillow up again and tore it in half before he realized what he was doing.

"Mr. Hooks . . . a Mr. Micelli from the Securities and Exchange Commission in Washington, DC, is on line two."

"Goddamn government regulators," Hooks barked. "Have him talk to the comptroller."

"The comptroller is out to lunch. Mr. Micelli insists he talk to you because you're the only corporate officer available."

"Jesus. Okay, put the son-of-a-bitch on." He snatched up the phone. "Yes?"

"Mr. Hooks?" A young, respectful voice. Good. "Sorry to bother you, sir, but I have a few questions on the 10-Q form your company recently filed."

"Well, who are you?"

"Oh, I'm sorry, I thought I had explained that to your secretary. I'm with enforcement at the SEC. There are a few items on the 10-Q form your company filed that I—"

"This is a $400 million net worth company. I don't have time to waste on the phone with some clerk in Washington. Why can't you wait and talk to the comptroller?"

"It's just that . . . You see, Mr. Hooks, you're the one who signed the form and I have to ask *you*. As you know, because the 10-Q reports to the SEC and the IRS on how your publicly-traded company is doing financially, it's essential the public be accurately informed. I'm sure you agree that there can't be any misleading statements on it."

Hooks felt the sweat prickle out on his brow, his nose. "What are you saying, 'misleading statements?' We never make misleading statements. What's your question?"

"I'll get right to it, Mr. Hooks. Many of your investors have lost a lot of money. Someone sent us a written complaint. It appears as though you have substantially overstated the company's profits. Do you have an explanation for that? We've already seen several lawsuits filed."

"Whoever complained is full of . . . of . . . crap! What's his name?"

"Sorry. I couldn't tell you that even if I were allowed to; the letter was anonymous. However, it was written in such detail and backed with enough legal points and authorities that we were compelled to look into it."

"Anonymous, eh? I see." Hooks didn't care if Micelli sensed his contempt. After all, he'd helped the President of the United States get elected. He'd even advised on the appointment of the director of the SEC—this kid's boss!

Hooks' secretary stepped into his office, wearing a questioning look.

Hooks held the phone away from his mouth just enough to ensure he could be clearly overheard. "Who does this little prick think he is to call me—the president of this company—and take up my time with stupid questions? He's asking about idiot comments from anonymous complaints." He brought the receiver back to his lips. "What did you say your name is?"

"Micelli, Sir. M-I-C-E-L-L-I."

"What are you—a clerk, a civil servant, what?"

"I'm a deputy enforcement officer, a lawyer for the SEC."

"A lawyer; I should have figured. How long have you been out of law school?"

"Approximately two years."

"Well, listen. Don't bother me with your dumb questions. Call *our* lawyer, Egan James. He'll straighten your . . . he'll straighten you out. Anything more?"

"I guess not," Micelli replied in the same polite tone. "For now."

Hooks slammed down the receiver. "Where the hell is Egan?"

Andrea half-dragged and half-bounced her Turbo-trainer bike down the stairs and onto the secluded patio of the townhouse she and Susan rented and shared. Everything—the leaves, red bougainvillea, ceramic pots, the deck tile and especially the smooth surface of the Jacuzzi spa—reflected the Saturday morning sun. She set a large glass of orange juice near the bike alongside Thompson's *Darkness*

and Scattered Light. Wearing a bikini top, jogging shorts, and her high top Reebok aerobic shoes, she settled in place, reached for the book and started pumping the pedals.

Moments later the phone rang inside the townhouse. Reluctantly she climbed off the bike and answered. Wrong number. Just in case, she took the wireless phone out to the patio, set it down and recommenced pumping the pedals, the open book still on the handle bars. Soon sweat rolled down her nose and back and into the cleavage of her bikini top. Impulsively she unhooked the top and tossed it aside. The sun felt wonderful on her bare skin. Maybe the theory was true—about a little vitamin D on the boobs reducing health risks.

The phone rang again. Still pumping her legs, she picked it up and pushed the *on* button.

"Hey, mystery lady," a voice said.

She stopped pumping. "Rich?"

"Have you seen *Cats*?"

"Cats? Oh, you mean the musical? Yes, I have. Why?"

"You're out of breath. I hope I'm not interrupting anything . . . private. Can you talk?"

"I'm sure my Turbo-trainer could use a break."

"Oh, thank God. My jealousy barometer was pointing to 'thunderstorm.'"

"Wait. You break up with me via letter, date other women, don't contact me for eight months . . . and now you're jealous?"

He sighed. "Okay, I deserved that. Look, I have tickets to the matinee of *Cats* this afternoon. Did you like it when you saw it before?"

"Loved it."

"Then—if it's okay—we could see the show, then have a little dinner afterwards before I catch the redeye back to DC."

She realized that despite being off the Turbo-trainer for a couple of minutes, her heartbeat had not slowed down. What had her father said? *Andi, don't put your mind ahead of your heart.*

"You've got a date."

⚓

"This is my lucky night," Rich said as he guided his rental car into a parking space directly in front of La Gran Tapa restaurant.

Inside, the hostess checked their reservations and escorted them to a quaint window table open to the street.

"I loved *Cats* the first time, but I liked it even better tonight," Andrea said as Rich seated her.

"Same here." He sank into the opposite chair and stared at her. "God, it's good to see you again. You, me, live theater . . . almost like old times."

She looked him in the eye. "A little slower, please. As they say, a lot of water has gone under the bridge . . . and it's not easy paddling back upstream."

"Forgive me if I sound presumptuous . . . but you seem to be forgetting that *you* dumped *me*."

"I didn't—"

"You refused to marry me, Andi. Twice. Without any explanation. I had to wire my ego back together somehow."

She lowered her gaze.

The waitress chose that moment to reappear. From the menu Andi chose baby octopus in a lemon garlic sauce; Rich decided on *paella*.

"Let's try this again," he said after the waitress left. "What have you been up to the last few months?"

"Working a lot," she said. "Oh, and one other thing. Do you want to know why I brought along such a big purse?"

"I did wonder about that; you usually carry a—what is it?—a clutch."

She opened the purse, pulled out a book and handed it to him. He raised his eyebrows and examined the cover. "*Fusing Order and Chaos*. What's this?"

"Look closer."

"Wait. You *wrote* this! Well, co-wrote it. Andi, you mentioned working on a book a couple of times, but . . . when did it come out?"

"It's literally hot off the presses."

"This is amazing." He flipped pages. "But not exactly light reading, is it? And look at this bibliography!"

"It's got a little bit of everything. Economics, politics, philosophy, psychology . . . even physics."

"Is this one for me?"

"It certainly is."

"Then autograph it, Little Miss Whiz Kid, so I can prove I know you."

"Sure thing." On the title page she wrote: *To Rich with love, Andrea.* "Do you want to be the leader of my fan club?"

"Of course. How many members are there?"

"One. Look, I did better than just autograph it. Read the dedication."

Rich flipped the page and raised his eyebrows.

"I called you 'Rich Morrison' instead of 'Senator Richard Morrison' because you're famous enough already. Hope you don't mind."

He snorted. "Half the people in this state couldn't name their senators if you paid them five hundred dollars for each correct answer." His expression turned serious. "Andi, I'm honored. Truly. And I can't wait to read this. But . . . who is 'Bric Locket'? What kind of name is that?"

"A mysterious one."

"Oh, God."

"Seriously, he prefers to keep a low profile, even though the main ideas in the book are his. I just contributed a few concepts and did lots of research."

"Why do I suspect you're underselling yourself?" Rich broke off as their food arrived. After the waitress left he went on: "Eight months ago this was just an idea I heard you mention from time to time; now it's a published book. That's really an accomplishment."

While they ate she explained that the publisher had provided a quick turnaround because it was a small house. "But that's not all good news. We didn't get paid a penny in advance, and there's not going to be any promotion beyond what we do ourselves. Plus, like you already noticed, the book is not exactly mass market material."

He was holding the book open in one hand while eating with the other. "Maybe not, but even at a glance I can see this is big stuff. You and I are going to have a lot to talk about."

"Bric says we should market it as a sedative for insomniacs."

"I'll let you know soon enough; I'll read it on the way back to D.C." He glanced at his watch. "Speaking of which, I have barely enough time to drop you off and still catch my plane."

⚓

While stopped at a red light just a block from her house, Rich started tapping the steering wheel with his fingertips. Without looking at her he said, "How come you never mentioned this Bric guy before? You must have been working with him pretty closely."

"On and off."

"Is he . . . an old friend?"

"Let's just say we're very close."

The light turned green; Rich punched the accelerator down hard enough to make the tires bark. "Is that why you won't marry me, Andi? Because of Bric Locket?"

She laughed. "Now that's *funny*!"

"Why?"

"For one thing, he's old enough to be . . . to be my father. For another. . . ." She paused as the car pulled to a stop in front of her house. Turned in her seat. "For another, he *is* my father."

"Really? A retired Army guy was involved in writing this book? Wait. He died."

"No, I'm not talking about William Burns. I'm talking about my *real* father."

"Your. . . ."

She climbed out of the car, bent down and leaned her head through the window opening. "There's too much for me to explain right now; you'll miss your flight.".

"I know, but . . . God, you're *still* a bundle of mysteries!"

"You have no idea. But Rich . . . would you keep confidential what I just told you?"

"Of course. But why?"

"I'll explain that later, too."

He shook his head. "I knew you were going to say that."

"We could have someone look into her past, you know." Phil Dobson sat across from Rich in the living room of Rich's apartment inside the Loop. "In fact, I would say that half your staff recommended we do that while you were running for the Senate."

"I said 'no' then." . . . Rich poured Phil a bit of Scotch . . . "and I say 'no' now."

Phil accepted the glass with a shrug. As Rich's chief political advisor, he had developed the hide of an alligator. "Investigating her now could save you a ton of heartache . . . not to mention your career . . . somewhere down the road."

"Look, I didn't ask you over to discuss my some-time girlfriend and her mysterious co-writer. I want to know your opinion of their book."

"Well. . . ." Phil sipped the Scotch. "I took my time reading it, but I have to say . . . it's kind of all over the place."

"Is it? Seems to me everything comes back to the same theme: the necessity of finding the best point of synthesis between competing and cooperating for any kind of system . . . including political ones. To me that's a huge deal. You know that John Forbes Nash math wizard guy with the beautiful mind who got the Nobel Prize? . . . In business game theory, he called it 'equilibrium.'"

Yeah, I read that Russell Crowe might play him in a movie," said Phil."

Now Rich pored himself one and continued, "Except for the built in separation of powers in our constitution, which generally give rise to good faith differences, I hate the bad faith distortions that give rise to unnecessary polarization in our political discourse. That does nothing but derail progress."

"I agree. But that's my point. Even if there really *is* such a thing as an optimum synthesis in government, how could we ever apply it? Let's use a specific example. Your constituency is mostly conservative, which Burns and Locket would put on the right-wing or competitionistic side of the spectrum, as they call it. Right?"

Rich nodded.

"Then there are the independents, who are all over the board. Average them out and call them centrists. But what about the left-wingers? The cooperationists? In our political system they tend to belong to the other party. So even if there's a point of synthesis that would fuse the best of all three worlds together, how can we ever *find* that point, far less put it to use?"

"That's a fair question, but it's been done before. Like they say in the book, the formation of the United States itself is an example of *the synthesis* at work. The process was messy and contentious, but in the end the Founding Fathers managed to merge the competitiveness of the several states under the Tenth Amendment with the cooperativeness of Central Government under the Constitution itself."

"That was millions of citizens and thousands of regulations ago. Not to mention a war of independence. Nowadays things have gone too far the other way. Now people either want totally unregulated free enterprise capitalism or big government socialism. There are basically only those two points of view; an either/ or proposition."

"That's exactly the polarization I'm talking about. But *Fusing Order and Chaos* proves there's also a synthesized point of view that prescribes an economic and political system closest to what works throughout nature and the universe."

"The universe . . . and you don't think the book is all over the place?"

"The search for unifying principles has always been at the core of human inquiry."

"That's very intellectual stuff, Senator. That kind of thing doesn't fly in Descanso or Fresno. Voters live off their gut reactions."

"True. But half the problem lies in recognizing the *necessity* of achieving synthesis, and that's an emotional thing. Look. A free market economy is indispensable; the book makes that clear. So does history. But an economy has to be linked to a carefully-delineated government safety net for individuals and the social group, too. It's a reconciliation of the best aspects of capitalism—protection of individual rights—and the best aspects of social systems— lifelines for the needy. No hammocks, but no true hunger. Health and safety, but no government slavery."

"You know our constituency won't see it that way. They may regard it as a subversive attempt to promote European style socialism, or quasi-socialism."

"No, No," responded Rich. "This concept is right of center, basically conservative but not always, depending on the subject, but not way over into extreme versions of libertarianism- the irreconcilably flavored extremes of it.

"The book points out something I've found to be true: many people in democracies are trying to achieve such a synthesis. All our voters have to do is look around for a minute. For example, consider the recent weakening of antitrust laws—all that does is allow monopolies to kill off competition. Or what about the decision to deregulate the savings and loan industry? How did *that* work out?

"Those are both examples of over-competition. On the other hand we have over-cooperation: the squandering of taxpayer revenues as bureaucracy expands its domain—which it always does— or the administering of affirmative action programs in ways that deny equal protection and opportunity for all in favor of particular classes, races or minorities or even majorities." Palming his fist, Rich went on.

"The problem is that few people recognize the underlying *reason* to achieve a political-economic synthesis that favors competition but not at the complete expense of cooperation; . . . because that particular synthesis would be, and is, the natural characteristic of *all* developing systems throughout life and the universe."

Phil raised his hands, palms forward. "I get your point. In fact, I agree. The question is . . . how do we get the *voters* to agree?"

"Let's conduct an experiment. We'll introduce the book to people at the extremes of the political spectrum, both right and left. But don't volunteer that anyone on the other side is reading it."

"So they don't just dismiss it out of hand?"

"Right."

"Then what?"

"I'm betting that one of two things will happen. Either both sides reject the book's thesis, or both sides are inspired by it."

"Instead of one side being gun-ho for it and the other side blowing it off entirely."

"Exactly."

"Because the principles are universal?"

"That's my conviction."

"Well, it's an interesting idea. Any recommendations for the first guinea pigs?"

Rich smiled. "I might have a suggestion or two."

Feet propped on his desk, a corporate report in his hands, Herbert Hooks sat in his overstuffed leather chair in his expansive office. He jumped when the intercom beeped.

"Mr. Hooks?" his secretary said in her matter-of-fact tone.

"Yeah?"

"There are some gentlemen out here who say they're from the United States Justice Department. I asked if they had an appointment, and they showed me their badges and said they don't need one."

Hooks dropped his feet to the floor. "Where's Egan? Where the hell is *Egan*?"

"He's still at lunch."

"Jesus, it's 2:30. Call the steam room at the Athletic Club. When did I talk to that asshole kid at the SEC? About a month ago?"

"I don't remember. Shall I—"

"Tell them I'll be right out." A gastric pain struck Herbert Hooks' lower abdomen as he got up and walked to the door of his office. When he opened it he came face to face with four men dressed in business suits. The first one thrust a badge into his face.

"Mr. Hooks?"

"Yes."

"I'm Special Agent Wilson from the Department of Justice, and this is Deputy Agent Arnheim from the Enforcement Division of the Securities and Exchange Commission. I'd also like to introduce Frank Stevens, court appointed Receiver, and John Abramson from the Federal Bureau of Investigation."

Hooks felt a frog swell up in his throat. "Uh . . . What's this about?"

"As of this moment this company is under the control of a federal receivership, by *ex parte* order of U.S. Judge Roger Winchester. Assistant United States Attorney Andrea Burns made the court appearance for the Government. We're at this moment taking over the books and records and installing Frank Stevens as temporary receiver to run the company. You will have your chance to oppose the receivership at a hearing in fifteen days."

Hooks' mouth opened and closed.

SEC Agent Arnheim stepped forward. "The New York Stock Exchange has been notified. The indications are that as of close of trading today this company is suspended from trading. And the SEC is compiling information for action to take place within twenty days." He handed Hooks a paper with a signature and an embossed federal seal at the bottom. "Mr. Hooks, this is a subpoena for you to appear before the SEC for a deposition."

"We are, at this time," Wilson added, "also handing you a search warrant and a subpoena *duces tecum* for the production of all documents of this company, which we are placing under the control of the receiver as of now. Before you ask any questions or make any statements, I'm going to state your rights. You have the right to remain silent. Anything you say can and will be held against you. You have a right to an attorney . . ."

"What right have you to just break in here and seize this company?" Hooks bellowed. "I'll have my Congressman and Senator . . . I'll have the President of the United States on your asses if you don't turn around and march right back out of here! Why wasn't I notified?"

"Ms. Burns made a showing to the judge on that," said Wilson. "She felt that if advance notice were given and the company tipped off, inside shareholders might dump their stock before the New York Stock Exchange could suspend trading."

"Well, my lawyer is going to straighten you out, and the judge will too! You have no grounds."

"A *prima facia* showing was made indicating that massive fraud was committed by the officers of this company—this *publicly traded* company," Wilson said. "And the federal court has temporarily ordered that the receiver be appointed. You may have your lawyer contact Ms. Burns with questions. Andrea Burns. As I said, she is the Deputy United States Attorney for the Southern District. Now, sir, please step aside."

"You—You—"

"Which office belongs to your corporate counsel?" Arnheim asked. Dazed, the banker pointed to Egan James' door. One of the agents went inside, looked around, and opened the credenza. The interior was packed with files. The agent began pulling them out.

After a two-hour lunch, Egan responded to a message left at his athletic club and he used the phone just outside the steam room. *At least it's not Samantha calling for once*, he thought as he waited for the receptionist to get Herbert's secretary on the line. His wife had a bad habit of interrupting him whenever he was doing anything comfortable or relaxing. In other words, anything that didn't involve her.

Then he heard the voice of Hooks' secretary . . . but for some reason she was speaking in nearly a whisper. "I was ordered not to call out or talk to anyone," she said.

"Huh? What's going on?"

"I can't talk. I have to get off the line. I guess I'm working for *them* now."

"'Them?' Who?"

"They won't let me say anything."

"This is ridiculous. Where's Mr. Hooks?"

"They have him in his office. They're looking at files and asking him things."

"*Who* has him?"

"They said I'm not supposed to say."

Egan slammed down the receiver. He toweled the sweat from his crew-cut sideburns, then phoned Lou Helms, a criminal defense lawyer who had once been an Assistant US Attorney.

"Lou, I don't know what's going on, but apparently agents or police officers are going through my company's files. They've got Herbert Hooks, our president, in his office, questioning him."

They agreed to meet at the entrance to the company's corporate offices in fifteen minutes. After a hectic drive Egan arrived at the building a minute early, parked in front and started pacing back and forth on the sidewalk. Helms arrived exactly on time.

"Relax," Helms said. "You look like you're going through an earthquake. Let's just go in and find out what's happening."

Upstairs, men in shirtsleeves and ties were poring through documents and making copies on a portable machine they had rolled into the conference room. Horrified, Egan spotted files and papers from his own office stacked all over the room. Agents stroked through the documents with thick labeling pens, marking packets and putting different-colored stickers on them. Other agents were already returning copied files to their drawers. Everyone looked up when the two men walked in.

"I'm Louis Helms," the lawyer said, "specially representing the company. May I see the court papers?" He looked at a heavy-set man with a sweaty brow and said, "Are you Mr. Hooks?"

"Yes." Hooks patted moisture from his face with a handkerchief.

"I don't want you to utter another word."

The banker nodded.

Agent Arnheim handed the subpoenas to Helms, but looked at Egan. "And who are you, sir?"

Egan attempted to match his stare. "Company legal counsel and Executive VP."

"Ah, Mr. James." Agent Wilson stepped up beside Arnheim and smiled. "I have a subpoena and a search warrant for you, too." He held out a two-page document. "These are duplicates of what Mr. Hooks got a little while ago."

Hooks lurched forward. "This whole investigation is a fraud! It's nothing but the result of a screw-up by that . . . that wet-behind-the-balls kid-lawyer at the SEC, the one I set straight over the phone a couple of months ago."

"Mr. Hooks," Helms said in a softly warning tone. "Please."

Arnheim smiled at Hooks. "You must be referring to Mr. Micelli. It is possible you pissed him off . . . sir."

Helms looked the subpoenas over, then got permission to take Egan and the banker to a back office, where he shut the door. "Okay.

I can't stop them from continuing their search, but they're not entitled to interrogate either of you if you don't want to be interviewed."

"I have nothing to hide," Hooks snarled. "Maybe if I tell them what I know, they'll leave us alone."

"I would *strongly* suggest you not do that." Helms stared at him. "The Justice Department and the SEC are not in the habit of taking over public companies unless they have uncovered *very* serious questions of business failures, fraud or possible criminal activities."

"But—"

"Excuse me," Egan said. "There's something I need to do. I'll be right back."

He walked down the hall and peered into his office. The agents glanced at him and returned to their excavations. Holding his breath, he leaned over just enough to slide his credenza file drawer open a few inches. When he saw his personal file still in its place, he breathed easier. He should never have fallen into the habit of leaving that drawer unlocked. He couldn't even remember the last time he'd tossed its little silver key in the air.

As an agent pushed past him with a box full of files Egan noticed his empty briefcase standing just inside the door rather than in its customary place leaning against a leg of his desk. Well, that was a lucky break.

He picked the briefcase up with one hand while with the other he snatched his personal file out of the credenza. In less than a second he had placed the latter inside the former and left the office.

Three hours later the agents packed up their copy machine, had all relevant material carted away, and disappeared as suddenly as they had come.

Hooks and Egan looked at each other. Helms said, "I want to see both of you in my office tomorrow. Call my secretary and arrange an appointment."

When Andrea stepped into her office after lunch the next day, she almost stumbled over a row of neatly-stacked storage boxes. She examined the labels and raised her eyebrows. "That was fast. . . ."

She wondered what her father would say about this turn of events—her being involved in a case against two of the men responsible for him residing in the penitentiary. Then her mind instructed her not to be influenced by the personal connection; she conjured a mental block against history.

She had purposely not talked to her dad in a while. She knew he would be more than interested in all of this, but feared something might go wrong. What if her suppositions had no basis? What if Hooks and James slipped away somehow? The case would be reported in the paper. She decided to send her dad some clippings when the news broke.

Over the next two days she kept eyeing the boxes as she caught up on other work, then finally started in on them. She pulled out file after file and made notes on yellow pads as she tried to track transactions. In order to get evidence for the Federal Grand Jury as quickly as possible, she worked late each night. One evening as she laboriously scanned documents page by page, she looked up at the clock and noticed it was midnight. *Well, then, I guess I came in early today.* Sighing, she turned back to look at what she held in her hand—one of Egan James' bulging file folders. Most of his papers were in terrible disarray, and mixed up with pages torn out of magazines, obscure scribbled notes, lingerie advertisements from Victoria's Secret catalogues. The man was a pack-rat. The last thing she wanted to do was look at more of his crap . . . but it was her job.

Sighing again, she removed a large rubber band from around the folder and carefully placed the pile of contents on her desk. She flipped through them . . . then stopped suddenly. Went back a page. Stared.

Before her lay a photocopy of a faded letter bearing a familiar signature. *What's Egan doing with one of Dad's letters?*

It got stranger. The addressee was Laura Evans; the date October 26 of 1978. The body of the letter referred to the first three chapters of a proposed novel. . . .

Andrea shot to her feet as though zapped by lightning. "Unbelievable! The lost transmittal letter!" she shouted. *Where did James get this? How long has he had it?* And then . . . *Egan James was a DDA back then. Did he obstruct justice by deliberately withholding this piece of evidence?*

She knew John Woods would never stoop so low to convict someone. Not even her father doubted Woods' honesty. It was Egan, Egan all along . . . and he even hung onto the evidence all these years like a . . . like a trophy.

Early the next morning she phoned Brockton and used her US Attorney status to have Anthony called to the phone during closed phone hours.

"I hope you're going to tell me something good," he said.

"Well, it's not too bad."

"Okay. Please go on."

"You know that transmittal letter you wrote ten years ago when you sent the first few chapters of your novel to Laura?"

"The one that would have exonerated me? Are you kidding? I'm not sure a day goes by that I don't think about it. Why?"

"Oh, nothing. I found it."

There was a long pause. Then, "It sounded like you said you found it."

"I did say that. I did find it."

"Wh . . . where? How?"

"A few days ago our office seized Egan James' files in conjunction with a 1933 Act, 10B5 securities fraud case I'm working on. I sent you some newspaper clippings about it, but you probably haven't received them yet. Anyway, the transmittal letter turned up last night while I was going through some of James's old documents."

"You mean he *kept* it?"

"I can see him gloating over it at night. Dad, I'm going to *get* him." She gripped the phone so hard her fingers cramped. "I'm going to nail him for you, just like I always said I would. It's time to lay a little force on Egan James' overly-competitive, greedy ass."

"Jesus. Jeez. This is . . . But listen, Andrea. Be careful. Whatever you do, do it ethically. Stick with the rules. You wouldn't want to give James and Hooks any chance to get the government's case dismissed."

As if seeing her father face to face, she nodded. "Don't worry. It's clear Egan obstructed justice during your trial. He kept your proof of innocence hidden right there in his desk. I'm taking everything to John Woods."

"Andrea . . . you can't get personally involved."

"This has nothing to do with the case I'm investigating with the US Attorney's Office, and I'm not letting it affect my thinking on that. But I get your point. Can I at least show it to Sarah, my next ranking assistant US Attorney? I won't try to influence her; I'll just let her know that it might apply to a questionable trial from a decade ago and let the chips fall where they may."

"Whatever you do, just keep your rules of ethics in mind. Don't risk your job or your career on me."

"No offense, Dad, but I wouldn't discuss the details of an ongoing case with anyone . . . even you."

Anthony hung up the phone and walked back to his cell. As he passed the guard station he picked up his mail and found copies of the newspaper articles Andrea had mentioned. In his cell he poured over every word. Egan James and Herbert Hooks had allegedly conspired to pump up the value of corporate stock in their publicly-traded company. None of the allegations surprised Anthony; he was sure of each one before he even read it.

Andrea had highlighted some names at the top of the long list of investors who'd sunk large sums into the Hooks-James parent corporation. When he looked closer, he realized why she'd done it: they were Samantha's snooty relatives. He tried not to smile. Those folks were probably not feeling so superior right now—the moment the SEC halted trading, the house of cards had fallen and Hooks' company stock had dropped almost to zero.

His smile broadened when he read that the SEC's investigation had been set off by an anonymous letter. *According to sources, this letter was clearly written by a person knowledgeable in the law.* Anthony read that line three times.

A sidebar detailed a court motion brought by James' and Hooks' lawyers against the investigative reporter to force him to reveal his sources. Apparently he had reported information that went beyond what he could have learned by just examining the public records. The judge granted the motion, but the reporter showed he had gotten his leads from a second anonymous letter that had been received by a freelance co-journalist named Laura Evans.

24 Souvenir of a Pack Rat

Beams of golden morning light filtered through the mist just outside the window as Andrea knocked on the frame of Sarah's office door.

Sarah looked up. "Hi, Andi, what's going?"

Andrea eased into the office. "When I was looking through some of the old case files from Hooks' office I ran across a rather interesting letter that came from Egan James' desk. He's like the classic pack rat. I had to plow through though all kinds of ancient stuff." Andrea shut the door and handed the photocopy to Sarah. "Do you recall the conviction of the president of the County Bar years ago? His name was Anthony Darren."

"I do recall it. In fact, that was one of the first things I heard about local lore when I got here."

"Well, that letter is signed by Darren, and I think it might have a bearing on that case. Do you think Mr. Woods would be interested in looking at it?"

Sarah raised her eyebrows, then peered at the faded writing on the page. "I don't see how."

"As I remember, Darren claimed he'd lost a transmittal letter about a novel that would have cleared him. This sure looks like it might be that. You're my senior; what do you think?"

"It does seem strange that this came from Egan James' files. Maybe the pack rat keeps souvenirs. I'll show it to John. Do you mind if I keep this and start a file?"

"No problem. I've made a copy."

Although Sarah considered Woods a good boss, he wanted to make the most of his time and sometimes seemed harried and short-tempered. She asserted herself into his office anyway.

He looked up, impatience filling the crags of his face. "What is it?"

"I'll just take a few minutes, John. I have a copy of a letter dated close to ten years ago that I thought you might want to see."

"Not unless it's from a long-lost uncle leaving me a billion dollars."

"Not exactly. Do you remember Anthony Darren, the former president of the County Bar Association? There was a boat-sinking incident. . . ."

"Of course. Why? He's still in prison. What do you have there?"

Without further explanation Sarah handed him the page. As he read, Woods slowly rose from his swivel chair, holding the letter in both hands. He stared at it in silence for a full minute.

Finally he lowered it. "I'll be a son-of-a-gun. That poor bastard Darren. If he'd produced this when the whole mess started, I would have dismissed his case. Are you sure this is authentic? Where did you get it?"

"Actually, Andrea found it while she was going through the documents subpoenaed from Egan James' files."

"*James*?" Woods dropped the letter and it fluttered to his desk. He walked to the window and stood looking out over the city. "Anthony Darren said all along that well before that tuna boat sank he'd written some chapters and a synopsis of a novel with a similar storyline and sent them to an editor or agent for consideration—along with a transmittal letter that showed his fictional idea came first. Without the transmittal letter all evidence pointed the other way . . . and he could never produce the letter. Nobody believed it existed, not even me." He paused. "God, I hate to say this or even think it . . . but I might have put an innocent man in prison."

"James was a deputy DA at the time?"

Woods turned. "He led the investigation team. He even ended up marrying Anthony Darren's fiancé after Darren went to prison. But if he's had this letter all these years, that means he's almost certainly guilty of obstructing justice."

"So . . . do you think this letter could get Darren a pardon, then?"

Woods thought a moment. "Off the top of my head I'd have to say probably not. There was other evidence against him, including statements by a cellmate of the man who supposedly scuttled his own tuna boat. So it's not a slam-dunk he's innocent. Also, pardon applications can become political hot potatoes; people start letter campaigns against them. On the other hand, this letter could lead to additional evidence in his favor."

He turned back toward the window. "Sarah, how's your schedule?"

"Tight, as usual."

"Look, it's going to be hard to financially justify your time, but, I'm assigning you to investigate what it would take to get Anthony Darren pardoned. Could you do most of that work on a volunteer basis, after hours? And if you'd like to get Andrea's help, that's fine with me so long as it doesn't interfere with the Hooks-James case."

"Glad to help," Sarah sighed. What else could she say?

Poor Andi, she thought as she headed back down the hall. *She's going to regret she ever brought this up. . . .*

The floor of the porch creaked beneath Andrea as she approached a door mottled with peeling varnish. She pushed the bell and her index finger came away spotted with rust. *He'll never recognize me*, she thought. *The trial was so long ago*. Besides, she had never been introduced to Joe Cruz, and had no reason to believe he'd even remember her name.

From Laura she had learned that after Cruz was released from prison, he and his wife, Sylvia, had continued on in the same old house with its beautiful view of the bay where he had always lived—until the bank came to get it. But a group of friends, disregarding his protests, had raised the funds to save the house from foreclosure although not, clearly, decomposition.

After a minute the front door squeaked open a few inches, and a man's voice said something inaudible. Although bright sunlight warmed Andrea's head and shoulders, everything beyond the doorway appeared black. "Mr. Cruz?" she said. "I'm an assistant US Attorney, and—"

"Leave us alone. I'm off parole now." The door began to close.

"—and I'm here to get evidence to help Anthony Darren."

The door halted. "To help Anthony?"

"Yes, sir."

At that the door flew wide open and an older, thinner, and grayer version of the Joe Cruz she remembered from the trial gestured for her to come in.

Andrea followed him into what appeared to be a den littered with envelopes and copies of letters. The place looked like a post office mail room. Joe, who wore jeans and a light sweater with holes at the elbows through which a white t-shirt showed, saw her expression. "Sorry for the mess. I've been writing letters soliciting support to have Anthony's case reopened, to prove he's innocent."

"That's exactly why I'm here."

"Because of my letters?"

"Well . . . because of *a* letter."

"Would you like some iced tea?"

A minute later they were sitting on a couple of spots on the couch cleared of paper. As Andrea's vision adjusted to the gloom she noticed the shadows of sadness around Joe's eyes. His cheeks were far more gaunt and pale than she remembered, but his biceps and forearms still bulged, probably from his current job of hauling nets around the docks. *He must be about fifty by now.*

"A few days ago," she said, "John Woods asked my partner Sarah and me to read through the trial transcripts of your old case."

"John Woods? Isn't he the bastard who prosecuted Anthony in the first place?"

"Actually, Mr. Cruz, he's a very honest man. It looks like he was manipulated into taking the case on at all. Do you remember a missing transmittal letter having to do with a novel Mr. Darren was writing?"

"How could I forget? And call me Joe."

"All right, Joe. The transmittal letter? We found it."

Joe's mouth opened, and for a few seconds his face froze. Then he muttered, "Our prayers have been answered." The first smile Andrea had seen from him began to rise upon his face. "How did you find the letter? And was there anything else?"

"I can't disclose how we found it, and no, so far we've found nothing more. And unfortunately we'll need a *lot* more to get Mr. Darren a pardon. That's why Sarah and I decided to split up the work and interview any crew members of *the Sea Diva* who might still be around."

"I wasn't a crew member," he said bitterly. "I *owned* that beautiful lady. Well, the bank owned her."

Andrea forged on. "My job is to find anyone who may have overheard any statements made by your chief engineer, Poncho Pascalle. Can you direct me to anyone who may have talked to him before he was lost?"

"Nobody who's still alive or in touch, although there are plenty of people who *think* they've seen his ghost since he died. Maybe he's talked to them."

"I'm sorry . . . did you say they saw him after he died?"

"A ghost, Ms. Burns. Fishermen are even more superstitious than baseball players. Some guys I know who have gone back to the area where *the Sea Diva* went down swear they've seen Poncho's ghost out there swimming in the waters." Joe looked genuinely disturbed. "It doesn't help that his body was never found."

"Is that unusual?"

"Not really. Not that far out to sea. And it was a stormy night. A terrible storm. . ."

His face closed down; his gaze lost focus. His own son had died in that same tragedy, Andrea recalled.

"It gets stranger," he said so suddenly she jumped. "One of my ex-crewmen said he saw Poncho just last year but not out at sea; in Costallegre, in the port where *the Sea Diva* made her last stop."

"But still a ghost?"

"This particular gentleman isn't like most fisherman; he's not the sort to believe in ghosts."

"You mean . . . Poncho might be *alive?*"

Joe shook his head, the lines in his face pulled down by disappointment. "I didn't say that. Moby Jack does drink a bit much."

"Could we at least talk to this guy? What's his name again?"

"We call him 'Moby Jack' Callucci. Big guy, half garden-variety American, half Italian . . . and lately always about half-smashed. About a month ago I got a call from a bartender friend out on Shelter Island. Said Moby was there and getting out of hand. By the time I got there, he was pouring a beer over another friend's head and swearing he'd seen Poncho on the streets of Puerto Nuevo."

"Puerto Nuevo? The town in Baja with all the lobster restaurants?"

"No, no, the capital city of Costallegre. Moby said he saw Poncho on the street and tried to catch up to him, but some other guys came up and hustled him—Moby—into a cantina. I don't know if I believe him. Moby's not the kind who's going to let anyone push him anywhere he doesn't want to go. Of course, if it was a cantina, he probably *did* want to go."

"Where is Moby now? Do you know?"

"Probably still in town."

Andrea gestured at a phone. "Why don't you call him?"

"Now?"

"Now!"

Joe picked up the receiver, dialed, spoke to someone in Spanish, hung up, called someone else. After several repetitions of this he took his hand off the receiver and said, "Okay, the bartender on Shelter Island says Moby is at the Red Sails right now, having some shooters. They're crossing their fingers he doesn't start tearing the place up. I asked them to let Moby know we're coming over—but it sounds like we'd better hurry."

The bar was situated in a restaurant that resembled a New England whaling captain's house, complete with a widow's walk on top. In the dim interior of the almost-empty bar sat a man with curly amber hair. As he got up to greet them, his body stretched into a human tower rising toward the ceiling. Andrea could see why they called him Moby. From the trial transcript, she remembered he had been the witness the prosecution had successfully blocked from testifying by convincing the judge his story was hearsay.

"How you doing, Moby?" Joe asked a little warily.

"Drowning my sorrows," the giant said. "Or my happiness; I can never remember."

Joe looked at Andrea. "He's fine."

They sat down at the bar and Joe ordered three beers.

"Seriously," Joe said. "How's it going?"

"Ah, same old thing. The industry is about gone. Been trying to find work where I can fly choppers."

Joe leaned toward Andrea. "I bet you're wondering how he even fits into a chopper."

"Well. . . ."

"Flexibility," Moby Jack said, upending his beer glass.

"Moby, this lady is a U.S. Attorney. She's trying to get Anthony Darren a pardon."

"You're kiddin' me!" Moby almost toppled off his stool. "Ma'am, I could kiss you!"

"Jesus, Moby, don't ruin it before she even gets started."

Moby waved a huge hand. "Jealously is an ugly thing."

Joe signaled the bartender to bring another beer. "Mobes, remember when you told me about seeing Poncho Pascalle's ghost in Costallegre?"

"I remember you saying I was drunk."

"Weren't you?"

"Well, yeah, but I saw him anyway." He turned toward Andrea. "I saw him as plain as I'm seeing you now. I'd just come around a corner—this was down in Puerto Nuevo—and there he was. Looked startled as hell, then took off. Next thing I knew these little guys swarmed all over me and hustled me into a cantina."

"Little guys," Joe said. "I heard they were the size of football players."

"Well, maybe *French* football players."

"And they took you into a cantina?" Andrea asked.

"Yeah. I didn't resist that much because they were more pushy-friendly than aggressive. Probably nervous about me kicking their asses. They bought me a beer, I bought them some beers. They kept saying the guy I thought was Poncho wasn't Poncho. Said he was a guy called . . . Gato something."

"Mariano 'El Gato' Cardenas?" Andrea said.

"Yeah. Hey—how'd you know?"

"I just read an article about him in *Time*. He's one of the rebel leaders in Costallegre."

"Yeah, that's what those French football players said too. El Gato's trying to overthrow that friggin' commie Bramoso, which is not something an American should get involved in. But to hell with that. I heard we paid for Bramoso's college education on a scholarship exchange deal. So when he goes back home, what does he do? Takes over the revolution in Costallegre, throws out democratic reform and makes the place commie."

"Moby, do you really, honestly think the man you saw was Poncho Pascalle?"

Moby scowled at her. "Young lady, just because we're sittin' here having some suds together doesn't mean I'm blitzed. Do I look in-eh-bri-a-ted to you?"

"No," she lied.

"Let's walk over to St. Lucia Church. I'll swear on the altar it was Poncho I saw that night."

"I heard that some of the fishermen who've been out where the *Diva* sank thought they saw Poncho's ghost swimming in the sea. So you can't blame us if we seem a little, cautious."

Moby laughed. "And you have trouble believing *my* story? Did Joe tell you the rest of what those fishermen say?"

"There's more?"

Joe put a hand across one eye as if scratching his brow.

"There was this guy on the *Diva* named Alfonso Martin. Poncho's assistant engineer, a lying asshole who fed a bunch of B.S. to the jury during the trial. Well, a year ago he was on a different fishing boat in that same area, and a storm caught 'em. Just like the storm that hit the night *the Sea Diva* went down. The wind howled like a pack of sea witches, people say, and the rain was horizontal. They say Martin came up from below, real seasick. That wasn't like him. But anyway, one minute he's hanging over the rail, the next thing a monster wave rolls over that side of the ship and he's gone. Nobody else, just Martin—but when they look overboard they see *two* heads in the waves. One of them was laughing. They swore it was Poncho."

Andrea looked back at Joe, found him scratching his other eyebrow.

"So what happened?" she asked Moby. "To Martin, I mean?"

"Disappeared. Never found him."

"Just like Poncho, right?" Joe said. "How is any of this helping us help Anthony?"

Andrea ignored him, spoke to Moby. "If you really believe Poncho is alive, do you think we could find him? Talk to him?"

"Ma'am, there's a revolution going on down there. That's a very dangerous part of the world. Do you really need him?"

"I'm afraid his testimony might be pretty much essential to getting Anthony pardoned."

Moby's gaze rose to the ceiling, then shifted to Joe. "Well, then, what the hell are we waiting for? Let's hop down to Costallegre."

"El Gato," Sarah said when Andrea reported her discussion with Joe and Moby Jack. "Doesn't that mean 'The Cat?'"

Andrea nodded.

"So a man who's supposed to have drowned hundreds of miles at sea might actually be a revolutionary hero called The Cat who might actually be the key witness in getting an innocent man out of prison. Does that about sum it up?"

"I know, it sounds absurd but Moby Jack is absolutely convinced Pascalle is still alive down there in Costallegre. I think we have to proceed on that assumption. Joe and Moby Jack are more than willing to go down there and look for him; it won't cost us a cent of money or a second of time."

"Joe Cruz is a convicted felon; it's not like he can just go where he wants."

"That's why I think it's best if the INS gets him permission to go down."

"And *then* what? Costallegre is a military dictatorship that's not terribly fond of its rebels. So Joe's going to just waltz down there and bring El Gato back without any interference? Do you really think that's likely? I don't think the US even has diplomatic relations with Costallegre."

"What if Joe gets a statement from Poncho down there, under oath? That could be added as evidence to the transmittal letter, right?"

Sara frowned. "Andrea, even a statement taken under oath could be hearsay if it can't be subject to cross-examination. You know that."

Andrea hung her head. "You're right. I do know that."

"Honey, may I ask you something?"

"Of course."

"Why is this so important to you? I mean, I appreciate you wanting to correct an injustice and all, but . . . you seem to be going way out on a limb on this one."

Andrea licked her lips. "John seems to think it's important, too."

"Yeah, well," Sarah stared at her for fifteen or twenty seconds, then shook her head. "Okay. Before you ask, a deposition is also out of the question. It's a war zone in Costellegre; US citizens aren't really even supposed to travel there, so it would obviously be too inconvenient for opposition to send a representative to a depo."

"I understand."

"And one last thing: even if we arranged for something wonderful to happen in Costellegre, if the pardon application gets opposed up *here* we'd be forced to physically bring Poncho back to the U.S. to testify. From what I hear, that's pretty much impossible."

"Got it. But, can we at least ask what John thinks?"

Sarah sighed. "I'll go make the pitch."

Back in her tiny office, Andrea tried to work, but soon realized all she'd done was shuffle papers while waiting for the buzz of her intercom.

She was concentrating on the intercom so hard she jumped entirely out of her seat when her door flew open. Sarah burst in, hands clasped above her head in a victory pose. "John gave the go-ahead!"

"What?"

"You were right about one thing—he's *very* determined to get Darren cleared."

"That's terrific, Sarah! So now we've got to get Joe a passport. . . ."

"Ah, that. I'm afraid you might need the help of a friendly local Senator to swing that."

"Oh, no, I . . . wouldn't feel comfortable asking Rich to help. Besides, he won't be back in town for a couple more weeks."

"There's such a thing as a telephone. Look, if you won't ask him, I will. He won't forget all the campaign work I did for him."

"Still, would you mind keeping me out of this? If Rich decides to help, I want him to do it because it's the right thing, and not because of me. Do you understand?"

"Not even a little bit."

"But you'll keep me out of it?"

"If that's what you want, sure. I'm always happy to grab glory for myself!"

Rich sat at his desk in Washington listening to Sarah's story, then smiled as if she were there with him. "So you're asking me to arrange passports and visa clearances into a hostile nation for an ex-convict and a probable future convict; is that about it?"

"Um . . . is it too much to ask?"

"Actually, no; not if there's the slightest chance this Poncho Pascalle is really El Gato."

"But . . . I thought this had to do with Anthony Darren."

"Oh, it does; if he's innocent, I hope you get him a pardon. But there could be an important by-product from the trip as well."

"Really?"

"Costallegre is being torn to pieces by civil war, with no end in sight. Cuba supplies Bramoso's forces and the CIA almost certainly supplies the insurgents. Left against Right, Communism against Capitalism . . . but as usual it's the people just trying to live their lives who get caught in the middle. Somehow the opposing sides need to be brought together so they can work out a cease fire, maybe even a peace treaty."

"But what does that have to do with—"

"El Gato represents the people in the middle. He's their hero. He's the bridge to bringing Bramoso and Adamson together."

"Bramoso and *Adamson*?" Sarah grinned. "The two presidents? You really do think big."

"I think it can be done. I happen to know them both. I think they can find common ground." He didn't mention that he had already sent them each a copy of *Fusing Order and Chaos* and received their independent comments. Not surprisingly, each man favored the opposite end of the spectrum described in the book but at least they agreed that the spectrum existed, and that its overall size and influence mattered. It was not an *either-or* proposition, but where to place the needle on the spectrum.

I wonder what El Gato would think if he read *Fusing Order and Chaos*? Hell, I wonder if he even reads English.

He focused on Sarah again. "You say Joe Cruz thinks of Poncho Pascalle as an older brother, right?"

"According to Andrea."

"Then if Poncho really is El Gato, Joe's the perfect man to find him and persuade him to . . ."

"To what?"

"To stop being a legend and become flesh and blood again. Perhaps we can provide him an equally important reason to come to the U.S.—for his country. For 'their revolution' may become the only reason his compatriots would let him go, especially at these critical times. . . ."

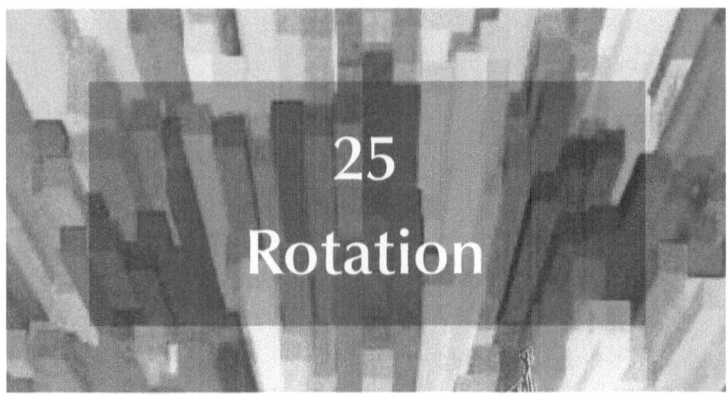

Anthony Darren was lying on his bunk scribbling notes on a pad when the clang of his cell door startled him. He raised his head.

"Get your ass up," Sluggo said. "The warden wants some face time with the Word Man of Alcatraz."

Despite his best efforts to keep his hopes at a safe level—somewhere around his ankles—Anthony couldn't stop his heartbeat from increasing as he preceded the guard along the catwalks to the prison elevator, then across the yard, up the cracked concrete steps, into the administration wing, and down the dreary hall to the Warden's office. While he waited to be buzzed in the forbidden thought sprang across his consciousness: *Has progress been made on my pardon?*

The buzzer sounded and the secretary ushered him into the abode of the prison's head man: mahogany-paneled walls, intricate crown molding, carpet the color of newly-scabbed blood. The warden, wearing a preoccupied, severe expression, sat at his desk reading some kind of report. He glanced up at Anthony.

"Mr. Darren, I've decided it's time to rotate you out of your librarian job. You've monopolized it for some time; someone else might benefit from it, too. So, effective immediately, you are assigned to the maintenance crew. Any questions?"

Anthony felt the blood drain from his face, dizzying him.

"I hope it wasn't my articles on the penal system?" he croaked.

"Was that a question? I can't say; but along with other factors, it appears that you've learned nothing since our last conversation on the topic of prison reform. So let's see what you can come up with on improving sanitation procedures."

Anthony felt his throat close. He could not have spoken even if he'd had something to say.

"You're excused back to your cell." The warden lifted a sheet of paper as if to hide his face.

That afternoon, mop and bucket in hand, Anthony began his new job cleaning prison bathrooms and latrines. At dusk he trudged along behind the prison trash truck as it stopped at each pick-up station.

During the night he and another convict spent three hours emptying heavy cans of refuse into the maw of a trundling garbage truck.

When he finally got back to his cell, shuffling like a man twice his age, Anthony looked around and realized, with a strange lack of surprise, that all the papers and notes for his new book were gone.

Andrea rushed through the crazy-angled architecture of the Horton Plaza shopping mall, passing walls of mauve, tan, blue, and yellow, climbing half-floor staircases and traversing bridges as quickly as she could. It was almost twelve-twenty, and Laura's phone message had read *Meet me at the Horton Plaza Food Court at noon*.

Finally she arrived at the food pavilion, where colorful storefronts advertised shops of every unique food imaginable. She passed Mexican aromas, Italian, French, southern American, good old American, and Chinese, until she spotted Laura at a non-fat yogurt and fruit counter.

Laura motioned her to move around a corner into a secluded, shadowy coffee house.

"Did you become a spy while I wasn't paying attention?" Andrea asked with a nervous smile. "What's with all the intrigue?"

"Order something and I'll tell you."

A minute later they were stirring drinks at a stand-up bar. "Well?" Andrea said. "Come on, Laura, you're making me nervous."

"You should be nervous. Look, I've been freelancing for *The Daily*

Currier the last couple of weeks, and from office scuttlebutt I found out someone—apparently either Egan James' or Herbert Hooks' lawyers—has hired an investigator to check you out. He's been asking reporters off-the-record questions about you."

Andrea stopped stirring. "What kind of questions?"

"Personal ones. Sounds like they're trying to dig up dirt on you."

"Those bastards."

"You must be rattling their cages pretty hard. But let me tell you something else. Hooks has influence with the editor's staff at the *Currier*. He's friends with owner, Wellington Aspen; they belong to the same good ol' boy clubs."

Andrea nodded. "That explains all the articles about wasting taxpayer money on 'Grand Jury wild goose chases' that have been coming out lately." She sipped her coffee. "My boss has even heard from a few Congressmen on the subject. The audacity of these people! One of the bastions of freedom in the US is supposed to be the federal court system."

"You would hope so," Laura replied. "But on the other front, what's happening with trying to find that ghost witness for Anthony?"

"Joe finally got permission to take off for Costallegre with that giant, Moby Jack Callucci. Even with Rich's help it was tough getting Joe clearance; the bureaucracy was unbelievable."

"Are they still taking along a copy of your book in case they find El Gato?"

"I can't believe it, but yeah. They've both read it but they aren't sure they'll be able to explain it in Spanish. Joe is good in street Spanish, but unfortunately *Fusing Order and Chaos* is written in a fairly esoteric style, and I don't have the time or money to get it translated."

"Then what good is it going to do, even assuming they find El Gato and give it to him?"

"Hopefully one of his men can translate it. But remember, for Joe and Moby, getting the book into El Gato's hands is a secondary goal; their main reason to go down there is to persuade El Gato to come back to the U.S. and help my father."

"Do you think it would make a difference if El Gato knew that the presidents of both his country and ours have already read the book?"

"If El Gato is Poncho Pascalle, he'd probably be more impressed if he knew who really *wrote* the book. But only you, Anthony, and I know who Locket really is, and Dad wants to keep it that way."

Laura frowned. "I thought you told Rich . . . "

"Sorry; let me rephrase. Yes, Rich knows that Locket is my father . . . but he doesn't know that my father is also Anthony Darren."

"Isn't it time you told him the full story, Andi?"

"I can't, not yet, because that would put him into a conflict of interest on my father's application for a Presidential pardon."

"How?"

"It's public knowledge that Rich is the President's friend, and that Rich and I are dating. If a pardon for Dad does get granted there can't be any question that it was given solely on merit and not because Rich has a relationship with me."

"I'm sorry, sweetie; that's got to be rough."

"It is. I'm so tired of living two lives."

"How is—" Laura fell silent as a portly older man wearing a sports jacket and well-shined shoes shuffled past behind them. He carried nothing, not even a shopping bag.

"You think he's the PI?" Andi whispered after a moment.

"Looks more like a CPA, but what do I know?" Laura tossed her coffee cup into a nearby trash can. "What I was about to say is, how is the Hooks case coming along? You look exhausted."

Andi shrugged. "I have to be thorough. I have to do it right."

"Well, I hate to burden you even more, but you should know that when I saw Anthony last week he looked just as exhausted as you. Maybe more. I'm afraid he's withering away again now that they've taken away his library job."

Andi sipped her coffee. "I've got at least one spot of good news. Sarah and I have been spending nights and weekends working on the application for Dad's pardon, and thanks to Sarah, the Justice Department has agreed to grant Poncho immunity if he is in fact alive and agrees to testify."

"Andi, that's wonderful!"

We managed to get hold of some of Poncho's relatives down in Castellegre by telephone and told them Joe and Moby Jack were coming down, and their reaction was disappointing. They said they have no idea who El Gato is. They predicted Joe and Moby would never find him. In fact they said that if Joe and Moby came down and started asking questions they would almost certainly be arrested and shot."

"It's that bad?"

"They might have thought their phones were tapped. But anyway, nobody would agree to help."

"Shhh; look." Laura tilted her head toward a man walking down the aisle with an ice cream cup in his hand: the portly fellow with the nice shoes. Again they waited until he passed before either spoke. "I'm feeling as paranoid as a Castellegran," Laura said. "But tell me . . . are Joe and Moby Jack going down there anyway?"

Andrea's mouth slanted in a sardonic smile. "What do you think?"

"I think the good people of Puerto Nuevo have no idea what's about to hit them."

Piles of documents and scattered yellow pads layered a large table and crowded the elbows of the four men: Herbert Hooks and his personal attorney, white-haired Morton Smith; Egan James; Lou Helms.

The intercom interrupted them. "Mr. Helms, please pick up line one."

Helms punched a button. "Helms here. . . . It's okay, I'm working on that right now. What did you find out?" He listened for a minute. "Say that again. Okay, thanks for the tip. Be in touch. 'Bye."

"What's that all about?" Hooks asked.

Helms' face was impassive, but his eyes tracked from Hooks' face to Egan's. "That was my private investigator. Do you two remember a case about a decade ago where an attorney—the President of the County Bar, in fact—got convicted for sinking a tuna boat? Never mind, I'm sure you remember since you"—he looked at Egan—"helped investigate the case and you"—the eyes shifted toward Hooks—"financed the tuna boat in question."

"The Darren-Cruz case," Hooks said. "That's when Egan and I met. What about it? Why the hell are we wasting our time talking about that?"

"I'll tell you why. You guys keep complaining about deputy U.S Attorney Andrea Burns being overzealous on our current case, right?

I don't blame you; she's been giving me and Mort fits; she acts like she's on a vendetta. Right?"

"What about it? " Hooks snapped. "What does the Darren- Cruz case have to do with Andrea Burns?"

The attorney leaned forward with his hands braced on the conference table. "Andrea Burns is Anthony Darren's *daughter*, you dumb shit!"

Hooks sat back.

Egan flinched.

"I hate surprises on cases," Helms said. "Have you two been holding back on me?"

Before either could answer, the phone buzzed again. Helms grabbed the receiver. "Helms here. Hmmm. What time? Okay, get me a complete copy right away. What do you mean, how? Go across the street and pay the copying costs to the clerk, that's how!"

Snapping down the receiver, he turned back to the conference table. "Well, guys, guess what? You've just been indicted."

Andrea and Rich lay in each other's arms on a terrycloth pad in the secluded patio of Andrea's townhouse. Next to the Jacuzzi flickered three candles that surrounded a half-empty bottle of champagne still cooling in a sparkling bucket of melting ice. Two glasses stood guard, glistening, almost empty, an occasional tiny bubble rising lazily through the reflection of their naked forms. A bouquet of yellow tulips lay on a fresh, folded towel on the deck pad next to a card with the hand-written caption *CONGRATULATIONS Miss Prosecutor, defender of Liberty and Justice for all!*

With the turbulence gone, the spa shimmered smooth. The water droplets on their bare bodies shone in the candlelight while they slept in each other's arms.

Andrea awoke first and ran upstairs to retrieve their robes. After putting on hers, she padded back out to the patio and coaxed Rich from his sleep. As he rose she slipped his arms into the sleeves and cinched the sash for him.

"Tell me the exact charges again," he said. "I love the sound of it."

"Securities fraud and insider trading. But just because Hooks and James have been indicted doesn't mean they're going to end up behind bars; I still have a lot of work ahead."

"But not tonight."

She slid her arms around him. "No. Not tonight."

"What are we waiting for?" he whispered.

"What do you mean?"

"To get married. What are we waiting for?"

She hesitated, then slipped her hands under the collar of his robe and kneaded the muscles of his neck and shoulders. "Honey, I love you like crazy but I'm still afraid I could hurt you if we get married before I resolve a certain something."

"Andi, tell me what it is, will you please? I'm in misery not knowing what's in the way. I can't fight it anymore. I *have* to know."

She rested the top of her head against his chest for a moment, then leaned back and looked into his eyes. "All right. But first: promise you will not under any circumstance use your political position to help me with my . . . situation."

"Well, that's a switch from the usual kind of request I get," Rich said with an ironic quirk to his lips. "But sure, I promise."

"Remember how Sarah asked you to write a letter to help arrange for Joe Cruz and Moby Jack Callucci to go down to Costallegre?"

"Of course."

"You volunteered to do that because you believed in John Woods' opinion that an innocent man might be rotting in prison. Right?"

"Anthony Darren. That's right."

"And you have no idea I'm involved in any of it."

"What do you mean? How are you involved?"

"Sarah and I have been working together on Anthony's pardon application."

"You have? Then why didn't *you* ask me to help push Joe Cruz's visa through?"

"Because if I'd done that, it might have caused you problems later on."

He took hold of her shoulders and held her away. "How? Don't go getting all mysterious on me again. Just tell me how trying to help get Anthony Darren out of prison might cause me problems later."

"Because Anthony Darren is also Bric Locket."

"Wait. You told me Bric Locket is your. . . ." He blinked once, twice, then threw back his head and let out a great booming laugh. "Oh, Jeez. What a fool I am, not putting all this together long ago! It's not like the clues haven't been there. Anthony Darren is your father. Bric Locket is your father. No wonder I've been running in circles." He lowered his head and smiled into her eyes. "You're worried that having a convicted prisoner as a father would make you an unsuitable mate for a United States Senator? Do you really think so little of me?"

"It's not that. Well, maybe partly that. But my father is applying for a Presidential pardon, remember? If I married you now, people might accuse you of trying to influence the Administration to get a political favor. That could hurt your reputation and your chance for re-election. It would certainly kill my father's chance for a pardon. So now do you see the problem?"

He squinted one eye. "I'm trying to."

She hugged him again. "Just bear with me a little longer, sweetheart. A little longer."

"Little lady, I intend to bear with you the rest of my life, just as soon as you agree to it."

26 Costalegre

Joe and Moby Jack wearily climbed the stairs to their modest hotel room in Puerto Nuevo. The hotel consisted of concrete blocks and wood floors, a hodgepodge of styles and materials slapped together over many years, one section at a time. From the balcony Joe looked down a boulevard lined with Mexican Fan palms to the harbor with its wild variety of anchored boats and ships: heavy tankers, tuna seiners, cargo ships and Costalegran military vessels. Most of the gunships appeared to be secondhand U.S. patrol boats, now flying Costalegran flags.

"What do you think?" Moby Jack said.

"Well, none of the gunships are pointing their cannons at us. After two weeks I take that as a good sign."

"We haven't even been arrested yet."

"Yet." Joe squinted at the sky. "I'm going to try to call Andrea again."

"Good luck."

At the payphone in the scuffed lobby Joe made another international call—his fifth so far. The phone rang and rang on a sea of static. Finally, "Hello?"

"Andrea! Is that you?"

"Joe! God, I've been worried. Where are you?"

"Puerto Nuevo. Our hotel looks right out of the movie *Casablanca.*"

"Any luck?"

Joe sighed. "No. We've been all over the place trying to track down Poncho's family, including way up into the hills. But most of his people are gone, just like they said, and the rest basically slammed doors in our faces. So we switched gears and started talking with everyone we could—villagers, shopkeepers, street vendors, all these kids wandering around loose. But it's the same with everyone. Mention 'Poncho Pascalle' and they look at you like you're speaking Swahili; mention 'El Gato' and they cross themselves. Hell, Moby Jack pressed forty bucks on our hotel manager and asked *him* if he knew anything about El Gato, and the guy shoved the money right back. And this in a country where people are eating lizards to stay alive."

"It's that bad?"

"You wouldn't believe how much this country has gone down since my last visit. All those kids I mentioned? Despite the poverty, there's a population explosion like you can't believe."

"I do believe it. That was one of the predictions in *Fusing Order and Chaos*, remember?"

"Yeah, well, it's dead on. When we get back, Moby and I want to meet your mysterious buddy Mr. Locket, see how you guys figured all this out."

"I'll make sure of it."

"But meanwhile, we're not giving up. We figure word must be getting around that two *Norte Americanos* are looking for El Gato, so we're going to push that even harder. If we can't get to him, maybe we can get him to come to *us*. Moby Jack is going to park himself every night down in the outdoor cafe in front of our hotel in full view of passersby. He sticks out like a giant redwood tree on a Texas bean farm."

"That sounds dangerous."

"Moby's getting impatient; he wants something to happen."

"That sounds even worse."

"No, he's actually been amazing. Once when we were up in the hills we got stopped at a *Federale* checkpoint—soldiers in black berets, camouflage uniforms and automatic weapons. They wanted to turn us back, but Moby told them we were on our way to Puerto Nuevo to talk with shipyards about future repairs for tuna vessels. The country needs investment so badly they let us right through." He paused. "I have the feeling Moby's done this kind of thing before."

"Joe, you're not secret agents. You're a giant redhead and a Portuguese bullfighter trying for a comeback."

"You got that right. But we're staying with it anyway."

A few days later Anthony took his turn on the prison phone. At the mere sound of Laura's voice he felt a pilot light inside him click to full flame. "Anything new on your side?" he asked.

"Well . . . yes and no. Sarah says someone's been poisoning the well regarding your pardon. For a while it was moving along fine, but suddenly word's gotten out that the U.S. Attorney's office is working on it, and now all these 'important people' are sending letters urging the President not to grant it. Now, who do you suppose could be behind *that*?"

"I can't imagine." Anthony rested his forehead against the wall. He wondered if he would have created a visible hollow in the bricks there by the time he left this place. If he ever left. "Tell me . . . are my chances less than fifty percent?"

"We honestly don't know. They're down, but we don't know how far. I'm so sorry, sweetheart."

"Okay . . . how about Joe and Moby? What's up with them?"

"Last we heard they haven't had any success getting closer to El Gato. But they're still trying."

"Ah. . . ." Anthony felt hopelessness step up alongside him, eager for an embrace. The hands on the wall clock near the guard station ticked ahead minute by minute, hour by hour, day by day, by weeks, months, years—and to these ticking hands his eyes were drawn in a hypnotic glaze. Life and time were passing him by endlessly, wastefully. . . .

"Anthony? . . . Are you there?"

He leaned back, pulling his head off the wall. "Not really."

The next day Anthony tried dialing the phone number Hector had given him. An automatic message droned that the number had been changed. The new number had been changed, too, but finally he got through to Angelita Lopez Sanchez in Los Angeles.

At first she didn't know who he was. Then she said, "Ah, I remember Hector talking about you. He feels he is forever indebted."

Anthony breathed a sigh of relief. "The last thing Hector said to me was that he might be 'flying south for the winter.' Two friends of mine just made that same trip and have been trying to contact a man down there known as El Gato. Do you think —"

"El Gato?"

"Yes. Do you think Hector could connect them to—"

"Oh no! No one talks to El Gato. It's like trying to talk to a ghost. He's a mystery man."

Anthony took a slow breath. "Would you ask Hector anyway, Angelita? It's very important."

"I'll try," she said. "If he can help, okay, but I don't think he can. It will be dangerous. I must go now, Mr. Darren."

"Good-bye, Angelita, and thanks. Tell Hector that the Professor may need his *papeles*."

"I understand. *Adios*."

The avenue, which extended several blocks from the waterfront and always seemed filled with music and laughter, was the same as Joe remembered. Seamen from ships flying the flags of countries all over the world walked up and down the cobblestones. Cantina sounds mingled with sensual laughter of beautiful women working the red light bars of this colorfully notorious strip. Here, Moby had told Joe, was where he had run into Poncho's ghost.

As they walked into each cantina, one after the other, Joe saw all eyes shift to his partner. Dressed in a T-shirt and shorts, his body as trim and hard as the aluminum beer kegs behind the bars, Moby joked and talked with bartenders and patrons alike in Spanish which, while not exactly fluent, was definitely colorful. Within a few minutes he had patrons laughing. In the first locale they called him "Rojo Grande," Big Red, and the nickname proceeded them down the strip.

Joe soon noticed one big change from the past: on every corner and in every cantina stood two or three Costalegran soldiers in full military regalia: shiny black boots, starched green camouflage uniforms, black berets. Each had an AK47 slung over his shoulder, a pistol on his belt and the swagger of the well-armed.

Halfway down the boulevard the two Americans entered a bar filled mostly with apparent locals. Joe spotted the guards right away . . . and vice-versa. "Moby," he said for the third time, "we've got to stay cool in this joint."

"Lighten up, man. Our mission is to mingle, right?"

Joe nodded reluctantly. He reminded himself that Moby had managed to survive two tours of duty in Vietnam, including almost two thousand helicopter liftoffs. Why should either of them worry?

There were a lot of working girls in the bar—"Women of Horizontal Refreshment," as Moby Jack liked to call them. One of them introduced herself as Socorro, put an arm around Joe's neck and made all sorts of erotic promises. He shifted nervously. Another sat herself on Moby's lap. Within a few minutes Moby had both girls laughing and kidding. "You should pay me rather than the other way around," he told them.

Socorro's friend shook her head and made a counter proposal.

As Joe looked around the room, trying to keep an eye on the scattered soldiers without appearing to do so, he also tried to monitor the conversation beside him so things would not get out of hand. Moby's biography included too many examples of brawling and clearing out entire bars on the waterfronts of San Diego and Balboa, Panama.

Socorro shifted her hand to Joe's knee. He was trying to draw himself away without insulting her when an angry voice to his right made him jump. A man who looked like a Costalegran cowboy, complete with Stetson and tooled-leather boots, leaned over Joe to yell something at Socorro. His Spanish was too rapid and colloquial for Joe to follow, but his demeanor needed no translation as he reached over and yanked on Socorro's free arm. She struggled to hold onto Joe's knee as she shrieked at the cowboy to get away. Joe hesitated. *The girl is not part of my mission. I'd be very happy if she took off with the cowboy. . . .*

Moby tapped Joe on the shoulder. "Is this guy bothering you?"

"No. No, just play it cool. Don't start anything here. Please. Those *Federales* look like they're itching to use their AKs."

But then a sharp slap cracked the air, and Joe knew instantly that restraint time was over. The girl's head rocked sideways. The cowboy's hand, still open, readied for another blow. Moby stood up, seeming to almost hit the ceiling. His muscles flinched through his white T-shirt as he raised his chair and slammed it down , sitting down in the same motion, next to the cowboy's. Then Moby gave it a mighty backward push, driving the cowboy's chair back a full three feet. Moby sat, placing his thick back between the girl and her aggressor.

He gave Joe a wink. "See? *No problemo*."

Joe's gaze shifted. "Look out!"

Moby Jack twisted in his chair, and his bulging arm, lightly matted with reddish fuzz, swung around fast as a mongoose smelling a cobra. His meaty hand caught the cowboy's wrist just below the extended blade of a serious sheath knife clenched in the cowboy's hand. All movement halted instantly.

Then Moby rose to his entire six feet six inches and, with a quick jerk, snapped the cowboy's arm out of its socket.

A cry like a branded calf screeched from the man's throat. Moby dangled him by the useless arm for a few seconds, regarding him with what appeared to be disappointment, then plucked the knife out of his hand and released him. The wailing cowboy stumbled out through the curtained exit, cradling his mangled arm. Moby tossed the knife onto the table and sighed. "That didn't even make me thirsty."

Then he looked at the two AK-47 muzzles pointing at him from inches away and said, "Now *that* makes me thirsty."

"Moby. . . ." Joe said.

The crowd receded to the perimeter of the room. *This* is *the Old West*, Joe thought.

"Hey you, Rojo Grande," one of the soldiers said in Spanish. "Walk outside with your hands in the air."

"Roger, Wilco." Moby raised his hands slowly and turned toward the door. Joe, pumped full of dread, followed them out— along with most of the bar patrons. Outside, the crowd surrounded the soldiers and Moby, and nobody seemed entirely sure what to do next. One of the soldier's began raising a field radio to his mouth.

Just then a patron from the cantina stepped into the gap between the crowd and the soldiers. "Wait, wait," he said. "This was all a mistake, I think. A misunderstanding. There's not even a victim anymore." The man was short in stature but almost as broad across the shoulders and chest as Moby. He produced an apologetic shrug, as if the whole event was somehow his fault.

"Rojo Grande here almost tore someone's arm off," the soldier without the radio said. "He has to be arrested."

"The other man had a knife. Almost a sword."

"And Rojo Grande was defending a maiden's honor!" someone from the crowd shouted. That produced a lot of laughter and a flamboyant curtsy from Soccoro. The soldier with the radio grinned and put the radio back on his belt. The other soldier looked confused.

"Can I lower my arms now?" Moby Jack asked. "They're getting tired."

"Don't any of you recognize Rojo Grande?" the thickset man said. "He's a famous football athlete and a hero in the US."

"American football?" the second soldier said. "That's not real football."

"True," said the thickset man. "But look at him—can you see him playing the real thing with feet that size?

A louder roar of laughter. Now both guards were smiling.

"My cousin played football for the University of Texas," a bystander told Moby in Spanish. "His name is Diego Alvarez. Did you know him?"

"Heard of him. Played guard. Good man."

"Rojo Grande was an All-American end for Notre Dame," said the thickset man, whom Joe was beginning to think of as the Mediator.

"The Irish! My favorite American football team!" another patron cried. "Except there's a lot of Hispanic Catholics at that school, too. It's not just Irish."

"You're right, some of the best," said Moby. "All nationalities, races and religions fighting together on the same team but they all have the Irish spirit."

"That is true," agreed the bystander, "the Irish spirit!"

The Mediator pumped a fist in the air. "Irish spirit! Irish spirit! Irish spirit!"

Within seconds the crowd—including the soldiers—had picked

up the chant, and the entire mob barged back into the cantina for another round or two of beers and shooters.

Much later, Joe escorted Rojo Grande through staggering layers of well-wishers and out onto the street. While they were figuring out which direction was uphill, the familiar stocky figure came out behind them and stood staring up at the stars. "You two looking for El Gato?" he asked in English only slightly dusted with a south-of-the-border accent.

Joe's brain cleared in recognition as if someone had dumped freezing water on his head; even Moby seemed to focus. "Yes," Joe said. "How did you know?"

The Mediator gave him a direct look. "I understand you're also going around talking to members of Poncho Pascalle's family. Why? Poncho died years ago."

"We're not so sure of that,' Joe said. "And if he is alive he can help a friend, *El hermano leche*."

"And who is that milk brother?"

"My name is Joe Cruz, but the help would be for a mutual friend who is in prison in America for a crime he didn't commit."

"And what would this friend's name be?"

Joe hesitated. From his own experience he knew that prisons made a person more, not less, vulnerable to victimization for all kinds of reasons. "I'd rather not say."

The Mediator nodded as if that was a wise decision. "You're staying at the Vista Marina, right?"

"Yes."

"I have to check a few things. . . . Be prepared to receive a message."

"When?" Joe and Moby said simultaneously.

"Be patient, *señores*. It might take a while." Lifting one muscular arm, the Mediator gave an open-hand, chest-high salute, and then stepped quietly off into the shadows.

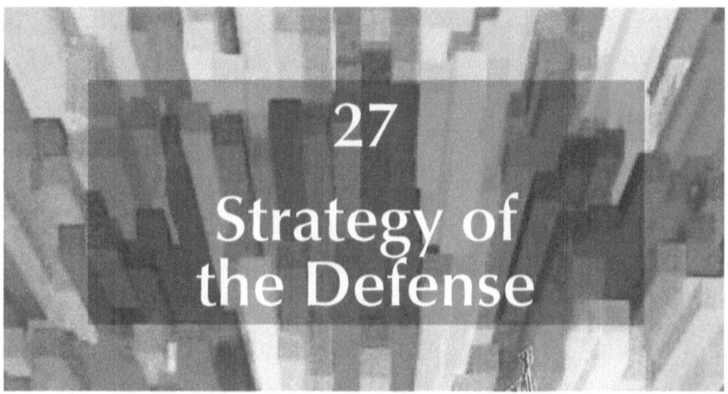

27
Strategy of the Defense

Andrea hurried to complete preparations for the James-Hooks trial. A federal prosecuting lawyer has to work within the Constitutional rules guaranteeing the accused a speedy trial—which, in the case of Federal court, means trial within seventy days following arrest or indictment unless a defendant waives that safeguard. In practice, most defendants seek more time in order to prepare better cases against a prosecution that's already gotten their ducks all lined up.

But in this case, as complicated as it was, James' and Hooks' attorneys seemed perfectly content to go to trial as soon as possible. A puzzle—until Andrea got back to her office and learned that attorneys Helms and Smith had moved to disqualify her as prosecutor on the grounds that she had a conflict of interest.

The news hit her like a double blow across the knees. First, because she could think of only one "conflict of interest" that might apply and second—worse—because no one but she was prepared to prosecute this case. If she didn't do it, the government would either have to dismiss in exchange for a plea bargain on a lesser charge, or risk losing the case entirely. Andrea feared they would go for the lesser charge.

She'd intended spending two or three hours that evening refining her opening statement, but now she couldn't concentrate on it. Instead she called Anthony, even though monitors were probably listening in.

As Anthony listened to her explanation his eyes slowly closed.

"Well, if they found out you're my daughter, they obviously plan to argue you're trying to get revenge against James and Hooks."

"But I don't even *know* those guys, Dad. The securities case has nothing to do with you and them. I'll dig through the American Bar Rules of Ethics, but I don't think there's anything right on point."

"Andi," he said softly, "you *are* biased."

For a moment she said nothing, then he heard her sigh. "Have I blown it? Oh, God, I should never have kept this a secret from John."

"Calm down," Anthony said. "Let's talk it out, just like we did all those hypothetical cases while you were in school." He paused, thinking. "Okay. I'd say they have a pretty strong argument for conflict of interest, so I'm not sure arguing against that will do you any good. On the other hand, from what you've said it sounds like they've known about the supposed conflict for quite a while. You know they're obligated to bring a motion like this in a timely manner; they have no right to sandbag you and put prosecution in a position where no one else is ready to try the case. Which means the judge has a dilemma."

"What dilemma?" The despair had left her voice.

"Any judge worth a salt is bound to also suspect that the defense knew, or at least should have known, about this conflict of interest earlier. So, if I may make a suggestion, *use* that. Bring it up before the judge. I doubt defense counsel will lie outright if the judge asks them, point blank and under oath, to tell him the date they first learned of this possible conflict. Neither of these guys is going to commit perjury for a client, so they'll admit they found out long ago. Actually, John Woods will probably have to argue the point; you're too involved."

"Okay, I'll suggest it to him. Anything else?"

"If the judge decides to disqualify you anyway, have John request that as a compromise you bring in a co-counsel who will act as lead in the trial, and that you and this co-counsel try the case together."

"Okay. If that's the way it works out, maybe Sarah can act as co-counsel."

"Perfect. Just don't have John make that suggestion except as a last resort, all right? By the way, who's the judge?"

A pause. Then: "Would you believe the same judge who sent you to prison?"

"Winchester? Really?"

"He might be biased himself, but I suspect this isn't the sort of circumstance where he's likely to disqualify himself, is it?"

"No, it isn't. I just wish I could be there, but sometimes the eagle flies and empty the aerie lies."

"What's that supposed to mean?" she asked.

He looked down the length of the corridor, at all the barred doors of the "houses," the grimy tiles, the hand-printed walls. And, eventually, a closed and locked door. "Nothing," he said. "Just one of those little quotes I picked up along the way."

To that she had no response.

"Darren," Sluggo said as he clattered along behind Anthony on the way back to Anthony's cell, "how come you get so many fuckin' phone calls? I got better things to do than guard your ass."

"Sorry, didn't know I was such an inconvenience."

"Your mouth is going to buy you trouble if you keep it up, asshole." Sluggo pulled open the door, waited for Anthony to go in, then began sliding the bars shut.

"Hey!" Anthony had lifted a corner of his mattress. "What's going on? Someone's been in here! My manuscript—it's gone *again*!" He spun and stepped into the gap before the door could finish closing. "I'm tired of this bullshit, Sluggo!"

"You accusing me of stealing your chicken-shit chicken scratches, Darren? Jesus, you're the dumbest fuckin' prisoner I ever seen. Now step to the back or I'll slam this door in your face."

"I'm not moving until I get my papers back."

Sluggo jerked the gate. Anthony caught it and shoved it the other way, hard.

Sluggo's face darkened. "Okay, that does it, dipshit." Instead of reaching for his pepper spray, Sluggo grabbed Anthony by his shirt and charged him across the cell, slamming him against the wall. Anthony absorbed the impact, then clutched Sluggo's hands and bent his wrists back.

He had to admit he enjoyed the expression of pain that bloomed on the guard's face. Enjoyed the way the guard's knees half-buckled. Enjoyed the way Sluggo began backing up, duck-walking in reverse.

"Let go, you son of a bitch!"

Enjoyed . . .

Jesus, what are you doing? You call this balance, synthesis, any fucking smart thing at all? Sometimes the eagle flies, and sometimes he gets shot out of the goddamned sky.

Anthony released the guard and stepped back.

Sluggo rubbed his wrists, then stepped quickly into the corridor, slammed and locked the door. "You just bought yourself time in solitary, fuckhead. You think you're so smart, so special? Let's see how you like a week or two alone with your fuckin' thoughts."

As he walked away, the clanging of metal cups and catcalls crescendoed throughout the block. Anthony slumped onto his bunk. *Nice move . . . con.*

At 7 a.m. John Woods was taking off his coat in his office as Andrea stepped in and closed the door behind her.

He glanced at her and went to his desk, got out his pipe and tobacco.

She watched him for a moment, then cleared her throat. "John . . ."

When she failed to continue, he shot her a questioning look.

"John . . . I'm very concerned that the defense is moving to disqualify me. With trial starting this morning, if they succeed we won't have anyone else ready to take over."

"I'm aware of that," Woods said. "You're the best I have at the moment on this kind of matter. You're our specialist as a securities fraud prosecutor. On top of which Roger, Bob, Sarah, Al and Earl are all already in trial on other cases." Woods got the pipe going and leaned back in his swivel chair, his gaze drilling through her. "So, what conflict of interest do you think they'll come up with, Andrea?"

She licked her lips. "Something having to do with the old case of United States of America vs. Anthony Darren and Joseph Cruz."

Woods squinted. "I prosecuted that case; I don't see any connection. But go on."

"You remember when you gave Sarah the go-ahead to work on a pardon for Anthony Darren?"

"Yes."

"Do you feel that I tried to influence you in any way in that decision?"

Woods tapped the pipe stem on his front teeth. "Not at all. As I recall, Sarah initiated the study based on a transmittal letter you found among Egan's records. And those records were copied by a federal agent before you ever touched them. So what's the point?"

She felt almost dizzy now. "John . . . do you recall rumors that Anthony Darren had a daughter out of wedlock when he was a young man?"

"Yes. Yes, I remember that. In fact, at the suggestion of Egan James I believe I tried—a bit over-zealously, perhaps—to introduce into evidence that Darren may have abandoned this girl. Why? Where is this taking us, Andrea?"

"The daughter in question is me."

The pipe threatened to fall off Woods' lip. "What?"

"I am Anthony Darren's daughter. Andrea Darren; that should be my name."

Shrouded in smoke, Woods rotated his chair until he was facing the window. "Jeez, Andi, why didn't you tell me this before?"

"I'm sorry. I didn't . . . my father didn't want it to hurt my career."

He turned back. "Well, sit down, young lady. Let's figure this out. Looks like I'm going to court with you this morning."

"Whose motion is this?" Judge Winchester asked after everyone was seated around his desk.

"Motion of the defense," Helms said.

Helms, Smith and Woods engaged the judge in small talk while they waited for the court reporter to set up her steno machine, but Andrea couldn't join in; her mind would let her do nothing but agonize over how the judge would react and what he would decide.

Not long after the defense attorneys finally commenced their argument, the judge's expression told Andrea he was flabbergasted.

" . . . and so," concluded Helms, "Ms. Burns should be disqualified from trying this case. She is the daughter of a man my client,

Egan James, helped convict for conspiracy to sink a ship, as well as for murder under the Federal Code. It's obvious she has a personal vendetta going here."

The judge turned to Woods. "John, what has the US Attorney's Office got to say about this?"

Woods replied in a sanguine voice. "Your Honor, it is Egan James and not Andrea Burns who is meant to be on trial here— just as ten years ago it was Anthony Darren on trial, and not Andrea Burns. Yes, she is the daughter of Anthony Darren—but no rules of ethics have been breached. She has no financial interest in this case. She is not a relative of anyone on trial here, and the outcome of this trial has no effect on her father's status. Your Honor heard all the evidence in the case of the sinking of *the Sea Diva* ten years ago, and Your Honor is the judge who sentenced Mr. Darren; therefore it is obvious that *you* have no conflict of interest in this case. For similar reasons we can infer that I, who prosecuted Mr. Darren in that same case, also have no conflict of interest."

The furrow in Winchester's brow only deepened.

Woods continued. "At no time did Andrea Burns suggest or make any attempt to influence me one way or the other whether or not to prosecute this case. The facts were presented for indictment based upon readily available information, and grand jurors asked their own independent questions. At all times Ms. Burns simply let the chips fall where they may."

The judge looked directly at Andrea, then back at Woods.

"In fact," Woods went on, "things should be the other way around, Your Honor. It is the government that should move to bar the *defense* from ever raising before the jury this issue of 'vendetta' or of a father-daughter relationship. But most importantly, we've been sandbagged. The defense clearly waited until the last minute to make this motion. Their conduct of hiding in the weeds constitutes a waiver of alleged conflict. We have no one else prepared to try this case. If we don't start today we'll have to let these defendants go—in other words we have been seriously prejudiced by their tactics."

And so it went, back and forth. An hour later Winchester said, "I've heard enough. I want to look up a few things, check a few points and authorities. Come back at eleven and I'll give my ruling."

⚓

In the hallway Andrea paced the floors alone for a while, then phoned her office to check messages. Millie said, "You've had several calls. A Mr. Cruz called long distance to tell you they're 'still stuck,' whatever that means, and to ask if you have any ideas. Also—"

"Never mind. I've got forty minutes until I have to be back in court. Can't stand waiting here; I'm coming to the office."

The wind shuffled bougainvillea blossoms in random directions across the pavement as she made the five minute walk. The water of the bay lapped at the docks, close enough for her to smell the salt, but today she couldn't enjoy it. She couldn't predict how the judge would rule any more than she could pick the spots where the bougainvillea blossoms would land.

Among the messages on her telephone desk was one from a *Los Angeles Post Tribune* columnist. She returned the call and asked for Mr. Edward Spencer. If it was about the trial she would have no comment, but she always tried to be diplomatic with reporters. They had their job to do, and First Amendment rights of free press were guaranteed by the United States Constitution. Besides, why tick off the press?

When Spencer got on the phone, he sounded as though he were clutching a bag of candy behind his back. "What is your reaction to the President's comments, Doctor Burns?"

"I'm sorry, I don't follow you."

"The President just told a group of reporters that he'd recently read a book he thought would be worthwhile reading. That's a significant remark. He mentioned the title: *Fusing Order and Chaos*. That is your book, isn't it?"

Andrea hesitated. "Well, mine and Bric Locket's. Mostly Bric's. Which President is this? UCLA? UCSD?"

"The President of the United States of America." Spencer sounded amused. "Ever heard of him?"

"Well, naturally I'm very pleased," she said dizzily. "We hope the book's concepts can be used by people of different political, social, and economic views as a tool for synthesizing their differences."

"Doctor Burns, there's no record of this Bric Locket having

published anything anywhere before. How can we get hold of him for an interview?"

"I'm sorry, Mr. Spencer, he's a very private person. He prefers not to give interviews. And besides, he's away on a very extended stay working on another book."

"Well, can you tell me anything about his background then? I've read the book, and it's quite dense with citations. What are Mr. Locket's credentials?"

"Sorry again. For personal reasons and because the book takes such strong political positions, he feels he shouldn't disclose his identity at this time. Maybe someday."

"I see. 'Bric Locket' is a pseudonym. Well, perhaps you'll let him know that just last night the Southern California Literary Society placed *Fusing Order and Chaos* on its list of nominees for 'Best Non-fiction by a Previously Unpublished Southern California Author.' I know because I'm on the board."

Andrea had been feeling so far down that the impact of Spencer's words shot her into outer space. She could think of only one thing to say: "Thank you."

"The prize is given each year to an outstanding work by a new writer. There are four other books in the running for this particular award, so nothing is guaranteed. Still, just being nominated is an honor. Do you have any comment on this? . . . Doctor Burns?"

"Yes. Yes, of course I'm thrilled, and I know Bric will be as well. How can we ever thank you for your consideration?"

"Ms. Burns, we didn't do anything. It's you and Mr. Locket who created the stir with your theories. The awards dinner will be held in Los Angeles on the evening of June 2nd at 7 p.m. Although it's not mandatory you attend, we hope you will do so as our guests. Mr. Locket as well, if he would be so kind. The members of the Society would certainly love to meet him."

"I would very much like to be there. Thank you so much, Mr. Spencer. If by then I've completed a trial I'm about to start."—*I hope*—"I'll attend for sure. As for Mr. Locket, it's unlikely he'll make it, but I'll see that he receives your invitation."

"Thank you, Ms. Burns. Please do urge him to attend. It would be an honor to meet him."

After hanging up, she took a moment to catch her breath, then tried to call Rich, Laura, Sarah, and Anthony to give them all the terrific news. But she was unable to connect with any of them, and had to hurry back to court unsatisfied.

At precisely eleven o'clock the clerk announced that Judge Winchester's decision would be rendered from the courtroom rather than in chambers. The court reporter got herself and her steno machine situated. A minute later Winchester entered, stepped up to the bench, sat down in his regal chair, and welcomed them.

"First," he said, "I am ordering excluded from the courtroom anyone who is not a lawyer for a party in this case." The only spectator in the gallery sighed, got up and left. "Marshal, please bar the door. Unless anyone wishes to object, I'm ordering the transcript of this hearing sealed. This session will be heard *in camera*."

The attorneys blinked at one another but no one spoke.

"All right, does anyone have anything to add to their previous arguments?"

"No, Your Honor," said each side.

The judge began to read. "In the matter of United States of America vs. James and Hooks regarding defendant's motion to disqualify counsel, and after arguments and points and authorities having been submitted by the USA and the defendants, I find that counsel Andrea Burns has a potential conflict of interest and I am inclined to disqualify her from proceeding with this case."

Everything stood still. Andrea felt herself sinking toward the center of the earth. Without looking, she knew Egan James' face wore that little smirk she so hated, and that Herbert Hooks was mopping his guilty face.

With an almost apologetic look at John Woods, Winchester said, "Do you have anything further to say, Mr. Woods, before I confirm this tentative decision to disqualify?"

With his usual aura of calm, Woods rose and approached the lectern between the counsel tables. "Your Honor, I have a suggestion. Respectfully, I request the court to inquire of Defense Counsel, under oath if necessary, as to precisely *when* they learned that Ms. Burns is the daughter of Anthony Darren. If we can get the answer to this first question, I'll have an additional comment."

"I agree, counsel," the judge replied. "Mr. Helms, Mr. Smith, do I have to put you under oath?"

"No, Your Honor," said Lou Helms. He rose and replaced Woods at the lectern.

"No, Your Honor." Morton Smith joined Helms.

"Well," said Winchester, "when did you find out that Ms. Burns is Anthony Darren's daughter?"

Helms and Smith looked at each other. Finally Helms leaned toward the microphone. "Your Honor, we learned of the father-daughter relationship approximately seventy days ago."

Winchester's brows contracted. "And you waited until *now* to bring your motion? There is no excuse for that, counsel. However . . ." He turned his gaze toward Woods. "I believe the issue of fair trial is paramount here. Mr. Woods, you had further comment?"

Andrea struggled to sit still, to project the same calm mien as her boss. But she knew that everything now swung on a thread already stretched to the breaking point.

Woods returned to the lectern. "On the issue of fair trial I have a suggestion. I propose, Your Honor, that I be permitted to assign co-counsel for the prosecution, and that such counsel be designated as lead counsel; that such co-counsel make all arguments to the jury but that Ms. Burns be allowed to put on the case, make arguments only to the court, examine witnesses and introduce exhibits."

Half-smiling, the judge peered over his reading glasses at the defense table. "What do you say to that Mr. Helms, Mr. Smith?"

"Object strenuously to that idea, your honor," Smith said.

"I concur," added Helms. "A conflict is a conflict. Ms. Burns should not be allowed to act even as co-counsel."

The judge hesitated. "Balancing the interests of opposing parties, I do not believe any prejudice would come to the defendants if separate co-counsel were to act as lead prosecution attorney. And I am satisfied that the defendants, with due diligence, could have brought this motion to disqualify Ms. Burns at an earlier time. Tardiness of the motion has prejudiced the government's position and perhaps is a waiver of the conflict. That is my ruling."

He shifted his gaze to Andrea. "I am also imposing an order that Ms. Burns not discuss this case with Anthony Darren. Although I am not *ordering* it, my advice to Ms. Burns is that she have no discussions on *any* subject with Mr. Darren for the duration of this trial—except a last note incorporating this advice."

Another shift. "I *am* ordering that the Defendants shall not raise this issue to the jury, nor discuss this matter publicly during the trial. The transcript of this hearing and my ruling is sealed."

"Does that mean there's a 'gag' order?" asked Smith.

"That is correct, Counsel—Mr. Woods, who would you assign as co-counsel?"

"The government assigns Sarah Billings from my office."

"I'll give her a few hours to prepare," the judge said with a turned-up chin and raised eyebrows, as if to acknowledge that the time allotted was woefully insufficient. "We will recess until 3:00 p.m. today."

28 Rebel Connection

From the depths of sleep Moby heard tapping—and instantly he was crouching on the floor next to his hotel bed like a red-maned lion, heart thundering in his chest. Through the door he heard a whisper: "Rojo Grande, José. Let's go. *Andele* . . . hurry!"

Soundlessly he opened the door, and in stepped the Mediator. "Jeez, it's still dark outside," Moby mumbled, slipping into his clothes before Joe could roll out of bed. While Joe dressed, Moby dropped to the floor again, this time to pop off his usual fifty morning pushups. All along, the Mediator urged them on. "The taxi is waiting!"

From the balcony Moby peered down at the rumbling, exhaust-smoking car, its headlights off. Then he and Joe followed the Mediator down with their things and climbed into the rattletrap without disturbing the pre-dawn stillness.

Soon they were rumbling through overhanging trees and the heavy brush of the jungle above Puerto Nuevo. The driver rounded a curve before he turned on the headlights. Twenty minutes later he turned them off again and coasted onto a dirt road. A thousand feet farther along, surrounded by black foliage, he parked. And they waited.

The distant rattling of perhaps a truck echoed through the jungle. Half a minute later a dark-painted pickup, headlights out, brakes squeaking, rolled to a stop next to them. One man jumped off the truck bed. Another sat in the cab, the glow from his cigarette indicating a cavalier disregard for snipers.

The driver got out holding an M-16. He spoke quietly to the Mediator and together they pulled a pile of blankets from the cab. Heaps of straw and baskets of vegetables filled the truck's back corners. The Costalegrans motioned to Joe and Moby; they climbed into the truck bed and lay down on the straw. The Mediator pulled the blankets over their heads.

An instant later the blankets whipped back again, revealing the black sky. The driver handed his rifle to Moby. Rojo Grande checked the magazine and safety, then held the cool barrel against his face as the blanket flew back over him. He felt the straw and vegetables piling on top of him. The truck started moving and settled into a cushioned, vibrating ride through the jungle. A short time later Joe began snoring lightly.

After a while Moby felt the truck rolling to a stop, and heard the sound of voices. *Check point.* Next to him he sensed Joe lying awake and rigid. Releasing the rifle's safety, Moby willed himself to be still and silent and ready.

Then something sharp and unyielding sank into his left thigh. Before he could even think about whether or not to react, the point withdrew, leaving behind a wet, burning pain. *Shit . . . I got stabbed!* Then the same thing happened to his right bicep. Moby's tongue stuck to the roof of his mouth while he waited for it to happen again. It didn't. Instead, the weight of vegetables pressing on him lightened here and there as soldiers no doubt helped themselves to the produce.

At last the truck lurched forward again, and Moby let the tension slowly drain away. The incisions on his leg and arm burned and stung abominably, but he ignored it. He'd endured far worse, and probably wouldn't bleed to death.

He was half-asleep when the truck stopped again. This time there was no conversation or poking about with blades; the weight of the vegetables and straw lifted off him and a blinding flashlight struck him in the eyes. In the dim morning light two men motioned him out of the truck. He shook the residue of sleep from his head and jumped to the ground next to Joe. They were led into a solitary stucco ranch house surrounded by shadowy trees and meadows.

"Holy shit, Moby," Joe said. "You got *stabbed?*"

"You didn't?"

Joe shook his head.

"They were testing the produce for quality," Moby said with dignity. "I obviously passed."

A woman with slightly graying hair, gracious eyes and a warm smile served them bean and chicken soup, then began dressing Moby's wounds.

The Mediator and the men from the truck seemed relaxed now. As dawn broke over the trees they spoke to the couple of the house in warm and friendly Spanish. Two small, laughing children with dark eyes and almond-colored skin climbed on Moby's knees and shoulders. Moby stood, pretended he was a tree. They could have been climbing a giant redwood, only these branches threw them into the air and caught them as they squealed and giggled.

Soon everyone gathered outside. One man lifted a small outboard motor onto the truck bed, which the others filled with heavy, well-stuffed gunny sacks. Then Moby Jack, Joe, the Mediator and the remaining revolutionaries piled into the back. The truck moved out into the early morning sunlight, rocking along a dirt road.

The jungle thinned, became scraggly, then vanished into dunes of untracked sand. The truck wove through them and finally stopped on a beach at the edge of a crystal-clear estuary. Moby climbed to the top of a dune and stood at full height, his hand shading his eyes, scanning a landscape of unparalleled majesty. Other estuaries, visible in all directions, led to a pristine blue bay. For miles, mangrove trees enveloped the watery ribbons. As far as he could see, only their truck and its team seemed to inhabit this unspoiled wilderness.

The revolutionaries waded to the stand of mangroves that rose from the shallows of the estuary on roots that looked like millions of plumbing pipes, and pulled a native longboat out of cover. One opened a torso-sized blue plastic canister and emptied into it fifths of tequila and vodka, half a bottle of Cointreau, thirty or so sliced limes and three double handfuls of cracked ice. Smiling, he sealed the thermos, wrapped it in his arms and vigorously shook it. The other men busied themselves loading supplies into the boat.

Finally the Mediator clamped the small motor to the stern and motioned Moby and Joe aboard. To the buzz of the motor they glided off under the mangrove canopy. The rays of the sun filtering through the foliage reflected sparkling patches off the glassy surface of the water. Thousands of oysters, blood clams and other mollusks clung to the tree roots.

A darkly tanned man standing on the bow swirled a small net over his head as though to lasso mysterious swimmers below. Then he signaled with an open hand, and the boat slowed. The net spun, flew out gracefully and landed in a perfect butterfly splash. He hauled it emerging from the water, flashing silver and gold. Moby and Joe grabbed it and emptied three wriggling fish into the boat.

The boat moved on. The temperature rose with the sun. When the boat finally reached open water at the mouth of a large bay, more pristine wilderness greeted Moby's eyes. In his tortuous Spanish he asked if he could dive in. The boat stopped and the bow man gestured to a wooden box. Moby flipped it open and was delighted to find fins, masks, knives, snorkels and even a Hawaiian sling-spear gun.

"See if you can shoot some food for camp tonight," the Mediator said.

"But try not to shoot me," Joe added as he unbuttoned his shirt. "I'll be the big, beautiful merman looking for lobsters and such."

Everyone but the Mediator stripped to their shorts, strapped on knives, and one by one splashed into the clear water. The Americans went to work instantly, swimming about as they had done countless times as teenagers growing up in the families of commercial fishermen. The bottom of the boat began filling with oysters, clams, speared fish and flapping lobsters.

The hunters climbed back in; the boat motored on. The Mediator took his knife and began popping open the clams and oysters. He squeezed on sprinkles of lime juice, dashed them with hot salsa, and offered the raw delicacy to Moby and Joe. They slurped meat from the shells one by one—like eating popcorn—sucking down the juices, smacking their lips and washing down their hors d'oeuvres with the Fisherman's Margaritas from the big blue canister.

Finally Joe leaned back in the sunlight, his ringlets of hair still beaded with water, and Moby watched the lines in his friend's face begin easing away for the first time in many years. *Good for you, old buddy*, he thought. *You're finally lightening up again.*

They reached the other side of the bay and continued on through another labyrinth of water paths beneath a mangrove canopy before the boat finally emerged into a tree-walled amphitheater dominated by a sand island crowned with trees. Moby saw a short man, broad through the hips and shoulders, standing on the beach with his fists on his hips. He wore faded blue-green surfer shorts, a wrinkled white T-shirt and a faded LA Dodgers cap, gray hair curling up around its edges. The man's smiling white teeth were clamped at a crazy angle on a lighted cigar.

"Joe," Moby asked, "is that who I think it is?"

"Looks pretty good for a dead guy," Joe said.

Moby rose to his feet so fast the boat almost overturned. "Poncho! Poncho, you sumbitch!"

Poncho waved a thick arm. "Took you long enough to get here, you ol' crazy buddies!"

Wading hip-deep into the water, Poncho Pascalle grabbed the rail and helped drag the boat up the beach. Moby and Joe jumped out and the three men embraced, slapping each other's backs; then Moby lifted both the others off their feet and swung them in a semicircle.

"Put me down, you gorilla," Poncho said. Then, his feet again on the sand, he brushed his eyes with the back of his hand. "Joe, Moby, it's good to see you guys. Joe, you are still my brother. So how come you never visit?" he laughed.

Joe gripped Poncho by the shoulders. "I think they turned off your phone service down here."

"Damn them. I told them I would pay my bill next week."

Moby laughed. "Poncho, you did the best disappearing act in history. You've got to tell us about it."

"Of course, lots to catch up on."

Poncho led Joe and Moby to the center of camp. Half hidden in trees and behind make-shift lean-tos squatted a camouflaged amphibious armored vehicle, a .50 caliber muzzle protruding from its steel-plated shields. A comfortable-looking thatched palm roof cabana, elevated on stilts, nested under the trees to the rear of the clearing. The forest canopy shadowed several two-man military tents pitched in the background.

Several rebel soldiers came out and the entire group gathered around an overturned oil drum that had been converted into a wood-burning stove, its top steel-wooled to a high sheen. Lobsters, oysters, clams and fish were carried over from the boat and piled onto it. Soon rich-smelling steam rose, and with the addition of spicy vegies, cilantro, lemon and peppers the camp cook's machete clanged a marimba-like rhythm against the drum's hot surface.

Meanwhile other soldiers off-loaded the long boat, hauling ashore gunnysacks of canned goods, beans, beer, soft drinks and other supplies. Moby shook his head. "You boys sure got it rough out here in the sticks."

Poncho's smile faded. "Yes, it is good until the helicopters come, or the gunboats."

Moby grimaced his apology.

The cook passed around a wooden tray stacked with hot tortillas. The men lined up, scooped spatulas of seafood onto their tortillas and dashed them with lime juice and salsa. Moby and Joe selected spots in the circle of men and sat down on drift logs, barefoot in the sparkling sand. Looking around at this meal-sharing motley crew, Moby felt a tingle of familiarity. It came from the primordial wilderness surrounding him; it came from the pride of being accepted into this team of revolutionaries; it came from whispers within—whispers from warrior genes in his own cells, genes from ancestors extending back, from life to life, perhaps across a hundred thousand years. Above all it came from personal memories of other camps like this, other groups of hard men dedicated to hard causes.

It made him feel alive.

As the setting sun's orange glow strobed through the rim of trees, most of the men moved away into shadow, leaving only Joe, Moby and Poncho at the edge of the water holding beers and a bottle of tequila. They sat on bulging gunny sacks and empty crates around a ship's hatch cover that had probably washed in from the Pacific. Beside them a small fire crackled between high rocks.

Then Joe said, "Okay, Poncho. It's time. Moby Jack already told me what he remembers about that night on *the Sea Diva*, and I listened to Alfonso Martin's lies in court. Now I want." He cleared his throat. "I want to know exactly what happened. Exactly how my Michael died."

In the firelight Poncho's face looked like a bas relief carved on an Aztec temple. "I will tell you the whole thing, Joe. But first, you tell me: did you radio the code? Did you radio the code for me to sink *the Sea Diva*?"

"Of course not. In fact I called with the code to *not* sink the *Diva*. The tortoise shell code. But Captain Di Santi couldn't find you, so I told him to give you the message. I repeated it to him so many times—tortoise shell, not turtle shell; tortoise shell, not turtle shell—I think he was sure I'd gone crazy."

"Di Santi never gave me no message."

"Figures. I'm sure he thought it was pretty insignificant, in the circumstances."

"He sent Alfonso Martin to tell me instead."

"He *did*?"

Poncho spat into the fire. "The little *cabrón* must have been standing there in the radio shack listenin' to your whole transmission. Then he come an' tried to trick me into sinkin' the *Diva* by intentionally givin' me the wrong code."

"On the order of Herbert Hooks, no doubt."

Poncho nodded. "I didn't believe him; I knew you'd never sink your beautiful new ship. So after Alfonso talked to me I started to go up top an' radio you back. But then I got a bad feelin', an' went back below . . . an' there was Alfonso, duct-taping a hand grenade to a fuel line on the day tank. An' the grenade, the pin? —it had a long wire on it. And there was Alfonso with a giant chisel an' hammer, getting' ready to bust the fittin' where the fuel line connects to the day tank."

"Which would fill the engine room with diesel," Moby said.

"Right. Then he'd climb up the ladder and pull the wire. That lets go the handle of the grenade, which is . . . probably not high explosive; probably phosphorus, yes? Otherwise why bother spilling fuel? So it goes off an' lights the diesel fumes, which blow up the main fuel tanks . . . an' that's it; after that *the Sea Diva* is finished."

For a moment even the cacophony of jungle noise seemed miles away. Then Joe said, "Where would Alfonso Martin have gotten a phosphorous grenade? I mean, that's not the sort of thing a saboteur carries around just in case."

Poncho stirred. Cleared his throat. "He got it from me. I mean, from my storage."

Joe looked at him. "So that's one thing he didn't lie about. The illegal arms cache."

"For my brothers and sisters in Castellegre. For the revolution."

"But in my boat. You were using my boat to smuggle *arms*!"

"I did it before." Poncho's head suddenly seemed too heavy for him to hold up. "An' I didn't know my assistant was spyin' on me, watchin' me. For Hooks."

Joe tilted his head back and stared up at the bouquets of stars. "Okay. Go on."

"I tried to pull the grenade off the fuel line. Then I saw what else Alfonso had done. I looked down an' saw that the cover had been taken off the sea chest."

"Why the sea chest?" Moby asked.

"Its at the bottom of the ship; inside it are the suction ports that supply cooling to the main engine and generators, an' water for the fire hoses. Alfonso had wrapped shaped charges aroun' the suction ports; if he set them off water would pour into the sea chest and flood the boat fast."

Moby nodded. "And at the same time the flash-bang grenade would start a fire big enough to keep the crew away."

"Fire and water," Joe told the stars.

"That little prick Alfonso," Poncho said, his head still down. "I tried to get the grenade off there, but Alfonso came and fought me like a snake. I grabbed him by the throat. But I forgot about the chisel. He hit me in my shoulder with it, my ribs. I didn't care; I was just goin' to squeeze his head off. But the storm . . . the boat rock so hard he pull away and hit me right here with that goddam giant chisel." He pointed at the top of his head.

Moby winced.

"Lucky I have the thick skull. Fall on the catwalk but not quite pass out. Fading in and out, you know? But I hear hammering. Smell fuel. See Alfonso start up the ladder." He paused. "Then . . . Michael comes."

Joe's head lowered.

"He's comin' down to visit me, say goodnight. He likes to do that. I hear him say, 'What's going on?' An' Alfonso . . . Alfonso says, 'The chief's set a dynamite charge to sink the ship. I try to stop him, but it's too late. Get the hell out! It's goin; any second!'

"But Michael doesn't get out. He grabs me under my arms and drags me aroun' a bulkhead. Saves my life because the grenade goes off, so hot I feel my boots cookin'. Then . . . the shaped charge goes off too. Michael says, 'We're takin' on water! We're takin' on water! Jesus!' An' then he . . . that boy, he picks me up in a fireman's carry and goes up the ladder. Joe, I outweigh that boy by fifty pounds and he carries me up the fuckin' ladder like a pillow."

Joe closed his eyes.

"I can barely see. I smell smoke, water, feel the boat swaying. Wind, spray, rainin' like bullets. Michael puts me on the deck. I see him go to the CO2 fire lever an' throw it over. Nothin' happens. More of Alfonso's work, I think. An' the fire's getting' worse; I can feel it comin' through the doorway. An' I think about the diesel tanks down there. But I still can't move.

"The storm is so big. Black sky, black water, and wind. Michael comes back to me an' says, 'Alfonso says you set a bomb to sink my dad's ship.'

"I say, 'He's full of shit; it's him an' that banker behind it.'

"An' he just nods and says, 'I knew it wasn't you. I'm goin to warn the others and get my stuff. Don' move; I be back.'

"I say, 'Forget your stuff an' get off this boat.'

"He says, 'No, no, I can't leave my papers. My dolphin papers.' An' he runs off." Poncho paused. "Joe, I'm sorry. I shoulda convince him. I shoulda said somethin' better."

Joe grunted. "He was always a hard-headed boy. Shouldn't have been on the *Diva* in the first place."

After a moment Poncho went on. "Later he comes back for me. I'm holdin' onto the rail with both arms the deck is listin' so bad, but here he comes with his sea bag on one shoulder, sayin' 'Don't you think we ought to be goin', Poncho?' An' he's tryin' to pick me up again when that beautiful lady starts slidin' under for good. We both go over the side. The water is warm as blood. Tastes like blood. I'm sinking. Michael pulls me up, grabs some shit floatin' aroun' an' wraps it aroun' me. He saves my life, Joe—again. But then I finally black out all the way an' that's it for that night."

"I saw the *Diva* go down," Moby Jack said. "Stern first, that big white bow rising up like a cliff, like an iceberg. Fire coming out of hatches and doorways. Then she slid down and it was over. Nothing left but steam."

"I saw none of that," Poncho said. "Nex' thin' I knew, I woke up lyin' in a lifeboat. One of our lifeboats; it only had enough air inside to barely hold me up. But there was canvas over it, an' food an' water inside. Michael must have found it an' put me in. But Michael, he was not there. I never saw him again." He paused. "Except at night sometimes, I see him floatin' out in the sea, wavin' his arm."

There was a long silence. Then Poncho sighed and went on. "I floated on that lousy piece of rubber for maybe two weeks. Then one day I saw a fishin' boat bearin' for me. She's flying a Costalegran flag. I think, *Why did God take Michael and let an old man like me live?* And I thought, *Costallegre.* God wants me to come back here, to do what I can to make my country free. That's the only thin' I can do to make Michael's death worth *somethin'*.'" He paused. "I know you have been in trouble with the law, Joe, because of me. Because I have not return to help you. But you called my sister in Costallegre. Everyone up north thought I was dead. You told her, it wouldn't help your case if I had lived. I was between a . . . what do you say . . . a rocca and a hard place? But I don' think they would believe me even if I do come back—me, an illegal alien, a gun runner."

Joe peeled a strip from the label of a beer bottle and said, "They would have thrown you in jail too."

"I was even more sure God had a plan for me after the fishermen tol' me I was given up for dead. Lost at sea. These fishermen and I have friends together, for the Republic and democracy. They agree not to report my rescue."

"And you became El Gato," Joe said.

"Not yet. First, we fought and took over the government and executed that dog Serape." His eyes tightened. "But then Rudy Bramoso took the revolution away from us. He started killin' us, the democrats, spreadin' lies, becomin' exactly like what we'd been fightin' against. So I went undergroun' again. Now I fight as El Gato—this time against Bramoso and the Communists. An' I'll keep fighting until I am dead or Costellegre is truly free."

Joe dropped his beer bottle onto the sand. "We're here to ask you to help with a different fight, Poncho. A fight for the freedom of Anthony Darren."

Poncho said nothing.

"He's been in prison for ten years because of something *we* did, or allowed to happen. So we have to make it right. Anthony is *this close* to being pardoned, but the court needs corroborating testimony about what really happened on board *the Sea Diva* that night. They need *your* testimony."

Poncho was already shaking his head. "I love you as a brother, Joe, an' I hate to say this but I warned you not to play Hooks' game. An' I fought that bastard Alfonso to stop him. I did everythin' I could to keep *the Sea Diva* afloat. I—"

Poncho closed his mouth. A muscle worked in the hinge of his jaw as he stared at his boots.

Poncho sighed. "I cannot go back to America, even for this. You know they gonna throw me in jail."

"The government has promised you immunity if you testify."

Poncho's eyebrows rose, but he shook his head. "It is not only up to me, Joe. I'm a soldier, with a duty, an' the DRF council would never approve me goin'. Not now. This is a . . . what's the word . . . crucial?—A crucial time for our cause."

Joe leaned toward him, the firelight blazing-up in his eyes. "That's all the more reason for you to go. In fact, that's the other reason we're here. We know a United States Senator named Richard Morrison who has some influence with Rudy Bramoso. They went to college together and still stay in touch even though their politics are at odds. The senator wants to arrange a secret meeting between your Democratic Revolutionary Forces and Bramoso's communist government."

Poncho's eyebrows rose. "A meeting? With that pig Bramoso?"

"Morrison believes there's more common ground between your two sides than you think."

"Yes. It's called Costalegre."

"There's a book you should read. You and the rest of the DRF leaders. Morrison read it; so did I; so did Moby Jack. So did the President of the United States and so did Bramoso. We think it could change everything."

Poncho frowned at Joe, then looked at Moby Jack with his eyebrows raised.

Moby grinned. "Yes, I read a book. And yes, I understood it. Mostly."

"This revolution isn't about things in books. It's about blood, freedom, justice!"

"Books have changed history many times," Joe said. "Sometimes for the better, sometimes for the worse. *Thoughts* change history. Isn't that what your revolution is about? Thoughts? Beliefs? Or is it just about bloodshed?"

"Easier to change history than to change the mind of Rudy Bramoso. Only a bullet can do that."

Joe raised his hands. "That's exactly the kind of attitude this book can change. What if I told you Bramoso's interested in finding common ground with the DRF? Genuinely interested."

"I would say you are crazy." Poncho grabbed a stick and stirred the fire to a tornado of orange sparks. "Where would this meeting be held?"

"In the United States, under the tightest possible security. Bramoso's going to go up there soon to address the U.N., so that would be the time."

Poncho frowned. "Why not meet down here?"

"Because it would be impossible to keep a secret here—and Bramoso doesn't want anyone to know he's even *thinking* about making accommodations, not until something solid comes of it. In the States, the Secret Service can make sure no word gets out."

More sparks spun toward the stars. "My *compadres* in the DRF will think the Americans are just tryin' to preach to them. The U.S. does not have a monopoly on knowledge of democracy, you know."

"That's not what this is about. Believe me."

"I would like to believe you, José. But I tol' you, such decisions are not mine alone."

Moby said, "Joe, could you leave us alone for a second?"

Joe looked up. "Sure." He rose and brushed off his pants. "I need to take a leak anyway."

After he'd disappeared into the darkness, Moby leaned closer to

Poncho. "Listen. Joe would never bring this up, but there's another reason you have to come back and testify for Anthony Darren."

"Moby, if Joe is like my brother, then you are like the cousin I always have to throw out into the yard."

"I know, but if you hear what I'm about to tell and you think about it, you'll have no choice but to help."

Poncho grunted.

"When Joe and Anthony Darren were young, they went swimming off the coast and Joe almost drowned in a riptide. Anthony saved him. Anthony risked his own life to save Joe's. Does that sound familiar?"

Pensive lines dug into Poncho's cheeks. "You are saying that I owe Joe a life because his son saved mine."

"Yeah. It sounds like a synthesis."

"A what?"

"Never mind. Just listen to your heart, Poncho. It knows what's—"

Footsteps crunched in the sand and Joe, lanky and still exhibiting the bullfighter's poise, stepped back into the smoky glow of the fire.

Poncho looked up at him. "Where is this book?"

"I have a copy for you. Unfortunately it's in English."

"I try readin' it first. If I think it's good, I'll see what the council thinks."

"That's all we can ask for." Moby Jack got up and from their sparse belongings retrieved the book—its back cover flapping.

Poncho frowned at the back. "*Unifying the opposites*? What is that?"

"You'll see." This is not a good start.

Poncho rose to his feet and faced Joe. "You know we will only settle for peace *with* freedom. If the others think there is a real chance for that because of this book, perhaps they will let me to go to America with you. We will see. But Joe . . . I make no promises."

"I understand."

Poncho held out his hand to each man. "Goodnight, *compadres*."

He disappeared into his tent. A moment later its sides flared to the glow of a kerosene lamp.

Moby woke at dawn with Poncho's heavy hand on his shoulder. He started to sit up, but realized that although Poncho's face looked grim and haggard, it showed no alarm. "I finish it," Pancho murmured.

"What? The book? Already?"

"It was—how do you say it?—thick. Not easy, but I finish. It gives me . . . much to think about."

"So you'll take it to the council?"

"Yes, but Moby . . . this is why I wake you and not Joe, I am not sure what they will think. These are hard men. Soldiers. Peasants, often. I am not sure they will understand the ideas in this book. I am not sure they will . . . trust it."

Moby rubbed his face. "But it's worth a try, right? You're going to take it to them and *try*?"

"Yes, I take. I will bring the Mediator, too; his English is very good; he might be able to tell it to the council better. Tell Joe . . . I will try."

29
Going South

Dear Anthony,

We are making progress on your pardon application. If we can verify that Poncho Pascalle is alive and we bring him back, after his testimony to Judge Winchester Sarah will request the judge to prepare a statement asking for your pardon.

I hope you're receiving my letters. I'll explain later, but Rich is still having a very tough time getting the peace meeting arranged. But don't let your hopes down. The President doesn't yet know, of course, who Bric Locket is. So that's not the problem.

Gossip time: Your old friend Samantha hasn't shown up even once at her husband's trial. Apparently she's quite the fair-weather spouse; I hear divorce is in the wind. She's been seeing the owner of a TV-promoted mortuary of late. I bet she'll have him in one of his own boxes before he knows it.

Laura and I are a little worried about you, though. I've been awfully busy with work, but I'll visit as soon as I get a verdict.

Sarah and I worked almost all night putting together the last bits of the case, but for reasons I can't discuss, she's on her own with the final argument. We both hope this trial ends soon. The court excused Sarah from being present when the verdict comes in so I'll be by myself in court when it's announced. Can't deny I'm edgy. Those opposing counsel are tough.

Sorry to rush—got to go.

Love, Andi."

Anthony swam as he could with one arm towing the inert mass of Joe. He kicked, panted, squinting toward a shoreline that seemed to be getting farther and farther away. Not La Jolla; a strange, climbing shore crusted with stucco buildings peering through forests of the darkest green.

"Joe," he gasped. "Joe, you've got to help."

"Can't." Joe lay calmly on his back, hands folded on his chest, face turned up to the sun.

"You have to. Kick. Do something, do something, or we're not going to make it."

"That's a shame," Joe said. "We're so close."

"The current's got us. It's taking us out to sea."

"Yes, it is."

"Do something, Joe!"

"I can't. I don't swim very well, you know that. That's why you need to swim for both of us. I know it sounds extreme, but that's life sometimes. Sometimes the middle isn't in the middle. Sometimes the eagle flies and empty the aerie lies."

Anthony felt the riptide truly take hold of him then, a weight muscular pulse, not at all like the same ocean moving crosswise but something full of intent and remorseless strength, a tentacle, an alien limb grasping his legs and hauling him away, away from shore, away from Joe, away into cold darkness. . . .

"Time to go, Darren."

Anthony thrashed awake in the gloom, struggled to sit up on the hard cot.

Sluggo stood silhouetted in the doorway. "I'm taking you back to your cell. Keep your ass out of trouble this time or you'll be back in the hole before that cot gets cold."

"I'd like to get my held-up mail on the way back," Anthony said.

"No. No regular privileges 'til tomorrow. If you have any mail you'll get it then. So move. You're doin' the trash run tonight."

"At least let me stop by my cell for my work boots and gloves. It's on the way."

"All right—but I want you out on that truck in four minutes. It's Sunday, so you're gonna be the only guy on foot."

Back at his old cell, Anthony sat on his bunk to lace up his boots. From somewhere came a whispering voice: "Don't look up."

He froze.

"The cat," the voice said in an Hispanic accent, "they won't let him out of the jungle because they have questions on the book. Hector says no one can explain it like the Professor."

Anthony couldn't control himself; he raised his eyes. He saw nothing but the ceiling of his house—his *cell*—and a small vent grille. He heard nothing more.

The cat, they won't let him out of the jungle because they have questions on the book.

He tried to parse out the message. *The cat* could only refer to El Gato. Apparently Joe and Moby Jack had actually managed to track down the mysterious guerilla and even got a copy of *Fusing Order and Chaos* into his hands. Was El Gato, Poncho Pascalle? It didn't seem to matter: whoever he was, "*they*" wouldn't let him come to the states; "they" didn't understand the book enough to trust it. Selling its concept; having his witness, were dependent on one another.

Hector says no one can explain it like the Professor.

Hector! Hector had come through, too. . . .

But now they needed a tutor down in Costallegre.

They needed *him*—for his sake and their hopes.

Anthony stared at his boots. *I want you on that trash truck in four minutes.* He thought about everything he'd been through in his life, and especially the last ten years. Everything he'd learned, thought about, written about. The consolidation of opposites, the search in all things for the exact point where the sweet spot existed—and then the fulcrum slids into movement, into progress, to the ultimate synthesis. The point of fusion.

What had he told Laura so long ago? We're human beings; we don't have to let things go to extremes before we find the best synthesis point for a human system. As people we can always look ahead, plan, adjust, avoid the biggest messes.

His boots smelled of garbage, his skin of the sweat of solitary confinement.

We can avoid the biggest messes.

Really? Always? What if you couldn't? What if an extreme situation is forced on you, despite all your planning and hard work? What did a person do then?

Sometimes the middle isn't in the middle. It's the course Socrates did not take. Sometimes the eagle flies and empty the aerie lies.

A strange lightness came over him—warm, peaceful, glowing. He floated to his feet.

Time to go to work.

⚓

"Andrea, Hal Goldman is holding on Line One."

"Thanks, Millie." Andrea pushed the button. "Hi, Hal. Looking for an update on the pardon?"

"Pardon? No. Andrea, don't tell me you haven't heard."

"Heard what?"

"Anthony's gone."

"Gone? What do you mean?"

"I mean he disappeared. From prison."

"He escaped?"

"Did you know he was going to do this, Andrea?"

"Good God, no. "

"This will ruin his chances on the pardon. And we're so close! He must have gone off his rocker."

"Hal, what should we do?"

"If he contacts you, tell him to get his butt back in prison, pronto. Do you have any idea where he might have gone?"

"No. I can't even imagine him doing this."

"Then perhaps all we can do is wait. But Andi, let me give you some advice. The authorities know you're Anthony's daughter now.

They're going to watch you like a hawk. If Anthony tries to contact you they'll run him down. Some of them would gladly shoot him; that way, won't have to worry if he gets pardoned. You understand? I'd be careful with phones from now on, if I were you."

His words sobered her. "Thanks, Hal."

The moment she hung up, the intercom clicked again. "Andrea? Call from England on line two."

Dad's sister, Andrea thought as she reached for the receiver again.

My aunt, and I've never really gotten to know her. Bad news travels fast and far.

"Don't get me wrong," Moby Jack said between mouthfuls of egg as they sat in the greenish light of another jungle dawn. "It's not that I don't like camping out in paradise. But, you know, it didn't take *me* ten days to read that damned book, and before that the last thing I read on purpose was *Green Eggs and Ham*."

"They must not be going for it," Joe said, staring into his tin cup. "Either they don't follow the ideas, or they don't like them. Either way, if they turn us down, what do we do next?"

Moby shrugged. "I don't much fancy the idea of trying to kidnap El Gato, do you?"

Joe had to smile. "No."

"So—" Moby looked up as one of Pascalle's lieutenants approached.

"The general returned late last night. He'll be with you soon."

"General?" Moby Jack frowned. "What general?"

Just then Poncho Pascalle strode toward them across the clearing. He held *Fusing Order and Chaos* in one hand and wore a serious look on his face, camouflage fatigues on his body, and on his head a royal blue beret accented with two gold stars. Behind him walked another man: slender to the point of emaciation, sunburned, his jaw covered with a week's worth of silvery stubble. He wore fatigues and a plain beret.

Joe and Moby Jack both rose almost involuntarily to their feet. "*General* Pascalle?" Moby said.

Poncho shrugged and held out the book. "Here. You can have it back. We don' need it anymore."

Joe's body sagged. "What does that mean?"

"It means I'm goin' to America with you."

"You what?"

Poncho grinned. "It almost didn' happen. My *compadres*, they didn' want to follow somethin' from a book. They thought I was *loco*. I tried to explain' everything, but they would not listen . . . said it was all American tricks, American propaganda . . . until I got some help to explain' it better."

He gestured toward his companion, who smiled wryly.

Joe looked at him. Looked harder. Almost fell backward into the fire pit. "*Anthony*?"

"In the flesh. Or what's left of it."

"I'll be screwed sideways!" Moby Jack blurted.

"What . . ." Joe said. "How. . . ?"

Anthony shrugged. "I decided I didn't like prison anymore. I decided it's all about extremes in there—extreme forced by prisoners, extreme forced by the administration and guards. So I went to my own extreme and established my own synthesis with the prison system: I left."

"But . . . *how*?"

"We have some time til dusk. I'll tell you while the crew finishes."

"Dusk?" said Joe and Moby in unison.

"I will explain," Anthony said.

They sank onto the sand around the fire pit, now with a new member, settling once again into a ritual as old as the simplest of societies and as new as global civilization: the Telling of the Story.

"A while back the warden took me out of my library job to punish me for some articles I'd written," Anthony said, staring into the fire, "and put me on garbage detail. But even there I kept thinking about *the synthesis*. I noticed how the truck took loose garbage—a bunch of individual pieces that had nothing to do with one another—and squashed them into a mass that would save space but make some too."

"The opposites again?" Mody Jack said. "You've definitely been in prison too long."

Anthony laughed. "You're right. But it got me thinking: being inside prison is a lot like being a piece of trash in a compactor. And that's when it hit me. That's when I knew how to escape."

"Huh?" Moby said.

"I didn't do it right away. I thought my pardon would be coming through; I didn't want to screw that up. But even so, I made preparations. As a sort of game, really."

"Preparations like what?" Joe asked.

"In a corner of the shed where they park the garbage truck there was one of those toolboxes people install across the beds of their pickups. You know the kind? Big steel reinforced boxes?"

All the men nodded.

"Day by day I shoved it a little closer to the garage door. Also, one night I fastened a piece of cable to one corner of it. And on another night I found an old car jack to toss inside with some rag-looking clothes. But other than that . . . I didn't do anything with it."

"That's when I realized I had never really been playing a game with my toolbox and cables; I'd been . . . preparing."

Two birds called back and forth in the jungle.

"Sunday nights are quiet on the prison garbage scene," Anthony went on. "On those nights there's only one prisoner on foot picking, dumping trash cans into the truck. So I made my move on a Sunday. When we drove by the garage that night I grabbed the toolbox, out of view of the driver, and threw it in the trash compartment of the truck . . . and I hooked the cable onto a handle on the outside. Then I waved goodbye to the driver, because he was heading straight out from there to the landfill. So he wasn't looking when I stepped behind the truck and climbed inside the toolbox. I shut the lid as best I could, but I knew it wouldn't go down all the way with me in there—that's why I had the jack, to brace it when the compactor came down. Then—"

"Wait, wait, wait," Moby Jack said. "You let the fuckin' truck *squash* you?"

"Not that much . . ."

"You crazy mother." Moby's face shone with something like awe. "So the truck drove right out with you in back."

"Pretty much. It stopped so the gate guards could inspect it, of course, but when they looked in back all they saw was the usual mess. To be honest, my biggest risk was suffocation. I knew it's about a thirty-minute drive to the landfill, so I just hoped the driver didn't stop for coffee or something along the way. Luckily he didn't; you can imagine how foul it was in there.

"Anyway, when we got to the landfill the bed tilted and everything poured out—except my box, because of the tether cable. The box just dangled there until I climbed out and unhooked it. Then I ran off and looked for more clothes. Found a pitiful few. Hid in the dark. When I finally took off the bulldozers were burying everything."

"A phone call got me help from a wonderful woman and that brave

Costallegren friend from prison I mentioned. Call it the reverse-illegal immigration underground. After that it was just a matter of . . . well, let's just say I had to do a lot more hiding in unpleasant, confined spaces to get here."

"My friend, Harry Houdini." Joe pounded Anthony on the shoulder. "Old buddy, it's great to see you . . . but now you're stuck. You can never go back home."

"Oh, I'm going back. I've got business to settle."

"But no pardon. You'll always be a fugitive."

Anthony shrugged. "That depends on the General."

Everyone looked at Poncho, who grinned. "Don' worry, I'm goin' to help as much as I can. The last few days I learned somethin' I maybe already knew, deep down. Human beings have two feelin's that are the leaders of all their other feelin's. One is to compete with each other and the many things out there. The other is to help each other as brothers. Sometimes we save each other's lives, sometimes we kill each other. These feelin's all the time seem to be fightin' against each other. But from what I understand, and what I already know in my heart, if you put them together you get more than if you stick with just one. It's like tunin' an engine; you got to find the sweet spot. So that's what I'm doin'—for Anthony, for my country, an' for myself."

"And your superiors are okay with it now?" Joe asked.

"Thanks to Anthony explainin' that book to them, yes. He'll be my secret consultant at the peace conference."

Joe turned a quizzical look on his friend. "How the hell did you become the world expert on this theory, anyway?"

"I was going to ask the same thing," said Moby.

Anthony shrugged. "There's lots of time to read in prison." Wish I could tell you more, but I don't want to risk having anyone at the peace conference find out their primary source of information was written by an escaped con.

"So now what?" Moby Jack asked.

"So now it's my turn to help out," Joe said. "Before we ever left the States I made a deal with a friend of mine who skippers a tuna boat—one of the last American boats. They've been fishing off the Galapagos, and now they're on their way back. If we ask them real nice, they said they'd be willing to pick up a small boat offshore."

"That's terrific," Anthony said. "But . . . what small boat?"

Poncho grinned. "Ah. Now it is *my* turn."

When the sinister shape eased out from under the mangroves, Anthony gaped. He instantly recognized the vessel's profile: thirty-six feet of Fiberglas hull with an open-backed flying bridge atop an enclosed cabin. In the bow there would be a couple of berths, and in the stern two massive inboard motors, each driving its own prop. A small skiff hung on davits above the transom. In short, it was some rich American's pleasure boat from fifteen or twenty years earlier.

But this model had been modified in ways that would never have landed it on the cover of *Yachting Magazine*. The hull was painted a stern ocean-camo gray, the twin engine tones sounded muffled . . . and both bow and stern displayed enormous .50 caliber machine guns.

"It's the Criscraft from Hell," Anthony said as they all clambered aboard.

Poncho grinned. "We call it our party boat. Armor in only strategic spots, but very fast and with very big guns. Like American PT boats from World War II, eh?"

"Nice!" Moby Jack shouted to the Mediator, who stood behind the wheel. "Does it come with a built-in cooler?"

"Sure," the Mediator said, straight-faced. "But it's full of ammunition."

Dusk had just begun to tint the sky when the party boat rumbled away from the beach and began maneuvering through the outlying labyrinth of estuaries and islands. Poncho said her initial destination was an isolated dock, maintained by friendly hands, where she would take on fuel for the trip out to sea.

Poncho took over the helm while the Mediator stood in readiness behind the forward machine gun. Inside the cabin, Anthony, Joe and Moby sat behind the open glass sliders to keep watchful eyes on the passing jungle.

"Lookee here," said Moby gleefully, pointing into the water.

Anthony and Joe rushed over to see two sea turtles locked together, one atop the other. "Someone should use that as the peace symbol for a flag," Moby said.

Joe grinned. "*The synthesis* at its finest."

Anthony punched him in the shoulder. "And you told me you weren't sure you understood the principle."

From the estuary they entered an arena of small islands, hundreds of them; some with beaches of white sand, others of shell, others of black sand or gravel or rock. All were crowned with thick foliage and bustling with animals. As the boat rounded through them, hugging first one shore after another, flocks of startled gulls and pelicans flapped away over the water and monkeys jumped comically from springing branches.

Finally the end of a wood-and-bamboo pier emerged around a point of land, and then the corrugated plastic roof of the fuel station. The place looked deserted.

"*Hola*!" Poncho called from the bridge as the boat slowed to walking speed. "Anyone there?"

No response. Poncho cut the throttles and the boat glided almost silently toward the dock.

Then Anthony, Joe and Moby were all hurled to the deck as Poncho slammed the props into reverse and the throttle to full power. Everything not fastened down—binoculars, chart scrolls, cans—flew through the air. As Anthony struggled to his feet he heard the unmistakable rattle of automatic rifle fire. Bullets popped through the surrounding Plexiglas and Fiberglas structures and cracked into the bulkhead above him, spewing splinters through the cabin.

Moby flew past him onto the stern deck and lunged for the.50 cal. He grabbed the handles and swung the muzzle toward stutters of flame issuing from various points in the trees.

"So much for 'in friendly hands,'" Joe grunted.

His voice vanished in a deafening roar as Moby swung the machine gun back and forth, spewing fire into the jungle. All the while the party boat continued racing from the dock in reverse. Then the cannon fire abruptly stopped. "Fuck!" Moby bellowed. "Jammed!"

As Anthony started to crawl back to help Moby clear the weapon, the party boat entered a series of increasingly wild maneuvers that hurled Anthony from side to side. *What the hell is Poncho doing? Nobody's even shooting at us right now!* Then he realized that the swerves were part of a larger pattern . . . the party boat was heading back toward the dock.

"What the shit?" Moby cried, pounding on the gun's charging bolt.

Anthony clawed up the ladder to the flying bridge. Poncho lay beneath the wheel in a thick smear of blood, eyes wide, chest heaving. Through the shattered windscreen Anthony glimpsed the Mediator sprawled on the foredeck in a tangle of his own loose limbs.

Anthony seized the wheel and punched the transmission into forward. The engines howled and shoved the stern deep into the water, but looking over his shoulder Anthony saw the dock coming up fast behind them.

"Brace!"

The boat jolted hard, and the screech of tortured Fiberglas clawed the air. Anthony glanced back and realized that the boat's stern, pushed deep by the reversed props, had slid under the decking and become wedged. Now, despite disgorging a massive surge of muddy water, the boat was stuck.

Plumes of gunfire flickered again from amongst the trees. Anthony dropped to the floor of the bridge as the Plexiglas side window turned opaque.

The incoming gunfire escalated, tearing through the side of the flying bridge and forcing Anthony to flatten himself even farther. *Where the hell is Joe*? he thought.

Then the party boat shivered to a more regular beat, and over the rattle of small-arms fire rose the throaty hammering of a .50 cal. Peering warily through the window, Anthony saw Joe standing spread-legged behind the bow gun, hurling a flood of flames and lead into the jungle. Expended brass glittered like yellow hail around his feet. He fired cover for Moby, who was dragging a loose plank off the dock decking.

Then Moby yelled at Anthony. "Reverse when I say, then forward full!" Anthony could barely understand him over the roar of the .50 cal, and did not comprehend what he had in mind at all, but nodded anyway.

Then he *did* understand as Moby thrust one end of the plank into a small space between the top of the transom and the underside of the pier. Throwing himself onto his back, he put his feet against the plank above him and shouted, "Reverse! Reverse, then forward!"

The plank bowed as Moby thrust up with all the power of his legs. Anthony reversed the motors, causing the props to dig deep and pull the stern down again. Foaming water poured over the transom and rose around Moby's straining body. Anthony slammed the transmission into forward, and almost flew off the bridge as the party boat erupted free of the pier and thundered off across the water.

Glancing back, Anthony saw Moby struggling to his feet as a trio of small patrol vessels appeared from the far side of the island. "They're coming!" Anthony shouted over the wind. "They're coming after us!"

Moby pounded at the stern gun with his hands a few more times, then racked the charging handle. "Cleared!" he cried. But after giving the patrol boats a long look, he left the gun and moved toward the bow.

Anthony kept his eyes on the patrol boats. They were several hundred yards back and spreading out, splitting the swells into a trio of frothing wakes. Anthony tried to think, to plan. According to Joe, the rendezvous with the fishing boat was supposed to take place at a point due west, about six miles off the coast. The tuna boat skipper expected Joe to make contact via light signals within the next forty-five minutes. That didn't leave much time to play hide and seek amongst these islands, which would be useless anyway; with three vessels, the pursuers could easily split up and outflank the party boat.

Moby appeared at the top of the ladder. "You okay?"

"Just enjoying a little cruise."

The giant gave a bright smile, then went to Poncho and bent over him. Anthony stayed at the wheel, trying to watch for islands ahead while keeping an eye on the patrol boats behind. The pursuers seemed to be falling back.

Moby rose. "Well, do you want the bad news, the terrible news or the really awful news?"

"Does it matter?"

"For starters, the Mediator's dead."

Anthony closed his eyes for a moment. "I was afraid of that." Dead bodies had a distinctive carelessness about them, something he remembered from 'Nam. "Damn it. How's Poncho?"

"Well, he took a glancer across the chest that probably broke a couple of ribs, but the real problem is the hole in his thigh. I had to put a tourniquet on that. He'll need help right away." Moby Jack paused. "Um, Joe got hit too."

Anthony's chest tightened. "How bad?"

"Not as bad as Poncho, but nasty. Right now he's as useless as the preverbal one-armed paper hanger."

"He took one in the arm?"

"No, the butt." Moby laughed grimly. "No screwing or ballet dancing for him for a while."

Anthony glanced over his shoulder again. No patrol boats in sight. He angled off between two islands; no sense in pointing the enemy directly toward their destination. "Moby," he said, "please tell me that's the last of the bad—"

The steering wheel kicked him in the solar plexus, and the world turned entirely into light and pain.

The light gradually swirled into a spiral galaxy surrounded by darkness. Anthony blinked, blinked, and realized he was lying on his back on the floor of the flying bridge. There was a terrible emptiness in his chest, a vacuum straining to be filled. Air . . . he needed air, but could not inhale. He thrashed around, eyes bulging, mouth gaping, and the darkness was swirling back in when air abruptly rushed down his throat in a great wheezing whoop. Lungs functioning again, he gasped in and out a few times, then got to his knees and finally his feet.

Moby rose next to him, red hair full of Plexiglas fragments. "Did I mention we were about to crash into submerged rocks?"

"Wh-what?" Outside Anthony saw stars, black water, and the smudges of distant islands. The engines still rumbled and the water behind the party boat churned, yet the vessel was not moving. "We're hung up on a reef? Is that what you're saying?"

"Poncho did suggest something about staying out of the shoals."

"Great." Anthony pulled back on the throttles and the party boat settled into the water with what sounded like a moan of relief. "Terrific. Now what?"

"Hang on; let me see how bad the damage is."

Moby dropped down to the hatch and began undogging it. Meanwhile Anthony, glancing around nervously for searchlights, used the shifter and throttle to try and jockey the cruiser off the rocks. He quickly realized that the rudders were jammed, fixed at an angle. Also, although the port prop seemed to bite the water with its usual power and the tachometer indicated the starboard shaft was also turning, he felt no pressure on that side. The blades of the starboard prop must have either sheared off against the rocks or smashed themselves into a steel fist.

"Um . . . Anthony. . . ." Moby pulled his red head out of the hatchway and looked up. "There's a mushroom of water about a foot and a half high coming through the bottom of the boat."

"Well, that's not good," Anthony said.

"I didn't think so either." Flashlight in hand, Moby Jack stuck his head ostrich-like back into the darkness, twisted his shoulders, then sat up. "Well, this ain't a helicopter so I can't be absolutely positive, but I'm pretty sure we're not going to any parties tonight. Time to hop in the dingy?"

"And row the next five miles? We'll never reach the rendezvous point that way, even if the patrol boats don't catch us." Anthony paused. "But if we can get off this reef and motor for just a couple of miles, then we can climb into the dingy and drift, try to signal Joe's tuna fishing friend. Seems to me that's our only chance."

Moby nodded. "Tell me what you want me to do."

"Hold on." Again Anthony played with throttles and shifters, even opposing the power of both engines by putting one in forward and the other in reverse. He pulled the wheel first to the left, then the right. Suddenly the boat slid backward off the reef.

"Moby! I think we're—" He fell silent as half a rudder blade floated to the surface to one side. "Shit. Okay, listen, stay down there and keep me informed about the water coming in. If I can get us closer to the pick-up point, they might see our signal."

"Better get moving, then. I can *hear* the water pouring in."

Anthony backed away from the reef, cranked the wheel left and shifted into forward. Saying a silent prayer, he inched the throttles higher. The boat wallowed ahead. Passed the area where it had been hung up without getting caught again. Exhaling in relief, Anthony throttled up a bit more. A bit more.

With only one prop running and only one off-center rudder to steer by, the boat was difficult to keep on any particular heading. Still, Anthony maneuvered it more or less westward while gradually throttling higher. He saw no option but to risk hitting another reef. Staying here, grounded or otherwise, would certainly mean getting caught by Bramoso's men. That would undoubtedly result in Poncho's execution, the failure of the peace conference . . . and the end of all hope for Anthony's pardon. Not to mention that Poncho and Joe both needed medical care as soon as possible.

"Water's still coming in pretty good," Moby called.

"Can you find anything to plug that hole? Even partially? Every minute we gain is good."

"Aye aye, Cap'n. I'll see what I can do."

Anthony turned his attention to the controls and to the water ahead. If he couldn't see the reefs, at least he could avoid the islands. And the patrol boats. He hoped.

After some time, Moby reappeared on the bridge, dripping with water and smeared with oil and muck. "Duct tape. Humongous six inch wide duct tape."

"What?"

"Made a big old ball of duct tape, like a pumpkin, squeezed it down to the size of a baseball and jammed it in the hole and plastered it over with more duct tape. Might stay for a while. At least it will give us more float time—slow the water coming in."

"Duct tape," Anthony said in wonder.

It held for about twenty minutes. Then Anthony felt the boat growing heavier, slower to respond. It fought the wheel like a rapiered bull and began listing heavily to stern.

Then the engine sputtered.

A minute later, it sputtered again. Anthony and Moby looked at each other.

Sudden silence, broken only by the lapping of the sea against the hull.

"I think this is a good place to stop and get off," Moby said.

When Anthony said they had to take the Mediator's body with them, Moby just nodded. After lowering the dingy into the water alongside the wallowing party boat, they zipped the Mediator into a sleeping bag and lifted his bag and him into the dinghy. They then helped Poncho and Joe in, moving slowly, carefully: one off-balance step and the overloaded little boat would capsize.

"Put me in the bow," Joe said. "I'll need to do the signaling. Ow! Moby, get your hand off my ass!"

"Sorry, sorry," Moby Jack said.

"It's not funny. . . ."

Anthony stepped in last, a spare sleeping bag tucked under his arm. He unshipped the long oars and put them in the oarlocks. "I'll row first," he said. "Then you, Moby."

Moby nodded. He was looking down at the Mediator's shrouded form. "From his good English, he sounded like he spent a lot of time in the States. Do you know his real name?"

Poncho replied. "Hector Lopez. He's the one convinced the Council they needed to listen to Anthony about the book."

"He was in prison with me for a while," Anthony murmured, pulling the oars harder, harder. "I helped him write his appeal. But peace for Costallegre was what he really wanted. That's all the more reason we can't let his death be a waste. We *have* to make it back. We *have* to make this peace conference work."

"Agreed."—Poncho.

"Agreed."—Moby Jack.

"Agreed."—Joe.

"And that's why you can't let anyone know you've seen me," Anthony added. "No one. No exceptions."

Joe turned his head. "But how can we say we don't know you when we all get picked up together? —If we get picked up."

"See this extra sleeping bag? I'm going to get in it. So you'll be taking the bodies of *two* deceased comrades aboard that tuna boat."

Moby winced. "Gotcha. Well, don't worry, we'll keep 24-hour watch over our dead *compadres*."

With dangerously little freeboard on their overloaded skiff, they rowed and watched, rowed and watched, rising and falling on the swells as they flashed their pitiful light toward the open sea.

The cold of the night settled into Anthony's bones, and he wistfully thought: if only they had an outrigger canoe; the rig that metaphorically stood for the ideal economy. Just enough regulation in the outrigger to keep the canoe from capsizing but with all the free market in the main hull to keep the economy moving fast and sure. A fast, beautiful asymmetric balance. Was he already suffering from hypothermia?

By the last few weeks of the trial, Andrea had learned not to get her hopes up when she called her office for messages during a recess: she knew there would be nothing but business calls to return. She hadn't heard a thing from her father since his escape from prison; she didn't even know if he was alive. But then, he probably assumed her calls were being monitored; she certainly did.

But on this occasion after Millie rattled off a typical list of incoming calls she said, "Oh —just one more message—a little strange. The caller said his name was 'Mister Joe.'"

"Joe?" Andrea felt her heart rise up inside her.

"Yes. He said to tell you everything is fine. He also said he has a 'Mister Poncho' with him; they just arrived this morning. He said he'll be calling back with a hospital room phone number, but I haven't heard from him again. Who are these guys?"

"Don't have time to explain now." Andrea grinned, feeling as if she were riding a gigantic Ferris wheel, standing up, arms stretched out wide, body arcing through the sky. "Which hospital?"

"Don't know," said Millie. "It didn't sound like he knew that himself."

Four days later, Sarah Billings stood, briefcase in hand, outside the courtroom of United States District Judge Roger Winchester watching two men creep down the hall toward her. One, short and stocky, swung along on crutches; the tall one limped and leaned on a cane.

"Hello, Miss Billings." Finally they got there and Poncho shook her hand. "Joe wants to come in and watch. Is that okay?"

"Good morning, gentlemen. Sure, that's fine. We have a few minutes—do you have any questions, General? Remember, you have federal immunity from prosecution so you can speak freely. By now the judge has read a whole stack of letters in opposition to Anthony's application, so don't hold anything back."

Poncho shook his head. "I have no questions, an' I won't hold nothin' back. Like I said, I just tell the truth."

"Is Andrea here?" Joe asked.

"No. The judge ruled she has a potential conflict of interest, so she's keeping her distance to avoid hurting another case we have going. But she did tell me that if you men know where Anthony Darren might be, you should get word to him that if he wants to have any hope on his pardon application, he *must* turn himself in. That means return to prison and wait."

The men glanced at each other. Neither responded.

Sarah brightened her voice. "Well, the health of both of you has certainly improved since I saw you at the hospital."

"The doc says we'll both limp for a while, but we'll be okay," Joe said.

"I'm glad to hear it." Sarah looked at her watch. "Okay, General—ready?"

He nodded.

"Then let's go in."

From his seat in the back of the gallery, Joe watched Judge Winchester take his seat at the bench. Now white-haired, Winchester looked far older than he had when Joe last saw him. *Tough shit*, Joe thought.

"Ms. Billings," the judge said sternly, "I have read your application papers, so there is no need for an opening statement unless you insist. Let's get on with this."

"Yes, Your Honor."

Poncho limped to the witness box, took the oath and hoisted himself onto the chair. Sarah immediately began questioning him on the circumstances of the sinking of *The Sea Diva*. Joe listened to every word and felt each one cut into his heart like a blade.

Finally Sarah picked up her yellow pad, walked to the lectern and looked directly at the general. "Did Mr. Cruz ever say if he had decided to sink the ship or not?"

"The last thing he tol' me was he was definitely *not* goin' to sink her."

"There's been talk about gun running and munitions. Was Mr. Cruz involved in any illegalities that might have had something to do with the sinking?"

"No, but I'd like to explain."

Sarah hesitated only a moment. "You may."

"One reason I come to this country as a young man was to be free from the dictatorship of old Serape in Costallegre. I helped my people throw out that dog, an' yes, to do that I sometimes brought weapons and ammunition down from America. But Joe had nothin' to do with that. Not ever."

"There was evidence that a grenade and other military-type explosives were used in the sinking."

"Alfonso Martin did that. But I did not know he had taken the grenades or charges. And Joe for sure didn't know."

"Do you know anything about a code that was to be used to indicate whether or not to sink the boat?"

"Yes. Before the boat left San Diego Joe and I arranged for a radio code—'bring back a sea turtle shell' means sink the boat, and 'bring back a tortoise shell' means don' sink her, return her to land. Alfonso overheard Joe send a code, but he tol' me the wrong one so I would sink *the Sea Diva*. But I know Joe would never sink his ship. He loves his ship."

In the back row, Joe closed his eyes.

After Poncho described everything that had happened in the engine room, the sinking of the boat and his later rescue at sea, Sarah looked at the judge. "Does the court have any questions?"

Winchester leaned forward. "I have read transcripts of that trial. As I recall, John Di Santi, the skipper of *the Sea Diva* testified that he received a radio call from Joe Cruz telling him to find you and to tell you to bring back a tortoise shell. He said Mr. Cruz was emphatic about that: a tortoise shell." The judge looked at Sarah. "Ms. Billings, correct me if I'm wrong; isn't this what the transcript shows?"

"Yes, Your Honor, that is correct."

The judge sat back. "And isn't that the key to the issue of Anthony Darren? The evidence you've been urging me to hear— that Joe Cruz sent the 'tortoise shell' code, as confirmed and corroborated first by the skipper, and now by General Pascalle?"

"Yes, Your Honor, I believe that is the issue. The court will recall that according to the testimony at the first trial, the tortoise shell story sounded very far-fetched and there was no one around to back up Mr. Cruz's claim that the radio communication was actually a code."

"But that's no longer the case, eh? We can now corroborate what Cruz has been saying all along."

"I believe so, your Honor."

Joe closed his eyes again, this time to send up a prayer.

A little later Sarah told the court she had finished with presentation of the evidence and asked whether the judge had any additional questions.

"Yes," he replied. "General, at any time did Joe Cruz say if he had told Anthony Darren about any scheme to sink the boat?"

"He said he *didn'* tell Mr. Darren about it," Poncho answered. "In fact he said Mr. Darren would drop him as a client if he heard about the game Joe was plannin' to play with the bank."

"So, General Pascalle, do you have any reason to believe that the argument Mr. Darren used in his defense—that he had written a fictional story about sinking a tuna boat that just happened to come true—was false?"

Poncho's brow wrinkled. "I don' quite follow you, Your Honor."

"I don't blame you; the jury obviously had the same difficulty. Let me try again." Winchester spoke slowly. "Anthony Darren was convicted of being involved in sinking *the Sea Diva* because the jury learned that long before Mr. Cruz hired him, Darren had already written detailed notes about a plot to sink a tuna boat for insurance. Mr. Darren insisted that this was a synopsis for a novel and that its similarity to real events was purely a coincidence, but the jury clearly did not believe him. So I ask you—do you believe Anthony Darren lied about his non-involvement in the sinking of that boat?"

"Absolutely not. I swear. I believe he tol' the truth. "

The judge sat back. "All right, I've heard enough. Thank you, General, for taking the personal risk to come back here and testify." He paused. "After all my years on the bench, I have found that most people have goodness in their hearts, and will cooperate and be witnesses as you have done." Eyes flashing, the old judge then bounced a palm in slow motion off the top of his desk. "You came to tell the truth."

Poncho braced his chest in a military posture.

"As I said, most people will be witnesses when called upon. On the other hand, one of the grossest examples of cowardice is a witness who intentionally avoids testifying because he does not want to stick his neck out, or is afraid of cross-examination.

"Joe Cruz had told your sister on the phone when they thought you were dead that you could not have helped him even if you had lived, and I know that the revolution held you in Costallegre, so you are excused from that prior duty of a witness in this case, but you made up for that in a big way now. The court thanks you."

He turned toward Sarah. "Ms. Billings, as you are aware, I have received a substantial number of letters in opposition to Mr. Darren's pardon application. However, not one individual has appeared in person to object. Not one is here today. Furthermore the facts very strongly indicate that Mr. Darren has been innocent all along, especially in view of the transmittal letter having been found. Therefore I will sign the request for pardon, but as you know, the final decision rests with the Administration."

Joe Cruz had to grab the back of the seat in front of him to keep from leaping up and howling in joy.

"Good luck, Counsel. We are now in recess." Winchester stepped down from the bench and shook hands with Poncho. "I have been told by reliable sources that you are a hero to your people. I commend you. A person such as you, a true revolutionary advocating the principles of liberty, is a rare gift indeed. I hope your wounds heal well before you leave."

El Gato gravely nodded.

"By the way, Counsel," Winchester said to Sarah, "Mr. Darren's situation is certainly not helped by the fact that he is now an escaped convict. A great many influential people oppose his application. He may have destroyed his chances, irrespective of whether he turns himself in."

"We are aware of that problem, Your Honor."

"Another question," said the judge. "What are the US Attorney's intentions regarding the possibility that justice was obstructed in the original trial?"

"After the conclusion of the present securities case, John Woods will consider commencing proceedings against relevant individuals for possible indictments."

Winchester nodded. "One last thing. I think I recognize Joe Cruz sitting there in the back row. I would entertain a motion should you wish to apply for a pardon for him also."

"Thank you, Your Honor. I was about to bring that up."

"Very well." Judge Winchester smiled at Joe, then swept out of the courtroom.

Using the chair and the crutch, Joe rose shakily to his feet. Poncho grinned up at him.

Sarah handed Poncho his crutches. "You did well, General Pascalle. Now let's get you off to D.C."

30 The Peace Conference

Andrea thrashed up from sleep and fumbled the telephone receiver to her ear. "*Dad*?"

"Alas, 'tis only me."

She smiled into her pillow. "Hi, Rich."

"Why are you still asleep? It's nine a.m. and I've been working for two hours."

"Only insane birds and low-brained vampires work this early. Besides, the world is round and I'm three hours on the other side."

"Speaking of time, when your trial is over and I get clear of this session, let's make up for the time we've lost lately. Okay?"

She rubbed her eyes. "Hope I live to see the day."

"Count on it. Oh, by the way, I've got some great news."

"'*By the way*' you've got some great news? Come on; I could really use it."

"I got the peace meeting time finally all confirmed."

"Rich! That's thrilling! How did you do it?"

"It wasn't easy. Apparently the State Department was worried I was intruding on their territory trying to score political PR points. I told them I'd be perfectly happy to step out if they wanted to take over—but both Bramoso and Pascalle insisted I be involved in the mediation. The breakthrough came when the President himself got on the phone with the Secretary of State."

"Any bruised egos?"

"Bet on it. But I volunteered not to use the meeting for any campaign purpose, so hopefully no one will brood too much." He paused.

"And I'll tell you something else wonderful that could come out of all this."

"*More* good news?"

"As you know, the pressure on the Administration from certain quarters to turn down Anthony Darren's pardon got worse once he became a fugitive."

"Rich, that's neither news nor good."

"Sorry. So far the President's still open-minded, but if he wavers I'll be able to tell him something that will make you both feel better. If this meeting between Bramoso and Pascalle manages to bring even temporary peace to Costallegre, *Fusing Order and Chaos* definitely had something to do with it. Both sides say the book is persuasive."

"That's awfully nice of you to say, sweetheart, but I have more important concerns than getting a little personal glory. Especially since I'm not really the one who deserves it."

"But that's the point! Andrea, for your father's sake it's time to advise the President that Bric Locket is also Anthony Darren. Then, if things turn out well, your father and his ideas could be the real heroes here. That would give the President all the additional ammunition he might need to ignore the political pressure about pardoning him."

"On the other hand," Andrea said, "if things go wrong the President will be accused of supporting a useless fugitive convicted of fraud and murder."

"Wow, you really know how to bring down the mood."

Andrea laughed, but only for a moment. "Also, I haven't spoken to my father since he escaped from prison, but I know he wouldn't want anything to influence his pardon request except the fact that he's innocent."

"Understood, Hon. I'll honor that." Rich chuckled. "Since you're my lawyer, I can tell you secrets and they'll be subject to attorney-client privilege, right?"

"Right."

Rich told her that Jose Salazar of Peru, the acting President of the Organization of American States, would preside at the forthcoming conference. Assistant Secretary of State Marshall Johnston, with Rich specially assigned to him, would also be there. The secret meeting would take place at the Peruvian Embassy in Washington DC the day following Bramoso's speech to the UN, coinciding with Memorial Day ceremonies. The Secret Service had arranged for the attendees to be driven to the Embassy in nondescript vehicles at fifteen minute intervals. They had even taken each of the conferees' measurements and provided tourist-type clothes in case the men wanted to leave the building.

Poncho, uncomfortable in a Navy blue suit and paisley tie, was the first negotiator to arrive at the Embassy. After he waited in the anteroom for ten minutes, Secret Service agents frisked him and escorted him to the conference chamber.

Next the agents ushered in Presidente Jose Salazar of Peru, Secretary Johnston, Senator Morrison, and others, everyone but Rudy Bramoso. The men all wore dark suits and ties, making a somber picket fence around a marble conference table, the stone shiny black with milk-white swirls.

Finally an agent gestured to a side door and Rudy Bramoso entered, wearing his customary military fatigues. Poncho struggled to keep the loathing from showing on his face. Here was the man who had killed two members of his family. Here was the man who was trying to kill an entire country. Here . . .

Not here, he thought. Not now.

He forced himself to rise, his body assuming the demeanor of his generalship, as Bramoso came around the table, greeting each man in turn. When he came face to face with Poncho, he did not extend his hand. Neither did Poncho. With curt glances, both men turned away and sat down.

Good enough, Poncho thought. At least we didn't shoot one another.

Cooperation, Rich thought. Come on, guys, now is the time for cooperation . . .

"Welcome, all of you," President Salazar said in Spanish from the head of the table. "Thank you for attending. We hope and pray that this meeting will lead to a fair and just settlement of the political disputes affecting our region."

Each man responded with thanks for having been invited and for the chairman's time and effort, but Rich noticed El Gato and Bramoso eyeing each other steadily across the table. *Ah, man.*

"To begin in an orderly fashion . . . ," Salazar said, outlining the protocol . . . He then nodded to Rodolfo Bramoso.

Bramoso lifted his chin. "The priorities are, first of all: the fascist Old Guard who once supported the dictator Serape has been attempting to retake my country. I cannot allow this to happen; not at any cost." He brought his fists slowly down onto the table and pressed until the knuckles showed white. "Second, these reactionary elements in our society are keeping the government from filling the peoples' basic needs for food, medical care, education, and decent shelter."

He ended the statement with ". . . nationalizing all business and bringing all services and citizens into the embrace of a full Socialist state."

He continued in this vein for the next fifteen minutes. Poncho, the El Gato, listened in stony silence, barely controlling his impulse to counter. But finally the general's turn came and all eyes focused on him. Poncho leaned forward, hands resting palms down on the smooth marble, and took his time looking from face to face. His gaze stopped at Bramoso. "For many years," he said, also in Spanish, "free speech, free elections and democracy were repressed by the Serape regime, as Signor Bramoso says—and we fought to change that. We cannot and will not go back. That said, to be honest my leaders don't care much what political or economic system my country chooses, so long as civil rights and freedoms are a first priority, the economy is a free market, and the government is limited to providing essential police and other protections and providing safety-net assistance to those in need and worthy of help. Because if you don't have these freedoms, then an ample supply of food, shelter and education will never become a reality—at least not without enslaving the people under a police state."

Rich was impressed by El Gato's eloquence in his native tongue, but he could see Bramoso's complexion darkening.

Poncho put the tips of his fingers over his heart. "Throughout history, custom and practice, communism has always, in the end, meant a socialist dictatorship. It becomes a dictatorship through complicated bureaucracy controlled by a select group. To keep power this group allows no free press, no free expression—no free speech. The bureaucrats hand jobs to their relatives and political associates; corruption infests them. Soon the bureaucracy and the social freeloaders develop symbiosis. Once all the bureaucratic fiefdoms have been established, mobility up the work and social ladders ends. This is what is already happening in my country now, and this is why my leaders and I will never accede to dictatorship in any form, or for any purpose, for our people."

Poncho swept an arm across the table. "None of the original goals of our revolution have been forthcoming since Bramoso commandeered control. I do not wish to see a return of Serape in any form, including this one. I already fought against it once."

Again he looked Bramoso straight in the eyes.

"We fear an all-powerful, all-controlling central government. We want the provinces to have more independence . . . then there will be less chance for a dictator to take control. We want checks and balances."

Bramoso shook his head and twisted his mouth into a mocking smile.

Rich listened to the continuing dialogue, but even more he watched the energy flow around the table. And he knew right away that Bramoso and Pascalle were not bending in the slightest, either of them. Ironically, they were like magnets pointing the same poles at one another, and thereby pushing themselves apart.

When his turn came to comment, Rich spoke in excellent Spanish. "I realize that all of you have as much or more knowledge about political systems than I, even about democracy. But wouldn't you agree that many of the differences that separate your positions have been the subject of dispute for perhaps as long as humankind has used political systems of any sort?"

Everyone stared at him. Good. They hadn't thought of that one.

He turned to Poncho. "General Poncho Pascalle Cardenas, you and your group stress freedom and individualism, with a free market economy as a high priority. You want the individual provinces of your country to have a strong say about their destinies, and for there to be as little national government control as possible. These are worthy goals . . . but isn't it a matter of degree?"

"In some things there can be no bending," Poncho said. And Bramoso nodded.

Great. "In my own country," Rich said calmly, "following the American revolution, the thirteen states joined together under the Articles of Confederation. They existed as a country under that system until 1789, and it was very similar to the system you suggest. But they found it did not work well. There was too *much* individualism—or to put it differently, as Mr. Locket did in his book—too much *competition* between the thirteen states." Morrison leaned forward. "Under the Articles of Confederation, before much longer the union would have surely disintegrated into separate competing entities. Fortunately, as each separate state grew in maturity and confidence—and after considerable debate, of course—they decided to adopt more cooperative rules for a stronger union."

Poncho gave a sour nod. "I remember reading that—I was forced to study American history in engineering school."

The men around the table chuckled. Rich smiled and spread his hands. "So, with James Madison leading the way, the states adopted the present United States Constitution, with the result being somewhat less state individualism in return for greater cooperation and subscription to the Federal Government and it hasn't worked out so bad, has it?"

Poncho said nothing, but some of the tension seemed to have gone out of his shoulders.

Rich turned toward Rodolfo Bramoso. "On the other hand, James Madison was afraid that a central government could become so strong it overpowered the autonomy of the states, personal individualism and personal freedoms. So perhaps it was fortunate that the United States began in an atmosphere of separate independence. That gave each state's roots and branches a chance to grow freely to a certain level of maturity, after which the state could more confidently consider the benefits of joining into a federation. Also, there were differences amongst the peoples and their religions that had to be protected. That is one reason the American revolutionaries instituted checks and balances into the government. They *synthesized* the cooperative, uniting nature of a central federal government with the competitive nature of individualism, including separateness for each citizen and state. Madison strove to codify this synthesis of the competing and the cooperating forces in the constitution of the new government."

Rich thought he saw a flicker in Bramoso's eyes.

"So, without belaboring the point," he went on, "I would pose a question: Do each of you believe a constitution *cannot* be created that allows for a balance between the rights of individuals and states verses central government? In other words, do you believe it's even *possible* to achieve a cooperative social system that also includes a competitive, free market economy? Because if you believe these options can be combined into a single unified system, then you may have the beginnings of a solution to the problem of Costallegre."

Bramoso' chin jutted. "You forget something: there can be no balance, no synthesis, as long as Serape's Old Guard continues to interfere with the revolution they once supported."

"We are *not* 'Serape's Old Guard,.'" Poncho snarled, barely managing to stay off his feet. "And your revolution is not the one we once supported. We once all fought for the same goal—to make Costallegre strong and free. Now we do not. There can be no synthesis if a dictatorship chokes off free speech and economic social mobility, and burgeons into a monstrosity that exists only to perpetuate itself in power."

"Nonsense," Bramoso snapped. "You think we do not want free elections? We want free elections—but this cannot be while the people are terrified of being shot in their beds if they do not vote the way the old Serape Guard wants them to. Only when the fighting ends can we have free elections."

"We want elections *now*!" Poncho roared. "And we will not stop fighting until we have them!"

Bramoso's face darkened. "Never will we agree to that. First you must lay down your arms. After a period of peace, *then* we will have elections."

"Ha! If we turn in our arms, you will round us up and execute us or throw us into prison. We are not fools!"

Bramoso slammed a palm onto the table, although the heavy stone absorbed and flattened the effect quite a bit. "Only fools would refuse to cease your treacherous violence. Fools, and traitors, and terrorists!"

"*You* are the traitor!" Poncho half stood from his chair. "You betrayed our revolution. You stole from us the freedom for which we gave our blood, and that of our brothers and sisters."

"Gentlemen!" The late afternoon sun revealed the jaundiced tinge to Salazar's face. He blotted his forehead with a handkerchief. "Please show mutual respect. It is time to recess now. Please, let us all return in one hour and a half."

Poncho waited until Bramoso and half the other men had left the room, then rose and stalked around the table toward the door. A yellow pad at Morrison's place caught his attention. In the middle of a page of doodling, printed clearly and boldly, was: "Peace + honor = Darren's freedom." Poncho stiffened. *No one here should even know Anthony is alive. Why would the Senator write down his name?*

The conferees went into separate rooms where they were given their respective 'tourist clothes'. The outside temperature was a humid eighty-five degrees—not much different from Costallegre— so Poncho put on green shorts, a white golf shirt, green baseball cap, white socks and jogging shoes. He wondered idly if Bramoso would dare to change out of his military fatigues. Like Castro, he loved to display himself as the eternal revolutionary.

Outside, Poncho walked a few blocks, then took a taxi to the Mall. In an odd way, his tourist garb pleased him. Never having visited the US capital before, he enjoyed looking like an ordinary American, a tourist. With a slight limp still in his stride, Poncho crossed the thick, fresh-cut grass leading to the gigantic stone pillar of the Washington Monument standing on a rise and pointing into the sky. Turning right from there, he followed a path surfaced with decomposed granite. He saw at the end of the Mall the Lincoln Memorial with the great reflecting pool extending from the steps at its base. As he walked, he felt the sense of being watched, but from where? The Mall was packed with people of all sizes, colors and modes of dress. He assumed that security cameras were everywhere.

But he knew he was being trailed. . . .

Anthony followed Poncho at a distance of forty or fifty yards, feeling secure and anonymous in the throng of Memorial Day revelers.

Hundreds of people ebbed and flowed between him and Poncho as the General took the path toward the Vietnam War Memorial, better known as "the Wall." Poncho probably didn't blend into the crowd as well as he thought he did . . . shorts or not, he still looked like a jungle guerilla wary for snipers.

Anthony hoped he fit in better with his Nationals baseball cap and American Flag t-shirt. As he walked, the rolling thunder of thousands of flashing motorcycles moving down the bordering boulevard resonated in sync with the beat of his heart. A saluting soldier in Marine Corps dress blues stood at attention in the center medium of the street, the bikers wheeling around him from opposite directions.

Passing over a rise, Poncho looked ahead and saw the Wall for the first time. His breath caught in his throat. It was a long, glistening black slab of marble that rose vertically like a schism in the earth, grass above and grass below. Its smooth sheen was covered with the carved names of the thousands of American soldiers who had died in that far country, their line in the sand now his line.

As Poncho approached the Wall, a man with a clipboard handed him a couple of pieces of paper. A few minutes later Anthony found himself holding the printed message about Memorial Day and a stub of pencil. He knew what to do with them, and asked for the locations of names of some fallen buddies.

Poncho was already standing next to the wall several yards away, pressing the thin sheet of paper against it and rubbing away with a pencil. All along the Wall, dozens of other visitors were doing the same thing.

But Poncho, he figured, would also be thinking of a different war and of its own dead heroes—men like Hector Lopez—who now lay far away, buried in the soil of his country. Men who had no memorial to commemorate their deeds, or even their existence.

"It's like we hit a brick wall," a voice muttered in Spanish, and Poncho appeared a couple of feet to Anthony's right. He slapped his sheet of paper against the Wall.

"You're finished? Is the meeting over?"

"No. It started badly, then got better, then went sour again. We're taking a break, then going back for one last try."

"What's the hang-up exactly?"

"It keeps coming back to extremes; most of the men, including Bramoso, say we must lay down our arms before we can have elections. It seems to them the collective rights should be paramount over individual rights."

"Think of some examples to counter that, General. Remember that you see it in art, you see it in nature."

"Do you see it in this wall, Anthony? All these dead boys. And for what? They fought, they died, nothing changed."

"Everything changed—just not in the ways we were expecting or looking for. Supporting the NVA weakened the Soviet Union so deeply that it never recovered. These names tell us we either impose *the synthesis* on ourselves in pursuit of a shared goal, or we emphasize extremes until the universe imposes *the synthesis* on us in ways we don't care for."

Poncho was silent for a full minute, his gaze locked on the Wall, the piece of paper fluttering in his hand. From some unseen location a band began to play *A Whiter Shade of Pale*, the opening organ chords shivering off monuments and trees, buildings and people.

"I must go now," Poncho suddenly said. "The meeting will be reconvening."

"Do you know what you're going to do?"

Poncho also placed his hand against the Wall. "Remind Bramoso—and myself—that in the end I hope we both want what is best for our country . . . . I don't know . . . The marble table has beautiful swirls, a manifestation of chaos, competition, but it is all locked together with uniformity, order, cooperation. That is why the table is beautiful. The government can be beautiful if we combine individual rights, that being competition, and some collective protections, that being the safety-net, a form of order or cooperation. That is nature—the miracle worker. We must find the way to the sweet spot."

Anthony realized that Poncho was now ahead of him. He had done all he could here. "Best of luck, General. *Hasta luego*."

"Hasta luego, el Professor."

Twenty minutes later Poncho sat at the conference table at the embassy and watched the other men come in, one by one. Again Bramoso was last. His face already looked tight and combative.

Poncho took a deep breath and looked down at the marble tabletop with its complicated swirls.

"Shall we resume?" Salazar asked. He sounded a bit deflated.

Do you know what you're going to do?

The Wall. Thousands of names etched into black stone, then rubbed onto white paper. White on black, black on white.

Poncho raised his head, looked straight into Bramoso's eyes. But this time he tried to see the man not as an opposite, an enemy, but as a another facet of himself. The idea was almost physically repulsive. *Him and me, the same? Never!*

Think of some examples, General. Remember that you see it in art, you see it in nature . . .

Yes, he had seem it. It was right in front of him; right in front of them all.

Again he raised his head. Looked at Bramoso.

"We need to find common ground," Poncho said.

Bramoso's brows contracted.

Poncho looked around the room, from face to face to face. "We all *need* to find common ground—the point of perspective that gives us the best view of *everything*. Or the point of synthesis, as a wise man has put it. Only from there can we progress. Let us try to achieve an ordered liberty, a moral liberty. By the words 'ordered' and 'moral' I refer to humane social responsibility based on the safety-net welfare system, not the cradle to grave welfare system. The latter can never be sustained by any government. It is unaffordable. Worse, it builds a dependent society. Remember the Costa Rican wild monkeys who are going extinct because the mothers had forgotten how to teach their babies to forage. The government was feeding them. So they stopped that."

The general went on, "By the word *liberty*, I refer to freedom, free market, human rights, and individual rights. Let us merge 'moral' and 'liberty' together into a supreme law –a supreme constitution. Let us acknowledge the wisdom of the great 17th century moral economist Adam Smith who spoke of the natural workings of the invisible hand—that is, of trust, confidence and fair dealing. Such is the natural manifestation of a metaphor that enables business and capitalism to work without excessive regulation. If free enterprise is to be shackled at all, those limited restraints must be sensible and necessary at the absolute minimum."

"Yes," General El Gato Pascalle went on. "Know the potential consequences when venturing a new reform, or don't do it. Don't chance it blindly, for surely the unintended consequent will emerge." They were paying attention to him now. Really listening, he could see. *I am no longer screaming from the edge of things.*

"How can such different men with such different views find that point of synthesis?" he asked. "How can we possibly share any common ground whatsoever? The answer is right in front of us."

He extended a forefinger and pressed it against the cold, hard surface of the tabletop. "Look at this piece of marble. What do you see? It is black and white swirled together. Not *blended*, you understand; not gray. It is two opposites that *remain* opposite and separate, yet together make a single thing, a beautiful and dynamic thing, a thing where liberty remains intact while the net saves those who truly cannot swim."

He spread his hands. "That is what we need to do, *El Presidente*. Gentlemen. We need to become like this marble. A synthesis of opposites. One strong and beautiful thing made of many weaker things—made of opposite colored swirls."

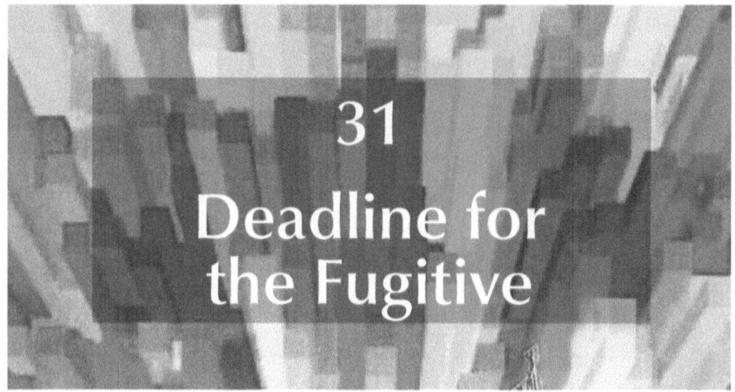

31
Deadline for the Fugitive

A single rap sounded at Warden Pritchard's office door just as he was preparing to leave for the day; in fact he had one arm already in a coat sleeve.

His secretary entered. "Sorry to interrupt, Warden, but we just received this cable . . . from the Office of the President of the United States."

"What?" Pritchard dropped the sleeve. "Who?" He ripped open the envelope, read the message and shook his head. Looked up. "Here, Marsha. Read it."

She read it , then said, "The president has given Mr. Darren his pardon, effective tomorrow, but only if he's then not a fugitive. This means he's in violation of the conditions of this pardon, right?"

Pritchard shrugged. "That's what you get when you continually flout authority. If anyone should know that, it's Darren. Well, if he's not back in his cell tomorrow he'll miss this boat for good . . . and he'll have nobody to blame but himself." The warden picked his jacket up again. "I have the feeling he won't be here; how about you?"

In her office law library, Andrea settled in a chair to do research for a brief. The sun was just breaking through the early morning mist, throwing mellow light on the table, but she couldn't appreciate it. She couldn't concentrate at all.

Too many loose ends. Rich was still locked in some room in DC with a bunch of international leaders, trying to stop a war. Her father was still MIA. Tonight was the literary Awards Banquet. And the jury was still out on the James-Hooks case.

At 8:30 Millie poked her head around the corner. "Andi, your jury's in."

Here goes one gigantic loose end. "Thanks, Millie." Andrea swallowed hard. "Buzz John for me, would you?"

Minutes later Andrea and Woods were entering the courthouse. Neither of them said anything as they walked into the familiar cavernous space of the Federal Courtroom. Then Woods gave her a fatherly smile and said, "Knock 'em dead."

He seated himself in the first row of the gallery outside the bar, while Andrea passed through the swinging gate of the bar and sat alone at the prosecutor's table.

A few minutes later the defendants, Egan James and Herbert Hooks, entered with their counsel, all wearing dark blue suits. As they took seats at their table, Andrea thought back to her decision to enter law school. For years she had wondered what it would be like to be a lawyer, and now she sat here representing the United States of America against four men—all tough, and three of them very experienced trial lawyers, and two of *those* amongst the very best around.

And the other two responsible for sending her father to prison.

But to her surprise she felt none of the buried fire that had erupted inside her the day she watched Anthony, her father, being led away in chains; the fire that had sustained her throughout law school and into her new job. Instead, she felt some other kind of energy, a kind of strength rooted outside herself; now, her concern was for the greater interests of the people of the United States. Somehow, without her even being aware of it, the responsibilities of her position as officer of the court had transcended her personal predilections.

The gallery filled quickly with spectators and reporters. She noticed with some disappointment that Laura was not among them. She realized she was even sort of half-looking for her father's face peering proudly, if furtively, from the crowd.

Then: "All rise."

Still buttoning his black robe, the judge stepped up to the bench. "Will the Marshal please bring in the jury," he said. The door between the witness stand and the jury box opened, revealing the secured back hallways, and the jurors trailed in from the inner sanctum of the deliberation room.

Andrea made eye contact with a few of the jurors as they stepped to their chairs. None smiled. None looked sad, or happy, or anything. They all wore faces of stone.

As soon as they were settled the judge asked the foreman to stand and state whether the jury had reached a verdict. A white-haired man in his early seventies rose, holding a sheet of paper in a hand that shook ever so slightly. "Your honor, the jury has reached a verdict."

"Would you please hand the written verdict to the clerk."

The paper was passed to the clerk, and then up to the judge. Andrea's heartbeat hammered in her ears at triple pace even as the crowded courtroom fell utterly silent. Seconds ticked by as the judge eyed the verdict. With no expression he handed the form back to the clerk, who returned it to the foreman.

"Mr. Foreman, please state the verdict," the judge said.

"We the jury, find the defendants Egan James and Herbert Hooks, guilty on all counts."

An uproar reverberated off the paneled walls. The judge's gavel cracked against the bench. "Order in this courtroom!"

James and Hooks turned ashen; their heads sagged. For the first time in Andrea's memory, Egan's sneer disappeared entirely.

Minutes later, out in the hall, John Woods swept her into a gigantic hug. One high-heeled shoe fell off as he lifted her from the floor. Her friends gathered round, smiling, trying to shake her hand while she hopped on one foot, then dropped the shoe again as Sarah rushed up. They hugged. Andrea blurted, "Congratulations, Sarah, for stepping in and doing such a great job!"

"No, you were the general; thank you for preparing the case so perfectly."

They accepted best wishes from all around, then Andrea excused herself, saying she had an urgent matter to attend to.

She arrived at her office shortly before ten a.m. Millie immediately cried, "Andrea, have you heard?"

"About the conviction?"

"Oh, no! I mean, congratulations on that, of course—as they say, you're the best . . . but no, it's about Anthony Darren."

"What? Has someone heard from him?"

"No, but we just got word from the government, they've given him a pardon!"

"Oh, my God."

"Look, here's a copy of the cablegram."

Andrea took the paper and read it. "But for this to be effective, he has to be back in prison." She looked up. "Millie, get Joe Cruz on the line. It's time for me to break phone silence."

Andrea snatched up the receiver and waited impatiently for someone to answer. Finally she heard, "Hello."

"Joe? This is Andrea. Do you know where Anthony is, or how to get hold of him?"

"Andrea, you can't call on this phone. Do you read me?"

"I don't give a damn. Anthony's been pardoned, but only if he is not in violation of prison regulations. He has to get back to Brockton, *now*!"

"But, I don't know where he is."

"Is he at least in the States?"

"Well, yes. He came back in the tuna boat with us."

"Same tuna boat?"

"Absolutely. We had to keep him stored in the fish hold for a while, and almost lost him to hypothermia. Then we kept him in a spare chain locker, except during the graveyard watches, and after we docked in port he was gone. Must have swam for it. When Customs boarded we told them we'd buried one of the bodies at sea."

"Joe, what are we going to do?" She tried to keep panic out of her voice. "We have to find him *immediately*."

"Let me think. Let me think. He told me that once Poncho testified, he'd turn himself in, but instead I think he took a flight back to DC . The General needed him there with him. He would only spend a day, then fly back immediately to Brockton."

"How could he—"

"Travel by air without ID? I can't really explain it right now, you know?"

Her mind had already leaped ahead. "Poncho's either still in that meeting or on a plane to LA. So he can't help."

"Okay, I'll start calling around. I'll let you know the second I find anything out. If we miss each other, I'll see you in L.A. tonight."

As Andrea was getting ready to rush out of the office, Millie brought her another phone message.

Andrea,

Some reporter friends called about the pardon and said Anthony would be discharged if he returns to prison in time. I'm on my way there to wait, so you won't be able to reach me.

I'll report in. Got my fingers crossed.

Love, Laura

When Andrea arrived home, a message waited on her answering machine. "I'm ecstatic about the verdict!" Rich's recorded voice crowed. "And I'm going to the banquet with you tonight.

"I've got some great news of my own—I'm coming right over to pick you up."

About forty-five minutes later Andrea looked out the window as a shiny black limousine pulled up at the curb. Her eyes momentarily misted as she thought how nice it would have been if her mother could ride in that car with them. She imagined Cheryl in her finest dress, sitting proudly opposite them, wearing a gardenia corsage Andrea had bought for her. But Cheryl would be so worried because Anthony was missing and in the worst trouble of his life. . . .

Andrea ran a brush through her hair, then rushed downstairs to the entry where Rich waited. She gazed down into his eyes as he followed her descent. He wore new jeans and a zip-up sweatshirt emblazoned with a giant American eagle encircled by the words, "Athletic Club of the United States Senate."

He threw his arms around her and lifted her to his chest. "Congratulations again." Then he set her down and held her at arm's length. "The verdict was the right one. It was great. You outmaneuvered those thugs. You're amazing."

She kissed him hard. "They were as guilty as the devil. If they'd been acquitted I don't know what I would have done. Now . . . what's *your* good news you wanted to tell me? Something about the peace talks?"

"Exactly. El Gato came through. Everything seemed to be breaking down, and then we took a break and when we came back Poncho knew exactly the right things to say. He was brilliant. There's still a long way to go before there will be true peace and stability in Costallegre, but Rudy's agreed to a ceasefire with the rebels. And when I say 'agreed' I mean written on paper and signed by both parties."

"Rich, that's *wonderful.*" She pulled his head down and touched her forehead to his. "All this success is overwhelming, Rich, but I'm really worried. Dad has to turn himself in, and we can't find him. I'm sorry, but I'll have to make more calls as soon as we get to LA."

"The car phone, Sweets; make as many calls as you want."

In the limo Andrea sat back, her head on Rich's shoulder while she let her mind absorb the peace and quiet. In her fantasy her mother sat on the opposite seat, all smiles and her typical loving, childlike expression.

"Mom," Andrea imagined saying, "do you know where we're going?"

"To a dinner in your honor."

"Well . . . I wouldn't go that far. It's for lots of writers, and it's unlikely that Dad and I will win an award even in our category. But just being nominated is an honor."

"I'm so proud of you." Cheryl's smile deepened. "Did you say your dad will be there? I can't wait to see him again. It's been so long."

Andrea snuggled against Rich as the limousine cruised toward the metropolis of Los Angeles.

Keys jangled at double time as Sluggo scurried along the elevated walkway to Anthony Darren's former cell. Two other inmates had been in and out of there since Darren did his magical disappearing act, but the house was supposed to be empty tonight. But someone had reported a "crasher" sleeping in there. These fucking cons, they'd do anything they weren't supposed to do.

As he approached the cell he saw that the barred door was shut. Through the grid he saw a man lying on the bunk, completely covered by a blanket. "Hey, you!" he called. No response. "Who the hell is that in there?"

The form began to rise slowly like something from a horror movie, the rough green prison blanket sliding slowly off its head. A suntanned forehead was revealed, then a pair of red eyes above a sardonic smile. "The Count of Monte Cristo at your service, *Monsieur*. I decided to stay over for brunch. Would you care to join me?"

Sluggo clutched the bars. "Darren? How the fuck did you get back in? Well, trust me, you ain't never gittin' out of here again! And who the fuck is the Count of Monte Carlo?"

"Cristo," Anthony said. "He's a guy who did time, came back and made good . . . and straightened out a few old crooks in his life along the way."

"Must be a fairy tale," Sluggo said sourly. "None a you guys make good. You're all alike. C'mon, butthead, you missed some time and you got some explaining to do."

Warden Pritchard's eyes scanned Anthony up and down as he stood in the Warden's paneled office in leg shackles and handcuffs. At least Sluggo had been dismissed.

"Mr. Darren," the warden said, "I recently received a letter from the President of the United States. You apparently do not know this yet . . . but you've been granted a pardon. You are a free man."

"I. . . ." Anthony felt the floor shift beneath his feet, goose bumps rise on his neck. "Are you sure?"

"You can read it if you like."

Everything seemed to be underwater. The warden handed him the letter. He looked at it but could focus on only six words: *I hereby grant you this pardon.* While he struggled with the rest of it the warden knelt, unshackled his legs, then unlocked the cuffs.

He held out his hand. Anthony shook it.

"No hard feelings, I hope," Pritchard said. "Nobody in here thinks they're really guilty, but I have to treat them as if they are. And by the way, the library has never run properly since I took you out of that job."

"You'll excuse me if I don't ask for it back," Anthony heard himself say.

Pritchard snorted a laugh. "Well, good luck. By the way, if you ever get that book you were working on published, I'd be pleased to own an autographed copy."

Anthony smiled. "You'll be getting that sooner than you think."

Pritchard looked perplexed, then shrugged. "I'm informed that a Ms. Evans will be arriving at the front gate shortly to pick you up. But first . . . would you tell me one thing? No, two things."

"If I can."

"First, how did you get out? And then how did you get back in?"

"To get out I rode out in a metal box in the back of the garbage truck. To get back in I just borrowed the same truck from the trash yard and drove right through the prison gate. You'll find the truck parked in the nurse's space, by the way. It's probably taking up two slots, and the Highway Patrol might be looking for it by now."

Pritchard almost smiled. "All right, I guess I'll cover you on that one." Then he buzzed his intercom and asked for Sluggo.

The guard entered, his round face wrinkled in confusion. "Yes, Warden?"

"Mr. Darren here has just been pardoned. See that he gets discharged with the least possible delay. As of this moment, he's a free man."

Sluggo's mouth gaped.

When Anthony went to pick up the personal belongings that had been taken from him when he arrived, he was shocked to find the plastic bag also contained a pile of typewritten pages—the manuscript of his new book that had vanished from his cell. After he fanned through the pages he looked up and saw Sluggo standing at the end of the hall, looking at him. The guard turned and walked away.

Wearing his new prison-issue business suit, Anthony stepped out of his cell and for the last time walked down the concrete deck. A rhythmic clapping of hands and tapping of drinking cups started up, following him, becoming louder and louder, until it thundered in cadence to his every step. Each beat became more and more deafening until the concrete walls themselves seemed to shake. Then he passed through the cellblock doors, and the ruckus faded behind him.

Laura was standing at the discharge gate. They hugged, and her wet cheek brushed his face. Together they walked to the visitor's parking area.

"I want to drive," he said.

"Are you sure that's a good idea? You haven't driven a car in ten years."

"No, but I recently drove a boat, and also a trash truck."

She laughed. "I'll let you take us as far as the freeway on-ramp, then we're switching places, buster."

Anthony drove carefully for two miles through dry brush-land to the interstate on-ramp, where he parked and stepped out. He started to pass Laura at the front of the car, then turned and grabbed her in a hard embrace, oblivious to the traffic whizzing by. In the wind and swirling dust they kissed, and the heat from the contact spread through him with the speed of a prairie fire.

"*Please* watch out for crazy drivers," he whispered. "We have a lot to live for now."

She drove out onto the freeway. Very carefully.

"Why Los Angeles?" he asked when he saw the sign pass overhead.

"Never you mind. Something special is happening, and there's a chance that Andrea will be there. I've been trying to contact her all day to tell her you're free, but I haven't been able to get hold of her." She smiled. "Maybe it was meant to be this way."

"That's great. But since we're going that far, do you mind if we stop along the way? I want to see the sister of my friend Hector Lopez. I want to tell her in person about her brother."

Laura put a hand over his. "Of course we can stop. You wouldn't ask unless it was important, but just a short visit?"

"Thanks, Laura. Very short."

When Andrea and Rich entered the dining hall, they saw that almost all the guests had already arrived. Light reflected from chandeliers and crystal sparkled through the room. Beautifully gowned women and formally attired men gave the occasion a special elegance.

An usher escorted them to a round, linen-covered table near the stage. Moby Jack waited with a glow of anticipation, his massive form amazingly debonair in a tuxedo. Beside him stood Joe Cruz,his bearing once again that of a proud bullfighter, holding hands with his beloved Sylvia. To their right stood Sarah, ever the cerebral fashion model, and Hal Goldman, now the soft gray eagle; and finally General Poncho Pascalle Emilio "El Gato" Cardenas, the ghostly jungle cat. All looked spectacular in formal dress.

Andrea hugged each of them in succession, and when she got to the General she whispered in his ear, "Have you heard from Anthony?"

"Yes. I saw him in Washington two days ago."

"Where is he now? I must talk to him."

"He said he was leavin' the day before yesterday, but he didn' say to where. If I hear from him I'll tell him to call you quick."

Laura's not here either. She sat down and asked that two places at their table be kept open. *For luck.*

All through dinner she kept looking up, imagining that Anthony and Laura were walking toward them. While everyone else commented on how fine each course of the meal was, to her the food tasted like straw.

Finally the award ceremony began. Andrea hardly heard what the master of ceremonies, Edward Spencer, was saying. He reviewed the works of the candidates, then began to give out the preliminary awards.

Andrea couldn't help staring toward the entrance, even though she wondered whether her father was still in hiding or being re-arrested.

Then she heard Spencer say, "And now, ladies and gentlemen, before we award the grand prize, we would like first to announce a special award for the best nonfiction work by a previously unpublished author. The candidates are. . . ." Andrea tuned out again. Where was her father? Where was Laura? Were they together somewhere?

". . . our review of this book, we agreed that the authors showed that our speedy rise to modernism has outstripped ancient tribal customs, mythology and spirituality—revealing a deeper truth, the primal wisdom that synthesizes order and chaos, cooperation and competition. Finding the sweet spot within this synthesis is both the quest, and birth of a new word. Achieving this synthesis gives us powerful methods for improving our lives in everything from building character in wayward children to solving trade wars between nations."

Andrea's heart jumped as she saw a handsome, well-dressed couple enter the room and be ushered discretely to a table near the entrance.

She wanted to cheer at the top of her voice. *Dad! Laura! You made it—obviously first back to prison and now to here!*

"So," Spencer intoned, "without further suspense, this award goes to two recipients, the co-authors of this remarkable book: Dr. Andrea Burns and Bric Locket, for *Fusing Order and Chaos*." He smiled down at Andrea's table. "I believe one of you is here to accept."

The ovation overwhelmed Andrea, the applause sending vibrations through her ears, her mind, her body. As if in a dream she let Rich lead her by the hand for a few paces toward the steps before releasing her. Well-wishers patted her shoulders as she passed.

On the podium she accepted a small plaque and the microphone. The room quieted.

"Members of the board and friends," she said, "this honor means more to me and my co-author than words will ever express, or than you will ever know. Our work on this project kept alive the hopes and dreams of Bric Locket, giving him the confidence to continue in the face of obstacles most of us will never have to face. This honor really belongs to him. And, he is here tonight!"

A fresh burst of applause rang out as the audience looked in all directions. "I ask that he come to the rostrum," Andrea said. Again, applause enveloped the room as Anthony rose from the far corner of the hall. Rich looked with amazement at the trim man approaching the stage. Anthony and Andrea embraced—father and daughter.

"Ladies and gentlemen," she said, "please meet Bric Locket. I'm sure most of you realize his name is a pseudonym. For those of you who have asked who he really is, now I can tell you that he is not only my co-author, he is also my beloved father, and his name is Anthony Darren."

Anthony's smile and eyes sparkled in the spotlights. He took the microphone and said, "And wasn't I lucky having you as a daughter. The synergism of family and friends is what this is all about!"

Everyone at Andrea's table got to their feet, applauding. The remainder of the audience rose to a standing ovation.

After the noise died down Andrea said, "May I also introduce some of our cherished friends among many who have been so very special to us. First, my Dad's love and my great friend, Laura Evans." She motioned Laura over. "Our teammates Joseph and Sylvia Cruz,

General Poncho Pascalle, Moby Jack Callucci, Hal Goldman, and Sarah Billings. My mother, Cheryl Crawford, who taught me perseverance, is here only in spirit."

Anthony touched her shoulder and took the microphone. "With your permission, I would like to pay special tribute to Hector Lopez, a man also here in spirit." He turned to the guests at Andrea's table. "And Joe, Sylvia, I want these people to know that Michael Cruz, your son, is here in spirit as well."

With hurt in his eyes and pride on his face, Joe raised an arm above the din of applause. Even brighter did the room glow.

Andrea said, "And not least for being last, I introduce Senator Richard Morrison."

The applause roared to thunder. She put a hand over her heart. "Rich, I accept, if you will still have me."

He clasped his hands over his head. "How about tonight?" he shouted.

"Tonight it is! Is there a preacher in the house?" Warm laughter greeted her.

Anthony put an arm around her. She whispered into his ear, "Egan James and Herbert Hooks were convicted today."

His gaze turned briefly distant. "Well, except for the inevitable appeal, it closes the book. For them I can only be sad." He saw Laura, her hands outstretched to him. He drew her in and gave her a kiss. Then, gathering his daughter to them both, he stood at full height in freedom and honor, fully part of a family at last.

ABOUT THE AUTHOR

V Frank Asaro, award-winning finalist USA Best Book 2015, for non-fiction and philosophy, is a lawyer, musician, composer, inventor and theorist; he also authored the non-fiction book, *Universal Co-opetition*, published Oct. 2011, now superseded by *A Primal Wisdom, 2d. Ed.*, published 2015 and *Althea Haunting*, a legal thriller/ghost story, published in 2016. He began developing the theory of co-opetition not long after he was selected out of law school as lawyer-clerk to the California Dist.Courts of Appeal. He went on to receive the highest-category law career peer review, *Preeminent®* Martindale Hubbell rating, and appeared in *Who's Who in American Law,* and *Who's Who in the World.*

Engaged in litigation most of his career, he honed skills proving or disproving facts and stories—a handy talent for a novelist. Moreover as a patent holder, he shows a creative knack. This he calls upon in weaving this most exciting tale of *The Tortoise Shell Game*, a fiction work in Admiralty—one of his fields. In those early days when he was an Appellate court law clerk, his creativity became a major component in developing the theory of the products liability holding of *Greenman v Yuba Power Products*—further expanded by the California Supreme court. A major part of the Greenman opinion is now the law in the English speaking and European Union countries of the world.

To contact: info@vfrankasaroauthor.com or
vfasaro@san.rr.com

www.ingramcontent.com/pod-product-compliance
Lightning Source LLC
Chambersburg PA
CBHW032143010726
47494CB00002B/338

* 9 7 8 1 9 4 0 7 8 4 4 9 6 *